Kate Hewitt has ～ ，
from drama teach h
worker, but writin e
also writes women e
the healing and redemptive power of love. Kate lives in
a tiny village in the English Cotswolds with her
husband, five children, and an overly affectionate
Golden Retriever.

Cara Colter shares her life in beautiful British
Columbia, Canada, with her husband, nine horses and
one small Pomeranian with a large attitude. She loves
to hear from readers, and you can learn more about
her and contact her through Facebook.

Deborah Fletcher Mello has been writing since forever
and can't imagine herself doing anything else. Her first
romance novel, *Take Me to Heart*, earned her a 2004
Romance Slam Jam nomination for Best New Author,
and in 2009, she won a *Romantic Times* Reviewer's
Choice Award for her ninth novel, *Tame a Wild Stallion*.
Born and raised in Connecticut, Deborah now considers
home to be wherever the moment moves her.

Summer of Love

March 2021
Second Chance at Sunset

April 2021
Once Upon a Wedding

May 2021
**Taking a Chance
on Forever**

June 2021
Summer Nights

July 2021
Finding Paradise

August 2021
Forever You

Summer of Love: Finding Paradise

KATE HEWITT

CARA COLTER

DEBORAH FLETCHER MELLO

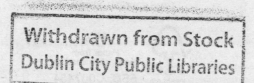
MILLS & BOON

First Published in Great Britain 2021
By Mills & Boon, an imprint of HarperCollins*Publishers* Ltd
1 London Bridge Street, London, SE1 9GF
www.harpercollins.co.uk

HarperCollins*Publishers*
1st Floor, Watermarque Building,
Ringsend Road, Dublin 4, Ireland

SUMMER OF LOVE: FINDING PARADISE
© 2021 Harlequin Books S.A.

Beneath the Veil of Paradise © 2012 Kate Hewitt
The Wedding Planner's Big Day © 2016 Cara Colter
Forever a Stallion © 2012 Deborah Fletcher Mello

ISBN: 978-0-263-30057-4

MIX
Paper from
responsible sources
FSC® C007454

This book is produced from independently certified FSC™ paper to ensure responsible forest management.

For more information visit: www.harpercollins.co.uk/green

Printed and bound in Spain
by CPI, Barcelona

BENEATH THE VEIL OF PARADISE

KATE HEWITT

CHAPTER ONE

Was she ever going to start painting?

The woman had been sitting and staring at the blank canvas for the better part of an hour. Chase Bryant had been watching her, nursing his drink at the ocean-side bar and wondering if she'd ever actually put brush to paper, or canvas, as the case might be.

She didn't.

She was fussy; he could see that straight off. She was in a luxury resort on a remote island in the Caribbean, and her tan capris had knife-edge pleats. Her pale-blue polo shirt looked like she'd ironed it an hour ago. He wondered what she did to relax. If she relaxed. Considering her attitude in their current location, he doubted it.

Still, there was something intriguing about the determined if rather stiff set of her shoulders, the compressed line of her mouth. She wasn't particularly pretty—well, not his kind of pretty anyway, which he fully admitted was lush, curvy blondes. This woman was tall, just a few inches under his own six feet, and angular. He could see the jut of her collarbone, the sharp points of her elbows. She had a narrow face, a forbidding expression, and even her hairstyle was severe, a blunt bob of near black that looked like she trimmed it with nail scissors every week. Its razor-straight edge swung by the strong line of her jaw as she moved.

He'd been watching her since she arrived, her canvas and paints under one arm. She'd set her stuff up on the beach a little way off from the bar, close enough so he could watch her while he sipped his sparkling water. No beers for him on this trip, unfortunately.

She'd been very meticulous about it all, arranging the collapsible easel, the box of paints, the little three-legged stool. Moving everything around until it was all just so, and she was on a beach. In the Caribbean. She looked like she was about to teach an evening art class for over-sixties.

Still he waited. He wondered if she was any good. She had a gorgeous view to paint—the aquamarine sea, a stretch of spun-sugar sand. There weren't even many people to block the view; the resort wasn't just luxurious, it was elite and discreet. He should know. His family owned it. And right now he needed discreet.

She finished arranging everything and sat on the stool, staring out to the sea, her posture perfect, back ramrod-straight. For half an hour. It would have been boring except that he could see her face, and how emotions flickered across it like shadows on water. He couldn't exactly decipher what the emotions were, but she clearly wasn't thinking happy thoughts.

The sun had begun its languorous descent towards the sea, and he decided she must be waiting for the sunset. They were spectacular here; he'd seen three of them already. He liked watching the sun set, felt there was something poetic and apt about all that intense beauty over in an instant. He watched now as the sun slipped lower, its long rays causing the placid surface of the sea to shimmer with a thousand lights, the sky ablaze with myriad streaks of colour, everything from magenta to turquoise to gold.

And still she just sat there.

For the first time Chase felt an actual flicker of annoyance. She'd dragged everything out here; obviously she'd intended to paint something. So why wasn't she doing it? Was she afraid? More likely a perfectionist. And, damn it, he knew now that life was too short to wait for the perfect moment, or even an OK moment. Sometimes you just had to wade into the mire and do it. Live while you could.

Pushing away his drink, he rose from his stool and headed over to Miss Fussy.

Millie did not enjoy feeling like a fool. And it felt foolish and, worse, pathetic, sitting here on a gorgeous beach staring at a blank canvas when she'd obviously come to paint.

She just didn't want to any more.

It had been a stupid idea anyway, the kind of thing you read about in self-help books or women's magazines. She'd read one on the plane to St Julian's, something about being kind to yourself. Whatever. The article had described how a woman had taken up gardening after her divorce and had ended up starting her own landscaping business. Lived her dream after years of marital unhappiness. Inspirational. Impossible. Millie turned away from the canvas.

And found herself staring straight at a man's muscled six-pack abs. She looked up and saw a dark-haired Adonis smiling down at her.

'I've heard about watching paint dry, but this is ridiculous.'

Perfect, a smart ass. Millie rose from her stool so she was nearly eye-level. 'As you can see, there's no paint.'

'What are you waiting for?'

'Inspiration,' she answered and gave him a pointed look. 'I'm not finding any here.'

If she'd been trying to offend or at least annoy him, she'd failed. He just laughed, slow and easy, and gave her a thorough once-over with his dark bedroom eyes.

Millie stood taut and still, starting to get angry. She hated guys like this one: gorgeous, flirtatious, and utterly arrogant. Three strikes against him, as far as she was concerned.

His gaze finally travelled up to her face, and she was surprised and discomfited to see a flicker of what almost looked like sympathy there. 'So really,' he asked, dropping the flirt, 'why haven't you painted anything?'

'It's none of your business.'

'Obviously. But I'm curious. I've been watching you from the bar for nearly an hour. You spent a long time on the set-up, but you've been staring into space for thirty minutes.'

'What are you, some kind of stalker?'

'Nope. Just bored out of my mind.'

She stared at him; tried to figure him out. She'd taken him for a cheap charmer but there was something strangely sincere about the way he spoke. Like he really was curious. And really bored.

Something in the way he waited with those dark eyes and that little half-smile made her answer reluctantly, 'I just couldn't do it.'

'It's been a while?'

'Something like that.' She reached over and started to pack up the paints. No point pretending anything was going to happen today. Or any day. Her painting days were long gone.

He picked up her easel and collapsed it in one neat movement before handing it back. 'May I buy you a drink?'

She liked the 'may', but she still shook her head. 'No thanks.' She hadn't had a drink alone with a man in two years. Hadn't done anything in two years but breathe and work and try to survive. This guy wasn't about to make her change her ways.

'You sure?'

She turned to him and folded her arms as she surveyed

him. He really was annoyingly attractive: warm brown eyes, short dark hair, a chiseled jaw and those nice abs. His board shorts rode low on his hips, and his legs were long and powerful. 'Why,' she asked, 'are you even asking? I'd bet a hundred bucks I'm not your usual type.' Just like he wasn't hers.

'Typecast me already?'

'Easily.'

His mouth quirked slightly. 'Well, you're right, you're not my usual type. Way too tall and, you know—' he gestured around her face, making Millie stiffen '—severe. What's with the hair?'

'The hair?' Instinctively and shamefully she reached up to touch her bobbed hair. 'What about it?'

'It's scary. Like, Morticia Addams scary.'

'Morticia *Addams*? Of the Addams Family? She had long hair.' She could not believe they were discussing her hair, and in relation to a television show.

'Did she? Well, maybe I'm thinking of someone else. Somebody with hair like yours. Really sharp-cut. He made a chopping motion along his own jaw.

'You're being ridiculous. And offensive.' Yet strangely she found herself smiling. She liked his honesty.

He raised his eyebrows. 'So, dinner?'

'I thought it was a drink.'

'Based on the fact that you're still talking to me, I upped the ante.'

She laughed, reluctant, rusty, yet still a laugh. This annoying, arrogant, attractive man amused her somehow. When was the last time she'd actually laughed, had felt like laughing? And she was on holiday—admittedly enforced, but she had a whole week to kill. Seven days was looking like a long time from here. Why not amuse herself? Why not prove she really was moving on, just like her boss Jack had urged her to do? She gave a little decisive nod. 'OK, to the drink only.'

'Are you *haggling*?'

Interest flared; deals she could do. 'What's your counter offer?'

He cocked his head, his gaze sweeping slowly over her once more. And she reacted to that gaze, a painful mix of attraction and alarm. Dread and desire. Hot and cold. A welter of emotions that penetrated her numbness, made her *feel*.

'Drink, dinner, and a walk on the beach.'

Awareness pulsed with an electric jolt low in her belly. 'You were supposed to offer something less, not more.'

His slow, wicked smile curled her toes—and other parts of her person, parts that hadn't curled in a long time. 'I know.'

She hesitated. She should back off, tell him to forget it, yet somehow now that felt like failure. She could handle him. She needed to be able to handle him.

'Fine.' She was agreeing because it was a challenge, not because she wanted to. She liked to set herself little challenges, tests of emotional and physical endurance: *I can jog three miles in eighteen-and-a-half minutes and not even be out of breath. I can look at this photo album for half an hour and not cry.*

Smiling, he reached for the canvas she clutched to her chest. 'Let me carry that for you.'

'Chivalrous of you, but there's no need.' She strode over to the rubbish bin on the edge of the beach and tossed the canvas straight in. The paints, easel and stool followed.

She didn't look at him as she did it, but she felt herself flush. She was just being practical, but she could see how it might seem kind of…severe.

'You are one scary lady.'

She glanced at him, eyebrows raised, everything prickling. 'Are you still talking about my hair?'

'The whole package. But don't worry, I like it.' He grinned and she glared.

'I wasn't worried.'

'The thing I like about you,' he said as he strolled towards the bar, 'is you're so easy to rile.'

Millie had no answer to that one. She *was* acting touchy, but she felt touchy. She didn't do beaches, or bars, or dates. She didn't relax. For the last two years she had done nothing but work, and sunbathing on the beach with a paperback and MP3 player was akin to having her fingernails pulled out one by one. At least that wouldn't take a whole week.

The man—she realised she didn't even know his name—had led her through the beach-side bar to an artful arrangement of tables right on the sand. Each one was shaded by its own umbrella, with comfortable, cushioned chairs and a perfect view of the sea.

The waiter snapped right to attention, so Millie guessed the man was known around here. Probably a big spender. Trust-fund baby or bond trader? Did it matter?

'What's your name?' she asked as she sat across from him. He was gazing out at the sea with a strangely focused look. The orange streaks were like vivid ribbons across the sky. He snapped his attention back to her.

'Chase.'

'Chase.' She gave a short laugh. 'Sounds appropriate.'

'Actually, I don't generally do much chasing.' He gave her a slow, oh-so-sexy smile that had annoyance flaring through her even as her toes—and other parts—curled again.

'Charming, Chase. Do you practise that in the mirror?'

'Practise what?'

'Your smile.'

He laughed and leaned back in his chair. 'Nope, never. But it must be a pretty nice smile, if you think I practise.' He eyed her consideringly. 'Although, the more likely possibility is that you just think I'm an arrogant ass who's far too full of himself.'

Now she laughed in surprise. She hadn't expected him to be so honest. 'And I could probably tell you what you think of me.'

He arched one eyebrow. 'And that is?'

'Uptight, prissy know-it-all who doesn't know how to have a good time.' As soon as she said the words, she regretted them. This wasn't a conversation she wanted to have.

'Actually, I don't think that.' He remained relaxed, but his gaze swept over her searchingly, making Millie feel weirdly revealed. 'Admittedly, on the surface, yes, I see it. Totally, to a tee. But underneath...' She rolled her eyes, waiting for the come-on. Everything was a chat-up line to a guy like this. 'You seem sad.'

She tensed mid-eye-roll, her gaze arrowing on him. A little smile played around his mouth, drawing attention to those full, sculpted lips. Lips that were lush enough to belong to a woman, yet still seemed intensely masculine. And it was those lips that had so softly issued that scathing indictment.

You seem sad.

'I don't know what you're talking about.' As far as comebacks went, it sucked. And her voice sounded horribly brittle. But Millie didn't have anything better. Averting her eyes, she slipped out her smart phone and punched in a few numbers. Chase watched her without speaking, yet she felt something from him. Something dark, knowing and totally unexpected.

'What's your name?' he finally asked and, knowing she was being rude, she didn't look up from her phone.

'Millie Lang.' No work emails. Damn.

'What's that short for? Millicent? Mildred?'

She finally glanced up, saw him still studying her. 'Camilla.'

'Camilla,' he repeated, savouring the syllables, drawing them out with a sensual consideration that didn't seem forced or fake. 'I like it.' He gestured to her phone. 'So what's going on in the real world, Camilla? Your stock portfolio sound? Work managing without you?'

She flushed and put her phone away. She'd just been about to check NASDAQ. For the fifth time today. 'Everything ship-shape. And please don't call me Camilla.'

'You prefer Millie?'

'Clearly.'

He laughed. 'This is going to be a fun evening, I can tell.'

Her flush intensified, swept down her body. What a mistake this was—a stupid, stupid mistake. Had she actually thought she could do this—have dinner, have fun, *flirt*? All ridiculous.

'Maybe I should just go.' She half-rose from her chair, but Chase stopped her with one hand on her wrist. The touch of his fingers, long, lean and cool against that tender skin, felt like a bomb going off inside her body. Not just the usual tingle of attraction, the shower of sparks that was your body's basic reaction to a good-looking guy. No, a *bomb*. She jerked her hand away, heard her breath come out in a rush. 'Don't—'

'Whoa.' He held his hands up in front of him. 'Sorry, my mistake.' But he didn't look sorry. He looked like he knew exactly what she'd just experienced. 'I meant what I said, Millie. It's going to be a fun evening. I like a challenge.'

'Oh, please.' His stupid comment made her feel safe. She wanted this Chase to be exactly what she'd thought he was: attractive, arrogant and utterly unthreatening.

Chase grinned. 'I knew you'd expect me to say that.' And, just like that, she was back to wondering. Millie snatched up a menu.

'Shall we order?'

'Drinks first.'

'I'll have a glass of Chardonnay with ice, please.'

'That sounds about right,' he murmured and rose from

the table. Millie watched him walk to the bar, her gaze glued to his easy, long-limbed stride. Yes, she was staring at his butt. He looked good in board shorts.

By sheer force of will she dragged her gaze away from him and stared down at her phone. Why couldn't she have one work crisis? She'd had a dozen a day when she was in the office. Of course she knew why; she just didn't like it. Jack had insisted she take a week's holiday with no interruptions or furtive tele-commuting. She hadn't taken any in two years, and new company policy—supposedly for the health of its employees—demanded that you use at least half of your paid leave in one year.

What a ridiculous policy.

She *wanted* to work. She'd been working twelve-, four-teen- and sometimes even sixteen-hour days for two years and screeching to a halt to come here was making her very, very twitchy.

'Here you go.' Chase had returned to the table and placed a glass of wine in front of her. Millie eyed his own drink warily; it looked like soda.

'What are you drinking?'

'Some kind of cola.' He shrugged. 'It's cold, at least.'

'Do you have a drinking problem?' she asked abruptly and he laughed.

'Good idea, let's skip right to the important stuff. No, I don't. I'm just not drinking right now.' He took a sip of his soda, eyeing her thoughtfully. Millie held his gaze. All right, asking that had been a bit abrupt and even weird, but she'd forgotten how to do chit-chat.

'So, Millie, where are you from?'

'New York City.'

'I suppose I should have guessed that.'

'Oh, really?' She bristled. Again. 'You seem to think you have me figured out.'

'No, but I tend to be observant. And you definitely have that hard city gloss.'

'Where are you from, then?'

He gave her one of his toe-curling smiles. His eyes, Millie thought distantly, were so warm. She wanted to curl up in them, which was a nonsensical thought. 'I'm from New York too.'

'I suppose I could have guessed that.'

He laughed, a low, rich chuckle. 'How?'

'You've got that over-privileged, city-boy veneer,' she responded sweetly, to which he winced with theatrical exaggeration.

'Ouch.'

'At least now we understand each other.'

'Do we?' he asked softly and Millie focused on her drink. *Sip. Stare at the ice cubes bobbing in the liquid. Don't look at him.* 'Why are you so prickly?'

'I'm not. It was a knee-jerk response. She *was* being prickly. She hadn't engaged with a man in any sense in far too long and she didn't know how to start now. *Why* had she agreed to this? She took another sip of wine, let the bubbles crisp on her tongue. 'Sorry,' she said after a moment. 'I'm not usually quite this bitchy.'

'I bring out the best in you?'

'I suppose you do.' She met his gaze, meaning to smile with self-deprecating wryness, but somehow her lips froze in something more like a grimace. He was gazing at her with a sudden intentness that made her breath dry and her heart start to pound. She wanted him to be light, wry, *shallow*. He wasn't being any of those things right now. And, even when he had been, she had a horrible feeling he'd simply done it by choice.

'So why are you on St Julian's?' he asked.

'Holiday, of course.'

'You don't seem like the type to holiday willingly.'

Which was all too true, but she didn't like him knowing it, or knowing anything. 'Oh?' she asked, glad to hear she was hitting that self-deprecating note she'd tried for earlier. 'And you know me so well?'

He leaned forward, suddenly predatory. 'I think I do.'

Her heart still pounding, Millie leaned back as if she actually felt relaxed and arched an eyebrow. 'How is that?'

'Let's see.' He leaned back too, sprawled in his chair in a manner so casually relaxed and yet also innately powerful, even in an ocean-side bar wearing board shorts. 'You're a lawyer, or else you're in finance.' He glanced at her, considering, and Millie froze. 'Finance, I'd say, something demanding but also elite. Hedge-fund manager, maybe?'

Damn it. How the hell did he know that? She said nothing.

'You work long hours, of course,' Chase continued, clearly warming to this little game. 'And you live in a high-rise building, full-service, on— Let's see. The Upper East Side? But near the subway, so you can get to work in under twenty minutes. Although you try to jog to work at least two mornings a week.' Now he arched an eyebrow, a little smile playing about his mouth. 'How am I doing so far?'

'Terrible,' Millie informed him shortly. She was seething inside, seething with the pain of someone knowing her at all, even just the basics. And she hated that he'd been able to guess it, read her as easily as a book. What else could he find out about her just by his so-called powers of observation? 'I run to work three mornings a week, not two, and I live in midtown.'

Chase grinned. 'I must be slipping.'

'Anyway,' Millie said, 'I could guess the same kinds of things about you.'

'OK, shoot.'

She eyed him just as he had her, trying to gain a little

time to assemble her thoughts. She had no idea what he did or where he lived. She could guess, but that was all it would be—a guess. Taking a breath, she began. 'I think you work in some pseudo-creative field, like IT or advertising.'

'*Pseudo*-creative?' Chase interjected, nearly spluttering his soda. 'You really are tough, Camilla.'

'Millie,' she reminded him shortly. Only Rob had called her Camilla. 'You live in Chelsea or Soho, in one of those deluxe bachelor loft apartments. A converted warehouse with views of the river and zero charm.'

'That is so stereotypical, it hurts.'

'With a great room that's fantastic for parties, top-of-the-line leather sofas, a huge TV and a high-tech kitchen full of gadgets you never use.'

He shook his head slowly, his gaze fastened on hers. He smiled, almost looking sorry for her. 'Totally wrong.'

She folded her arms. Strange how her observations of him made her feel exposed. 'Oh? How so?'

'All right, you might be right about the loft apartment, but it's in Tribeca—and my television is mid-size, thank you very much.'

'And the leather sofas?'

'Leather cleans very easily, or so my cleaning lady tells me.' She rolled her eyes. 'And I'll have you know I do use my kitchen, quite often. I find cooking relaxing.'

She eyed him uncertainly. 'You do not.'

'I do. But I bet you don't cook. You buy a bagel on the way to work, skip lunch and eat a bowl of cereal standing by the sink for dinner.'

It was just a little too close to the truth and it sounded unbelievably pathetic. Suddenly Millie wanted to stop this little game. Desperately. 'I order take-out on occasion as well,' she told him, trying for breezy. 'So what do you do, anyway?'

'I'm an architect. Does that count as pseudo-creative?'

'Definitely.' She was being incredibly harsh, but she was afraid to be anything else. This man exposed her in a way that felt like peeling back her skin—painful and messy. This date was over.

'As entertaining as this has been, I think I'll go.' She drained her glass of wine and half-rose from her chair, only to be stopped by Chase wrapping his fingers around her wrist, just as he had before—and, just as before, she reacted, an explosion of senses inside her.

'Scared, Millie?'

'Scared?' she repeated as contemptuously as she could. 'Of what—you?'

'Of us.'

'There is no *us*.'

'There's been an *us* since the moment you agreed to a drink, dinner and a walk on the beach,' he informed her with silky softness. 'And so far we've just had our drink.'

'Let me go,' she said flatly, her lips numb, her whole body buzzing.

Chase held up both hands, his gaze still holding hers as if they were joined by a live wire. 'I already did.'

And so he had. She was standing there like a complete idiot, acting as if she were trapped, when the only thing imprisoning her was her own fear. This man guessed way too much.

She couldn't walk away now. Admitting defeat was not an option. And if she could handle this, handle him as she'd assured herself she could, then wouldn't that be saying something? Wouldn't that be a way of proving to herself, as well as him, that she had nothing either to hide or fear?

She dropped back down into her chair and gave him a quick, cool smile. 'I'm not scared.'

Something like approval lit his eyes, making Millie feel

stupidly, ridiculously gratified. Better to get through this evening as quickly as possible.

'So shall we order?'

'Oh no, we're not eating here,' Chase informed her. Millie stared at him, nonplussed. He smiled, slow, easy and completely in control. 'We'll eat somewhere more private.'

CHAPTER TWO

'MORE private?' Millie's voice rose in a screech as she stared
at him, two angry blotches of colour appearing high on her
cheeks. He should be annoyed by now, Chase mused. He
should be way past annoyed. The woman was a nutcase. Or
at least very high-maintenance. But he wasn't annoyed, not
remotely. He'd enjoyed their little exchange, liked that she
gave as good as she got. And he was intrigued by something
underneath that hard gloss—something real and deep and
alive. He just wasn't sure what it was, or what he wanted
to do with it.

But first, dinner. 'Relax. I'm not about to about to abduct
you, as interesting as that possibility may be.'

'Not funny.'

She held herself completely rigid, her face still flushed
with anger. He'd had no idea his change of dinner plans
would provoke such a reaction—no; he had. Of course he
had. He just hadn't realised he'd enjoy it so much. Underneath
the overly ironed blouse her chest rose and fell in agitated
breaths, making him suspect all that creaseless cotton hid
some slender but interesting curves. 'You're right, it's not
funny,' he agreed with as much genuine contrition as he
could muster. 'We barely know each other, and I didn't intend to make you feel vulnerable.'

She rolled her eyes. 'We're not on some mandatory course

for creating a safe work environment, Chase. You can skip the PC double-speak.'

He laughed, loving it. Loving that she didn't play games, not even innocent ones. 'OK. Fine. By more private, I meant a room in the resort. Chaperoned by wait staff and totally safe. If you're feeling, you know, threatened.'

'I have not felt threatened by you for an instant,' Millie replied, and Chase leaned forward.

'Are you sure about that?' he asked softly, knowing he was pressing her in ways she didn't want to be pressed. He'd seen that shadow of vulnerability in her eyes, felt the sudden, chilly withdrawal as her armour went up. He knew the tactics because he'd used them himself.

It's not good news, Chase. I'm sorry.

Hell, yeah, he'd used them.

She stared at him for a moment, held his gaze long enough so he could see the warm brown of her eyes. Yes, *warm*. Like dark honey or rum, and the only warm thing about her. So far.

'Threatened is the wrong word,' she finally said, and from the starkness of her tone he knew she was speaking in total truth. 'You do make me uncomfortable, though.'

'Do I?'

She gave him a thin-lipped smile. 'I don't think anyone likes being told that it's obvious she eats a bowl of cereal by the sink for dinner.'

Ouch. Put like that, he realised it was insulting. 'I wouldn't say obvious.' Although he sort of would.

'Only because you're so perceptive, I suppose?' she shot back, and he grinned.

'So shall we go somewhere more private so you can continue to be uncomfortable?'

'What an appealing proposition.'

'It appeals to me,' he said truthfully, and she gave a little shake of her head.

'Honestly? What do you see in me?' She sounded curious, but also that thing he dreaded: vulnerable. She really didn't know the answer, and hell if he did either.

'What do you see in me?' he asked back.

She chewed her lip, her eyes shadowing once more. 'You made me laugh for the first time in—a long time.'

He had the strange feeling she'd been about to give him a specific number. *Since when?* 'That's a lot of pressure.'

Her eyes widened, flaring with warmth again. 'Why?'

'Because of course now I have to make you laugh again.'

And for a second he thought he might get a laugh right then and there, and something rose in his chest, an airy bubble of hope and happiness that made absolutely no sense. Still he felt it, rising him high and dizzily higher even though he didn't move. He grinned. Again, simply because he couldn't help it.

She shook her head. 'I'm not that easy.'

'This conversation just took a *very* interesting turn.'

'I meant *laughing*,' she protested, and then she did laugh, one ridiculously un-ladylike hiccup of joy that had her clapping her hand over her mouth.

'There it is,' Chase said softly. He felt a deep and strangely primal satisfaction, the kind he usually only felt when he'd nailed an architectural design. He'd made her laugh. Twice.

She stared at him, her hand still clapped over her mouth, her eyes wide, warm and soft—if eyes could even be considered soft. Chase felt a stirring deep inside—low down, yes, he felt that basic attraction, but something else. Something not quite so low down and far more alarming, caused by this hard woman with the soft eyes.

'You changed the deal,' she told him, dropping her hand,

all businesslike and brisk again. 'You said dinner here, in the restaurant.'

'I did not,' Chase countered swiftly. 'You just didn't read the fine print.'

He thought she might laugh again, but she didn't. He had a feeling she suppressed it, didn't want to give him the power of making her laugh three times. And it did feel like power, heady and addictive. He wanted more.

'I don't remember signing,' she said. 'And verbal agreements aren't legally binding.'

He leaned back in his chair, amazed at how alive he felt. How invigorated. He hadn't felt this kind of dazzling, creative energy in months. Eight months and six days, to be precise.

'All right, then,' he said. 'You can go.' He felt his heart thud at the thought that she might actually rise from the table and walk down the beach out of his life. Yet he also knew he had to level the playing field. She needed to be here because she wanted to be here, and she had to admit it. He didn't know why it was so important; he just felt it—that gut instinct that told him something was going on here that was more than a meal.

She chewed her lip again and he could tell by the little worry marks in its lush fullness—her lips were another soft part of her—that this was a habit. Her lashes swept downwards, hiding her eyes, but he could still read her. Easily.

She wanted to walk, but she also didn't, and that was aggravating her to no end.

She looked up, eyes clear and wide once more, any emotion safely hidden. 'Fine. We'll go somewhere more private.' And, without waiting for him, she rose from the table.

Chase rose too, anticipation firing through him. He wasn't even sure what he was looking forward to—just being with her, or something else? She was so not his type, and yet he couldn't deny that deep jolt of awareness, the flash of lust. And not just a flash, not just lust either. She attracted and intrigued him on too many levels.

Smiling, he rose from the table and led the way out of the beach-side bar and towards the resort.

Millie followed Chase into the resort, the soaring space cool and dim compared to the beach. She felt neither cool nor dim; everything inside her was light and heat. It scared her, feeling this. Wanting him. Because, yes, she knew she wanted him. Not just desire, simple attraction, a biological response or scientific law. *Want*.

She hadn't touched a man in two years. Longer, really, because she couldn't actually remember the last time she and Rob had made love. It had bothered her at first, the not knowing. She'd lain in bed night after endless nights scouring her brain for a fragment of a memory. Something to remind her of how she'd lain sated and happy in her husband's arms. She hadn't come up with anything, because it had been too long.

Now it wasn't the past that was holding her in thrall; it was the present. The future. Just what did she want to happen tonight?

'This way,' Chase murmured, and Millie followed him into a lift. The space was big enough, all wood-panelled luxury, but it still felt airless and small. He was still only wearing board shorts. Was he going to spend the whole evening shirtless? Could she stand it?

Millie cleared her throat, the sound seeming as loud as a gunshot, and Chase gave her a lazy sideways smile. He knew what she was thinking. Feeling. Knew, with that awful arrogance, that she was attracted to him even if she didn't like it. And she didn't like it, although she couldn't really say why.

It had been two years. Surely it was time to move on, to accept and heal and go forward?

She shook her head, impatient with herself. Dinner with someone like Chase was not going forward. If anything, it was going backwards, because he was too much like Rob. He was, Millie thought, more like Rob than Rob himself. He was her husband as her husband had always wanted to be: powerful, rich, commanding. He was Rob on steroids.

Exactly what she didn't want.

'Slow down there, Millie.'

Her gaze snapped to his, saw the remnant of that lazy smile. 'What—?'

'Your mind is going a mile a minute. I can practically see the smoke coming out of your ears.'

She frowned, wanting to deny it. 'It's just dinner.'

Chase said nothing, but his smile deepened. Millie felt a weird, shivery sensation straight through her bones that he wasn't responding because he didn't agree with her. It wasn't just dinner. It was something else, something scary.

But what?

'Here we are.' The lift doors swooshed open and Chase led her down a corridor and then out onto a terrace. A private terrace. They were completely alone, no wait staff in sight.

Millie didn't feel vulnerable, threatened or scared. No, she felt *terrified*. What was she doing here? Why had she agreed to dinner with this irritating and intriguing man? And why did she feel that jolt of electric awareness, that kick of excitement, every time she so much as looked at him? She felt more alive now than she had since Rob's death, maybe even since before that—a long time before that.

She walked slowly to the railing and laid one hand on the wrought-iron, still warm from the now-sinking sun. The vivid sunset had slipped into a twilit indigo, the sea a dark, tranquil mirror beneath.

'We missed the best part,' Chase murmured, coming to stand next to her.

'Do you think so?' Millie kept her gaze on the darkening sky. 'This part is more beautiful to me.'

Chase cocked his head, and Millie turned to see his speculative gaze slide over her. 'Somehow that doesn't surprise me,' he said, and reached out to tuck a strand of hair behind her ear. Millie felt as if he'd just dusted her with sparks, jabbed her with little jolts of electricity. Her cheek and ear throbbed, her physical response so intense it felt almost painful.

Did he feel it? Could it be possible that he reacted to her the way she did to him? The thought short-circuited her brain. It was quite literally mind-blowing.

She turned away from him, back to the sunset. 'Everybody likes the vibrant colours of a sunset,' she said, trying to keep her voice light. 'All that magenta and orange—gorgeous but gaudy, like an old broad with too much make-up.'

'I'll agree with you that the moment after is more your style. Understated elegance. Quiet sophistication.'

'And which do you prefer? The moment before or after?'

Chase didn't answer, and Millie felt as if the very air had suddenly become heavy with expectation. It filled her lungs, weighed them down; she was breathless.

'Before,' he finally said. 'Then there's always something to look forward to.'

Millie didn't think they were talking about sunsets any more. She glanced at Chase and saw him staring pensively at the sky, now deepening to black. The sun and all its gaudy traces had disappeared completely.

'So tell me,' she said, turning away from the railing, 'how did you arrange a private terrace so quickly? Or do you keep one reserved on standby, just in case you meet a woman?'

He laughed, a rich, throaty chuckle. This man enjoyed

life. It shouldn't surprise her; she'd labelled him a hedonist straight off. Yet she didn't feel prissily judgmental of that enjoyment right now. She felt—yes, she really did—*jealous*.

'Full disclosure?'

'Always.'

He reached for a blue button-down shirt that had been laid on one of the chairs. He'd thought of everything, and possessed the power to see it done. Millie watched him button up his shirt with long, lean fingers, the gloriously sculpted muscles of his chest disappearing under the crisp cotton.

'My family owns this resort.'

She jerked her rather admiring gaze from the vicinity of his chest to his face. 'Ah.' There was, she knew, a wealth of understanding in that single syllable. So, architect *and* trust-fund baby. She'd suspected something like that. He had the assurance that came only from growing up rich and entitled. She should be relieved; she wanted him to be what she'd thought he was, absolutely no more and maybe even less. So why, gazing at him now, did she feel the tiniest bit disappointed, like he'd let her down?

Like she actually wanted him to be different?

'Yes. Ah.' He smiled wryly, and she had a feeling he'd guessed her entire thought process, not for the first time this evening.

'That must be handy.'

'It has its benefits.' He spoke neutrally, without the usual flippant lightness and Millie felt a little dart of curiosity. For the first time Chase looked tense, his jaw a little bunched, his expression a little set. He didn't smile as he pulled out a chair for her at the cozy table for two and flickered with candlelight in the twilit darkness.

Millie's mind was, as usual, working overtime. 'The Bryant family owns this resort.'

'Bingo.'

'My company manages their assets.' That was how she'd ended up here, waiting out her week of enforced holiday, indolent luxury. Jack had suggested it.

'And you have a rule about mixing business with pleasure?'

'The point is moot. I don't handle their account.'

'Well, that's a relief.' He spoke with an edge she hadn't heard since she'd met him. Clearly his family and its wealth raised his hackles.

'So you're one of the Bryants,' she said, knowing instinctively such a remark would annoy him. 'Which one?'

'You know my family?'

'Who doesn't?' The Bryants littered the New York tabloids and society pages, not that she read either. But you couldn't so much as check your email without coming across a news blurb or scandalous headline. Had she read about Chase? Probably, if she'd paid attention to such things. There were three Bryant boys, as far as she remembered, and they were all players.

'I'm the youngest son,' Chase said tautly. He leaned back in his chair, deliberately relaxed in his body if not his voice. 'My older brother Aaron runs the property arm of Bryant Enterprises. My middle brother Luke runs the retail.'

'And you do your own thing.'

'Yes.'

That dart of curiosity sharpened into a direct stab. Why didn't Chase work for the family company? 'There's no Bryant Architecture, is there?'

His mouth thinned. 'Definitely not.'

'So what made you leave the family fold?'

'We're getting personal, then?'

'Are we?'

'Why did you throw out your canvas?'

Startled, she stared at him, saw his sly, silky little smile. 'I asked you first.'

'I don't like taking orders. And you?'

'I don't like painting.'

He stared at her; she stared back. A stand-off. So she wasn't the only one with secrets. 'Interesting,' he finally mused. He poured them both sparkling water. 'You don't like painting, but you decided to drag all that paraphernalia to the beach and set up your little artist's studio right there on the sand?'

She shrugged. 'I used to like it, when I was younger.' A lot younger and definitely less jaded. 'I thought I might like to try it again.'

'What changed your mind?'

Another shrug. She could talk about this. This didn't have to be personal or revealing. She wouldn't let it be. 'I just wasn't feeling it.'

'You don't seem like the type to rely on feelings.'

She smiled thinly. 'Still typecasting me, Chase?'

He laughed, an admitted defeat. 'Sorry.'

'It's OK. I play to type.'

'On purpose.'

She eyed him uneasily. Perhaps this was personal after all. And definitely revealing. 'Maybe.'

'Which means you aren't what you seem,' Chase said softly, 'are you?'

'I'm exactly what I seem.' She sounded defensive. *Great.*

'You *want* to be exactly what you seem,' he clarified. 'Which is why you play it that way.'

She felt a lick of anger, which was better than the dizzying combination of terror and lust he'd been stirring up inside her. 'What did you do, dust off your psychology textbook?'

He laughed and held up his hands. 'Guilty. I'm bored on this holiday, what can I say?'

And, just like that, he'd defused the tension that had been thickening in the air, tightening inside her. Yet Millie could not escape the feeling—the certainty—that he'd chosen to do it, that he'd backed off because he'd wanted to, not because of what she wanted.

One person at this table was calling the shots and it wasn't her.

'So.' She breathed through her nose, trying to hide the fact that her heart was beating hard. She wanted to take a big, dizzying gulp of air, but she didn't. Wouldn't. 'If you're so bored, why are you on holiday?'

'Doctor's orders.'

She blinked, not sure if he was joking. 'How's that?'

'The stress was getting to me.'

He didn't look stressed. He looked infuriatingly relaxed, arrogantly in control. 'The holiday must be working.'

'Seems to be.' He sounded insouciant, yet deliberately so. He was hiding something, Millie thought. She'd tried to strike that note of breeziness too many times not to recognise its falseness.

'So are we actually going to eat?' He hadn't pressed her, so she wouldn't press him. Another deal, this one silently made.

'Your wish is my command.'

Within seconds a waiter appeared at the table with a tray of food. Millie watched as he ladled freshly grilled snapper in lime juice and coconut rice on her plate. It smelled heavenly.

She waited until he'd served Chase and departed once more before saying dryly, 'Nice service. Being one of the Bryant boys has its perks, it seems.'

'Sometimes.' Again that even tone.

'Are you staying at the resort?'

'I have my own villa.' He stressed the 'own' only a little, but Millie guessed it was a sore point. Had he worked for what he had? He was probably too proud to tell her. She wouldn't ask.

She took a bite of her fish. It tasted heavenly too, an explosion of tart and tender on her tongue. She swallowed and saw Chase looking at her. Just looking, no deliberate, heavy-lidded languor, and yet she felt her body respond, like an antenna tuned to some cerebral frequency. Everything jumped to alert, came alive.

It had been so *long*.

She took another bite.

'So why are you on holiday, Millie?'

Why did the way he said her name sound intimate? She swallowed the fish. 'Doctor's orders.'

'Really?'

'Well, no. Boss's. I haven't taken any holiday in a while.'

'How long?'

That bite of fish seemed to lodge in her chest, its exquisite tenderness now as tough as old leather. Finally, with an audible and embarrassing gulp, she managed, 'Two years.'

Chase cocked his head and continued just looking. How much did he *see*? 'That's a long time,' he finally said, and she nodded.

'So he told me.'

'But you didn't want to take any holiday?'

'It's obvious, I suppose.'

'Pretty much.'

She stabbed a bit of rice with her fork. 'I like to work.'

'So *are* you a hedge-fund manager?'

'Got it in one.'

'And you like it?'

Instinctively '*of course I do*' rose to her lips, yet somehow the words didn't come. She couldn't get them out, as if someone had pressed a hand over her mouth and kept her from speaking. So she just stared and swallowed and felt herself flush.

Why had he even asked? she wondered irritably. Obviously she liked it, since she worked so hard.

'I see,' Chase said quietly, knowingly, and a sudden, blinding fury rose up in her, obliterating any remaining sense and opening her mouth.

'You don't see anything.' She sounded savage. Incensed. And, even worse, she *was*. Why did this stupid man make her feel so much? Reveal so much?

'Maybe not,' Chase agreed. He didn't sound riled in the least. Millie let out a shuddering breath. This date had been such a bad idea.

'OK, now it's your turn.'

She blinked. 'What?'

'You get to ask me a personal question. Only fair, right?'

Another blink. She hadn't expected that. 'Why do you hate being one of the Bryants?'

Now he blinked. 'Hate is a strong word.'

'So it is.'

'I never said I hated it.'

'You didn't need to.' She took a sip of water, her hand steady, her breath thankfully even. 'You're not the only one who can read people, you know.'

'You can read me?' Chase leaned forward, his eyes glinting in the candlelight. She saw the golden-brown stubble on his jaw, could almost feel its sandpaper roughness under her fingers. She breathed in the scent of him, part musk, part sun, pure male. 'What am I thinking now?' he asked, a steely, softly worded challenge. Millie didn't dare answer.

She knew what she was thinking. She was thinking about taking that hard jaw between her hands and angling her lips over his. His lips would be soft but firm, commanding and drawing deep from her. And she would give, she would surrender that long-held part of herself in just one kiss. She knew it, felt it bone-deep, soul-deep, which was ridiculous, because she barely knew this man. Yet in the space of an hour or two he'd drawn more from her than anyone had since her husband's death, or even before. He'd seen more, glimpsed her sadness and subterfuge like no one else could or had. Not even the parents who adored her, the sister she called a best friend. No one had seen through her smoke and mirrors. No one but Chase.

And he was a *stranger*.

A stranger who could kiss her quite senseless.

'I don't know what you're thinking,' she said and looked away.

Chase laughed softly, no more than an exhalation of breath. 'Coward.'

And yes, maybe she was a coward, but then he was too. Because Millie knew the only reason Chase had turned provocative on her was because he didn't want to answer her question about his family.

She pushed her plate away, her appetite gone even though her meal was only half-finished. 'How about that walk on the beach?'

He arched an eyebrow. 'You're done?'

She was *so* done. The sooner she ended this evening, the better. The only reason she wasn't bailing on the walk was her pride. Even now, when she felt uncomfortable, exposed and even angry, she was determined to handle this. Handle him. 'It was delicious,' she said. 'But I've had enough.'

'No pun intended, I'm sure.'

She curved her lips into a smile. 'You can read into that whatever you like.'

'All right, Millie,' Chase said, uncoiling from his chair like a lazy serpent about to strike. 'Let's walk.'

He reached for her hand and unthinkingly, *stupidly*, Millie let him take it.

As soon as his fingers wrapped over hers, she felt that explosion inside her again and she knew she was lost.

CHAPTER THREE

CHASE felt Millie's fingers tense in his even as a buzz travelled all the way up his arm. Her fingers felt fragile, slender bone encased in tender skin. A sudden need to protect her rose in him, a caveman's howl. Clearly it was some kind of evolutionary instinct, because if there was one woman who didn't need protecting, it was Camilla Lang.

He thought she might jerk her hand away from his, and he was pretty sure she wanted to, but she didn't. Didn't want to show weakness, most likely. He smiled and took full advantage, tightening his hold, drawing her close. She tensed some more.

This woman was *prickly*. And Chase had a sneaking suspicion she had issues, definitely with a capital I. Bad relationship or broken heart; maybe something darker and more difficult. Who knew? He sure as hell didn't want to. Didn't he have enough to deal with, with his own issues? Those had a capital I too. And he had no intention of sharing them with Millie.

Even so he drew her from the table, still holding her hand, and away from the terrace, down the lift, through the resort, all the way outside. He threaded his way through the tables of the beach-side restaurant and bar, straight onto the sand. She held his hand the whole time, not speaking, not pulling away, but clearly not all that pleased about it either.

There they were, holding hands alone in the dark.

The wind rattled the leaves of the palm trees overhead and he could hear the gentle *shoosh* of the waves lapping against the shore. The resort and its patrons seemed far away, their voices barely a murmur, the night soft and dark all around them. Millie pulled her hand from his, a not-so-gentle tug.

'Let's walk.'

'Sounds good.'

Silently they walked down the beach, the sand silky and cool under their bare feet. Lights of a pleasure yacht glimmered in the distance, and from far away Chase heard the husky laugh of a woman intent on being seduced.

Not like Millie. She walked next to him, her back ramrod-straight, her capris and blouse still relentlessly unwrinkled. She looked like she was walking the plank.

He nearly stopped right there in the sand. What the *hell* was he doing here, with a woman like her? Didn't he have better ways to spend his time?

'What?' She turned to him, and in the glimmer of moonlight he saw those warm, soft eyes, shadowed with a vulnerability he knew she thought she was hiding.

'What do you mean, *what*?'

'You're thinking something.'

'I'm always thinking something. Most people are.'

She shook her head, shadows deepening in her eyes. 'No, I mean…' She paused, biting her lip, teeth digging into those worry marks once more. If she didn't let up, she'd have a scar. 'You're regretting this, aren't you? This whole stupid date.'

He stopped, faced her full-on. 'Aren't you?'

She let go of her lip to give him the smallest of smiles. 'That's a given, don't you think?'

Did it have to be? How had they fallen into these roles so quickly, so easily? He wanted to break free. He didn't want to be a flippant playboy to her uptight workaholic. He had a sudden, mad urge to push her down into the sand, to see her clothes wrinkled and dirty, her face smudged and sandy, her lips swollen and kissed...

Good grief.

Chase took a step back, raking a hand through his hair. 'We're pretty different, Millie.'

'Thank God for that.'

He couldn't muster a laugh. He had too many emotions inside him: longing and lust, irritation and irrational fear. What an unholy mix. He'd asked her out because it had seemed fun, *amusing*, but it was starting to feel way too intense. And he didn't need any more intense. He took a breath and let it out slowly. 'Maybe we should call it a night.'

She blinked, her face immediately blanking, as if her mind were pressing delete. Inwardly Chase cursed. He didn't want to hurt her, but he knew in that moment he had.

'Millie—'

'Fine.' Her back straighter than ever, she started down the beach away from the resort. He watched her for a second, exasperated with her stubbornness and annoyed by his own clumsy handling of the situation.

'Aren't you staying at the resort?'

'I'm finishing our walk.'

He let out a huff of laughter. He *liked* this woman, issues and all. 'I didn't realise we'd set a distance on it.'

'More than ten seconds.' She didn't look back once.

She was far enough away that he had to shout. 'It was more like five minutes.'

'Clearly you have very little stamina.'

There was more truth in that then he'd ever care to admit. 'Millie.' He didn't shout this time, but he knew she heard anyway. He saw it in the tensing of her shoulders, the half-second stumble in her stride. 'Come back here.'

'Why should I?'

'On second thought, I'll come to you.' Quickly he strode down the beach, leaving deep footprints in the damp sand, until he reached her. The wind had mussed her hair just a little bit, so the razor edges were softened, blurred. Without even thinking what he was doing or wondering if it was a good idea, Chase reached out and slid his hands along her jaw bone, cupping her face as he drew her to him. Her skin felt like cool silk, cold silk, icy even. Yet so very, unbearably soft. Eyes and lips and skin, all soft. What about her, Chase wondered, was actually hard?

She was close enough to kiss, another inch would do it, yet he didn't. She didn't resist, didn't do anything. She was like a deer caught in the headlights, a rabbit in a snare. Trapped. Terrified.

'Sorry,' he breathed against her mouth, close enough so he could imagine the taste of her. She'd taste crisp and clean, like the white wine she'd drunk, except it would be just her. Essence of Camilla.

She jerked back a mere half-inch. 'Sorry for what?'

'For acting like a jerk.'

Her lips quirked in the tiniest of smiles. 'To which point of the evening are you referring?'

'All right, wise-ass. I was talking about two minutes ago, when I said we should call it a night.' He stroked his thumb over the fullness of her lower lip, because he just couldn't help himself, and felt her tremble. 'I don't think I was too much of a jerk before that.'

Millie didn't answer. Chase saw that her lips were parted, her pupils dilated. *Desire.* The brief moment of tenderness suddenly flared into something untamed and urgent. Chase felt a groan catch in his chest, his body harden in undeniable and instinctive response. His hands tightened as they cradled her face, yet neither of them moved. It was almost as if they were paralysed, both afraid—no, terrified—to close the mere inch that separated them, cross that chasm.

Because Chase knew it wouldn't be your average kiss. And he was in no position for anything else.

With one quick jerk of her head, Millie slid out of his grasp and stepped backwards. 'Thanks for the apology,' she said, her voice as cool as ever. 'But it's not needed. It was interesting to get to know you, Chase, but I think we've fulfilled both sides of the deal.' She smiled without humour, and Chase couldn't stand the sudden bleakness in her eyes. Damn it, they were meant to be *soft*. 'Good night,' she said and headed back down the beach.

Millie walked without looking where she was going or caring. She just wanted to get away from Chase.

What had just happened?

He'd almost kissed her. She'd almost let him. In that moment when his hands had slid along her skin, cradling her face like she was something to be cherished and treasured, she'd wanted him to. Desperately. She would have let him do anything then, and thank goodness he hadn't, thank God he'd hesitated and she'd somehow found the strength to pull away.

The last thing she needed was to get involved with a man like Chase Bryant.

She left the beach behind and wound her way through the palm trees to the other side of the resort. She'd go in the front entrance and up to her room, and with any luck she wouldn't see Chase again all week. It was a big place, and he'd told her he was staying at his villa.

So why did that thought fill her with not just disappointment, but desolation? It was ridiculous to feel so lost without a shallow stranger she'd met a couple of hours ago. Absolutely absurd.

Clearly what this evening had shown her, Millie decided

as she swiped her key-card and entered the sumptuous suite Jack had insisted she book for the week, was that she was ready to move on. Start dating, have some kind of relationship.

Just not with a man like Chase Bryant.

The words echoed through her, making her pause in stripping off her clothes and turning on the shower. *A man like Chase Bryant.* She'd pigeon-holed Chase from the moment she'd met him, yet he'd surprised her at every turn. Just what kind of man *was* he?

A man who asked pressing questions and told her things about herself nobody else knew. Who turned flippant just when she needed him to. Whose simple touch set off an explosion inside her, yet who kept himself from kissing her even when she was so clearly aching for his caress.

A man who made her very, very uncomfortable.

Was that the kind of man she didn't want to get involved with?

Hell, yes.

She wished she could dismiss him, as she'd fully intended to do when she'd first met him: spoiled and shallow playboy, completely non-threatening. That was the man she'd agreed to have dinner with, not the man he *was*, who had set her pulse racing and tangled her emotions into knots. A man who touched her on too many levels.

Was that what she didn't want? Getting involved with someone who had the power to see her as she really was, to hurt her?

Well, *duh.* Obviously she didn't want to get hurt. Who did? And surely she'd already had her life's share of grief Millie stepped into the shower, the water streaming over her even as her thoughts swirled in confusing circles.

Her mind was telling her all that, but her body was singing a very different tune. Her body wanted his touch. Her mouth wanted to know his kiss. Every bit of her ached with a longing for fulfilment she thought she'd forever suppressed.

She let out a shudder and leaned her head against the shower tile as the water streamed over her.

She could stay analytical about this. So she didn't want to get hurt. She didn't have to. How much she cared—how much she gave—was in her control. And here she was—and Chase was—on a tropical island for a single week, neither of them with very much to do...

Why not?

Why not what?

She dumped too much shampoo into the palm of her hand and scrubbed her hair, fingernails raking her scalp as if she could wash these tempting and terrible thoughts right out of her mind.

Just what was she contemplating?

A week-long affair with Chase Bryant. A fling. A cheap, sordid, sexual transaction.

She scrubbed harder.

She didn't do flings. Of course she didn't. Her husband had been her only lover. Yet here she was, thinking about it. Wondering how Chase would taste, how he would hold her. What it would feel like, to be in his arms. To surrender herself, just a little bit of herself, because even if he sensed she had secrets she wasn't going to tell them to him. She just wanted that physical release, that momentary connection. The opportunity to forget. When Chase had been about to kiss her, she hadn't been able to think about anything else. All thoughts and memories had fled, leaving her nothing but blissful sensation.

She wanted that again. *More.*

Millie rinsed off and turned off the shower. She could control this. She could satiate this hunger that had opened up inside her and prove to herself and everyone else that she'd moved on.

She just needed to tell Chase.

Chase watched the poker-straight figure march down the beach as if in step with an invisible army and wondered why on earth Millie was looking for him. For there could be no mistaking her intent; she'd arrowed in on him like a laser beam. What, he wondered, was with all the military references going through his mind?

Clearly Millie Lang was on the attack.

And he was quite enjoying the anticipation of an invasion. He sat back on his heels on the deck of his sailboat, the water lapping gently against its sides, the sun a balm on his back. Millie marched closer.

Chase had no idea what she wanted. He'd stopped trying to untangle his thoughts about their date last night, from the almost-kiss he hadn't acted on, to the hurt that had flashed in her eyes to the fact that it had taken him three hours to fall asleep, with Millie's soft eyes still dancing through his mind. Definitely better not to think about any of it.

'There you are.'

'Looking for me?'

She stood on the beach, feet planted in the sand, hands on hips, a look of resolute determination on her face. 'As a matter of fact, I am.'

'I'm intrigued.' He stood up, wincing a little at the ache in his joints. He couldn't ignore the pain any more. She watched him, eyes narrowed, and he smiled. He could ignore it. He would. 'So, what's on your mind, scary lady?'

Her mouth twitched in a suppressed smile, and then she was back to being serious. 'Is this your boat?'

He glanced back at the sailboat, doing an exaggerated double-take. 'What—this?'

'Very funny.'

'Yep, it's my boat.'

'Did you sail here?'

He laughed, reluctantly, because once he might have. Not any more. He didn't trust himself out on the sea alone. 'No, I flew in a plane like most people. I keep the boat moored here, though.'

'I suppose the Bryants are a big sailing family and you started at the yacht club when you were a baby.'

He heard an edge to her voice that he recognised. She hadn't grown up rich, suspected the proverbial silver spoon. 'More like a toddler,' he said, shrugging. 'Do you sail?'

Lips pressed together. 'No.'

'You should try it.'

She glanced at him suspiciously. 'Why?'

'Because it's fun. And freeing. And I'd like to see you out on the water, your hair blowing away from your face.' She'd look softer then, he thought. Happier too, maybe.

'You would, huh?'

'Yeah. I would.'

'Well, you already told me how you felt about my haircut.'

He chuckled. 'True. Feel free to let me know if there's anything you don't like about my appearance.'

She eyed him up and down deliberately, and Chase felt a lick of excitement low in his belly. He liked that slow, considering look. Millie Lang was checking him out. 'I will,' she said slowly, 'but there isn't anything yet.'

'No?' He felt it again, that licking flame firing him up inside. Was Millie *flirting*? What had changed since last night, when she'd been as sharp and jagged as a handful of splinters? When he'd let her walk away because he told himself it was better—or at least easier—that way.

And then hadn't stopped thinking about her all night.

'Come aboard,' he said, and stretched out a hand. She

eyed it warily, and then with a deep breath like she was about to go underwater she took it and clambered onto the boat.

It was a small sailboat, just thirty-two feet long with one cabin underneath. He'd bought it with his first bonus and sailed halfway around the world on it, back when he'd been a hotshot. Now he cruised in the shallows, like some seventy year old pensioner with a bad case of gout and a dodgy heart. No risks. No stress. No fun.

'It's…nice,' Millie said, and he knew she didn't know a thing about boats. Who cared? He liked seeing her on deck, even if her clothes were still way too wrinkle-free. Today she wore a red-and-white-striped top and crisp navy-blue capris. Very nautical. Very boring. Yet he was intrigued by the way the boat-neck of her top revealed the hard, angular line of her collarbone. He wanted to run his fingers along that ridge of bone, discover if her skin was as icily soft as it had been last night.

'I could take you out some time,' he said. 'On the boat.' Why was she here? He stepped closer to her, inhaled the scent of her, something clean and citrusy. Breathed deep.

She turned to him, her hair sweeping along her jaw, and his gaze was caught by the angles of her jaw and shoulder, hard and soft. Her top had slipped a little, and he could see the strap of her bra: beige lace. No sexy lingerie for this lady, yet he still felt himself go hard.

'You could,' she said slowly, and he knew she was gearing up to say something—but what?

He folded his arms, adopted a casual pose. 'So?'

'So what?'

'Why are you here, Millie?'

Again that trapped look, chin tilted with defiance. This woman was all contradiction. 'Do you mind?'

'Not a bit.' And that was the truth.

She turned away, rubbing her arms as if she were cold. 'How long are you on this island, anyway?'

'A week, give or take.'

'You're not sure?'

'I'm being flexible.'

'And then you go back to New York?'

'That's the plan.' This was starting to feel like an interrogation. He didn't mind, but he wondered what she was getting at.

'I've never come across you in New York,' she said, almost to herself, and Chase just about kept himself from rolling his eyes.

'It's a pretty big city.'

She turned to face him. 'And we move in completely different circles.'

'Seems like it.'

'So there's no chance we'd see each other again.'

Maybe he should start feeling offended. But he didn't; he just felt like smiling. Laughing. Why did he enjoy her prickliness so much? 'Is that what you're afraid of?'

She met his gaze squarely. 'I'd prefer it if we didn't.'

He rubbed his jaw. 'If that's what you'd prefer, why are you on my boat?'

'I meant after. After this week.' Her words seemed heavy with meaning, but he still didn't get it.

'OK. I think I can manage that.' Even if he wasn't sure he wanted to.

'It would be easier,' she said, sounding almost earnest now. 'For me.'

Now he was really confused. 'Millie, I have no idea what you're talking about.'

'I know.' She pressed her lips together, gave a decisive nod. OK, Chase thought, here it comes. 'I'm attracted to you. You probably know that.'

He lifted one shoulder in a shrug that could mean anything. He didn't want to ruin this moment by agreeing or
disagreeing; he just wanted her to keep talking.

'And I think you're attracted to me. Sort of.'

She looked so pathetically and yet endearingly vulnerable that Chase had to keep himself from reaching for her.
What he would do when he had her in his arms, he wasn't
completely sure. He did know one thing. 'I'm attracted to
you, Millie. More than I'd ever expect.'

She let out a short laugh. 'Because I'm not your usual
type.'

'No, you're not. Does that matter?' He wasn't even sure
what he was asking. Where was she going with this conversation?

'No, I don't think it does.' She didn't sound completely
sure.

'But, trust me, I am.' If she risked a glance downwards,
she'd know.

'Well. Good.'

'Glad we're on the same page.'

She let out a breath and looked straight in his eyes.
Vulnerability and strength, hard and soft. 'I hope we are.'

'Maybe we'd find out if you clued me into where this
conversation is going.'

'Fine.' She took a deep breath, plunged. 'I want to sleep
with you.'

CHAPTER FOUR

To HIS credit, Chase's jaw didn't drop. He didn't laugh or raise his eyebrows or even blink. He just stared at her, expressionless, and Millie felt herself flush.

She'd decided on the straightforward approach because, really, what else could she do? She didn't flirt. She couldn't play the seductress, and in any case she knew instinctively that Chase would see through any gauzy ploys. No, all she had was a straight shot, and she'd fired it. Direct hit.

'OK,' Chase finally said, letting out a breath. 'That's... good to know.'

She gave a shaky huff of laughter. 'I'm glad you think so.'

He rubbed his jaw, the movement inherently sexy. She could see the rippling muscled six-pack of his abs, the glint of sun on his stubble, his strong arms and lean fingers. Yes, she was definitely attracted to him. 'So,' he said. 'What brought this about?'

Of course he'd start asking questions. Most guys would take what she said at face value and drop their pants. Not Chase. She should have realised this wasn't going to be simple.

She shifted her weight, tried to act at least somewhat nonchalant. 'What do you mean?'

'Why me?'

'You're here, you're interested and I'm attracted to you.'

He arched an eyebrow. 'I take it this isn't your normal behaviour?'

She swallowed, kept his stare. 'No, not exactly.'

'So why now?'

How much truth to tell? She decided to fire another straight shot. 'Look, I don't want to get into messy details. This isn't about emotion, or getting to know each other, or anything like that.'

'I appreciate your candour.'

'Good.' She felt that flush creep back. This had seemed like such a good idea last night, when she couldn't forget how much she'd wanted him to kiss her. When having a fling with Chase Bryant had seemed like the perfect way to move on from the spectres of her failed life. To forget, at least for a little while.

From here it wasn't looking so good.

'So?' she finally prompted, a definite edge to her voice.

'Well, I'm flattered.' Chase leaned over the boat to haul in some kind of rope. Millie waited, everything inside her tensing. He straightened, tossing the rope into a neat coil on the deck. 'But I'm not that easy a lay.'

She blinked, tried desperately to arrange her face into some sort of blankness. 'Oh? You could have fooled me.'

He looked almost amused. 'Now what gave you the impression that I was a man-whore, Miss Scary?'

'I didn't mean that.' Her face, Millie suspected, was bright red. 'I only meant you asked me out last night and so you must be…you know…open.'

'Open?' Now he really seemed amused.

'To a—a no-strings type of…' She trailed off, unwilling to put any of it in words. Affair? Fling? *Relationship?*

'Thing?' Chase supplied helpfully, and she nodded, bizarrely grateful.

'Yes. Thing.'

'Interesting.' He reached for another rope, and Millie felt the boat rock under her feet.

'So do you think you could give me your answer?' she asked, trying not to sound impatient. Or desperate.

'An answer,' Chase mused, and Millie gritted her teeth. He was tormenting her. On purpose.

'Yes, Chase. An answer.'

'As to whether I'll sleep with you.'

She heard the grinding screech as she gritted her teeth even harder. 'Yes.'

He smiled as he coiled another rope on the deck. 'The short answer is yes.'

She let out a quick, silent breath. 'And the long answer?'

'We'll do it on my terms.'

He turned to her, completely relaxed, utterly in control. Millie felt her heart flip over in her chest. It wasn't exactly a pleasant sensation. So, Chase would sleep with her. She would sleep with him. They would have sex.

Her body tingled. Her heart hammered and her mouth dried. Just what she had started here? And how would it finish?

'Relax, Millie. I'm not about to drop my pants.'

Even if that was what she'd wanted from him originally: a simple, quick, easy transaction. Now she didn't know what she wanted. She swallowed, tried to ease the dryness in her throat.

'So what are your terms?'

'Don't worry, I'll keep you informed as we go along.'

Too late Millie realised they were moving. They'd gone about twenty feet from the shore and Chase was doing something with the sails or rigging or whatever was on this wretched boat. She didn't know the first thing about sailing.

'What—what are you doing?' she demanded.

'Sailing.'

'But I don't—'

'I told you I wanted to see you on my boat,' Chase said with an easy smile. 'With your hair blowing away from your face.'

'But—'

'My terms, Millie.' His smile widened. Millie suppressed a short and violent curse. Just what had she got herself into? 'Relax,' he said. 'You could even enjoy yourself.'

'That *was* kind of the point,' she muttered, and he laughed.

'Glad to hear it.'

She watched Chase let out the sail, the white cloth snapping in the brisk breeze. They were quite far out from the shore now, far enough for Millie to feel a sudden pulse of alarm. She was alone on a boat in the middle—well, *sort* of the middle—of the Caribbean with a man. With Chase.

She didn't feel frightened, or even nervous. She felt... alert. Aware. *Alive.*

'OK,' she said, taking a step towards him. 'So where are we going?'

'Do we need a destination?'

'I'm kind of goal-oriented.'

'So I've noticed.'

Her hair was blowing in the breeze, but not away from her face. In it. Strands stuck to her lips and with an impatient sigh she brushed it away. Chase grinned in approval.

'There.'

'What?' she asked irritably. 'Is this some kind of weird fetish you have? Women and hair?'

'I just like seeing you look a bit more relaxed. More natural.' He paused, as if weighing his words. 'Soft.'

'Don't.' The single word came out sharp, a cut. 'Don't,' she said again, and this time it was a warning.

'What?'

'Don't—don't try to change me. This isn't about that.'

She couldn't stand it if he thought he was on some wretched mercy mission, making her relax and enjoy life. He had no idea. No clue whatsoever.

'What *is* it about?' Chase asked calmly. 'Sex?'

'Yes. I thought I made that clear.'

'You did.' Just as calmly he strode towards the sail and started doing something with it. Millie couldn't tell what. 'And I made it clear this would be on my terms. Watch out.'

'What—?'

She saw something heavy and wooden swing straight towards her face and then Chase's hands were on her shoulders, pulling her out of the way. She collided with his chest, her back coming against that bare, hard muscle. Her heart thudded and his hands felt hot on her shoulders, his thumbs touching the bare skin near her collarbone.

'What was that?' she asked shakily.

'The boom. I had to tack.'

'Tack?'

'Change direction. I should have warned you, but all this sex talk was distracting me.'

She had no answer to that. All she could think about was how warm and heavy his hands felt on her shoulders, how he'd only have to move his thumbs an inch or two to brush the tops of her breasts. How she wanted him to.

'We're good now,' he said, dropping his hands. 'We should have a pretty nice run. Let's sit down.'

Numbly Millie followed him to a cushioned bench in the back of the boat. Chase reached into a cooler and took out a bottle of sparkling water, offering it to her before he took one himself.

'Cheers. Sorry I don't have champagne to toast this momentous occasion.'

'So why don't you drink, exactly?'

'More doctor's orders. Reduce stress.' He spoke with that

deliberate lightness again. He wasn't telling her the truth, or at least not the whole truth.

Millie swallowed and took a sip of water. Her thoughts were racing as fast as the boat that skimmed lightly over the aquamarine sea onto an unknown horizon. *What was going to happen here?*

'So. Tell me more about these terms of yours.'

'The first one is I decide when we do the deed. And where. And how.'

She swallowed. 'That's asking for a lot of control.'

'I know. And I'm not asking. I'm telling.'

The bottle felt slippery in her hands. 'I'm not really comfortable with that.'

'OK.' He shrugged, everything so easy.

'What do you mean, OK?'

'The deal's off, then. No sex.'

She bit her lip. 'I didn't mean that.'

Another shrug. 'You want to sleep with me, you agree to my terms.'

'You make it sound so—cold.'

'No, Scary, you're doing that all on your own. You're the one who wants to have some hurried grope and then brush yourself off and move on with life.'

'I never said that.'

'Am I wrong?'

She looked away. 'It wouldn't have to be *hurried.*'

'What is this, some milestone? First time you'll have had sex since you broke up with your long-time boyfriend?'

She kept her gaze on the sea, frills of white amidst the endless blue. 'No.'

'Divorce?'

'No.'

He sighed. 'Something, though, right?'

'Maybe.'

'Fine. You don't want to tell me. No messy details.'

'That's right.'

'But I'm telling you I'm not interested in some soulless, sordid transaction. If you want that, hire an escort service. Or go hang out in the bar for a little while longer. Someone will pay or play.'

She blinked and set her jaw. 'As tempting as that sounds, I'm not interested.'

'Why not?'

'Because—' She hesitated. She felt as if he were stripping away her defences, and yet she didn't know how he was doing it. She kept darting around to cover her bases, but they were already gone. 'Because I don't want that.'

He leaned forward, his voice a soft, seductive whisper. 'What do you want, Millie?'

Reluctantly, she dragged her gaze towards him. His eyes glittered gold and the wind ruffled his hair. He looked completely gorgeous and so utterly sure. 'I want you.'

He held her gaze, triumph blazing in his eyes, a smile curving his mouth. *Damn it*. Why had she said that? Admitted so much?

'And I want you,' he told her in a low, lazy murmur. 'Rather a lot. But I want to be more than a milestone, and so we're doing this my way.'

More than a milestone. Already she was in over her head. She'd been so stupid, convincing herself that she could handle Chase, that he'd agree to some one-night stand. On the surface, he should have. But from the moment she'd met him he'd never been what she'd thought he was. What she wanted him to be.

So why had she pursued this? Why was she still here, still wanting to do this deal? Did she really want him that much? *Yes*.

'Fine. We'll do it your way. But I want to know what that is first.'

His smile turned to a pie-eating grin. 'Nope.'

'Nope?'

'Nope. Information is given on a need-to-know basis only.'

Her fingers tightened on her bottle of water, her knuckles aching. 'I need to know, Chase.'

'I'll decide that.'

She could not believe how horribly autocratic and arrogant he was being. She could not believe she was taking it. Why on earth was she not telling him to piss off and take her back to the shore? Was there some sick, depraved little girl inside her who wanted to be told what to do?

Or did she just want him that much?

Yes, she did.

'Fine,' she said, forming the word through stiff lips. He nodded, no more. She took a sip of water to ease the dryness in her throat. 'So what now?' she asked once she'd swallowed and felt able to speak again.

'You take off your clothes.'

Her bottle of water slipped from her nerveless fingers and Chase reached forward to catch it.

'Easy there, Scary. I was joking. Right now we relax, enjoy the sun and sea. I'll let you know when clothes or lack thereof come into the equation.'

She shook her head slowly. 'Why are you doing this?'

'Doing what?'

'Toying with me.'

He arched an eyebrow. 'Is that what it feels like?'

'Pretty much.'

He didn't answer for a moment, just took a long swallow of water so she could see the brown column of his throat, the breadth of his chest tapering down to lean hips. He was beautiful. 'Well,' he finally said, his gaze meeting hers with too much knowledge, 'I suppose it's because you've been trying to toy with me.'

She took a startled step back. 'I have not.'

'Oh, really? You march over to my boat and practically demand to sleep with me. You think I'm just going to lie down and let you have your wicked way with me?'

'No…not exactly.'

'You think you can tell me how, when and where I'm going to have sex with you?'

'That's what you're trying to do with me!'

'Exactly. And I'm not going to be entered into your smart phone and then deleted when you're done. I'm not a hedge fund, Millie. I'm not an account or a client or a to-do item to tick off. And, more importantly, neither is what's between us.'

She felt as if he'd wrapped an iron band around her chest and *squeezed*. Breathing hurt. 'There's nothing between us.

'That is bull and you know it.'

'What do you *want*, Chase?'

'You. Just like you want me. But I think we have very different definitions of just what that means.'

She dragged a breath into her constricted lungs. Spots danced before her eyes. She was in way over her head now; she was drowning and she had no idea how to save herself. 'I think we must,' she finally managed, and Chase just grinned.

Chase watched Millie process what he said and wondered if she was going to pass out. She'd gone seriously pale. And admittedly he'd laid it on pretty thick. He didn't even know why he was pushing so hard. He'd thought last night had been too intense, and yet today he'd upped the ante a hundred fold. He'd acted on instinct, telling her he was going to call the shots, not just because he didn't want to be her toy-boy but because he knew on a gut level she needed to let go of that precious control. And he wanted to be the one to make it happen.

As for what was *between* them… She was right. There was nothing between them, not really.

Yet.

So what did he want?

He took another long swallow of water, desperate for a cold beer. A distraction. He was scaring himself with all this talk. Asking for more than he'd ever intended to want, never mind have.

Maybe he was acting this way because ever since his diagnosis everything in life had felt important, urgent. Precious. And if he felt a connection with a woman well, then, perhaps he should just go for it. Take it as long and far as he could.

Except did he even know how long or far that could be. He didn't have a lot of options here. A lot of freedom.

He was, Chase reflected, a lousy deal.

Yet Millie only wanted this week, and really that should suit him perfectly. A week, he had.

A week, he would give.

And it would be the most incredible, intense week either of them had ever experienced.

'You OK there, Scary?'

She glanced at him, still looking dazed. 'Are you doing this on purpose?'

'What?'

'Pushing my buttons. Making me uncomfortable.'

He paused as if he had to think about it, which he didn't. 'Yes.'

She shook her head. 'OK, let me spell it out for you, Chase. I don't want to be pushed. I don't want buttons to be pressed. I want a week-long fling, some really great, mind-blowing sex, and that's *it*. And, if you don't think you can deliver, then maybe you should just take me back to shore right now.' She was trembling.

'Mind-blowing, huh?'

'Yes. Definitely.'

'I think I can deliver.'

'And nothing *more* than that,' she stressed, as if he didn't get it already.

'That's a problem.'

She blew out an impatient breath, pushing her hair behind her ears. She looked younger when she did that, although he guessed she was about his age, maybe a little younger. Mid-thirties, probably. 'Why is that a problem?'

'Because I don't think sex can be mind-blowing if a few buttons aren't pressed. In a manner of speaking, of course.'

She looked so disbelieving he almost winced. 'Are you telling me you haven't had cheap sex before? One-night stands? Flings?'

'No, I'm not saying that.' He'd had more than his share of all the above. He wasn't particularly proud of his past, standing on this side of it, but he'd own up to it.

'Then why are you insisting on something more now?'

He stretched his legs out in front of him, laced his hands behind his head. 'I suppose it depends on what you think of as more.'

'Stop talking in riddles.'

'OK, here it is, totally straight. We're both here for a week, right?'

'Right.'

'A week out of time, out of reality, and we'll never see each other again in New York or elsewhere. Yes?'

'Yes.'

'See, we *are* on the same page.'

'Spit it out,' she said, her teeth gritted, and he couldn't keep from grinning. He loved riling her.

'So you give me one week, and I give you mind-blowing sex. Deal?'

'I'm not signing until you tell me the fine print,' she said tautly, and he laughed aloud.

'You give me one week,' he repeated. He leaned forward, the urgency and excitement he felt coming out on his voice, his body. He felt it thrum between them with the pulse of an electric current. 'One week. Seven days. But you give me *everything*, Millie. You give me all of yourself, no holding back, no hiding. All in. And in return I give you mind-blowing.'

She stared at him silently for a long moment, her eyes wide, pupils dilated—with fear or desire? Probably both. Hell, he felt both. He couldn't believe he was doing this. He couldn't believe how much he wanted to.

'That,' she finally said, 'is a *lousy* deal.'

'You really think so?' He felt a tiny flicker of disappointment, but still that urgent hope. She was here. She was still talking, still wanting.

And, God knew, he wanted her. A lot.

'I told you I didn't want to get into messy emotional stuff. I don't want to *know* you, Chase.'

The flicker of disappointment deepened into actual hurt. He pushed it away. 'Except in the biblical sense, you mean.'

She let out a huff of exasperated breath. 'You're totally reneging on what we agreed on.'

'Nope. You are. My terms, remember?'

Her lips parted, realisation patently dawning. He waited. 'I thought you meant—well, the physical aspect of—of things. Like, maybe something a little bit kinky.' A beet-red blush washed over her face like a tide.

'We could go there if you like,' Chase offered. The prospect held an intriguing appeal. 'And I did say the when,

where and how, it's true. But now I'm giving you some of those need-to-know details.'

She said nothing, just turned to stare out at the sea. They were in open water, the wind starting to die down. He should tack again, but he just waited. This moment was too important.

'I don't want to talk about my past,' she said slowly, forming each word with reluctance. 'I'll give myself in other ways, but not that.'

'That's kind of a big one.'

She turned to face him, and he felt as if a fist had struck his soul. She looked incredibly, unbearably bleak. 'Then you can take me back right now.'

Chase held her gaze, felt a twisting inside him. She was truly beautiful, he realised, but it was a stark, severe beauty, all clean angles and pure lines. And sadness. So much sadness. 'No need for that,' he said as lightly as he could. 'I agree.'

Her breath came out in a rush. 'Good.'

'So it's a deal?'

Her mouth trembled in an almost-smile. 'I guess it is.'

Chase stood up and walked towards the rigging. It was time to change direction. 'Then let our week begin.'

CHAPTER FIVE

MILLIE watched Chase steer the boat—he'd done something with the sail again—and tried to slow the hard beating of her heart. It was impossible.

She couldn't believe she had agreed. She couldn't believe she'd *wanted* to agree. They weren't her terms, not by a long shot, but maybe she could live with them. One week. No talking about the past. *Mind-blowing sex.*

Yes, she could live with them. Even if she felt a kind of numb terror at the thought of what lay ahead.

'So, are we going somewhere now?' she asked, rising from the bench to join him at the sail. This time she watched for the boom.

'Yep, land ahoy.' He pointed straight ahead to a crescent of sand amidst the water. It didn't look like much.

'What is that?'

'Our own version of *Survivor.*'

'You mean a deserted island?'

'I knew you were quick.'

'What are we going to do there?'

He gave her a knowing look. 'What do you think?' Millie gulped. Audibly. 'Relax, Millie. We're going to eat lunch.'

'Oh.' Another gulp. 'OK.'

'Although,' Chase mused as he navigated the boat towards that slice of beach, 'I almost think we should just do

would be a good idea.'

She felt a flare of anticipation—and relief. 'Maybe that

Chase gave her another knowing look. 'I said almost.'

She folded her arms. 'Well, when are we going to—?'

'Need-to-know basis only,' Chase reminded her breez-ily. Then he was mooring the boat and the island—it really wasn't much—loomed before them.

He jumped out first, splashing through the shallows to moor the boat more securely, before turning to her and hold-ing out his arms. 'Want to jump?'

She stood on the deck, one foot poised uncertainly on the railing, unsure just how she was going to get out of this thing. 'No, thank you.'

'I'll let it go this time, but remember our terms, Scary—you've got to give me everything.'

She stared at him, saw him looking both serious and smug, and then without warning or even thinking she took a flying leap from the boat and landed right on top of him.

With a startled *'Oof!'* Chase fell back into the sea, pulling her with him. She was soaked instantly, and she felt the hard lines of his body press into her own soft curves. Excitement and awareness flared like rockets inside of her, obliterat-ing thought.

Then through the sudden haze of her own desire she saw that Chase was wincing in what could only be pain. Mortification replaced lust and she tried to clamber off him. 'Did I hurt you—?'

'No.' He held her still on top of him and sucked in a breath. 'Surprised me, though.' He adjusted his arms around her, sliding his palms down her back so her hips rocked against his. 'Not that I mind.'

The water lapped around them, salty and warm. Her warm face

was inches from Chase's and she could see droplets of water clinging to his cheek and lips. Unable to resist touching him—and, really, why should she resist now?—she put the tip of her finger to one of the drops on Chase's cheek. He sucked in another breath, his gaze holding hers like a vise. Daringly, Millie touched another droplet on his lips. His mouth felt soft and warm, hard and cool all at the same time. Sensation zinged through her, frying her senses. Just one little touch and she was already drowning in a sea of desire. Chase hadn't moved, just kept his hands on her hips, cradling her with aching closeness. She felt the hard thrust of his arousal against her thighs and instinctively shifted, though whether to bring him closer or farther away she didn't even know. Couldn't think.

The moment spun out and Millie felt the breath dry in her lungs as she waited for him to move.

And then he did.

'So.' Slowly, smiling, he eased her off him. 'Lunch.'

So they weren't going to go for it right then. She felt a bewildering mixture of disappointment and relief. Of course, he *had* said he preferred the moment before rather than after. There was still so much to look forward to.

Millie struggled up from of the water, watching as Chase rose out of the ocean like some archaic deity, water streaming in rivulets off the taut muscles of his back. He sluiced the water from his face and hair and then turned to her. 'You got a suit under there?'

'A suit?' She glanced down at the now-soaked striped top and capris her secretary had ordered her as part of her holiday wear. She hadn't had time to go shopping. 'Umm... No.'

'Shame. I was looking forward to seeing you in a string bikini.'

'I don't own a string bikini.'

'Let me guess—sensible one-piece.'

'I burn easily.'

'Remind me to apply another layer of sunscreen on you after lunch. But first, we dive.'

'Dive?' she repeated incredulously. 'But I just told you I don't have a swimsuit.'

Chase shrugged. 'You'll have to swim in your underwear. Or naked, if you prefer.'

'*What?*' This came out in a screech. Chase raised his eyebrows.

'Millie, we *are* going to sleep together, right? See each other naked? Touch each other in all those intimate places? Bring each other screaming to ecstasy?'

She was blushing. Like fire. *Way* too many details. 'That doesn't mean I want you to see me in my underwear in broad daylight,' she managed.

'Maybe I've decided to make love to you in broad daylight.' He pointed to the slender strip of sand. 'Maybe right there on that beach.'

Millie followed the direction of his pointing finger and could already see the two of them there on the beach, bodies naked, sandy and entwined. She could imagine it all too easily, no matter that she still felt shy about taking off her clothes. 'Even so,' she muttered. 'It's different.'

Chase let out a long-suffering sigh. 'So you want to swim in your clothes?'

'No.' She recrossed her arms, shifted her weight. She didn't know what she wanted. She'd agreed to this, she'd known it would be uncomfortable, and yet some bizarre and perverse part of herself still wanted it. Wanted him. Wanted the intimacy with him, even if she felt sick with nerves. But if she really did want it why was she still resisting? Why was she fighting Chase on every little point? They'd already established he wasn't going to ask her about her past. They wouldn't see each other after this week.

They were going to have sex.

'Fine.' In one abrupt movement she slid her wet top over her head and kicked her way out of her capris. The clothes bobbed and floated on the surface of the sea, and belatedly she realised they were the only clothes she had here. She didn't relish the prospect of walking down the resort beach in her undies. Lifting her chin, she glared at him. 'Satisfied?'

'I wouldn't say I'm *satisfied*,' Chase said slowly, his gaze wandering over her in leisurely perusal. 'But pleased, yes.'

Millie shivered even though the air was sultry. She felt ridiculous standing there in her bra and panties, both a sensible, boring beige, even though Chase was only wearing a pair of shorts. They were both near-naked and yet...

When had someone last seen her this close to bare? A man? Rob, of course, was the *only* man who had seen her in her underwear, besides her obstetrician. The thought was both absurd and excruciating.

Standing there under Chase's scrutiny, she was agonisingly conscious of all her faults. She was too skinny, due to the black-coffee breakfasts and skipped lunches. Her appetite had fallen off a cliff since the accident. And, while supermodels looked good stick-thin, Millie knew she didn't. Her hip bones were sharp and she'd dwindled down to an A-cup. And then of course there were the stretch marks, just two silver lines below her belly button—would he notice those? Would he ask? She'd remind him if necessary, and often.

Chase smiled and reached into the boat, bringing out two dive-masks. Millie eyed them dubiously.

'Why are we diving, anyway? I thought we were eating lunch.'

'We have to catch it first.'

Her jaw dropped. 'You have got to be kidding me.'

He arched an eyebrow. 'Do I look like a kidder?'

'Well, since you asked...'

'Seriously, it's easy. We're looking for conch—you know the big, pink shells? The pretty ones?' She nodded. 'We'll find a couple of those, I'll pry out the meat and we'll have conch salad. Delicious.'

'Raw?'

'Haven't you ever eaten sushi?'

'Only in a Michelin-starred restaurant in Soho.'

'Live a little, Millie.'

She frowned. 'I don't want to get food poisoning.'

'The lime juice in the dressing has enough acid to kill any nasties,' he assured her. 'I've eaten this loads of times.'

And just like that she could imagine him here, looking so easy and relaxed, with the kind of curvy blonde he usually dated. *She'd* have a string bikini. Or maybe she'd go bare. Either way Millie felt ridiculous standing there in her underwear, having no idea what to do. And, worse, she felt jealous.

Chase tossed her a mask. 'Look for the shells. We only need one or two.'

Dubiously she put the mask on. This was so out of her comfort zone, which was precisely why Chase had chosen to do it. When he'd said lunch she'd envisioned a picnic on the boat, gourmet finger-food and linen napkins. As if.

Still, she wouldn't give Chase the satisfaction of seeing just how uncomfortable she was. Squaring her shoulders, she adjusted her mask and followed Chase into the water. He was already cutting easily through the placid sea and with a deep breath Millie put her face in the water and gazed down into another world.

Rainbow-coloured fish darted in the shoals and amidst the rocks, prettier than any she'd seen in an aquarium. The sea water was incredibly clear, so the whole ocean floor seemed to open up in front of her, stretching on endlessly. Her lungs started to burn and she lifted her head to take a breath.

'You OK?' Chase had lifted his head too, and was glancing at her in concern.

'I'm fine.' She felt a strange stirring inside that he'd asked, something between gratitude and affection, that he was worried. He might be pushing her, but he wasn't going to let her fall.

And she wouldn't let herself either.

Chase kicked forward. 'Let's swim a little farther out.'

She followed him out into deeper water, and they swam and dove in silent synchronicity, the whole exercise surprisingly relaxing, until she finally saw a conch, pearly pink and luminescent, nestled against a rock. Taking a deep breath, she dove down and reached for it, her hand curving around its smooth shell as she kicked upwards to the surface.

Chase was waiting for her as she broke through. 'I got one!' Her voice rang out like an excited child's, and she gave him an all-too-sloppy grin.

'It's always a thrill. I got one too. That should be enough.'

They headed back to shore and Millie sat on the beach and watched while Chase retrieved a knife, cutting board and a few limes and shallots from the boat.

'You come prepared.'

'It's a quick, easy meal. But delicious.'

The sun dried her off, leaving salt on her skin as she sat with her elbows on her knees and watched him at work. She should have known he wouldn't let her sit back and do nothing for very long. Giving her a sideway glance, he beckoned her over.

'You can help.'

'You want me to slice some limes?' she asked hopefully, and he grinned.

'I thought you'd like a challenge. You can clean the conch.'

Bleh. Still, she wasn't going to argue. She eyed her wet tee-shirt drying on the boat, conscious that she was still only in her bra and pants. At least they were both sturdy and definitely not see-through. Chase caught her glance and shook his head.

'Your unmentionables are more modest than some of the bikinis I've seen, you know.'

'I'll bet.'

'Come on, Scary. You can do this.' He handed her a knife and instructed her on how to insert, twist and bring out the entire conch. Grimacing, Millie tried, and finally succeeded on her third try.

'Well done. Now we just need to fillet it. I'll do that, if you like.'

'Please.'

'You slice the limes.'

They worked in companionable silence for a moment, the sun warm on their backs. When everything had been sliced and diced, Chase fetched a wooden bowl from the boat and tossed it all together. He divided the salad between two plates and presented one to Millie with a courtly flourish.

'Your lunch, madam.'

'Thank you very much.' She took a bite, her eyes widening in surprise at how tasty it truly was. Chase smiled smugly.

'Told you.'

'Don't rub it in.' Unthinkingly she nudged him with her foot, a playful kick, and Chase raised his eyebrows. Too late Millie realised it could have looked like she was flirting. But she hadn't been, not intentionally anyway. She'd just been... enjoying herself.

And when was the last time she'd done that?

'A penny for your thoughts,' Chase said lightly. 'Or how about a bottle cap? I don't actually have any spare change.'

She glanced up and realised she'd been frowning. 'This is delicious, but it does seem a pity to eat such beautiful creatures.'

'They are pretty,' Chase agreed. 'They're actually endangered in US waters. But don't worry, they're still plentiful here. And the resort monitors the conch population around the island to make sure it never falls too low.'

'How eco-friendly of them. Is that a Bryant policy?'

He shrugged. 'A Chase Bryant policy. And economically friendly as well. If we don't conserve the island, there's no resort.'

Her salad finished, Millie propped her chin on her hands. 'But I thought you don't have anything to do with the resort.'

'Not really. But I'm interested in environmental policy, so...' He shrugged, but Millie wasn't fooled.

'Something happened?'

He tensed, and although it was barely noticeable Millie still felt it. Curiosity and a surprising compassion unfurled inside her. What had gone wrong between Chase and his family?

A second's pause was all it took for him to regain his usual lightness. 'Do I need to invoke the "no talking about the past" clause of our contract?'

'That was my past. Not yours.'

'I assumed it went both ways.'

She smiled sweetly. 'Fine print.'

Chase polished off the last mouthful of his meal before collecting their dishes and tossing them back into the boat. 'Fine. I was a bit of a reckless youth, made a few significant mistakes, and my father decided he'd rather I had nothing to do with the family business.' He shrugged, as if it were such ancient history that none of it mattered any more. 'So I went my own way, and am happy as a clam. Or a conch.'

Millie gazed at him, sensing the cracks in his armour.

He was just a little too deliberate with his light tone, and his story was far too simple. She wasn't about to press him, though. She'd been the one to insist that this week wasn't about emotional honesty or intimacy. But then, what *was* it about? It had been half a day already and they hadn't even kissed.

Yet she'd relaxed and enjoyed herself more than she'd ever thought possible.

'Come on,' Chase said, standing up and reaching a hand down to her. 'Let's explore the island.'

'That should take all of two minutes.'

'You'd be surprised.'

He hauled her to her feet, his strong, warm hand encasing hers, his fingers sliding over hers, skin on skin. Millie nearly shivered from the jolts that raced up and down her arm at that simple touch. When they did have sex, it was going to be amazing.

Mind-blowing.

Her heart slammed against her ribs as the realisation hit her again. Was she ready for this? Did she have any choice?

'Stop hyperventilating,' Chase said mildly. 'If it sets you at ease, I prefer a bed, or at least a comfortable surface. A beach seems romantic, but the sand can get into all sorts of inconvenient places.'

'You've tried it?' Millie tried not to feel nettled. *Jealous.* She'd never had sex on a beach.

'Once or twice,' Chase answered with a shrug. He was leading her away from the boat, towards a small grove of palm trees. 'Trust me, it's overrated.'

Millie's mind buzzed. OK, a bed. What bed? Her bed at the resort? At his villa? How were they going to *do* this? Well, obviously she knew *how*, but how without it being completely awkward or embarrassing? She hadn't had sex in over two years and then only ever with one man. What on earth had she been thinking, suggesting a fling? She was the least flingy person she knew.

She also knew it was way too late to be thinking this way. She should have considered all the uncomfortable practicalities before she'd made the suggestion to Chase. Before they'd agreed on a deal.

Before she'd suddenly realised just what this all meant, and that there was no such thing as simple sex.

Yet, even though she *was* hyperventilating, she knew she didn't want to back out. She wanted Chase.

Did his sailboat have a bed?

'Yes,' Chase called back and Millie skidded to a halt right there in the trees.

'What do you mean, *yes*?'

He stopped and turned, so aggravatingly amused. 'Yes, the sailboat has a bed.'

Her jaw dropped. 'Did I say that out loud?'

'No, but I could follow your thought process from here. I hate to say it, but you're kind of predictable.'

'You didn't expect me to jump on top of you from the boat,' Millie pointed out, and Chase cocked his head.

'True. I like when you surprise me.'

She'd liked it too. She'd liked feeling his hard body under hers. She'd enjoyed touching him. Just thinking about it now made her blood heat and her body pulse. Why was she waiting for him to kiss her? What if she kissed him?

'Don't get ahead of yourself there,' Chase murmured. 'Our first kiss needs to be special.'

She let out a most inelegant snort. 'What are you, a mind reader?'

'You were staring at my lips like they were the latest stock market report. It didn't take a huge amount of mental ability to guess what you were thinking.'

Disgruntled, she tugged her hand from his. 'So where are we going, exactly?'

Chase took her hand back, folding her fingers in his once more. 'I'll show you.'

They walked through the palms for a few more minutes, wending their way through the drooping fronds, the ground sandy beneath their feet. Then Chase stopped, slipping his arm around Millie's waist to draw her to his side. He did it so easily, so assuredly, that she didn't even think about any awkwardness as her leg lay warm against his, his fingers splayed along her hip.

'Look.'

She looked and saw a perfect little pool right there in the middle of the trees, a tiny jewel-like oasis, its surface as calm as a mirror. Millie knelt down and cupped the water with two hands; it was clear and cool. She glanced up at Chase. 'It's fresh?'

'Yep, fed by an underground spring, I think.' She shook her head in wonder, amazed that such a tiny island would have a source of fresh water. 'Drink,' Chase said. 'I've drunk it before, it tastes great. You could sell it for five bucks a bottle in the city.'

She took a sip, suddenly self-conscious at how Chase was watching her. When had taking a drink of water become sensual? Provocative?

'You know what the most amazing thing is, though?' he said, and she sat back on her heels.

'What?'

'You've been walking around in your underwear for most of the day and you haven't even noticed.'

She let out an embarrassed little laugh. 'And, now that you've reminded me, I'm going to notice.'

He grinned. 'Actually, what I was really going to say is that a couple of hundred years ago there were some shipwrecked sailors on a little atoll just a few hundred yards away, without any fresh water. They didn't discover this place and they died of thirst.'

She dropped her hands. 'That's awful.'

'I know. If they'd just tried swimming around a little bit, or even making a raft or something, they might have survived.' He shook his head. 'But they were just too scared.'

Millie narrowed her eyes. 'And I'm supposed to make the connection, right?'

He stared at her in exaggerated innocence. 'Connection?'

She stood up. 'If those sailors had just been a little more adventurous, they would have survived. Really lived. All they had to do was swim a little farther than they were comfortable with.'

'I don't think they could swim at all, actually. Most sailors back then couldn't.'

She folded her arms. 'I don't need the morality tale.'

'It was obvious, huh?'

'Like a sledgehammer.'

'And I made the whole thing up to boot.'

She let out a huff of outraged laughter. 'You did?'

'No, I didn't. It's actually true. Well, a legend around here anyway.' He grinned and Millie didn't know whether to throttle him or kiss him. She felt like doing both, at the same time.

'You're unbelievable.'

'So I've been told.'

His gaze rested on her like a heavy, palpable thing, assessing, understanding. Knowing. She drew a breath.

'Look, Chase, I know I'm uptight and you think I need to relax. I probably seem like a joke to you.'

'You don't,' Chase said quietly. 'I promise you, Millie, this is no joke.'

She looked away, discomfited by the sudden intensity in

his voice. 'I don't want to be your project,' she said quietly. 'The reckless playboy teaches the uptight workaholic how to relax and have fun. Shows her how to really live.' She bit her lip hard, surprised by the sudden catch of tears in her throat. 'That isn't what I want from you.'

Chase took a step closer to her. 'Then maybe you should tell me what you do want.'

She forced herself to meet his gaze. 'Mind-blowing sex, remember?'

'I remember. And I remember the deal we made. One week, and you give me everything.'

He'd come closer, close enough so she could feel the heat of him, inhaled the scent that she was starting to realise was just Chase. Sun and musk and male. She drew a shaky breath. 'I don't know how much I have to give.'

He touched her chin with her hand, his fingers like a whisper against her skin. 'Someone hurt you. I get that. But this can be different, Millie.'

She shook her head, swallowed the hot lump of tears. 'No one hurt me, Chase. Not the way you think.'

'No questions about the past, I know,' he said, the hint of a smile in his voice. 'And this week isn't meant to be some lesson. It's just us—enjoying each other.'

Her breath came out in a soft hiss. 'OK.'

He stroked her cheek, and she had to fight not to close her eyes and surrender to that little caress. 'And I enjoy seeing you open up like a flower in the sun. I like seeing your face surprised by a smile.'

'Don't.'

'Is that scary, Millie? Is that out of your comfort zone?'

She swallowed. 'Yes.'

His other hand came up to cradle her face, just as he had last night. Had it only been last night? She felt as if she'd known this man for years. And he knew her.

'How long has it been,' he asked, 'since you were happy?'

'Two years.' The answer slipped out before she could think better of it. 'But really longer. Two years since I've known.' She stared at him, knowing he was drawing more from her than she'd ever intended to give, and also knowing that she wanted to give it. One week. For one week she wanted intimacy. Physical, emotional, intense. All of it. *All in*.

Chase was gazing back at her, his expression both tender and fierce, and then slowly, deliberately, he dipped his head and brushed his lips with her own.

A soft sigh of surrender escaped her as her lips parted underneath his. His lips were all the things she'd thought they would be: soft, hard, cool, warm. And so achingly gentle.

He brushed his lips across hers a second and third time, like a greeting. Then he touched his tongue to the corner of her mouth, and then the other corner, as if he were asking her how she was. A wordless conversation of mouths. Her lips parted wider, accepting. *I'm good*.

He deepened the kiss, his hands tightening as they cradled her face, and Millie's hands came up to bunch on the bare skin of his shoulders. Yet even as sensation swirled through her another part of her was stepping back and analysing everything.

His hands felt bigger than Rob's. His body was harder. His kiss was more demanding and yet more gentle at the same time. More assured. Yet could she even remember the last time she and Rob had kissed? That last day, all she'd had were harsh words, impatient sighs...

She hadn't even said goodbye.

Chase lifted his head, pulling back a little bit so Millie blinked in surprise. 'Your lack of response is a bit of a buzz-kill, you know.'

'What?' She gaped like a fish. 'I wasn't—'

'No,' Chase agreed, 'you weren't. It started off rather nicely, but then you went somewhere else in your head.' She couldn't deny it, and his gaze narrowed. 'What were you thinking about, Millie?' She swallowed, said nothing. 'You were thinking about some other guy, weren't you?'

'No!' Millie protested, then bit her lip. She couldn't lie, not to Chase. 'I couldn't help it.'

For the first time since she'd seen him, he looked angry. Or maybe even hurt. Emotion flashed in his eyes like thunder and then he deliberately relaxed. 'I know you think too much. You've got to turn off that big brain of yours, Millie.'

'I know.' Did she ever. The whole reason she'd embarked on this fling of theirs was to keep herself from thinking. Remembering. Tormenting herself with guilty regrets.

'Let's go back to the boat,' Chase said. 'We should get back to St Julian's before dark.'

Silently Millie followed him back through the grove to the slender beach and then onto the boat. Chase didn't so much as look back at her once, or help her onto the boat. Any warmth between them seemed to have evaporated. Millie fetched her clothes, now thankfully dry but stiff as a board and caked with salt, and clutched them to her. She stood uncertainly on the deck while Chase set the boat free from its moorings, his movements taut with suppressed energy—or emotion? Was he angry with her?

'Is there somewhere I can change?'

'Don't bother.' He didn't even look at her as he reached for another line.

'What?' She didn't like seeing Chase this way, the hard lines of his face transformed into harshness—or maybe just indifference. Gone was the charming, charismatic man she'd come to like—and trust. 'I don't want to walk into the resort in my underwear,' she said, trying to joke, but Chase turned to her with a dangerously bland expression.

'You can put your clothes on after.'

'After?'

'After we have sex. That's what you wanted, isn't it, Millie? No messy emotions or entanglements, no getting to know each other.' He spread his arms wide, a cool smile curling his mouth. 'Well, here we are. Alone in an ocean, and there's a perfectly good bed in the cabin below. No reason not to hop to it.'

Millie stared, swallowed. 'You mean now?'

'Right now.' He jerked a thumb in direction of the ladder that led below deck. 'Let's go.'

CHAPTER SIX

WHAT the hell was he doing? Being a total bastard, judging by the look of shocked horror on Millie's face. But he was angry, even if he shouldn't be. The thought of Millie thinking of some other jerk while he was pouring his soul into that kiss filled him with a blind rage.

'Well?' Chase arched an eyebrow and put his hands on his hips. 'What are you waiting for?'

Her teeth sank into those worry marks on her lower lip. She clutched her clothes tighter to her chest. 'Somehow, with the way you're looking at me, I don't think it's going to be mind-blowing.'

'Leave that to me.'

She shook her head. 'I don't like angry sex.'

He gave her a level look. 'I'm not angry.' He wasn't, he realised with a flash of cringing insight. He was hurt. He hadn't expected to care so much, so quickly.

Millie gave just as level a look back, even as her eyes flashed fire. He might not be angry, but she was. Well, fine. Bring it on.

'All right.' She lifted her chin a notch, her eyes still flashing, and stalked past him to the ladder. Chase watched her descend below deck, her body taut and quivering with tension. Or maybe anger, or even fear.

Did it matter? Wasn't this what she wanted, a quick bout

of meaningless sex? She could get him out of her system, or so she undoubtedly hoped.

And maybe he'd get her out of his. He'd spent the afternoon coaxing smiles from her even as he enjoyed himself more than he'd ever thought possible. Every smile, every laugh, had felt like a discovery. A victory.

He thought they were building something—admittedly something fragile and temporary, but *still*. Something. And the whole time she'd been thinking of some stupid ex.

'Are you coming?' she called from below, her voice as taut as her body had been.

Chase's mouth curved grimly at the unwitting *double entendre*. 'You'd better believe it.'

He hauled himself down the ladder and saw that Millie stood in front of the double bed. She turned to him, her chest heaving, her nipples visible beneath the thin, silky material of her bra. She arched her eyebrows and curved her mouth in a horrible rictus smile.

'All right, Chase. Let's see what you've got.'

He swallowed, acid churning in his gut. How had they got here? The afternoon had been full of tenderness and teasing, and now they were acting like they hated each other.

Millie's eyes glittered and he knew she wouldn't back down. She never backed down from a challenge; he'd learned that already.

And hell if he'd back down either. She was the one who had said she didn't want to get to know him. Wasn't interested in emotional anything. Right now, right here, he could give her what she wanted. The only thing she wanted.

And, damn it, he'd want it too.

'Take off your bra.' A pulse beat hard in the hollow of her throat but she undid it and tossed it to the floor. Her breasts were small and round, high and firm. Perfect. Chase swallowed. 'And the rest.' She glared at him as she kicked off her underwear, her chin still tilted high.

'Is this what you call foreplay?'

He almost laughed. She was magnificent. Naked, proud, defiant, *strong*. He shook his head. 'I just like to see what I get in this deal of ours.'

'Only fair I get the same opportunity, then.'

He arched an eyebrow, aroused in spite of the anger. Or maybe because of it. Hell, he didn't know anything any more. 'What are you saying, Scary?'

'Take off your pants.'

He did.

They stared at each other almost in grim silence, both of them totally naked, nothing between them. The air seemed to crackle with the tension, with the expectation.

Hell.

What now?

Millie folded her arms. Waited. Chase felt like a circus seal, or a damn monkey. She clearly expected him to *perform*.

He hadn't wanted it to be this way. He'd wanted to gain her trust, even her affection, and help her to lose control in the most amazing way possible. Right now she was clinging to that precious control with her french-manicured fingernails and it was slipping crazily away from him.

He didn't want this.

He wasn't going to back down.

'Get on the bed.'

She gave him a little smirk, almost as if he were being *so* predictable, and lay on the bed. She even put her hands behind her head as if she were incredibly relaxed, but she was trembling.

Damn.

Again Chase hesitated. *Don't do this.* He didn't want to

ruin what they had by losing her trust, affection, *everything*, in a bout of absurdly unsexy sex. Except who was he kidding? They didn't *have* anything.

This was all they had—this, right here on the bed.

'Let me tell you,' Millie drawled, her hands still laced behind her head, 'this is turning out to be the worst sexual encounter of my life, and forget about mind-blowing.'

Chase saw that she still trembled.

He sat on the edge of the bed and slowly ran his hand from the arch of her foot along her calf to behind her knee, his fingers instinctively seeking further, finding the soft, smooth skin of her inner thigh. More softness. He felt her muscles tense and quiver beneath his touch. Her breath hitched.

'I'm not going to play this game,' he said quietly and she stared at him, her whole body going rigid.

'This was *your* idea.'

'Yeah, I'll grant you that. But you went for it because this is what you want.'

'You think *this* is what I want?'

'There's no emotional intimacy or getting to know you in this scenario, is there?' He slid his hand higher, savouring the sweet softness of her thigh. Another couple of inches would be even sweeter.

She stared at him, mesmerised, trapped. He stilled his hand. 'You know I'm right, Millie.'

In answer she reached up, lacing her fingers behind his head, and pulled him down for a hungry, open-mouthed kiss. Her tongue delved inside and she arched upwards, pressing her body against him.

Shock short-circuited Chase's brain for a second. Then his libido ramped up and he kissed her back just as hungrily with an instinct he was helpless to repress—even as he acknowledged this wasn't what he wanted. He didn't even think it was what Millie wanted, not deep down. She was trying to stay in control, seizing it desperately, and he couldn't let her.

But then her hand wrapped around him and he stopped thinking about what he couldn't do. His body was telling him what he could.

'Millie.' Her name was a groan against her mouth and he reached up to try to remove her death grip on the back of his head. *'Wait...'*

But she didn't want to wait. She was all over him, eager, urgent, desperate, making him feel the same way. His self-control was slipping away. How did a man argue for a more emotional experience when the woman beneath him was determined to drive him wild? For the feel of Millie's hands on him, her legs hooked around his hips as she angled upwards, was making him crazy. Through the fog of his own lust he tried to remember where he'd put the condoms.

'Quickly...' Millie whispered, her voice a ragged whimper, and Chase stilled. He heard too much desperation and even sadness in her voice, and he didn't want that. No matter how much his body screamed otherwise.

'Millie.' He pushed away from her a little bit, enough to see her pale, dazed face. 'Let's hold on a moment, shall we?' he said unevenly, even though his greatest desire at that point was to forget emotion and sensitivity, and even a condom, and just drive right into her.

'No, I don't want...' Her face went a shade paler, and then she lurched upwards. 'I think I'm going to be sick.' In one abrupt movement she rolled off the bed and raced to the head. Chase listened to her retching into the toilet in a kind of stunned disbelief.

This was starting to feel like the worst sexual encounter of his life too. He reached for his shorts and pulled them on, grabbed a spare tee-shirt from the drawer and waited on the edge of the bed.

A few minutes later a pale and shaky-looking Millie emerged. From somewhere Chase found a smile. 'I don't think that was because of the conch.'

She gave him a rather wobbly smile back, although her eyes were dark with pain. 'No, it wasn't.' Somehow the anger, tension and even the desperation of moments before had evaporated, but Chase didn't know what was left. He felt bewildered, like someone had skipped ahead in the scene selection on a DVD. He was clearly missing some plot points to this story.

'Here.' He handed her the tee-shirt and she slipped it on. Her hair was tousled, the shirt falling to mid-thigh. With a little sigh she sat on the edge of the bed, about as far away from him as possible.

'Sorry about that.'

'To which part of the evening are you referring?' he quipped, parroting her own words from last night back to her.

Millie gave a tiny, tired smile and leaned her head against the wall. She closed her eyes and with a pang of remorse Chase saw how exhausted she looked. Today had been quite the rollercoaster.

'To the part where I threw up in your bathroom a few minutes ago.'

'On a boat it's called a head.'

'Whatever.' She opened her eyes. 'That was another buzz-kill, I suspect.'

'To say the least.' They stared at each other, unspeaking, but Chase was surprised at how *un*-awkward it seemed. Maybe you got to a point with a person where things didn't seem so embarrassing or strange. If so, he'd got to that point pretty quickly with Millie. 'You want to tell me what's going on?'

'Remember the no-talking clause?'

'That clause was voided when you threw up. I was about six seconds from being inside you, Millie.'

She bit her lip and he reached over and gently touched those worry marks. 'You're going to get a scar from doing that if you don't cut it out.'

She sighed and shook her head. 'Maybe this whole thing was a bad idea, Chase.'

He felt a lurch of what could only be alarm. He didn't like feeling it. At this point, he should be agreeing with her. This *was* a bad idea. Neither of them needed the kind of mind games this week seemed to play on them. He'd convinced himself he wanted intense, but this? This was way too much.

Yet even so he heard himself saying, 'Why do you say that?'

'Because I'm not ready.'

She'd felt pretty ready beneath him. With effort Chase yanked his thoughts from that unhelpful direction. 'Ready?' he repeated.

'For this. A fling, an affair, whatever you want to call it. I wanted to be ready, I wanted to move on, but I don't know if I can. I can't stop thinking—' She stopped abruptly, shook her head.

It was no more than he'd already guessed, yet he didn't like hearing it. Didn't like thinking that some guy still owned her heart and mind so much he couldn't even get a toe-in. Jealousy. That was what he felt, pure and simple. Determinedly Chase pushed it away. 'We went about this all wrong, Scary,' he said. 'And that was my fault. I'm sorry.'

Surprise flashed across her features, like the first beam of sunlight after a downpour. 'For what?'

'For getting angry. I didn't like the fact that you were thinking of whatever guy did a number on you when I was kissing you.' He smiled wryly. 'It's kind of an insult to, you know, my masculinity.'

'Sorry.'

'It's OK. I should have got over it. Instead I pushed you—and myself—in a direction I had no intention of going.'

Her mouth curved in the faintest of smiles. 'Angry sex, huh?'

'It's really not that great.'

'Kind of like sex on a beach.'

'Exactly. Both overrated.' He sighed and raked his hand through his hair. 'Look, let's hit rewind on this evening. Go back on deck and forget this happened.'

'Well,' she said, sounding almost mischievous, 'I don't think I'm going to forget the sight of you naked in a hurry.'

Chase grinned. 'Me neither, Scary. Me neither.' Still smiling, he reached for her hand and felt a clean sweep of thankfulness when she took it. How bizarre that all that tension, anger and hurt had melted and reformed into something else. Something deeper and truer. Friendship.

'I hope,' Millie said as he led her from the cabin, 'we're not diving for dinner.'

'Definitely not.' He felt himself warm from the inside out, and he gave her hand a squeeze before helping her up the ladder.

Millie walked to the cushioned bench in the back of the boat on wobbly legs. She felt exhausted, both emotionally and physically, by the events of the day and especially the last hour. Chase Bryant was putting her through the wringer. Or maybe she was doing it to herself, by trying to have the desperate, mindless sex she'd thought she wanted until her body had rebelled and thrown up a whole lot of conch.

Chase was right, of course. It wasn't the conch that had made her sick. It was the memories. She couldn't turn her brain off, as much as she wanted to. Couldn't stop remembering, regretting. She'd wanted to have this fling so she could forget, but it wasn't happening that way at all. It was making things worse. Chase was opening up things inside her, stirring to life everything she'd wanted to be forgotten and buried, *gone*.

She watched as he set sail, part of her mind admiring the lean strength of his tanned, muscled body even as the rest whirled and spun in confusion. She hadn't expected him to become so angry earlier. And she hadn't expected him to be so understanding just then.

For a moment there on the bed, the cabin silent except for the draw and sigh of their own breathing, she'd actually wanted to tell him things. Confide all her confusion, sadness and guilt. But that would mean telling him about Rob. About Charlotte. And she never spoke about Charlotte. Even now the pain ripped through her, all too fresh even though it had been two years. Two years since the phone call that had torn her world apart, taken everyone she loved.

Shouldn't two years be enough time for the scars to heal? To finally feel ready to move on?

She felt the cushion dip beneath her and blinked to see Chase sitting next to her. She'd been so lost in her own miserable thoughts she hadn't seen him coming.

He touched her mouth and even now, after everything that had and hadn't happened, she felt that quiver of awareness, the remnant of desire. 'Scars, Scary. I'm serious.'

She let out a trembling little laugh. 'It's hard to stop something you're not even aware you're doing.'

'What deep thoughts are making you bite your lip?'

'They're not particularly deep.' She turned a little bit away from him, forcing him to drop his hand. 'Are we heading back to the resort?'

'No. To my villa.'

She turned back to him, felt a frisson of—what? Not fear. Not excitement. No, this felt strange and suddenly she knew why. She felt hope. Even after the absolute disaster below deck, Chase was giving her—*them*—a second chance.

'What are we going to do there?'

He regarded her speculatively for a moment. 'I'm going to cook for you while you soak in my jacuzzi. Then we're going to eat the fantastic meal I've whipped up, watch a movie, maybe have a glass of wine. Or sparkling water, as the case may be.'

'That sounds surprisingly relaxing.'

'Glad you think so.'

'And then?'

'And then we'll go to sleep in my very comfortable, king-sized bed and I'll hold you all night long.'

He spoke breezily enough, yet Millie heard the heartfelt sincerity underneath the lightness, and she felt tears sting her eyes. She blinked hard.

'Why are you being so nice to me?'

'Hasn't a man been nice to you before, Millie?' He spoke quietly, as if he felt sad for her. She shook her head.

'Don't pity me, Chase. I've—I've had a perfectly fine relationship before.'

'That sounds incredibly boring and unromantic, but OK. Good for you.'

She let out a trembling laugh. He *never* let up, but then neither did she. 'This doesn't sound very intense, though,' she told him. 'I thought this week was all about excitement.'

'There are different kinds of intense. And I think a quiet evening at home will be intense enough for you.'

He rose from the bench and Millie watched as he steered the boat, one hand on the tiller. The wind ruffled his short hair, his eyes narrowed against the setting sun. He paused, his hand still on the tiller, to watch the glorious descent of that orb of fire towards the now-placid sea. Shock jolted through her because for a moment Chase looked like she felt. Desperate. Sad. Longing to hope.

Then he straightened his shoulders and turned back to her with a smile, all lightness restored. 'Almost there.'

Half an hour later Millie was soaking in the most opulent tub she'd ever seen, huge, sunken and made of black marble. Chase had filled it right to the top with steaming water, half a bottle of bubble bath, and then left not one but two thick, fluffy towels on the side. Then with a smile and a salute he'd closed the door and gone to cook dinner.

When, Millie wondered, had she ever felt so incredibly pampered? So *loved*?

She froze, even in all that hot, fragrant water. *Don't even think that,* she told herself. *Don't go there.* The dreaded L-word. She'd loved Rob. She'd loved Charlotte. And here she was, two years later, heartbroken and alone.

She slipped beneath the foaming water and scrubbed the sand from her hair. The thoughts from her mind. She wanted to enjoy this evening, all the lovely things Chase had promised her. It had been so long since she'd had anything like this.

Since she'd felt anything like this.

Don't think. One week. That was all they had, all she wanted to have. One week of enjoyment, of fun and, yes, of sex. Despite today's disaster they could still have it. Enjoy it.

And then walk away. Move on, just like she wanted to, because anything else—anything real or lasting—was way too frightening. She'd loved once. Lost once. And it wasn't going to happen again.

One week suited her perfectly. One intense, wonderful week.

When Millie came out of the bathroom she saw, to her surprise, her suitcase laid out by the bed. How on earth had Chase been able to get into her room and take her stuff?

The answer was obvious: he was a Bryant. For a little while there she'd forgotten; he'd just been Chase. Annoyance and affection warred within her. It was nice to have her clothes, but it was a little *too* thoughtful. Sighing, she discarded her towel and reached for one of the boring outfits her secretary had chosen, this one a beige linen dress with short sleeves and no shape. She glanced down at it and gave a grimace of disgust. She wished, suddenly and fiercely, that she owned something sexy.

But then she'd never owned anything sexy. She and Rob hadn't been about sexy. Their sex life had been good enough, certainly, but they had both been so focused. There had been no time or inclination for sexy or silly or fun.

Everything that Chase was.

Was that why she'd chosen him for her first fling? Because, despite initial appearances, he was utterly unlike her husband?

Her thoughts felt too tangled to separate or understand. And maybe, like Chase said, she was over-thinking this. Straightening the boring dress, Millie headed out into the rest of the villa.

It was a gorgeous house, made of a natural stone that blended into its beach-side surroundings, the inside all soaring space and light. She found Chase in the gourmet kitchen that flowed seamlessly into the villa's main living space with scattered leather sofas and a huge picture-window framing an expanse of sand and sky.

'That smells delicious.'

'Chicken with pineapple and mango salsa,' Chase informed her, whipping a dish cloth from his shoulder to wipe something up on the granite work surface. Millie felt her heart—or something—squeeze at the sight of him. He'd changed into a worn blue tee-shirt and faded jeans, and he looked so natural and relaxed standing there, different bowls and pans around him, the smells of fruit and spice in the air.

She and Rob had never cooked. They'd eaten takeaway every night or ready-made meals from the gourmet supermarket. Why cook, Rob had used to say, if you don't have to? And she had agreed. After a ten-hour day at work, the last thing she felt like doing was making a meal. And they'd both been proud of the way Charlotte, at only two years old, would eat all the things they ate. Brie and smoked salmon. Spicy curries and pad thai. She'd loved it all.

A knot of emotion lodged in Millie's throat. Why was she thinking about Charlotte? She never did. She'd closed that part of herself off, shut up in a box marked *'do not open'*. Ever.

Yet here she was, memories springing unbidden into her mind, filling up her heart.

'Millie?' Chase was glancing at her, eyes narrowed. 'You OK there, Scary?'

She nodded. Sniffed. How stupidly revealing of her, but she couldn't help it. She'd thought she could handle this week, but already she was finding she couldn't. She was thinking too much. Feeling too much. She'd thought Chase would make her forget, but instead he was helping her to remember.

'That bath was wonderful,' she said, in a deliberate and obvious effort to change the subject. 'I could live in it for a week.'

'The water might get a bit cold.' Chase reached for a couple of green chilies and began dicing them with practised ease.

'Fair point.' She took a breath and decided she needed to get on firmer footing. Find a little distance. 'As nice as it is to wear my own clothes, I'm not sure how they got in your bedroom.'

'A very nice bell hop drove them over while you were in the tub.'

'Don't you think you could have asked?'

He glanced up, eyebrows arched. 'Are we still going over this? My terms, remember?'

'You can't keep throwing that at me every time I object to something, Chase.'

'And that is because…?'

She blew out an exasperated breath. 'It's not fair.'

'True.'

'So?'

'We're not playing baseball, Millie. Or Parcheesi. There are no rules.'

She folded her arms. 'Are you on some huge power trip? Is that what this is about?'

'Does it seem like it?' He sounded genuinely curious, and Millie was compelled to an unwilling honesty.

'No, which is why I don't get it. I still don't really get what you want, Chase. Most men would take the sex and run.'

'Has that been your experience?'

'Don't go there. No questions about the past.'

'I told you what I wanted. One week.'

'One intense, all-in week.'

'Only kind that works for me.'

'Why?'

Chase didn't answer for a moment. He concentrated on his cooking, taking out some pieces of chicken from the bowl of marinade and tossing them into a pan shimmering with hot oil. Millie listened to the sizzle and spat as they cooked, a delicious aroma wafting up from the pan.

'Why not?' he finally said and flipped the chicken. 'I know it's easier and simpler on the surface, Millie, just to skim life. Don't dig too deeply. Don't feel too much. I've been there. That's most of my misspent youth.'

She swallowed, knowing he was right. Easier, simpler and safer. 'But now?'

'I want something more. I want the whole *carpe diem* thing. Seize life. Suck the marrow from its bones.'

'For one week.'

'Yep. That's about the size of it.'

'And you decide to do this with me?' She couldn't keep the disbelief from her voice. 'When you must know I'm the exact opposite of all that?'

He gave her a decidedly roguish smile. 'That makes it more fun. And all the more reason why it has to be on my terms. Otherwise we'd never get anywhere.'

Millie shook her head. How could she argue with him? How could she explain that she was afraid one week with Chase might be enough to peel back all her protective layers, leave her bare, exposed and hurting? She didn't want to admit the possibility even to herself.

She slid onto a stool and braced her elbows on the counter. 'So what made you change your mind? To stop skimming?'

He poured the rest of the marinade on top of the chicken, stirring it slowly. 'I think I might take this opportunity to invoke part B of the no-talking-about-the-past clause, which details that I don't have to talk about it either.'

'You have something to hide?'

She almost missed the dark flash in his eyes. She knew he was touchy about his family, but he'd told her the basics about that. Was there something else? Something he didn't want her to know?

'Not really,' he said, taking the lid off a pan of rice and spooning some onto two plates warming on the hob. 'Just some things I'd rather not talk about.'

'What about your youth was so misspent?'

'You trying to get to *know* me?'

'Maybe.'

He shrugged. 'Just the usual, really, for a spoiled rich kid. Expelled from half a dozen boarding schools, crashed my father's Maserati. The final straw was sleeping with his girl-friend.' He spoke so very nonchalantly, yet Millie sensed a thread of self-protectiveness in his voice. Maybe even hurt.

'That's pretty misspent.'

'Yeah, well, I like to do things right.' Now he ladled the chicken in its fragrant sauce over the rice, and Millie had to admit it all looked delicious. The man could cook.

'And what made you change? I assume you're not crash-ing Maseratis now?'

'Only the odd one here or there.'

'Seriously.'

'You want me to be serious?' He let out a long-suffering sigh and handed her a plate. 'In that case, I need sustenance.'

They sat in a dining alcove, the floor-to-ceiling windows giving an endless view of the ocean darkening to damson under a twilit sky.

'Your favourite part of the day,' Chase said softly, and a thrill ran through her—a thrill at the thought that this man was starting to *know* her. And that she liked it.

How terrifying.

'So?' Millie said, attempting to banish that thrill. 'Why the change?'

Chase speared a piece of chicken. 'Remember I told you my father decided he didn't want me in the family business?'

'That was, I assume, after the girlfriend incident?'

'Correct. That, of course, just made me more determined to be as bad as I could be.'

'How old were you?'

'Seventeen.'

Millie felt a surprising tug of sympathy for the teenaged Chase. Normally she'd just roll her eyes at even the thought of some spoiled rich kid going through cars and women at a break-neck speed, but when she knew it was Chase… When she knew he wasn't shallow or spoiled, had more depth than most people she met… Well, it felt different. She felt different.

'So you were super-bad, then?'

'More of the same, really. Parties, cars, women, drink. Some recreational drug use I'm definitely not proud of.' He still spoke lightly, but she saw shadows in his eyes. Felt them in her heart. What a sad, empty life. And her life, in a totally different way, had been sad and empty too. *Still was.*

'So what was your life-changing moment?'

He gave her a speculative glance. 'This is getting pretty personal.'

She swallowed and decided not to dissemble. 'I know.'

Chase speared another bit of chicken and chewed slowly before answering. 'My father died. I was finishing college, I'd been studying architecture more for the hell of it than anything else. I was still pretty much a waste of space.' He paused, and Millie almost reached out to him, touched him, even just a hand on his arm. She stopped herself and Chase continued.

'I found out from his will that he'd legally disowned me from inheriting anything. Cut me out completely. It was what he'd threatened to do years before, but I guess I didn't really believe he meant it until then. And, while I have to admit I was pretty disappointed that I wouldn't be getting any of his money, I felt something worse.' He glanced away, his expression shuttering. 'Disappointment. Disappointment in myself, and how little I'd made of my life.'

Then Millie couldn't stop herself. *All in, right?* She reached across the table and touched Chase's hand, just a whisper of her fingers against his, but it was big for her and she thought he knew that. He glanced down at their touching hands and then looked up, smiling wryly.

'Not that inspiring a story, really.'

'Actually, it is. You recognised your mistakes and did something about them. Most people don't get that far.'

'Did you?'

The blunt question startled her. All this intimacy and sharing was great until he turned the tables on her. She withdrew her hand. 'Maybe, in a manner of speaking.' She paused, her fingers clenching into an involuntary fist. 'But it was too late.'

'Why was it too late, Millie?' She shook her head. She'd said too much. 'All these secrets,' Chase said lightly. 'You know it only makes you more intriguing, right? Sexier too. And it makes me want to find out what you're hiding.'

'Trust me, it's not sexy. Or intriguing. It's just…' She let out a breath. 'Sad. In a lot of different ways. And the reason I don't want to tell you is because you'll look at me differently.'

'Would that be a bad thing?'

'Yes, it would.' She liked the way Chase teased her. Riled her. Yes, he made her uncomfortable, but he also made her feel real and alive. He didn't tiptoe around her feelings, didn't tinge every smile with pity or uncertainty. Didn't look at her like she was a walking tragedy.

The way everyone else did.

Maybe *that* was what had attracted her to him in the first place—the fact that he didn't really know her at all. And yet, Millie had to acknowledge, he did know her. The real her. He just didn't know what had happened in her life.

And she liked it that way.

Yet how could he really know her, without knowing that?

Tired of the tangle of her thoughts, she rose from the table. 'Didn't you say something about a movie?'

Fifteen minutes later, after friendly bickering about whether to see an action flick or worthy drama, they settled on a DVD. Chase sat down on the sofa and before Millie could debate where to sit he pulled her down next to him, fit her snugly next to him and draped his arm around her shoulders. Millie tensed for just a second and then relaxed into Chase's easy embrace. Why was she fighting this? The weight of his arm and the solid strength of his body felt good.

She tried to pay attention to the movie—the worthy drama she had insisted upon—but she was so tired that her eyelids were drooping halfway through. She must have dozed off, for some time later she stirred to find herself being scooped up in Chase's arms.

'I can't believe I sat through something with subtitles so you could fall asleep on me,' Chase said, and there was so much affection in his voice that Millie curled naturally into the warmth of him, putting her arms around his neck.

'Time for bed, Scary,' he muttered, and she heard a catch in his voice. As he carried her through the villa to the bedroom in the back, Millie had the sleepy, hazy thought that there was nowhere else she'd rather be. In Chase's house. In Chase's arms. Going to Chase's bed.

CHAPTER SEVEN

MILLIE woke early, just as dawn was sliding its first pale fingers across the floor. She always woke early; quarter to five was usual. Yet, instead of bolting upright and practically sprinting to the shower, she woke slowly, languorously, stretching before she rolled over, propping herself up on one elbow to gaze at Chase.

He was fast asleep, his hair rumpled, his breathing slow and even. He looked gorgeous, and since he was asleep she let herself study him: the strong, stubbly angle of his jaw; the sweep of golden-brown lashes against his cheek. His lips were lush and full, his nose straight. The dawn light caught the golden glints in his close-cropped hair. Her gaze slid lower. He'd taken off his shirt. She'd seen his chest already, of course. He'd practically been shirtless the whole time she'd known him. Yet now she could study the perfect, muscled form; the sprinkling of dark-brown hair that veed lower, broad shoulders tapering to lean hips. The sheet was rucked about those hips, and she couldn't tell what he was wearing underneath. Dared she peek?

'Boxers, Scary.'

Her gaze flew back to his face. He was blinking sleep from his eyes and giving her the slowest, sexiest smile Millie had ever seen. Her heart juddered in her chest but she didn't try to dissemble.

'I was wondering. You seem like the type to sleep in the buff.'

'Nope, I'm strictly a boxers man. Sleeping naked can create all sorts of awkward situations, like when your cleaning lady arrives a bit earlier than you expected.'

Her mouth curved. 'You seem to have experienced a lot of awkward situations.'

'It certainly makes life a bit more interesting.'

'I'll take your word on it.'

He reached out and touched her hair, his fingers threading through it. 'Your hair's not so scary when you've slept on it.'

'It's probably a mess.'

'I like it.' He tucked a strand behind her ear, then trailed his fingers along her cheek before resting his thumb on the fullness of her lower lip. 'Those worry marks look a little better.'

'Do they?' Her heart had started the slow, thudding beat of expectation. They were both in a bed. Nearly naked. Had Chase removed her dress last night? She couldn't remember, but she was wearing one of his tee-shirts. And nothing underneath.

Surely now…?

'As enticing a prospect as that is, I think we'll have breakfast first,' Chase said, and Millie let out a huff of breath.

'Stop reading my mind.'

'It's too easy. Every thought is reflected in your eyes.'

'Not every thought,' Millie objected. She knew she had some secrets and she wanted to keep it that way.

Didn't she?

'More than you think,' Chase said softly, and he drew her towards him for a lingering kiss. It was the kind of kiss you had *after* you made love, slow and sated. It didn't have the urgency she expected, that she *felt*. Because today was day three of her week's holiday and since she'd met Chase time had started slipping by all too fast.

'Soon,' Chase murmured against her lips and she groaned. '*Stop* that.'

'Actually, I think you kind of like it.'

She didn't answer, because she knew he was right, even if the way he read her so easily was seriously annoying. She liked being *known*. 'What are we doing today?' she asked as she followed him out of the bedroom into the kitchen. Sunlight poured through the picture windows and Chase, still only wearing boxers, was reaching for the coffee grinder. Within seconds the wonderful aroma of freshly ground beans was wafting through the air.

'I thought you could decide that,' he said as he poured the ground beans into the coffee maker.

'Me?'

'Yes, you. You're not just along for the ride, you know.'

'I sort of thought I was. Your terms, remember?'

'Exactly. And my terms state that today you decide what we do. Of course, I have the right to veto any and all suggestions.'

'Oh, I see. Thanks for making that clear.'

'No problem.'

What *did* she want to do today? As Chase got out fresh melon and papaya and began slicing both, Millie considered. What did she want to do with *Chase*?

'I want to paint you.'

He paused, a mug in each hand, eyebrow arched. 'Too bad your paints are in the rubbish bin, then.'

'I can draw you,' Millie said firmly, surprised by how certain she felt. 'I brought charcoals too. They're in my suitcase.'

'So you've changed your mind about the painting thing?'

'Technically I won't be painting.'

'You are such a literalist.'

'Yes,' Millie said quietly, and it felt like a confession. 'I've changed my mind.'

Chase stared at her long and hard, and the moment unfurled, stretched between them into something that pulsed with both life and hope.

'OK,' he said. 'Breakfast, and then you can draw. I assume you'd prefer a nude model?'

She laughed and shook her head. 'You can keep your boxers on. For now.'

After a breakfast of coffee, fresh fruit and eggs Chase scrambled while Millie sat at the table and imagined just how she would sketch him, she fetched her paper and charcoals and they headed outside.

The day was warm, the sun already hot, although a fresh breeze blew off the sea. Millie had changed into a polo shirt and capris, and Chase had, on her instruction, put on a tee-shirt and shorts.

'Are you sure you don't want me nude?' he said, sounding disappointed, and Millie shook her head.

'Far too distracting.'

'Well, that's something at least.'

'Just try to act natural.'

He gave an exaggerated sigh. 'Whenever someone says that, you can't act natural any more.'

'Try.'

'I bet you're a real ball-breaker at work.'

'That,' Millie informed him, 'is a horrible, sexist term.'

'But you are, right?' He positioned himself on the sand, hands stretched out behind him, legs in front. 'This OK?'

'Perfect.' She found a comfortable spot just a little bit away and laid the sketch pad across her knees. After staring at Chase this morning, she realised how much she wanted to draw him, to capture the ease and joy of his body and face so she could remember it always.

So she could have something of him even when this week was over.

She swallowed, also realising just how much she was starting to care for him. Forty-eight hours—forty-eight *intense* hours—were changing how she felt. Changing *her*.

'You going to put pencil to paper this time, Scary?'

'Yes.' Swallowing, she looked down at her paper, began to roughly sketch the shape of him.

'So you haven't been doing the art thing for a while,' Chase remarked, gazing out to the sea so she should capture his profile. 'Why did you stop?'

Millie hesitated. She knew she should remind him about the no-talking rule, but it seemed kind of pointless to keep at it now. She didn't even want to. She could still control what she told him. 'Life happened,' she said. 'I got too busy and drawing seemed kind of a silly pastime.' And totally out of sync with her and Rob's focused, career-driven lives.

'And then you finally took a holiday and thought you might like to try again?'

'Basically.'

'So why did you throw out the paints when I first met you?'

'All these questions,' Millie said lightly. 'You are *so* violating our agreement, Chase.'

'But you're answering them,' he pointed out. 'For once.'

She didn't speak for a moment, just sketched faster and faster, the feel and look of him emerging from her charcoal. 'I didn't like how obvious it seemed,' she finally said. 'Like I was trying to *find* myself or something.'

'Were you?'

She glanced up, the sketch book momentarily forgotten. 'I'm not lost,' she said sharply. 'I'm not *broken*.'

'You're not?' He still spoke mildly, yet she felt that spurt of rage anyway. Her fingers tightened around the charcoal.

'No.'

'Because I think you are.'

Shock had her fingers slackening again, and the charcoal fell to the ground. 'How dare—?'

'Why do you think you're here, Millie?' He turned to gaze at her and she saw a blaze of emotion lighting his eyes. 'Why do you think you were willing to have this crazy, intense week? And not just willing, but needing it?'

'I don't *need* it.'

'Liar.'

She shook her head, hating that he saw through her. Hating that she didn't have the strength to deny it any longer. She *was* lost. Broken. And she needed this week with him; she needed *him*.

And he knew it.

He kept his gaze on her, assessing, knowing, and she hated that too. The raw honesty between them in this moment felt more exposing and intimate than lying naked on a bed with him had yesterday.

She reached for the dropped charcoal, her fingers closing around it even though she knew she wouldn't draw any more. She couldn't. She stared blindly at the sketch pad, her mind spinning, her heart thudding.

'Our session is finished, I presume?' Chase drawled, and Millie nodded jerkily. 'And now you're going to go all haughty on me, aren't you? The Millie Lang armour goes up, and you get all scary and severe.'

'You're the one who calls me scary,' Millie said through numb lips. Every instinct in her was telling her to *run*. Save herself, or as much of herself as she could. How had she let it get this far? Chase had been so clever at seducing her into an emotional intimacy she had never intended to give or reveal. Damn it, all she'd wanted was *sex*.

And they still hadn't had it.

Maybe it was time to rectify that situation.

'I'm not going to go scary on you,' she told him, clutching her sketch pad to her chest. 'But you did say I could decide what we did today, and now I've decided.'

'And it's not sketching?' Chase still looked relaxed, still had his hands stretched out behind him like he was enjoying a nice morning in the sun.

'No, it's not.' Her voice still rang out, strident, aggressive. It sounded strong, even if she didn't feel it. 'I'll tell you what it is.'

'I bet I could guess…' Chase murmured and, furious that he still seemed to know her so well, she cut across him.

'It's sex. I want to have sex with you.'

Chase regarded her with lazy amusement, although he was far from feeling either lazy or amused. He knew Millie felt vulnerable and exposed, but damn it so did he. He hadn't meant to say any of that. Lost? Broken? He could have been talking about himself. What the hell had he been thinking, getting that honest? That *real*?

He hadn't been thinking at all. He'd just been acting on instinct, allowing the deep within him to call to the deep within her. And for a few charged seconds he knew they'd connected in a way that was far more powerful than anything they could do on a bed—or whatever surface they chose.

'You want to have sex with me,' Chase repeated. 'Sometimes, Millie, you have a one-track mind.'

'I'm serious, Chase. The whole reason we're having this stupid fling is—'

'Now our fling is stupid? I'm offended.'

'You know what I mean. I started this because—'

'*You* started it?'

'Stop interrupting me!'

'Because I'm the one who walked up to you on that beach, sweetheart. *And* asked you out.'

'I'm the one who suggested we sleep together.'

'I'll concede that point, but that's the only shot you're going to call.'

She stared at him, her face white, her lips bloodless. What had scared her so much? The fact that he saw her need, or that she sensed his own? And how did she think sex was going to solve anything?

On second thought...

'OK, Scary.' Chase rose from the beach, turning his face so Millie didn't see him grimace at the throbbing ache of his joints. It was getting worse. The new medication wasn't helping as much as he'd hoped. Hell, he was as broken as she was. He just hid it better.

'OK?' she repeated uncertainly, the wind blowing her hair into tangles even as she clutched the sketch pad to her chest like it was a body shield.

'OK, we'll have sex. I think we've had a fair amount of anticipation, don't you?'

'Yes.' She sounded uncertain. He wasn't surprised. She hadn't expected him to agree—well, guess what? Sex was probably the only place where he could make her let go of that all-too-precious control. Break the barriers she surrounded herself with, force her to be exposed and empty; only then could she be covered and filled.

Is that what you really want?

Yes. Certainty blazed through him, surprising him. He didn't know more than that, wouldn't look farther. *No more questions.*

Time to act.

'Come on,' he said, and reached a hand down to her. She

took it gingerly, her eyes so heartbreakingly wide, her teeth sunk deep into her lower lip.

'Where are we going?'

'I told you I prefer to make love on a bed, right?'

'Yes…'

'Cold feet?' he jibed softly, knowing she'd rise to that easy bait.

'No! Of course not!'

'Of course not,' he agreed. Yet her hand was icy-cold and her slender fingers felt like bird bones in his.

He led her back inside, through the house and then right to his bedroom door. Turned to her as he still held that icy, trembling hand. 'You're scared.'

She opened her mouth to deny it, then stopped. 'Yes.'

'You're thinking too much.'

'I know.'

'I think,' Chase murmured, 'I know a way to make you to stop thinking.' He kicked open the door and pulled her into the bedroom.

Millie felt weirdly numb as she followed Chase into the bedroom. It looked the same as it had a few hours earlier, when they'd lain in that nice, wide bed and talked and teased each other.

It *felt* totally different now.

Her heart was thudding so hard it hurt. Her mouth was dry. Her legs felt like jelly. She didn't think she'd ever felt this nervous before. Fizzing with both fear and a glorious anticipation. She wanted this, even if it scared her senseless.

Chase turned to her, his expression serious. Thoughtful. She closed her eyes and tipped her head back, waited for him to take over. Make her stop thinking.

He didn't do anything. She opened her eyes. 'What are you waiting for?'

He smiled. 'Sorry, Scary, this isn't the Chase Bryant Show.'

'You want me to do something?'

'I know you'd rather I just did everything, but since when have I ever let you have it easy?'

She let out a trembling huff of laughter. 'Sorry. It's... It's been a long time.'

'I kind of figured that out.'

She closed her eyes again, this time in embarrassment. With her eyes closed, she couldn't see him but she felt him step closer, felt the whisper of his fingers as he brushed her cheek, tucked her hair behind her ear. 'Telling you to relax isn't going to do a thing, is it?' She shook her head, felt Chase's hesitation. 'You sure you want to do this, Millie? You know you could back out now. I wouldn't— Well, yeah, I'd mind, but I'd understand. This is big for you. And scary. I get that.'

A hot lump of emotion lodged in her throat. Speaking was impossible. She just shook her head, eyes still closed. She heard Chase's soft breathing, felt his fingers gently brush her cheek again.

Finally she opened her eyes. He looked so concerned and tender as he gazed down at her that her heart seemed to seize up. Her emotions were fully engaged, much more than she'd ever intended or wanted. And, even though it terrified her, she knew bone-deep that she really *did* want this. She craved it. Not just the physical release, but the emotional intensity. *Intimacy.* How scary was that?

'I might not be doing much,' she whispered, 'but I'm not trying to leave, am I?'

'No. You're not. And thank God for that.' Slowly, deliberately, he drew her towards him, his hands cradling her face. Her heart pounded. This was it. He was going to kiss her, and then...

'Stop *thinking*, Scary.'

'I can't help it,' she groaned. 'I can't turn my mind off.'

'I realise.'

'I want to turn it off, Chase. I want to forget. I want to forget everything.' Her mouth was a whisper away from his. He gazed down at her, his eyes warm and soft with compassion as his thumbs stroked her jaw bone.

'But then you'll just have to remember again.'

'Just for a little while. I want to forget for a little while.' She drew in a shaky breath. 'Please. Make me forget. Make me forget everything.'

He smiled faintly even though she saw a shadow of concern in his eyes. 'That's kind of a tall order.'

'You're the only one who can.' And she knew she spoke the truth. '*Please*. Whatever it takes.'

In answer he kissed her, his lips brushing hers once, twice, as if getting the sense of her before he suddenly delved deep and she felt that kiss straight down to her soul. Shocks of pleasure and excitement sizzled along her nerve endings and she surrendered to that kiss, kissing him back, hands curling around his shoulders, nails digging in.

Yet even as she surrendered her mind took a step back. She started thinking. It was as if that kiss had taken over every part of her body and mind except that one dark corner where the memories crouched, waited till she was vulnerable to attack.

You never kissed Rob like this.

You shouted at him before he left for the last time.

You didn't kiss Charlotte goodbye. You didn't even look at her.

'*Easy*, Millie.' She opened her eyes and realised she'd been standing rigid, her nails like claws in Chase's shoulders.

'I'm sorry.'

'So am I.' Gently he unhooked her hands from his shoul-

ders. 'You were doing some serious thinking there.' Chase
stared at her for a moment, and then he took her by the hand
and led her to the bed. He stripped off his shirt and dropped
his shorts. Millie blinked. She'd seen him naked yesterday,
but he was still magnificent. Beautiful, everything taut and
sculpted and golden-brown.

'Now I'm naked,' he said.

'Clearly.'

'You still have your clothes on.'

'I'm aware.'

'I'm going to take them off.'

Her heart turned over. 'OK,' she said. He'd seen her naked
yesterday, but that had been her choice. Her action. Now, as
she stood still and he reached for the buttons on her shirt,
she knew it was his. She'd just relinquished a little bit of
control, just as he wanted her to. As she wanted to, even if
it was so incredibly hard.

Deftly Chase's fingers undid the buttons on her polo shirt.
'Raise your arms,' he said, and she did. He slipped the shirt
over her head, tossed it aside. Millie glanced down at the
plain white cotton bra she wore; the straps were frayed. *Why*
had she never indulged in sexy underwear? 'We'll leave that
on for now,' Chase said, his mouth quirking in a small smile.
'I kind of like it.'

She practically snorted in disbelief. 'You like my old,
plain white bra?'

'I know; weird, huh? But I've seen plenty of push-up monstrosities. This doesn't pretend or hide.' He touched her chin,
tilting her face so she had to meet his gaze. 'Unlike you.'

'My *bra* is more honest than I am?' she huffed.

'Pretty much,' he said, and undid the snap on her capris.

Millie's breath caught in her chest as Chase slid them
down her legs. His touch was feather-light and swift, hardly
a practised caress. And yet she felt as if she burned where his

fingers had so briefly touched her. He sank to his knees as he balanced her with one hand while he used the other to help her out of the capris, then tossed them over with the shirt.

She was in her underwear. Again.

And he was naked, on his knees in front of her.

She tried not to gulp too loudly as she gazed down at him, all burnished, sleek muscle. Slowly, so slowly, he slid his hands up her legs and then held her by the hips, his palms seeming to burn right through the thin cotton of her underwear as his fingers slid over her butt. She let out a stifled cry as he brought his mouth close to the juncture of her thighs and she tensed, anticipating his touch, fearing the intensity of her own response. But he didn't touch her, just let his breath fan over her, and that was enough.

Her knees buckled.

She *felt* Chase's smile and he stood up. 'Better,' he said, and she let out a wobbly laugh. Sensation fizzed inside her. The fear lessened, replaced by a warm, honeyed desire.

Then her mind started going into hyperdrive again, memories, thoughts and fears tumbling around like a washer on spin cycle.

'Stop thinking.'

'I *can't.*'

'Then I'll have to help you.'

'Yes.' *Please.*

Wordlessly he tugged her hand and led her to the bed. Her mind was still spinning relentlessly, and she had a sudden picture of her bed back in New York, her and Rob's bed, all hospital corners and starched duvet, and how she'd sank onto it when the phone had rung, and the police had told her there had been an accident…

'Lie down.'

'OK.' She felt only relief that he was interrupting her thoughts. She wanted to stop thinking. Stop analysing. Stop remembering so much. Why did being with Chase make her remember? She'd spent two years trying *not* to think, and now the thoughts came fast and thick, unstoppable.

She needed Chase to stop them.

She lay on the bed and he knelt over her. Millie felt herself tense. 'What are you—?'

'Trust me.'

And she knew she did trust him. Amazingly. Implicitly. Yet that thought was scary too. Chase reached for something above her head, and she saw he'd taken the satin pillow-case from the pillow.

He took the pillow-case off the other pillow and Millie waited, arousal and uncertainty warring within her.

'Care to tell me what's going on?' she asked as lightly as she could.

Chase slowly slid his hand from her shoulder to her palm, lacing her fingers with his own as he raised her hand above her head.

'I'm tying you up.'

'What?' She thought he was joking. Of course he was joking. Then she realised he'd done it, and her hand was tied to the bed post with a satin pillow-case. She stared at him with wide eyes, totally shocked. Chase simply knelt there, smiling faintly, his eyes dark and serious. Waiting.

Waiting for her permission.

She drew in a deep, shuddering breath, her whole body intensely, unbearably aware. She had no room for thoughts. She said nothing.

He bent down and kissed her deeply on the mouth, another soul-stirring kiss that had her arching instinctively towards him.

And then he tied up her other hand. She lay there, her hands tied above her head, her body completely open to his caress.

Vulnerable.

This felt far more intense than anything that had happened so far between them, and she knew why Chase was doing it.

He was taking everything from her. Taking it all, so he could give.

All in.

Slowly Chase slid his hands across her tummy, over her breasts, reaching behind to unhook her bra. 'Sorry,' he whispered. 'I do like it, but it had to go eventually.'

She still couldn't speak. Especially not when he tossed the bra onto the floor and bent his head to her breasts, his tongue flicking lightly over her nipples. She arched again, her head thrown back, pleasure streaking through her like lightning—but still the thoughts.

My breasts are too small.

Rob never liked them.

I don't deserve a man like this.

'Still thinking, huh?' He lifted his head and looked at her, his voice wry even as his eyes blazed.

'Sorry,' she whispered. She wanted him to help her forget, but maybe she couldn't forget unless she first released the memories. *Shared* them.

The most terrifying thought of all.

'Don't be sorry.'

'I want to stop thinking so much. Remembering.'

'I know you do.'

'Help me,' she implored. 'Help me, Chase.'

He gazed at her, his face suffused with both tenderness and desire. What a heady combination. She felt more for him in that moment then she ever had before, and then he took another pillow-case, folded it in half and placed it over her eyes. Millie gasped aloud. Chase waited, the pillow-case folded over her eyes but not tied.

She blinked, shocked and yet knowing she needed this.

Chase was helping her, helping her in a way she'd never have expected. It was strange and scary, yet amazingly *right*.

'OK?' he asked softly and she nodded. He tied the blindfold around her eyes.

Millie lay there, trying to adjust to this new reality. Her world had shrunk to the feel, sound and scent of Chase. Her mind had no room save for the sense of him. Her body tensed in a kind of exquisite anticipation, waiting for his touch. Wondering where he would touch her, every nerve taut with glorious expectation as she lay there, helpless, *hopeful* and utterly in his control.

And then she felt his mouth between her thighs, right on the centre of her, and she let out a shudder of shocked pleasure. She had not expected *that*.

Her body writhed beneath him and she felt a pleasure so intense it was akin to pain as her body surged towards a climax. '*Chase*,' she gasped, his name a sob. And then he stopped, taking her to the brink and no further, and she ached with the loss of him. '*Chase*,' she said again, and this time it was a plea.

She could hear his breathing, ragged and uneven, and his knees pressed on the outside of her thighs. She felt his heat, knew he was right above her. Where would he touch her next?

She let out a long shudder, every sense sizzling with excitement.

And then he began to touch her, a blitz of caresses that had her so focused on the sensation she could not form so much as a single coherent thought. First a butterfly brush of a kiss on her wrist. A blizzard of kisses on her throat. Then he kissed her deeply on the mouth and she responded, straining against the bonds that had brought her to this moment. He kissed her everywhere, light, teasing kisses, deep-throated demands, bites, licks and nibbles. She cried beneath him, first out of pleasure and amazement and then something deeper.

Something inside her started to break.

She'd told him she wasn't broken, and she hadn't been. She'd been holding herself together, only just, her soul and heart a maze of hairline cracks and fissures. And now, under Chase, she shattered.

Pain and pleasure, joy and sorrow, erupted from the depths of her being in helpless cries that became wrenching sobs, her whole body shaking with the force of them even as she lay there, splayed open to him, everything exposed. Everything vulnerable.

'Millie,' he said, and his voice was full of love.

'Yes,' she choked. 'Yes, Chase, *now*.'

Distantly she heard the rip of foil and knew Chase would finally be inside her. She'd never wanted anything so much, and yet she still gave a cry of surprise and joy when she felt him slide inside, fill her up.

She'd been so *empty*.

His arms came around her and Chase freed her so she enfolded her body around his, drawing him deeper inside as she buried her face in his neck and sobbed through her climax.

Chase surged inside her, deeper and deeper, and with his arms around her, holding her tightly and tenderly to him, he brought them both home.

CHAPTER EIGHT

CHASE felt his heart race as he held Millie in his arms and she sobbed as if her own heart were breaking.

God help him. God help them both. He'd never expected sex between them to be like *that*. Mind-blowing indeed. He was completely and utterly spent, emotionally, physically, everything.

Millie pressed her face against his neck, her body shaking with the force of her emotion. Chase didn't speak, knew there were no words. He just stroked her back, her hair, wiped the tears from her cheeks with his thumbs.

Millie's sobs began to subside into snuffles and hiccups, and she curled herself into him, as if she wanted to be as close to him as possible, her legs across his, her arm around his waist, her head still buried against his neck.

Chase held her, cradled her closer, even as part of him was distantly acknowledging that this had been one *hell* of a mistake.

She lifted her face from his neck and gazed up at him with rain-washed eyes. She looked so unbearably open; she'd dropped all the armour and masks. Nothing hid her from him any more, and he really wasn't sure how he felt about that. He shifted so he could hold her a bit more loosely, waiting for her to speak.

'I want to tell you,' she said quietly, hesitantly. 'I want to—to talk about my past.'

He didn't think he wanted to hear it. Chase adjusted her more securely against him, knowing she needed that. She needed him, God help them both.

'OK,' he said.

Millie glanced down, ran her hand down the length of his bare chest. Even now he reacted, felt the shower of sparks her touch created in him. He wanted to dismiss it as mere chemistry, but he knew he couldn't.

'My husband died two years ago,' Millie said, and everything, *everything* in him shrivelled.

Damn.

'I'm sorry,' he said quietly. He'd suspected some heartbreak; of course he had. How could he not? Sadness seeped from her pores. But a husband? A *widow*? He thought of all his light, deprecating jokes and inwardly winced.

Outwardly he ran his hand up and down her back, strokes meant to soothe and comfort even as his mind seethed.

'What happened?' he asked eventually, because for all her wanting to tell him everything she'd lapsed into silence.

'He died in a car accident. On the Cross Bronx expressway. A collision with an eighteen-wheeler. They think the driver fell asleep at the wheel.'

Chase swallowed. He couldn't think of anything more to say, so he just held her.

'I didn't tell you because for the last two years it's completely defined me. Everyone I know looks at me like I'm a walking tragedy.' Which she was. 'No one knows what to say to me, so they either ignore me or apologise. I hate it.'

He identified all too much with everything she said, albeit for a different reason. But he knew there was more she wasn't telling him.

'And then I feel guilty for thinking that way. Like I want to be happy, even when I know I never can be.'

'Everyone wants to be happy,' Chase said. 'You can be happy again, Millie.' But not with him. Now, he knew, was not the time to remind her they only had one week together. Four more days after this.

'I liked the fact that you didn't know,' she said quietly. 'That you treated me normally. I almost—I almost felt normal.'

'And then you felt guilty for feeling normal,' Chase supplied. What a depressing cycle.

'Yes, I suppose,' Millie said slowly. 'But more than that.' She stopped again and he knew he would have to prompt her. Coax the heartbreaking story with all its drama and tragedy out of her bit by bit.

But he didn't think he had the energy. That probably made him an incredibly shallow bastard, but he couldn't help it. He'd had his own share of depressing drama, tragedy and pain. He wasn't sure he could take Millie's.

And he knew she couldn't take his.

'We had a good marriage,' she finally said. 'I loved him.' And what was he supposed to say to *that*? She bowed her head, her hair brushing his bare chest. 'And I know no marriage, no relationship is perfect, but I look back and I see all the mistakes I made. We both made,' she allowed, her voice a throaty whisper, and Chase just let her talk. He didn't have much to offer her. He hadn't had too many serious relationships, and he'd never come close to marriage.

Yet.

Why the *hell* had he thought that?

'We grew apart,' Millie said after a moment. 'Because… because of different things. And the day he died I was sharp with him. I don't even remember what we argued about, isn't that stupid? But I didn't— I didn't kiss them—

him—goodbye. I don't think I even *said* goodbye. And Charlotte...' Her voice caught and Chase pulled her closer. He still didn't say anything. He had nothing to offer her in this moment, and he knew it. Maybe she did too.

After a ragged moment Millie slipped from his arms. He let her go, watched from the bed as she scooped up her clothes and headed towards the bathroom. 'I'm going to take a shower,' she said, her back to him so he could see all the delicate knobs of her spine, the slender dip of her waist and curve of her hip.

'OK,' Chase said, and as she closed the bathroom door he felt a shaming wave of relief.

Millie turned the knobs on the shower and rested her head on the cool tile. Her heart had stopped its thunderous racing and for a second she wondered if it still beat at all. After feeling so painfully, gloriously alive, she now felt dead inside. Numb and lifeless with disappointment.

So Chase didn't really want intense. Not the kind of intense she'd been offering as she'd lain in his arms and tried to tell him her story. Even as he put his arms around her, went through the motions, she'd felt the coldness of his emotional withdrawal. She'd violated the terms of their agreement—the terms *she* had made—and he didn't like it. Didn't want to go that deep or far.

Stupid, *stupid* her.

Drawing a shaky breath, she stepped into the shower, let the water stream over her and wash away the traces of her tears. She'd cried after the accident, of course. She'd done the counselling and the support groups and even *journalled*. But she'd never cried like that. She'd never given so much, so freely, and stupidly it made her want more. It made her want to tell him everything, about her marriage, the accident, *Charlotte*.

But within thirty seconds of speaking she'd realised Chase didn't want to know. He wasn't the only one who could read people.

Another shuddering breath and she reached for the shampoo. At least now she understood the terms: no talking about the past. Chase was all about the physical intimacy, having her melt in his arms, but the emotional stuff? Not so much. He'd liked pushing her but he didn't like the results. Well, she got that now. And it was just as well, because even if for a few shattering seconds she'd wanted to tell him everything, had maybe even thought she *loved* him, she understood now that wasn't where this was going. And when rationality had returned she'd known she didn't even want to go there. She'd loved and lost once. She wasn't going to attempt it again, and especially not with a man who was only in it for a week.

By the time she'd showered and dressed, Millie felt more herself. She'd found that icy control, and she was glad. She stepped out of the bathroom, saw the late-afternoon sun slant across the empty bed. They'd skipped lunch and, despite the emotional tornado she'd been sucked into all afternoon, she was hungry. Her stomach growled.

She wandered out to the kitchen and saw Chase talking on his mobile. She waited, far enough way so she couldn't eavesdrop, and a few seconds later he disconnected the call and gave her a quick, breezy smile.

'Good shower?'

'Fine. I'm starving, though.'

'I'm glad to hear it. I just made reservations at Straw Hat on Anguilla.'

'Anguilla? How far away is that?'

'An hour in my boat.'

'OK.' Maybe escaping the island would be a good thing. The door bell rang, and Millie watched as Chase went to answer it. She felt like everything was on fast forward, plans put in motion before she could even think.

'What's that?' she asked when he came back with several shopping bags with the resort's swirly logo on the side.

'A couple of dresses. I thought you might like something new.'

She gazed at him levelly. 'I have a whole suitcase of new clothes.'

Chase just shrugged. 'I don't think your wardrobe runs to fun and flirty.'

'Maybe I don't want *fun and flirty.*'

He sighed. 'Don't wear them if you don't want to, Millie. I just thought it might be nice for our big date.'

'Oh? So this is a big date?'

He narrowed his gaze. 'What's with you?'

'Nothing.' Somehow everything had changed between them, and not for the better. Chase wasn't as light and laughing as he'd used to be, as she *needed* him to be. He was tense and touchy, even if he was trying to act like he wasn't. And so was she.

'Fine. I'll take a look.' She reached for the bags and caught Chase's bemused look. 'Thank you,' she added, belatedly and ungraciously.

Chase's mouth quirked in a smile that seemed all too sad. 'No problem,' he said quietly, and she retreated to the bedroom.

Half an hour later she was on Chase's boat, wearing a shift dress of cinnamon-coloured silk as they cruised towards Anguilla.

Chase had shed his blazer and tie and rolled the sleeves up of his crisp white shirt to navigate the boat. He looked amazing.

They hadn't said much since the exchange in the kitchen, and the silence was making Millie twitchy. She wanted that fun, teasing banter back, the ease she'd felt in Chase's presence. She'd told him he'd made her uncomfortable, but it was nothing like this.

Moodily she stared out at the sea. The sun was already slipping towards the horizon. A third sunset. Only four more to go and their week would be over. And by mutual agreement, they would never see each other again.

Chase left the tiller to come and sit next to her, the wind ruffling his hair as he squinted into the dying sun. He didn't ask her what she was thinking, didn't say anything, and Millie knew he didn't want to know. He'd only pushed her when he thought she'd push back, not give in. It was the anticipation that had been fun for him, the moment before.

Not the moment after.

'So how come you have a villa on St Julian's if you didn't want to have anything to do with the Bryant business?' she asked when the silence had stretched on long enough to make her want to fidget.

Chase kept his gaze on the darkening sea. 'My grandfather bequeathed the island to my brothers and me, and my father couldn't do anything about it. As soon as I'd established myself I had the villa built. I hardly ever use it, actually, but it was a way to thumb my nose at my father—even if he was dead.'

'It must have hurt, to have him disinherit you,' Millie said quietly.

Chase shrugged. 'It didn't feel good.'

'What about your mother?'

'She died when I was twelve. Breast cancer.'

'I'm sorry.'

Another shrug. Clearly he didn't like talking about any of this, but at least he was giving answers. And Millie knew she wanted to know.

'And your brothers? Do you get along well with them?'

He sighed, raked a hand through his hair. 'More or less. Aaron is nice enough, but he views life as a game of Monopoly where he has all the money. Luke is my middle brother, and he's always been trying to prove himself. Total workaholic.'

'And where do you fit in?'

'Black sheep, basically, who only semi-made-good.'

'Are they married?'

'Nope, none of us seem eager to take the plunge.' He spoke evenly, almost lightly, but she still heard the warning. *Oh, fabulous.* So after this afternoon he thought she was going to go all doe-eyed on him, start dreaming of happily-ever-afters. She'd only done that for a *second*.

'And you get along?'

'More or less.'

It didn't sound like the best family situation. She was blessed to have parents and a sister who loved and supported her, but even they hadn't been able to break down her walls or keep her from hiding behind the rubble.

Only Chase had done that.

She let out a restless sigh, knowing she needed to stop thinking this way, wanting something from Chase he couldn't give. Ironic, really, that she'd assumed he was shallow, then believed he wasn't, only to discover he really was. And, while she'd wanted shallow before, she didn't want it now.

'And what about you? You have family around?' Chase asked.

'Parents and a sister.'

'Are you close with them?'

'Yes.' She paused, because even though she was close she hadn't told them as much about her marriage as she had Chase.

'Not that close, huh?' Chase said, sounding cynical, and

Millie shook her head. She couldn't bear for him to think that her family was like his, or that her life had been all sadness.

'No, actually, we are. My sister Zoe is fantastic. She stops by almost every week with my favourite snack, makes sure I'm not working too hard.'

'Your favourite snack?'

'Nachos with fake cheese.'

He let a short laugh. 'That is so low-brow. I was expecting dark chocolate or some exotic sorbet.'

'I don't play to type *that* much,' she said lightly, and for a moment everything was at it had been, the lightness, the fun. Then something shuttered in Chase's eyes and he turned away to gaze at the sea.

'We're almost there.' He rose and went to trim the sail as the lights of Anguilla loomed closer, shimmering on the surface of the tranquil sun-washed sea. They didn't speak as he moored the boat and then helped her onto the dock.

The restaurant was right on the sand, the terracotta-tile and white-stucco building one of a jumble along the beach. It felt surprisingly refreshing to be out of the rarefied atmosphere of St Julian's, to see people who weren't just wealthy guests. A rail-thin cat perched along the wall that lined the beach, and a few children played with a ball and stick in the dusky light.

Millie slowed her steps as she watched the children. One of the girls had a mop of dark curls. She looked to be about five years old, a little older than Charlotte would have been.

'Millie?' Chase reached for her hand and she realised she'd been just standing there, staring. Children had been invisible to her for two years; it was as if her brain knew she couldn't handle it and just blanked them out. She didn't see them in her building, in the street, in the park. It helped that her life was so work-focused; there weren't many children on Wall Street.

Yet she saw them now, saw them in all their round-cheeked innocence, and felt her raw and wounded heart give a death-defying squeeze.

'Millie,' Chase said again quietly and slowly she turned away from the raggedy little group. She wanted to rail at him, to beat her fists against his chest.

See? See what you did to me? I was fine before, I was surviving, and now you've opened up this need and hope in me and you don't even want it any more.

Swallowing, she lifted her chin and followed Chase into the restaurant. The place was a mix of funky Caribbean decor and fresh, well-prepared food. The waiter greeted Chase by name and ushered them to the best table in the restaurant, in a semi-secluded alcove.

'What's this? A huge ashtray?' Millie gestured to the rectangular box of sand in the middle of the table.

'Nope, just a little sand box to play with while we wait for our food.' He took a little spade lying next to the box and handed it to her with a glinting smile. 'Dig in.'

'Clearly meant for guests with short attention spans.' She scooped a bit of sand with the miniature spade and dumped it out again. 'So do you like being an architect?'

'All these questions.'

She glanced up sharply. 'It's called conversation, generally.' She heard an edge to her voice, knew he heard it too. So *now* he didn't like the questions.

Chase leaned back in his chair and took a sip of sparkling water. 'I like making things. I like having an idea and seeing it become a reality.'

'What firm do you work for?'

His mouth quirked upwards. 'Chase Bryant Designs.'

'Your own.'

'Yep, started it five years ago.' He spoke casually, but she heard a betraying note of pride in his voice. He'd made something of himself, and without help from his wealthy family. She wanted to tell him she admired that, that she was proud of him, but how stupid would that be? He'd just feel even more awkward. So she took a large gulp of wine, and then another, deciding that alcohol was a better option.

'Slow down there, Scary,' Chase said, eyeing her near-empty wine glass. 'Or I'll have to carry you home.'

'I'm not a lightweight.'

'No, indeed.' Now she heard an edge in his voice, and she pushed her wine glass away with a little sigh of irritation.

'Look, Chase, why don't you just come out and say it?'

He stilled. Stared. 'Say what?'

'You're done.'

'*I'm* done?'

'Yes. Ever since—' She paused, swallowed. 'It's obvious you've had your bout of intense sex and you're ready to move on. So maybe we should call it a day. A night. Whatever.' She grabbed her wine glass again and drained it, half-wishing she hadn't started this conversation.

Half-wishing even now he'd tell her she was wrong.

'You're the one who has been picking fights,' Chase said mildly. 'I bought you a dress and took you out to one of the best restaurants in the whole Caribbean. So, sorry, I don't get where you're coming from.'

She met his gaze squarely. 'You don't?' she asked quietly, no edge, no spite. Just raw honesty.

Chase held her gaze for a breathless beat and then glanced away. 'No, I don't,' he said quietly, and she felt that tiny tendril of hope she'd still been nurturing even without knowing it shrivel and die.

It hurt that, after all they'd experienced and shared, he wouldn't even own up to how things had changed. It hurt far too much.

She'd known this man for three days. Yet time had lost its

meaning in this surprising paradise; time had lost its meaning ever since she'd agreed to have this fling—this intense, intimate, all-in fling—with Chase.

For a second Millie almost rose from the table and walked out of the restaurant. She didn't need this. She didn't need Chase. Then the waiter came and they gave their orders, and the impulse passed, her strength fading away.

For it was weakness why she stayed. A weakness for him. That little tendril of hope might have withered and died, but its seed still remained in the stubborn soil of her heart, desperate to grow.

Chase watched the emotions—disappointment, hurt, sorrow—ripple across Millie's face like shadows on water, wishing he couldn't read her so easily. Wishing he wasn't screwing up so badly right now.

Nothing had been the same since the sex, and more importantly since the conversation after the sex. He'd pushed and pushed Millie, had wanted to see her lose that control, had wanted to be the one to make it happen. And when it had, and she'd taken a flying leap over that cliff, what had he done?

He'd backed away, and pretended he hadn't. Acted like he was still right there with her, flying through the air, when she knew he'd really high-tailed it in the other direction.

Coward. *Bastard.*

He took a sip of water and stared moodily around at the restaurant. He'd always enjoyed this place, found it fun and relaxing, but not this time. Now he didn't think anything would kick-start his mood. He wanted the fun back with Millie, the easy companionship they'd had. He hadn't even realised just how easy it had been, until now.

Now words tangled in his throat and he couldn't get any of it out. Couldn't even begin. What to say? *I'm sorry. I'm*

sorry I'm not there for you, when you thought I would be.
When you wanted me to be and I just couldn't do it.

Hell, this was all his fault. He should have listened to that cool, rational part of his brain that had told him to walk away from this woman before she drove him insane. Who said no to 'intense', no to a fling, no to anything with Millie Lang.

Instead he'd done the opposite, followed his libido and even his heart, and now he had no idea what to do. He hated seeing the deepening frown lines on Millie's face, the worry marks on her lip fresher and more raw than ever. As he watched a little bright-red pearl of blood appeared on her lower lip from where she'd bitten it.

Damn. Damn it to hell.

'Millie…' He reached over, placed his hand on hers. She looked up, eyes wide, teeth sunk into that lip. 'I'm sorry,' he said in a low voice. 'I've totally screwed this up.'

Tears filled those soft brown eyes and she blinked hard as she shook her head, teeth biting even deeper. 'No. I'm the one who screwed up. I shouldn't have said all that…after. That wasn't part of our deal.'

'I led you to it.'

She arched an eyebrow, somehow managed a smile. This woman was *strong*. 'By tying me up and blindfolding me?'

'Basically.'

'Have you ever done that kind of thing before?' she asked, curious, and he actually blushed.

'No.'

'Me neither.'

'Yeah, I pretty much figured that out.'

She let out a laugh that trembled just a little too much. 'Oh, Chase, I just want it back.'

He eyed her warily. 'Back?'

'You. Me. *Us.* I was having fun, you know, and that felt

really good.' She gave him a wobbly smile that felt like a dagger thrust to the heart. 'It felt amazing.'

And he knew she was right. It *had* felt amazing. More amazing than anything else he'd ever had or known. Why was he pushing it away?

Four more days.

'Come on,' he said roughly. He rose from the table, nearly knocking over their drinks as he threw down some bills. 'Let's get out of here.'

She rose also, taking his hand as he threaded his way through the table. 'Where are we going?'

'To a room. A room with a bed.'

'Or any convenient surface?' she murmured, and something close to fierce joy pulsed through him.

'That's about the size of it,' he agreed, and led her out into the night.

Millie didn't ask questions, didn't say anything at all as he led her away from the beach and towards the street. He hailed a cab, thanked God one screeched to the kerb in three seconds flat and then hauled her inside it.

Still no speaking. Would words break what was between them? Chase didn't know. Was afraid to find out. And yet he had words, so many words, words he needed to say and, more importantly, she needed to hear.

But, first, a room. A bed.

'Cap Juluca,' he told the cab driver, and Millie just arched an eyebrow. 'It's a resort here,' Chase explained, his voice still rough with want. 'I booked it in case we didn't feel like sailing back.'

And that was all that was said as they drove away from Meads Bay, down the coast, through the resort's gates, and then up to the main building. Chase kept hold of her hand as he checked in and then led her away from the main complex towards the private cove that housed their accommodation.

Millie skidded to a stop. 'A grass hut? Seriously?'

'A luxurious grass hut,' Chase said and tugged her inside.

Millie glanced around and he could see her taking in the polished mahogany floor, the comfortable rattan chairs, the gauzy mosquito netting. And the bed. A wide, low bed with linen sheets and soft pillows, the ocean lapping only metres away through the draped net curtains. The wind rustled through the woven grass that made up the roof and walls.

She turned to him. 'It's beautiful.'

'You're beautiful,' he said, a catch in his voice, and she shook her head.

'I don't need flattery, Chase. I know I'm not beautiful.' She sounded so matter-of-fact, it made his heart twist inside him.

'Why do you think you aren't beautiful?'

'Even you called me scary. And I know I'm not your usual type.' She let out a long, low breath. 'Look, I'm not asking for something from you that you're not willing to give. I promise.'

And he knew he'd driven her to that confession. Knew she thought he'd had cold feet and, hell, he *had*. Except now he felt his heart twist and turn inside him and he wanted her all over again, in his bed, in his life.

'Come here,' he murmured, and kissed her, slow and deep. She kissed him back, her hands fisting in his hair, her body pressed hard against his.

Somehow they made it to the bed, stumbling and tripping, shedding clothes. She pulled him down on top of her, hands sliding over skin, drawing him closer. 'I want to touch you,' she muttered against his throat, licking the salt from his skin. 'Last time I never got to touch you.'

And he wanted to be touched. He rolled over on his back, let out a shuddering sigh as he spread his arms wide, submitted to her desires. 'Touch me, Scary. Touch me all you want.'

She laughed and slowly ran her hand down his chest, across the smooth skin of his hip, and then wrapped her hand around his erection. 'All I want?'

'Hell, yes.'

She laughed again low in her throat, a seductress filled with power. He liked—no, he *loved*—seeing her this way, confident, strong, sensual. She kissed her way down his chest, lingering in certain places, blitzing quick caresses in others, and left his whole body on fire. His hands tangled in her hair as she moved lower.

'Millie...'

'You said all I want,' she reminded him huskily, and took him in her mouth.

Lord have mercy. He closed his eyes, all thought obliterating as she moved on him. All he could feel was Millie. All he could think was Millie.

Millie.

His hips jerked and he let out a cry; she moved so quickly he barely registered the change as she sank on top of him so he filled her up and she set the pace, her hands behind her, braced on his thighs. Chase didn't have much left in him. He grabbed hold of her hips and arched to meet her, his eyes closed, his head thrown back, everything in him a surrender.

A joy.

'Millie,' he said aloud, groaning her name. 'Millie.'

She came on top of him, her body tensing gloriously and then drooping over him as her hair brushed his cheek and she let out a long, well-satisfied sigh.

Chase let out another shuddering breath. This woman was going to kill him if she kept this up. He felt the thunder of his heart, and knew it was more of a danger than he ever really wanted to admit.

But it would be a wonderful way to die.

CHAPTER NINE

MILLIE gazed out at the ocean, little more than a *shooshing* of waves in the darkness. A tiny sliver of moonlight glinted off the dark waters. The air felt cool now, chilling her overheated skin. Chase had fallen asleep after they'd made love—no, *had sex*—and she'd dozed for a bit before, restless, she'd prowled out here and come to sit on the hard, cool sand by the shore, her knees drawn up to her chest.

The problem, she thought, was for her it *had* been making love. Love, that dreaded word, that fearful concept. She was falling in love with him and had a terrible feeling it was too late to stop the descent. And descent is what it was, straight down to hell, to that underworld of fear and guilt where every day you wondered if this would be your last one of happiness.

Plenty of people, she reminded herself, had second chances. Plenty of people were bereaved and moved on with life, found someone else to risk it all for. Plenty of people, but not her. She just didn't think she was made that way, couldn't imagine breaking her heart all over again.

And what about Chase? Even if he was interested in taking their fling past this week, he'd surely want more than she could give. Marriage, maybe even children. The thought had a shudder of both longing and terror ripping through her.

All foolish fairy-tales, anyway, because Chase wasn't interested in any of that. He'd wanted the fun back, just like she had wanted, but no more. And she got that now. They'd play by his rules from now on, and they would be her rules too.

'I wondered where you'd gone.'

Millie stiffened at the sound of Chase's sleep-husked voice. He made her think of rumpled bed covers and salty skin. The way she'd abandoned herself to him just a few hours ago and how she'd gloried in it.

'I couldn't sleep.'

She heard the whisper of sand as he came closer. 'No?'

'No. I'm afraid I'm a bit of an insomniac. Comes with the job, unfortunately.'

'Have you checked the stock market today?' Chase asked, only half-teasing, but Millie stiffened in sudden realisation.

She hadn't. She hadn't checked the stock market in over forty-eight hours. Good Lord.

'Of course,' she answered breezily, but it was a beat too late.

'Liar,' Chase said softly, and came to sit beside her, clad only in boxers, his bare thigh inches from her own. She'd been intimate with him in so many ways, yet the feel of his leg next to hers still gave her the shivers.

'If I haven't checked, it's only because I can't get reception on your boat.'

'You're a terrible liar, you know that? You haven't checked because you haven't thought of it, and that scares you more than anything.'

Millie said nothing. She was falling in love with him, and even though her body still tingled from where it had been joined to his she knew it was the last thing he wanted.

'The stock market will live without me for a few days.'

'I suppose the more relevant question is, will you live without it?'

She angled her head so she was half-facing him, but she

couldn't make out his expression in the darkness. 'I'm here, aren't I?'

'Why did you leave my bed?'

'Oh, is this some caveman thing? Or is it just playboy pride?'

'Playboy pride?'

'You know, you've got to be the one who walks away first.' She tried to keep her voice light and teasing—banter, damn it—but she knew she'd failed. Chase didn't answer, and when he finally spoke it was too soft, too sad.

'I'm not walking away, Millie.'

'Yet. You have four more days, remember, and I take contract violations very seriously.'

Chase didn't say anything and Millie felt herself start to go brittle. Keeping up her side of the bargain was exacting a high price. Why couldn't he play along? Wasn't that what he wanted?

'When did things start to go wrong with your husband?' *What?* Millie froze, stared straight ahead. 'Is that why you still feel guilty?'

She drew a strangled breath. 'Why are you asking me these things now?'

'Because I should have asked them before. When you wanted to tell me.'

'Should have,' she repeated, and Chase gave a little nod. 'I know.'

She shook her head, decisive now. Needing to be. 'Look, Chase, I fully admit I was kind of vulnerable after we—after we had sex.' It had been so much than just sex. So much more than what she'd thought she wanted. 'That was kind of the whole point of the exercise, wasn't it?' she added, still trying, desperately, to tease.

'Are you calling the best sex you've ever an *exercise*?'

The best sex she'd ever had. And she couldn't deny it,

because it was true. Even if it hadn't been just sex. 'You know what I mean.'

'I know I wanted you to lose control but then I didn't know what to do when you did. I'm sorry for that.'

'Yeah. Well.' She scooped up a handful of damp sand and let it trickle through her fingers. 'It doesn't really matter.'

'How can you say that?'

'Because it's true. That—that conversation was just a momentary weakness. I'm over it now.'

'I'm not.'

She felt the first prickle of annoyance. 'Why are you doing this? I thought you'd be relieved.'

'You were going to tell me something else, something more than what you'd already told me.'

'No, I wasn't.'

'The real reason you carry all this sadness around. The reason you can't let it go.'

She felt her heart freeze in her chest, so for a moment she couldn't breathe. Couldn't think. 'If I seem sad, it's because my husband and—because my husband died. I think that would be obvious.' She turned to glare at him, forced herself to keep that angry stare.

Chase looked levelly back, eyes slightly narrowed, thinking. Figuring her out. 'If you won't tell me,' he said quietly, 'then maybe I should guess.'

'*Guess*?'

'Just like I did with your apartment and job and whole lifestyle.'

'Don't.'

'I know I messed up, Millie, but I want to make it right now.'

'It's too late.' She hugged her knees to her chest, amazed that even in the Caribbean she felt cold. *Icy.* 'Why bother anyway, Chase? We only have a few more days together.'

He had no answer to that, and she didn't expect him to. He still only wanted a week.

Chase stared at Millie's taut profile and tried to order his thoughts. He had to get this right. For an instant he'd wondered if he should stop pushing her, but a deeper instinct told him she needed this. Regardless of what did or didn't happen between them, she needed this reckoning. This release.

The only trouble was, he had no idea what sorrow she was still hiding.

'So.' He let out a long, considering breath. 'You said you and your husband grew apart over different things.' No answer. He really didn't have a clue how to go about this. Mentally he reviewed the facts he knew about Millie Lang: she was a hedge-fund manager; she'd been married; her semi-estranged husband had died in a car accident two years ago. Those were the basics, but what else?

She bit her lip when she was anxious. She was obsessive about work. She'd mentioned someone named Charlotte...

Charlotte.

Her words just now came back to him, and gears clicked into place. *If I seem sad, it's because my husband and—because my husband died.*

Someone else had died in that accident. Someone, he suspected, named Charlotte.

'Was your husband having an affair?' he asked quietly and she stared at him in blatant surprise.

'Why on earth would you think that?'

'You said you grew apart.' He racked his brain. 'Over different things.'

'Not that far apart.'

'So what did you disagree on?'

'It doesn't matter.'

'That is so far from the truth, Millie, that it's almost funny.' He laid one hand on her wrist, felt the desperate flutter of her pulse under his fingers. 'It matters so much you made me promise not to talk about your past at all.'

'I *told* you about my past.'

'Not all of it.' Of that he was certain.

'Enough,' she whispered, and it was a confession. There was more. There was more she wasn't telling him and, while he might not need to know, she needed to tell. He knew that, knew it with the same instinctive certainty that he'd known how to make her come alive in his arms.

He decided to risk a shot in the dark. 'Why do you never talk about Charlotte?'

Her mouth gaped open silently; he would have found her expression funny in almost any other situation. Now he found it heartbreaking. She looked like he'd just punched her in the gut. Like he'd broken her heart.

'Don't,' she finally whispered, and there was so much pain in her voice he almost backed down. He almost took her in his arms and told her he wouldn't ask anything more if she'd just smile and tease him again.

'Charlotte died in the accident with your husband,' he said instead, and heard how raw his own voice sounded. This was hard for him too. 'Didn't she?'

Millie just gave a little shake of her head, her gaze unfocused, and Chase knew she was still asking him to stop. He wouldn't.

'Who was she, Millie? Someone important to you, obviously.' She said nothing, just set her jaw and stared out to sea. Chase's first thought was that Charlotte had been her husband's mistress. Someone Millie refused to talk about or acknowledge. But as he gazed at her set profile he realised that was totally off. He knew Millie better than that. Charlotte wasn't somebody she'd hated; she was somebody she'd *loved*. Millie didn't talk about emotion or affection, and certainly not love. And, if she was willing to talk about her husband's death but not Charlotte's, then this Charlotte had to be someone even more precious to her.

Then it came to him. And it was so obvious and awful that for a moment he couldn't speak. He pictured Millie only hours ago, naked above him, and remembered those two silvery lines that had wavered just under her navel. He was a guy, and he didn't know a lot about that kind of stuff, but he still knew what they were.

Stretch marks.

'Charlotte was your daughter, wasn't she?' he said quietly, and in answer Millie let out a soft cry and buried her face in her hands.

Chase felt his heart pound and his own throat tighten with emotion. 'She died in the accident with your husband.' Millie's shoulders shook and Chase felt his eyes sting. 'Oh, Millie. I'm sorry. I'm so sorry.' Then he pulled her into his arms, just the comfort of his embrace, because he didn't have any words. She didn't resist, just buried her face in the curve of his neck as her body shook with the force of her sobs.

He thought she'd cried before, when they'd made love. He thought he'd breached all of her defences then, but he knew now she'd clung to this last desperate barrier. Her sobs were torn from deep within her, the raw, guttural sounds of an animal in pain.

Chase stroked her back, her hair, murmured words he wasn't even aware he was saying. 'Sweetheart, it's OK to cry. Let yourself cry, Millie. Let yourself cry, my love.'

My love. Distantly the words penetrated the haze of his own feeling. He loved her. Of course he did. It didn't even surprise him. It felt too right for that.

Chase didn't know how long Millie cried, how long he sat there holding her in his arms, the night soft and dark all around them. Time ceased to matter.

Eventually, after minutes or hours, Millie pulled away from him and sniffed.

'Rob wanted me to get an abortion. That's when things started to go wrong.' Chase didn't speak, just gazed at her steadily, his hand folded over hers. He wasn't going through the motions this time. He was feeling it, all of it, and it *hurt*. Loving someone—feeling her pain—it hurt.

Millie let out a shuddering breath. 'We'd been dating since college, but we waited to get married. We wanted everything to be right—our careers established, to be able to buy our own apartment. We'd thought about kids, but decided not to try till later. Rob was a lawyer, and he was completely focused on his career, like I was on mine. We both liked it that way.' She stared at him almost fiercely, as if he had disagreed. 'We *did*.'

'I believe you,' he said quietly.

'Then I fell pregnant, several years before we planned on starting a family. I was thirty.' She fell silent, lost in memory, and Chase just stroked his fingers over hers, light little touches to remind her that he was here. He was listening. 'I was surprised,' she said slowly, 'but I was OK with it. It was a few years earlier than we'd planned, but...' She shrugged. 'I thought we'd adjust.'

'And your husband didn't?'

'Rob wanted to become partner before we had kids. It was really important to him, and I understood that. We'd had a plan, and he wanted to stick to it.' She glanced at him with wide, troubled eyes. 'Don't hate him.'

Don't hate him? Of course he hated him. He hated everything about the selfish bastard. Chase squeezed her hand. 'I think it's more important that you don't hate him.'

'I don't,' she said quickly. 'I never did. I felt...sad. And guilty, like it was my fault for changing the plan.'

'It takes two, you know.'

She gave a tiny, mirthless smile. 'I know. But it was creating a lot of stress in our marriage, and so... I agreed to have the abortion.'

Chase's fingers stilled on hers. This he hadn't expected. 'You did?'

She nodded, biting her lip hard as a single tear tracked its way down her cheek. 'I did. I'd convinced myself it was for the best. That our marriage was more important than—than a baby.' She glanced down at her lap, wiping away that one tear with her fingers. 'I couldn't go through it. I went to the appointment, and I sat in the waiting room, and when they called my name...I was literally sick.'

'You have a habit of doing that in tense situations.'

She let out a soft huff of shaky laughter. 'Emotional situations. When it comes to buying and selling stock I have nerves of steel.'

'I bet.'

'I went home and told Rob I couldn't do it. And he accepted that. He did.' She glanced up quickly. 'I'm not revising history, I promise. He wasn't a bad man. I loved him.'

Chase said nothing. He didn't trust himself to offer an opinion on Rob. 'And then she was born,' Millie said softly. 'And she was beautiful. I never thought I was particularly maternal, and in a lot of ways I wasn't. I never got the hang of breastfeeding, and I couldn't even fold up the stroller.' She gave a little shake of her head. 'That thing always defeated me.'

'There are more important things.'

'I know. And I loved her. I did.' She sounded like she was trying to convince him, and Chase had no idea why. He'd never doubt Millie's love for her child. She might hate talking about emotions, but she had them. She could love someone deeply—if she let herself. And if the person she loved let her.

'I went back to work when Charlotte was three weeks old,'

Millie said after a moment. She sounded subdued now, her voice flattening out. 'I had to. Hedge-fund managers don't get a lot of maternity leave. It's still a man's field. And I worked long hours—ten- and twelve-hour days. We had a nanny, Lucinda. She saw a hell of a lot more of Charlotte than I did.'

'That doesn't make you a bad mother.'

'No.' Millie was silent for a moment, her eyes reddened and puffy, her face set in its familiar determined lines. 'But if someone had told me that I would only have her for two years, if I had ever realised how short my time with her would be…' She paused, looking up at Chase with such bleakness that he fought not to cry himself. 'I would have quit my job in an instant. In a *heartbeat.*'

'No one ever knows that kind of thing,' he said quietly. His throat was so clogged his voice came out hoarse. 'No one can ever know how long they have.' He certainly didn't.

'I know. But I wish I had thought of it. I wish I had realised. I wish—' Her voice broke, and she forced herself to continue. 'I wish I had said goodbye when Rob took her out that day. They were going to a petting farm out on Long Island. And I had to go into the office—on a Saturday—and was in a tizz about some client's meltdown. So I pushed them both out the door and didn't look back once.'

'Oh, Millie.' He took her in his arms again, this time because he needed to touch her. He pressed his cheek against the warm silk of her hair and closed his eyes, then repeated his question. 'Why don't you ever talk about Charlotte?'

'I can't. Couldn't.' Her voice was muffled against his chest. 'My family understood, they waited for me to talk first, and I never did. People at work felt too awkward, so they said nothing. I went to all the counselling and support groups and just talked about Rob. I could talk about that, I could say all the right things. But Charlotte…' Her voice choked. 'God, I miss her so much.' And then she began to cry again, silent, shaking sobs. 'I want to move on, I want to be happy again, but I'm terrified,' she said through her tears. 'Terrified of forgetting her somehow, and terrified to lose someone again.' She dragged her arm across her eyes. 'I could never go through that heartache again.'

Chase felt as if her words were falling into the emptiness inside him, echoing through all that silence. *I could never.* 'Of course you couldn't,' he murmured, and as he continued to stroke her hair, her back, holding her so achingly close, he felt the hope that had been blooming inside him wither and die.

Millie stared at the sand, wiping her cheeks of the last of her tears. Her body felt weak and boneless with exhaustion. She'd never cried so much, not even when she'd first learned of her husband and daughter's deaths. Yet they had been good tears this time. Healing tears. Telling Chase about Charlotte had been like lancing a wound. Painful and necessary, and now afterwards, she felt a surprising and thankful relief.

She glanced up at him, felt a rush of love at his serious expression, his eyes shadowed with concern. She loved him. She loved him for making her laugh, but she loved him more for making her cry. He'd known she needed to. He knew her so well, had known her since he'd first crossed the beach to ask her why she wasn't painting.

'Thank you,' she said softly, and Chase gave a small smile and nodded. She reached over and laced her fingers with his. He squeezed her hand and that reassured her. She wasn't exactly sure what he was thinking, or if he was freaked out now, the way he had been when she'd first told him about Rob. She didn't know what the future could possibly hold.

After all this, did Chase still want to walk away in another few days? Did she?

Loving someone was painful, messy, hard. And wonderful. Life-sustaining. Now that she'd felt all that again, could she even think of living without it?

'Let's go back to bed,' Chase said, and tugged her gently to her feet. Millie followed him back into the hut, slid into bed and pulled the cool linen sheets over both their bodies.

For a single second they both lay there, not touching, and her heart felt suspended in her chest. Then Chase pulled her to him, tucking her body to curve around his, his arm around her waist, his fingers threaded with hers.

Millie felt all the tension, anxiety and sadness leave her body in a fast, flowing river, and all that was left was tiredness—and peace. She closed her eyes, her lips curving in a tiny smile of true contentment, and slept.

When she woke she was alone in bed, and sunlight filtered through the net curtains that blew in the ocean breeze. Millie rolled over in bed, blinked up at the grass roof as memories and emotions tumbled through her. Then she smiled.

She slipped on her discarded silk shift, because even though the cove they were in was private she didn't know how private. Then she stepped out of the hut onto the sun-warmed sand and went in search of Chase.

There weren't many places for him to go, unless he'd gone over to the main part of the resort to fetch them some breakfast. He wasn't on their little stretch of beach, or anywhere in sight. Deciding he must have gone for breakfast after all, she went to the separate enclosure that housed the bathroom facilities, including a sumptuous, sunken tub of blue-black granite. She'd just stepped into the little hut, a smile still on her face, when she stilled. Tried to process the sight in front of her.

Chase lay on the floor, his face the colour of chalk, unconscious.

CHAPTER TEN

MILLIE didn't know how long she stood there staring, her mind seeming to have frozen in shocked disbelief. Too long, but finally she moved forward, knelt down, and tried to feel his pulse with fingers too numb to feel anything.

Finally she was able to detect his pulse, but she had no idea if it was normal. It seemed thin and thready, but maybe all pulses did.

'Chase.' She touched his face; his skin felt clammy. Her stomach cramped. '*Chase*.'

Nothing.

What had happened? What was *wrong* with him?

Taking a shuddering breath, Millie rose from the cold stone floor of the hut and hurried back to their sleeping accommodation. She scrabbled through her handbag for her mobile phone, the phone she hadn't checked in days.

'Please...' she whispered, and breathed a silent prayer of relief when she saw the row of bars that indicated reception. Then she dialled 911. She realised she didn't even know if Anguilla had emergency services, or a 911 number, so when she heard someone answer she nearly wept.

The questions the operator fired at her made her brain freeze again.

'Where are you located?'

'A resort...' She scrambled to remember the name. 'Cap something.'

'Cap Juluca?'

'Yes.'

'Can you tell me what happened?'

'I don't know. I went into the bathroom and he was just lying there, unconscious. I—I can't wake him up.' Terror temporarily closed her throat as memories attacked her.

There's been an accident. Critical condition... Come immediately...

When she'd got to the hospital, it had been too late.

Now, as if from a great distance, she heard the woman on the other end of the line tell her an ambulance would be coming within ten minutes.

'Please go to the scene of the accident and wait.'

The scene of the accident. The words caused an instinctive, visceral response to rise up in her and she almost gagged. She could not believe this was happening again.

The stone was cold under her bare knees as she knelt by Chase, held his cold hand and waited for the ambulance to come. Once he stirred, eyelids fluttering, and hope rose like a wild thing inside her, beating with hard, desperate wings. Then he lapsed back into unconsciousness and she bit her lip so hard she tasted blood. In the distance she heard the mournful, urgent wail of the ambulance.

The next hour passed in a blur of shock and fear. Still unconscious, Chase was loaded into the ambulance. Millie went with him, tried to answer questions she had no idea about.

Does he have any medical conditions you know about?

Does he take any medications?

Does he have any allergies?

She couldn't answer a single one. She felt swamped with ignorance, drowning in it. She loved him, she loved him so much, yet in this moment she couldn't help him. She could do nothing…just as before.

At one point in that endless ride to the hospital Chase regained consciousness, his eyelids fluttering before he opened his eyes and focused blearily on her. Millie's heart leapt into her throat.

'*Chase…*'

He smiled and relief flooded through her. It was all going to be OK. Everything, him, *them*, was going to be all right. Then he glanced around and she saw comprehension come coldly to him. That joyous light winked out and he turned his head away from her. Millie put her hand over his; Chase moved his away. She swallowed, trying not to feel the sting of rejection. They were in an ambulance; everything was confused, nerve-wracking. It didn't mean anything.

She ended up sitting in the emergency waiting room, exhausted and chilled despite the sultry Caribbean air, waiting for someone to tell her something. Anything.

Finally a nurse came through the double door and clicked her way across the tile floor. 'Mr Bryant may see you now,' she said, and with murmured thanks Millie followed her back through those double doors and into a utilitarian hospital room. Chase was sitting up in the bed, his face pale but otherwise looking healthy. Looking like himself. Relief poured through her just at the sight of him, healthy, whole, safe.

'Chase.' She started forward, wanting to cling to him but hanging back because she still didn't know what had happened.

'Hello, Millie.'

'Did they find out what happened to you? I saw you on the bathroom floor and I was so scared—but you're all right?' She glanced at him as if checking for signs of— what? Chase wasn't saying anything. He wasn't even looking at her. 'Chase?' she asked uncertainly, her voice seeming to echo through the room, and finally he looked at her.

'I have leukaemia, Millie.'

'Wh-what?' The words felt like no more than a jumble of syllables, nonsensical. 'Did they just *tell* you that? Because surely they'd have to do all sorts of tests first?'

He shook his head, the movement one of impatience. 'I've known for eight months and...' He let out a weary breath. 'Nine days. I passed out this morning because I'm on a new medication that can cause dizziness. I had a dizzy spell and hit my head on the tub.'

Millie just blinked. Her mind was spinning in hopeless circles, still unable to make sense of what he'd said. 'You have leukaemia?' she finally asked, as if he hadn't just told her.

'Chronic myeloid leukaemia.'

She sank slowly into a chair, simply because her legs would no longer hold her. She stared at him, speechless, while he gazed back all too evenly. She could not tell what he was feeling, but she was pretty sure it wasn't good.

'I'm sorry,' she finally said, and he inclined his head in cool acknowledgement. 'Why...?' Her throat was so dry she had to wait a moment to swallow and be able to speak. 'Why didn't you tell me?'

'You can really ask me that?'

'You didn't want me to know?'

'Obviously.'

She recoiled a bit, hurt by the coolness in his tone. Why was he pushing her away *now*? 'I can understand that, Chase, but I thought— I thought after I'd—' She stopped, unwilling to articulate what she'd hoped and believed when he was gazing at her so evenly, so *unhelpfully*. 'Tell me more,' she finally whispered.

'More?'

'About the leukaemia.'

He shrugged. 'What do you want to know? It's leukae-mia, Millie. Bone cancer. I take a medication which keeps it under control but my symptoms had started getting worse, so my doctor switched to a different inhibitor. That's why I was on St Julian's—to see how the medication affected me before I returned to New York.'

'You should have told me,' she said quietly, knowing it was the wrong thing to say—or at least the wrong time to say it. Yet she couldn't help herself. She'd bared herself to him, body and soul, and he'd kept all his secrets and emo-tions tucked firmly away.

'There was no reason to tell you.'

'No *reason*? What kind of relationship can we have if—?'

'We don't have a relationship, Millie.'

Millie stared, her mouth still open, her heart starting to thud. She didn't like the way Chase was looking at her, with steely certainty. Gone was any remnant of the laughing, light-hearted man she'd come to love. 'Chase,' she said, her voice so low it reverberated in her chest. She felt the awful sting of tears.

'We've had our intense week.'

'Actually,' she managed, and now her throat ached with the effort of holding all that emotion back, 'we have three more days.'

'They're keeping me in hospital overnight, so we'll have to cut it short.'

'You're *reneging*?' she asked, trying desperately to man-age some levity, and for a second she thought she'd reached him, saw a lightening in his eyes and prayed silently for him to stop this. To see what they had and know that it was *good*.

'Consider our contract terminated,' he said flatly and looked away.

Millie stared at him and clenched her fists in helpless

anger. She couldn't fight this. And why should she? Chase was keeping to their original terms. She was the one who had changed, who now wanted more. So much more.

'How am I supposed to get back to St Julian's?'

He hesitated, and she knew he was debating whether to tell her to charter a boat by herself. Then with a shrug he said, 'I'll take you back tomorrow, if you want to stay at Cap Juluca another night.'

'All right. Thank you.' She'd take it, because she wasn't ready to walk away for good. She needed time to think, to figure out her next move.

'It won't change anything, Millie,' he said, the words a bleak warning, and she gazed at him coolly.

'Everything's already changed, Chase. But I think you know that.'

In a numb fog of swirling despair she took a taxi back to the resort and arranged to stay another night. She paused on the threshold of the grass hut where they'd spent last night as lovers. Her heart wrung like a rag at the sight of that low, wide bed, the linen sheets now pulled tightly across, the scattered clothes now folded neatly on a wooden chest. She sank onto the bed, then sank her face into her hands. She felt so much sorrow, yet she couldn't cry. She had no more tears left; she'd given them all to Chase. They'd been tears for her pain, yet now she felt a grief for his.

Leukaemia.

He'd known for eight months. And he'd been keeping it to himself, of that Millie had no doubt. She wondered if even his brothers knew. She imagined Chase keeping up that light, laughing front even as he battled with his diagnosis. Had his lightness been his refuge, his way of coping? Or had it been his armour, the only way to keep prying people and their awful pity at bay?

She knew how it went. She understood how it felt to be defined by pain, and she even understood why Chase hadn't told her.

Yet it was different now. *They* were different, because she'd broken down her own barriers with Chase's help, and now she needed to help him break down his own.

How?

Millie left the hut for the smooth expanse of sand. From their private cove she couldn't see another building or person, just a few sailboats bobbing on the aquamarine waves. It was a gorgeous afternoon, a cloudless blue sky and a bright lemon sun. The sand sparkled under its rays. She wished Chase were here, wanted to see him with his feet planted in the sand and his face tilted up to that healing sun. She didn't like to picture him in a hospital room in a paper gown, living with the reality of his disease.

Even now she fought that reality. How could he be sick, when he looked so healthy? When he brimmed with vitality and life? Yet even as she asked herself these pointless questions another part of her mind remembered how he'd winced when she'd landed on him from the boat; how he'd squinted into the sunset with a grim focus. How he'd told her he wanted to seize life, suck the marrow from its bones.

Now she understood why. He didn't know how long he had to do it.

Part of her shrank in terror from that thought. Part of her wanted to run away, to forget. She didn't need the pain of losing someone again. She didn't know if she could survive it.

And yet. She had to fight for it, because life simply wasn't worth living without him. Without the love he'd given and shown her. The love she felt straight through to her soul.

Millie took a deep, cleansing breath. So she'd fight. And

that meant fighting Chase. Which meant she needed to throw down her armour…and find some weapons.

Chase stared at the doctor who had come in to give him the news. What news, he didn't yet know, but he knew enough not to expect anything good. Living with chronic leukaemia was a slow descent into disability. Into death.

'Your blood work has come back,' she said, closing the door behind her. Chase braced himself. He had his bloods done routinely and he knew what numbers he needed to stay in the chronic phase. If—when—he moved up to the accelerated phase, his days starting looking very numbered.

'And?' he asked tersely, because she was still scanning the lab report and not actually giving him information.

'They look fairly good.'

What did that mean? 'Fairly good' wasn't great. It wasn't fabulous or terrific or any of the other words he would have preferred. 'Fairly?' he repeated.

'Your platelet count is around two-hundred thousand. Which, as you probably know, is stable.'

Not that stable. It had been higher two weeks ago, when he'd first switched to the new inhibitor. It was clearly dropping, and that was not good at all.

'When you return to New York you should get your blood work done again,' the doctor said, and Chase just kept himself from saying, *Well, duh*. 'And reassess the effectiveness of your prescription.'

Again, obvious. Chase leaned his head against the pillow and felt the dread he'd banished for nearly a week creep back. The dread he hadn't felt since he'd met Millie, and fallen in love with her prickly self.

He quickly banished the thought, steeled himself to live without the exact thing that had been bringing him joy. *Millie.* There was no way, absolutely no way at all, he could burden her with this. *I could never go through that heart-ache again.* She'd spoken in a moment of raw grief and re-membrance, but Chase knew she'd meant it with every fibre of her being. She might think she felt differently right now, but he knew she didn't really want this. Him. If she shackled herself to him, there was every chance she would go through that same heartache—and who even knew how soon.

He spent a restless night in the hospital; he'd always hated the sterile rooms, the antiseptic smell, the sense of sorrow that permeated the very air like some invisible, noxious gas. His thoughts kept him awake too, for his irritating brain—or maybe it was his even more contrary heart—kept remem-bering and reliving every second he'd spent with Millie over the last four days.

Four days. He'd known her for four damned days. There was no way he should be as cut up about losing her as he was. He barely knew her. A week ago—one single week— he hadn't even known she'd existed.

And yet, a life without her seemed like a sepia-toned pho-tograph, leached of colour and even life. He couldn't imagine it, even as he grimly acknowledged that that was just what he'd be doing this time tomorrow.

Morning came, storm clouds a violet smudge on the hori-zon. A storm was going to kick up, the nurse told him, which meant rough sailing from here to St Julian's. He debated calling it off, telling Millie he couldn't sail in this weather, but he wasn't about to back down now. Besides, if he knew Millie—which he knew he did—she wasn't going to give up without a fight. He'd seen how shocked she'd looked when he'd ended it yesterday, had known she'd been think-ing they'd have something after this week. And how could she not, after all they'd shared? She'd cried in his arms. He'd held her heart. And now he was breaking it, which made him a stupid, heartless jerk because he should have known from the first that this was a likely outcome.

He'd known he was a lousy deal, and yet he'd convinced himself that one week would work. Would be enough for a woman like Millie—or a man like him. And they could both walk away with their heart and souls intact.

Ha.

As he left the hospital, the sky still cloudless blue despite the gathering storm clouds on the horizon, Chase had a sudden, fierce hope that he could turn this around. The statistics for the long-term survival rate of CML were good. *Excellent*, his doctor had assured him as she'd handed him rafts of literature. Chase had hated even the titles: *Coping with CML; Accepting Your Diagnosis*. Talk about a buzz-kill. It had all felt incredibly negative, while putting a desperately positive spin on something that just sucked. Basically, what happened with CML or any disease? You degenerated and then you died. End of story.

And so this was the end of his and Millie's story, brief chapter that it had been.

I could never go through that heartache again.

Well, Chase thought, she wouldn't. He'd make sure of it.

He kept up all of his steely resolve until he actually saw Millie. She was waiting for him in the grass hut where they'd made love and just seeing her there reminded him of how she'd lain on top of him, how she'd taken him into herself. How he'd felt so good. So loved.

Now she sat on the edge of the bed, her face pale and set, her silk shift-dress hopelessly wrinkled which, considering the usual state of her clothes, had to be driving her crazy.

Except she didn't seem aware of it at all.

She stared at him with eyes the colour of her dress, brown, warm and soft, just like she was. How had he ever thought she was hard or severe? Scary, he'd called her, and it had

turned into an endearment, but it just seemed silly now. She
was softness, warmth and light. She was love.

'You've been biting your lip again.'

She touched the deep red marks in the lush softness of
her mouth. 'Old habits die hard, I guess.'

Chase thought about making some quip back, but then
decided he didn't want to do the banter. It wasn't going anywhere; they weren't. Except back to St Julian's, and on to
New York. The rest of their lives apart.

'You ready to go?'

'Fortunately I didn't bring much.'

He didn't say anything, just took one look at the handbag
she'd left at her feet. It was one of those bulky hold-all types
and he reached for it. She flung out one fluttering hand.

'I can get it.'

Chase stiffened. 'I can manage a single bag, Millie.
Despite how you saw me earlier, I'm perfectly—' Healthy?
No. 'Fine.' For the moment.

'I know you are,' she said quietly. 'I wasn't saying that,
Chase.'

'Let's go.'

She stared at him for a second, her eyes still so dark and
soft, and just one look had Chase's steely resolve start to
rust and crumble. He wanted to take her in his arms. No, he
wanted her to take *him* in her arms. He wanted to cry in her
arms like she had in his.

The thought appalled him.

'Coming?' he demanded tersely, and with a single nod
she rose from the bed.

They didn't speak as they walked through the lush gardens of the resort, or in the cab the concierge called for
them that took them back to where his boat was moored in
Meads Bay. No words even as he helped her into the boat
and set sail.

No, Millie waited until they were out on open water running towards St Julian's to begin her attack. And that was what it felt like, the same as when she'd begun her battle to sleep with him. Now she battled to stay.

'Did they do blood work in the hospital?'

'Some.'

'What were the results?'

Chase shaded his eyes against the sun, gazed at the thickening clouds boiling on the horizon, spreading out. Damn. The storm was moving faster than he'd anticipated. He was a confident sailor, but after a sleepless night spent in hospital, not to mention his reaction to his new meds, he wasn't thrilled about riding out a storm. Especially not with Millie.

'Chase?' she prompted softly and he sighed.

'I don't really want to talk about this, Millie.'

'Why not?'

'Because there's no point. We had our week and now we're finished.' He took a breath, made himself be harsh. 'You don't have any part of my life any more.'

'I'm not sure I had any part of your life.'

He didn't say anything, didn't even shrug. She was probably right, even if it hadn't felt that way to him. It felt like she'd had a huge part of his life, a huge part of his *self,* but he wasn't about to hand her that ammunition.

'Chase, I think you care for me.'

Again no response. Silence was easier. He kept staring out at the horizon, until he felt a hard shove in his shoulder. He turned, astonished, to see Millie glaring at him.

'*Don't* give me the silent treatment. That is so cowardly.'

He felt a bolt of sudden rage. 'Are you calling me a coward?'

'If the shoe fits.'

He opened his mouth to issue some scathing retort, but

none came. She was right. He *was* being a coward. 'I'm sorry,' he finally said. 'You're right.'

'Wait, you're actually agreeing with me?'

He sighed, not wanting to joke with her even as he craved it. Craved her. 'Millie…'

'Don't do this, Chase. Don't throw away what we have.'

'We don't have anything.'

'Now you're a coward *and* a liar.'

'Call me what you want.'

'Look me in the eye and tell me you don't care for me,' Millie ordered.

Obliging her would be the easiest way out of this. 'Millie, I don't care for you.'

'In the eye, I said.'

He'd been staring at her chin. Reluctantly he raised his gaze to those dark, soft eyes—and felt himself sink into their warmth. Damn it. He couldn't say it. He knew he couldn't. He swallowed. Stared. Said nothing.

Millie smiled. 'See? You do.'

Fine, he'd be honest. 'You're right, I do. It was an intense few days, and naturally that created feelings in both of us.'

'So now you're trying the "it's not real" route.'

'How can we know it's real?' Chase argued. 'We've been on an island paradise, Millie. We haven't seen each other in action, in our homes and jobs and lives. How do we even know this will stand the test of a stressful week, much less time?'

She bit her lip. 'Well, there's only one way to find that out.'

He'd walked right into that one. 'I don't want to.'

'What are you afraid of?'

Dying. Dying alone. 'Millie, you said yourself you didn't want to go through that heartache again. You couldn't.'

Her eyes widened, lips parting. 'Is that what this is about? You're protecting me?'

'I have a terminal disease, Millie. Death is, at some point, a certainty.'

'Guess what, Chase? I have a terminal disease too. It's called life, and death is also a certainty for me.'

He almost smiled at that one, but he shook his head instead. 'Don't be flippant. I'm serious.'

'So am I.' She took a breath, launched into her second line of attack. 'I did the research.'

'What, on your phone?'

'As a matter of fact, yes. The long-term survival rate for CML patients is eighty-seven percent.'

He'd read the same statistic, probably on the same encyclopaedia website. 'For those who have it detected early enough.'

'Did you?'

'Maybe.' The doctor had given him a good prognosis, but then his platelets had fallen and the first inhibitor had stopped working. He could be staring at an accelerated phase within the year, or even sooner. He could be in that other thirteen percent.

'And after five years of living with CML,' Millie continued steadily, 'the rate rises to ninety-three percent, which is the same kind of life expectancy as a person without CML. Stuff happens, Chase. Accidents, diseases, life. There are no guarantees.' Her voice wavered slightly. 'Trust me, I know that.'

'I know you do. Which is why I don't want you to go through it again.' He decided he needed to be brutal, even if it hurt both of them. 'Millie, if we were married, if we'd known each other and been in love with each other for years, then yes, I'd expect you there by my side. I'd want you there. But we've known each other five days. Five *days*. And, yes, they were intense—and I'll admit it, they were some of the best days of my life. But that's all they were. Days. And with that little history you don't shackle yourself to someone who is a losing proposition.'

She blinked. Bit her lip. 'Shouldn't I be the one to decide that?'

He sighed wearily. She was the strongest, most stubborn woman he'd ever met, and even though he admired her tenacity he couldn't cope with it any more. 'We can't talk about this any more.'

'We *can't*?'

'No.' Grimly he pointed to the sky. It had been a sweet, clear blue half an hour ago, but now those violet clouds had boiled right up over the boat. The brisk breeze that had them on a good run back to St Julian's was picking up into a dangerous wind. 'A storm's coming,' he said. 'We need to secure the boat and you need to get below.'

CHAPTER ELEVEN

MILLIE stared at the thunderous clouds overhead and felt her stomach freefall. This didn't look good. The intensity of their conversation evaporated in light of a far more intense reality.

'What do you want me to do?' she asked, and Chase didn't even look at her as he responded.

'Get down below.'

'But you'll need help up here.'

'Millie, you aren't an experienced sailor. Having you up here is more of a liability than a help.' He glanced at her and she saw real fear in his eyes. 'Get down below.'

Millie hesitated. 'I don't want you to be up here alone.'

'I assure you,' he said coldly, 'I am perfectly competent.'

'You know, always assuming I am making some reference to CML is really annoying,' she flashed back. 'I wouldn't want anyone up here alone, Chase. It's dangerous. And I can be very good at obeying instructions.'

His mouth *almost* quirked. Or so Millie hoped. 'You could have fooled me.'

'Tell me what to do.'

'I'm sure that's the last time I'll hear *that* phrase from your lips. All right, fine.' He let out a long breath. 'We need to secure the boat.'

'Batten down the hatches?'

'Exactly.'

'Um…what does that mean, exactly?'

Chase rolled his eyes. Millie smiled. Even though a storm was coming, even though they were at an emotional impasse, she still loved being with him. Loved how he could always make her smile.

'You can close all the portholes and stow any loose items in a safe place—there's a chest at the end of the bed. I'll pump the bilge dry.'

Millie had no idea what *that* meant, but she hurried to obey Chase's instructions. The first raindrops splattered against the porthole in the galley as she closed it. She threw a bunch of books and clothes in the fixed chest Chase had mentioned, and then went back on deck. The wind had picked up and Millie felt its bite. She thought vaguely of all the news reports of deadly tropical storms and hurricanes she'd read or listened to over the years and suppressed a shiver of apprehension. Judging by Chase's expression, they were in for a wild ride.

'What now?' Millie asked, raising her voice so Chase could hear her over the wind.

'You keep the bilge dry and I'll keep us steady so we take the waves on the bow. I've located our position and we're about twenty minutes off St Julian's. I don't want to get any closer until the winds die down. The last thing we want is to founder on the rocks.'

'Right.'

Chase showed her how to pump the bilge, and as the wind picked up and the waves began to crash over the bow they worked in silent and tandem focus. Millie was too intent on her job to feel the fear that lurked on the fringes of her mind. She was soaked and cold, the silk dress plastered to her body. Several times the boat rocked and she fell over, jarring hard. She looked back at Chase and saw him at the tiller, soaking wet and steady. Strong. Even in the midst of this fierce storm her heart swelled with love.

Millie didn't know how long they remained there, keeping the boat afloat and steady as the winds howled and the waves broke over the bow. At some point Millie realised she was needing to pump less and the boat wasn't rocking so much. The storm, she realised, had passed over them.

As the sea around them began to calm, Chase turned around to give Millie a tired smile. He looked haggard, the strong angles of his face and body almost gaunt with tension.

'We did it,' he said and Millie smiled.

'So we did.'

'Thank you.'

She nodded, her throat tightening. Now they were back to the argument that had seen them locked in battle, but at least she would fire the next shot. 'We seemed to weather that storm pretty well.'

Chase narrowed his eyes. 'I'd say so,' he agreed neutrally.

Millie took a breath. 'And if we can manage to do that, then—'

'We can weather the storms of life?' He rolled his eyes. 'Scary, are you really going to go there?'

She took a step towards him. 'I'll do whatever it takes, Chase.'

He gazed at her with a quiet kind of sorrow for a moment. 'I know you will. That's what worries me.' He sighed and stared out at the now-placid sea. 'Come below. We should change into dry clothes.'

Millie followed him below deck and changed into a spare tee-shirt and shorts of his while he did the same. Dry and tense with anticipation, she watched as he sat down on the edge of the bed and patted the empty space next to him. Not exactly the move of a seducer.

On jelly-like legs, Millie walked over and sat next to him.

Chase took her hand in his. Millie tried not to gulp. He was going to make her cry again, she thought numbly, and this time it wouldn't heal. It would hurt.

'Millie.'

'Don't give me the let-me-down-gently speech, Chase. We're both too tough for that.'

He gave her a small smile instead. 'You're right. You're strong, Millie, and incredibly stubborn.'

'Don't forget scary.'

'And severe. A lot of S-words there.' He sighed, sliding his fingers along hers, as if even now he just enjoyed the feel of her. 'You're tough enough to take the truth.'

She bristled, readied for battle. 'And which truth is that, Chase?'

'The truth that since my diagnosis my platelets have been falling. I'm still in the chronic phase of CML, but if you did your internet search then you know that once you hit the accelerated phase it's not good. In fact, it's really bad.'

'There are no guarantees in life, Chase.'

'No, but it's a guarantee that, once I hit that phase, there's no turning back. It's simply a matter of time until I have a blast crisis, and from then on my days are numbered. And those days are hard. We're talking chemo, radiation, hospice, a long, drawn-out sigh towards the end. It's not pretty.'

She swallowed, visions of Chase growing weak and frail filling her head. 'I know that.'

'Here's some more honesty,' he said quietly. 'We had a very intense time. You especially, in telling me about Charlotte and your husband. You hadn't talked like that or cried like that since the accident, and it's bound to make you feel differently about me.'

'You think my feelings aren't real?'

'I'm saying there's no time to test if they're real. We go back to New York and start dating and in a week, a month, who knows, I'm in the hospital and all bets are off. That's not fair, Millie.'

'I should be able to decide.'

'Are you telling me you actually want that?' Chase demanded. He almost sounded angry now. 'You're prepared to be my damn *care-giver* when you barely know me? Waste what could be the best years of your life on someone who's running out of time? Not to mention to go through the whole grief thing again?'

She swallowed. Said nothing. Because, when he put it as bleakly and baldly as that, it did sound absurd. And awful. And for a heart-wrenching moment she wasn't certain of anything; she knew Chase saw it in her face, heard it in her silence.

'See,' he said quietly, and he sounded pained, as if her silence had hurt him. 'It's not going to work, Millie.'

And Millie, her heart turning over and over inside her, was afraid he was right. 'I want it to work,' she whispered, and he squeezed her fingers.

'Let's just remember what we had.'

She swallowed, her throat too tight for her to speak. And then with a sad smile he let go of her hand and went back on deck.

Three days later Chase was travelling first-class back to New York. He gazed down at the blueprint he'd been working on, the blueprint that had completely, completely absorbed him a week ago, but all he could see was Millie. Millie's soft, dark eyes and sudden smile. Millie leaning over as she lay on top of him and kissed him, that severe hair he now loved—just like he loved all of her—brushing his bare chest.

Forget about it, he told himself, and resolutely banished the image—just as he'd done three minutes earlier. Sighing, he shoved the blueprint away and raked a hand through his hair. Those last hours with Millie had been horribly awk-ward and yet so precious. After they'd sailed back to St Julian's, he'd moored the boat and walked her through the resort. Neither of them had spoken. They'd both known it was over, and now there was just the mechanics of depar-ture.

'I'll leave your clothes at the front desk,' Millie had said, for she'd still been wearing his tee-shirt and shorts.

'Forget about it.' His voice came out rough, rougher than he intended, because it hurt to speak. It hurt to think. It shouldn't have hurt so much, because it was what he wanted, yet it did. It hurt, absurdly, that she had so readily agreed.

She nodded slowly, then came to a stop in front of an out-door roofed corridor. 'My room's down here.'

'OK.' He nodded, unable to manage anything more. She blinked at him.

'Chase…'

He knew he'd break if she said anything more. He'd break and then they'd start on a desolate path he had no intention of taking either of them down. 'Goodbye, Millie,' he said, and without thinking—because he needed to touch her, to taste her once more—he drew her in his arms and kissed her hard on the mouth, sealing the memory of her inside him. Then he turned and walked away quickly, without looking back.

Now Chase reached for the blueprint once more. It was of a university library in New Hampshire, and he didn't have the entrance right. He wanted soaring space without being grandiose, and of course the building—as with all his build-ings—needed to be made of local and renewable materials. The colour of the oak he was using for the shelving reminded him of Millie's eyes.

Damn. He pushed the blueprint away once more. No point

in attempting to work. At least in sleep he wouldn't think of her.

He'd dream.

Several days later Chase sat in the office of his haematologist while she scanned the results of the battery of tests he'd undergone as soon as he'd returned to the city.

'The good news?' she said, looking up, and Chase nodded. 'Your levels are stable.'

'And the bad news?'

'They're a little lower than I would have liked, but there could be a lot of reasons for that.'

'Like the fact that the new medication isn't working?' Chase drawled, and his doctor, Rachel, gave him a wry smile.

'Chase, I know there is a tendency to expect the worst-case scenario in these situations, as a kind of self-protective measure.'

Spare him the psycho-babble. 'It's been my experience that the worst case is what often happens.' Like his mother getting breast cancer and dying within six weeks. Six *weeks*. Or his dad dying of a heart attack before they could reconcile, before Chase had even *considered* reconciling. He'd been so busy trying to show his dad how little he cared and he'd thought he had so much time. Time to prove himself. Time to say sorry for being such a screw-up.

And most of all like meeting Millie when it was too late, when his days were most likely numbered. Yeah, the worst case could happen. Most times it did.

'This is not the worst case,' Rachel said quietly. 'Trust me. This inhibitor isn't working as well as I'd like, it's true, but there's another one we can try. And, while your levels have dipped, they're not rocketing in the wrong direction.'

'But lowering levels is a sign of an accelerated phase,' Chase said, and it was not a question.

Rachel sighed. 'It can be, *if* you are exhibiting several other factors.'

'Such as?'

'There would be cytogenetic evolution with new abnormalities.'

'I don't even know what that means.'

'The point is, just because one medication isn't working doesn't mean you've become unresponsive to all therapies.'

'But it's not good.'

'I still maintain that we diagnosed CML at a very early stage, and the statistics are extremely positive for patients with your profile.'

'But, ultimately, I'm not a statistic.'

'No, you're not. But neither are you a worst-case scenario.'

Chase drummed his fingers on the arm rest of his chair. He hated not knowing. He hated feeling like a ticking time bomb about to explode.

'Live your life, Chase,' Rachel said quietly. 'Don't live it in fear of what might happen.'

'What will likely happen.'

'I'm not saying that.' She reached for her note pad. 'I'm writing you a prescription for a different inhibitor. We'll monitor your levels closely, once a week for the next month, and see how we go.'

'Great.' More doctor's appointments. More wondering. Rather belatedly Chase realised he was acting like a total ass. 'Sorry, Rachel. It hasn't been the greatest day.' Or week, since he'd walked off that plane and into his barren life.

Rachel smiled sympathetically. 'Work going OK?'

Chase fluttered his fingers in dismissal. 'Fine.'

'Personal relationships?'

He smiled thinly. 'What personal relationships?'

Rachel frowned. 'You need people to support you through this, Chase.'

That was exactly what he didn't need. He hadn't told anyone at work about his diagnosis. He hadn't even told his brothers, because he doubted they really wanted to know. The three of them hadn't exactly been there for each other since his parents had died.

No, he'd only told Millie.

'It's fine,' he assured his doctor, even though it felt like nothing in his life was fine. Everything, Chase thought moodily, sucked.

'I know a holiday can make you feel a little behind, Millie, but this is ridiculous.'

Millie glanced up from her computer monitor where she'd been scanning the closing prices of the Hong Kong Stock Exchange. She'd invested one of her client's assets in some new technology coming out of Asia, and it was looking good so far. Very good. So why wasn't she happier?

'You like me to work, Jack,' she said, glancing back at the screen.

Jack sighed. 'Not sixteen-hour days. I pride myself on a tough work ethic, but yours borders on obsessive. It's not good for you, Millie. You'll burn out. I've seen it happen. It's not pretty.'

'I'm fine, and I'm happiest working.' *Lies.*

'How was the holiday, anyway?'

It had been two weeks since she'd returned from St Julian's. Two long, lonely weeks where every moment when her brain wasn't fully occupied with work she'd caught herself thinking of Chase. Dreaming of him, his touch, his smile.

It wasn't real. It was just five incredible days, that's all.

She'd told herself that a hundred times already, and she still didn't believe it.

'Millie?'

Belatedly she realised she hadn't answered her boss. 'My holiday? Oh, you know...' She fluttered her fingers. *Amazing.* 'It was fine.'

'Everything's fine, huh?'

'Yep.'

'What did you do?'

'What do you ever do on a holiday?' *Dive for conch. Make love. Cry in someone's arms.* 'Sunbathe, swim...' She trailed off, her gaze determinedly still fixed on the screen.

'I always pegged you as more of an active holidayer. I figured you'd learn to scuba dive or parasail or something.'

'Nope.'

'Millie.' Jack put his hand on her desk, distracting her from her blind study of the screen. She glanced up and saw how paternally compassionate he looked. And Jack never looked paternal, or compassionate. He was too driven for that, just as she was.

Was trying to be.

'What is it, Jack?'

'You OK? I mean, really OK? I know with what happened... You know...the accident...' Besides a heartfelt 'I'm sorry' at Rob's and Charlotte's funerals, Jack hadn't talked about her bereavement. She'd been giving off clear don't-ask-me signals, and he'd obeyed them. Everyone had. Easier all round.

So why was he asking now?

She must really look like she was losing it.

'Thanks for asking, Jack,' Millie said quietly. 'But I'm... OK. I'll always carry that sadness with me, but it's not as bad as it once was. It gets better every day.' That much, at least, was true. Ever since she'd confessed and cried in Chase's arms, she'd felt lighter. Better. Grief never went away completely, but it was no longer the suffocating blanket that had smothered her for so long. She could breathe. She was free.

She didn't have Chase.

It wasn't real.

It *felt* real. Lying awake at night, remembering how he he'd touched her and made her smile, it felt all too heartbreakingly real.

'Well.' Jack cleared his throat. 'I'm glad you're OK. So stop the sixteen-hour days, OK?'

Millie just smiled and clicked her mouse to the next page of the report. She had no intention of stopping.

Stopping meant thinking, and thinking meant thinking of Chase. And there was no point in torturing herself any more than she had to.

A week later her sister Zoe phoned her during her supposed lunch hour—spent at her desk—and informed her she was coming by for dinner.

'I'm kind of busy, Zo.'

'Exactly. I thought you'd come back from this holiday a little more relaxed, Millie, but you're worse than ever.'

'Gee, thanks.'

'I'm serious. I'll be by at seven.'

Since it was Zoe, Millie agreed. Zoe had been the one person she'd felt she could be almost real with after the accident. Zoe knew there had been tension between her and Rob, although she didn't know the source. She'd understood Millie didn't want to talk about Charlotte, and she'd never pressed. She just came over and brought corn chips and fake cheese, made margaritas.

Zoe buzzed up promptly at seven; Millie had got in the door three minutes earlier. She was still in her power suit and spiked heels, and Zoe raised her eyebrows at the sight of her.

'Raar. I bet men find that get-up *so* sexy.'

'That is so not the point.'

Zoe dumped her bag of provisions on Millie's sleek and spotless granite worktop. 'I know, but men are such weaklings. I bet all your work colleagues have fantasies about you unbuttoning that silk blouse as you murmur stock prices.'

Millie let out an unwilling laugh. 'Zoe, you are outrageous.'

'I try. So.' Zoe took out a bag of tortilla chips and spread them on a pan. 'What happened in Hawaii?'

'I went to the Caribbean.'

'Right.' She reached in the bag for a tub of bright-orange cheese product. Yum. 'So what went down there, Mills? Because something did and I'll get it out of you eventually.'

'No, you won't.' Of that Millie was certain. She had far more self-control than her fun-loving sister did.

'Was it a man? Some hot island romance?'

Millie watched as Zoe squeezed the cheese all over the chips, and thought of Chase telling her how low-brow her snack of choice was. Even now the memory made her smile. 'Actually, it was.'

'What?' Zoe looked up, astonished, and squirted fake cheese across the kitchen right onto Millie's pristine white silk blouse.

'You are so paying for this dry-cleaning bill.'

'Done. And you are so telling me what happened.'

'There's not all that much to tell.' Millie dabbed ineffectually at the bright-orange stain. She was already regretting her impulse to confide in her sister. Talking about Chase hurt too much.

'Did you actually get it *on* with some *guy*?' Zoe asked, so incredulous that Millie had to smile.

'I did.'

'Was he hot?'

'Totally.'

'I am totally jealous.'

'You should be.'

'So it was a fling? A holiday romance?'

'Basically.' Millie tried for insouciant and failed miserably. She turned away under the pretext of running water onto a cloth to dab on her blouse, but really to hide the tears that had sprung unbidden in her eyes.

And of course she didn't fool Zoe.

'Oh, hon.' She put one hand on her shoulder. 'What happened?'

'It's complicated.'

'Knowing your history, I'd expect that.'

Millie sighed. 'Let me tell you, I am pretty tired of complicated. And I'm tired of sad.'

'I know you are,' Zoe murmured.

Millie swallowed, blinked and turned around. 'He had some issues.'

'Oh no, not a guy with issues. You're better off without him, trust me.'

Millie smiled wanly. Zoe was infamous for dating toerags who left her on some pathetic pretext of how being hurt by their ex-girlfriends, or their mothers, or their first-grade school teachers had made them commitment-phobic. 'Not like that.'

'Then how?'

'He…' She paused, not wanting to reveal Chase's condition. It wasn't her secret to share. 'It doesn't matter. The point is, he didn't want to continue it because he didn't want me to get hurt.'

'That is so lame.'

'He meant it, though,' Millie said quietly.

Zoe shoved the pan of cheese-covered tortilla chips in the oven. 'Oh, really? Because when a guy says something about how he doesn't want you to get hurt, what he really means is *he* doesn't want to get hurt.'

'No—' Millie stopped suddenly and Zoe planted her hands on her hips.

'Am I right, or am I right?'

Could it be possible? Chase had seemed so sincere, so sorrowfully heartfelt when he'd held her hand and told her the truth. Mentioned words like *care-giver* and *hospice* and *blast crisis*. And she'd believed him, because she wasn't stupid; a future with Chase was scary. And uncertain. And yet even now, weeks later, it still felt like her only hope.

What if he'd sent her away because *he* was afraid? Because he wanted to send her away before she walked away on her own? Because he thought she wouldn't handle it, wouldn't *want* to handle it?

'You might be right, Zo,' she said slowly. 'I just never thought of that.'

Zoe peered in the oven to check on their chips. 'For a financial genius,' she remarked, 'you can be kind of stupid about some things.'

Millie had to agree.

CHAPTER TWELVE

MILLIE straightened the tight-fitting black cocktail dress and threw her shoulders back. Show time.

It had taken nearly two months to track down Chase. She could have found him sooner; she'd found his office address on the internet and she could have shown up there any day of the week. But she wasn't about to blunder into battle; she needed to do this right. And it had taken her that long to figure out just how that could happen.

Now she stood on the threshold of the lobby of one of Manhattan's boutique museums, this one dedicated to Swedish modern art. The result was spare, clean lines, a soaring ceiling and a lot of funky sculpture. And Chase, who had designed the museum's new conservatory on the top floor, was in attendance at this opening night party.

Millie had been to plenty of parties in the city. Rob had liked to work the Manhattan social scene, often stating that he accomplished more in one evening at a party like this one than a week at the office. Millie had enjoyed the parties they'd attended for the most part, but she hadn't been to one in two years. And she'd never gone alone.

More importantly, she'd never gone to one with the sole intent of seducing the guest of honour.

She took a deep breath and scanned the crowd for Chase. Time to start putting her plan into action.

* * *

Chase gazed around at the milling guests in their tuxedos and cocktail dresses—all black, which was practically required at dos like these. Normally he liked working the charm, enjoying the hors d'oeuvres and the low-grade flirting, but he felt only weary of it tonight.

Hell, he'd been weary of it for the best part of three months since he'd left Millie—and his heart—on St Julian's.

That sounded like a song, he thought moodily. A bad one. He took a sip of champagne. By all accounts he should be happy. The new conservatory was a huge success in art and architectural circles and, even more importantly, the new inhibitor Rachel had prescribed him was actually working. For how long, of course, no one could say, but she was happy with his levels and he felt physically better than he had in months. He was even allowed to drink.

So why was he still so miserable?

'Hello, Chase.'

Chase turned slowly, disbelievingly, at the sound of that familiar voice. He blinked at the sight of Millie, *his* Millie, standing there so calm and cool, a flute of champagne held aloft.

'Aw, Scary, you changed your hair.'

Her lush mouth curved in the faintest of smiles. 'You didn't like it before.'

He took her in, *drank* her in, for despite her hair, which was now tousled and short, she looked so wonderfully the same. Same soft, dark eyes. Same lush mouth. Same straight, elegant figure clad in the kind of dress he'd expect her to wear—a black silk sheath with a straight neckline and cap sleeves, saved from severity by the way it highlighted every slender curve. His hands itched with the desire—the *need*—to touch her.

'How have you been, Chase?'

'Fine. Good. You?'

'The same, I'd say.' Her mouth quirked up at the corner, like she was teasing him. So he wasn't being the most sparkling conversationalist. All his energy was taken up with just looking at her. Memorising her. 'It's good to see you,' Millie said quietly and Chase nodded jerkily.

'You too.'

She raised one slender arm to gesture to the milling crowds, to the Manhattan skyline visible through the walls of glass. 'I like the space. Very open and modern.'

'Thanks.' He sounded like an idiot. A wooden idiot.

'I know you're the guest of honour here, but do you think you could be free for a drink at the end of the evening?' Vulnerability flashed in her eyes; he saw it, he felt it. 'For old times' sake.'

Chase knew it wasn't a good idea. What did he and Millie really have to say to each other? His new medication might be working, but he hadn't changed his mind about their future, or lack thereof. He was still a ticking time bomb.

And yet, one drink. Just to hear how she was. To be able to *look* at her. Nothing more. 'Sure.'

'Good.' Now he saw relief flash in her eyes, and he knew she still cared. Hell, so did he.

Maybe this was a bad idea.

'When will you be free?'

'I'm free now.' He'd already made his remarks, shaken the requisite number of hands. He was ready. *So* ready; maybe it would be better to just get this over with. Final closure.

Because that was what it really was, right?

'Well, let's go then.' And, turning around, Millie sashayed out of the conservatory. Chase followed.

They didn't speak in the lift on the way down, or out on the street when Millie raised one arm and had a cab coasting to the kerb within seconds. Chase didn't hear the address she gave as they climbed into the cab; he was too diverted by the sight of her long, stocking-clad legs. She was wear-ing *suspenders*, and he'd seen an inch of milky-white thigh as she slid across the seat.

His blood pressure was sky-rocketing. He could feel the hard thud of his heart, the adrenalin racing through his veins. He'd missed her. He'd missed her way too much. And he wanted her right now.

'Where are we going, out of interest?' His voice, thank-fully, hit the wry note of amusement he was going for.

'My apartment.'

Brakes screeched in his mind. 'What?'

She gave him a far too innocent smile. 'Why waste twenty bucks on two glasses of wine in a noisy, crowded bar? This is much more civilised.'

And much more dangerous. Was Millie *playing* him? He'd always thought her too blunt to be sneaky, but maybe not. What did she want out of this evening?

What did he?

They didn't say anything more until the cab came to a stop outside a luxury high-rise near the UN complex. Chase reached for his wallet but Millie had already swiped her card.

'My treat,' she murmured and, swallowing hard, he fol-lowed her out of the taxi and into the lobby of her building, all black marble and tinted mirrors.

She fluttered her fingers at the doorman and then ush-ered him into the lift. Tension was coiling in Chase's body, seeking release. Something was going on here, some kind of plan of Millie's, and he didn't know what it was.

He had a feeling he was going to find out pretty soon.

She didn't speak until she'd reached her apartment, un-locked the door and led him into just the kind of place he'd expected her to have. Very tasteful. Very boring.

'Before you ask, an interior decorator did the whole thing. I didn't have time to go antiquing.'

'Still pulling sixteen-hour days, Scary?'

'More or less.' She took a very nice bottle of red out of a wine rack in the ode to granite and stainless steel that served as her kitchen. 'This OK?'

'Fine, but let me, or I'm going to start to feel surplus to requirements.'

She handed him the bottle and a corkscrew. 'Trust me, Chase, you are not surplus to requirements.'

'What's going on, Millie? Besides a friendly drink?'

'I have a deal to offer.'

A deal. Of course. He wasn't even surprised and yet his blood still sang. The cork came out with a satisfying pop and he poured them both glasses. 'What kind of deal?'

'One night.'

His hand involuntarily jerked, and a blood-red drop of wine splashed onto the counter. Millie swiped it and then licked the wine off her thumb. Chase went hard. 'What do you mean, one night?' he asked in as mild a voice as he could manage. Millie didn't answer, just accepted the glass he handed her and took a sip. 'Cheers,' he said and tried not to drain his glass.

Millie drank and then lowered her glass, gazing at him straight-on. 'One night—my terms.'

Hell. 'Which are?'

'Need-to-know basis only, of course.'

Of course. 'Why are you suggesting this, Millie?'

'Because I can't get you out of my head. It's affecting my work, my life—what little there is of it. And I'm gambling that it's been the same for you.' He didn't answer, which was obviously answer enough. 'One night, Chase, that's all. To help us get each other out of our systems and move on.'

He almost asked if that was what she wanted now, but stopped himself. What was the point? It was what he wanted. It had to be.

'And if I don't agree?'

'Stay and enjoy a nice glass of wine with an old friend.'

And *that* sounded so appealing. 'And if I do agree?'

Her mouth curved. 'Need-to-know basis, remember?'

'Is this some kind of revenge?'

'Revenge?' She let out a low, husky laugh. When had Millie become such an accomplished seductress? So unbearably sensual? 'Definitely not. Consider it…returning the favour.'

He swallowed. Stared into his wine glass. Wondered why the hell he wasn't busting out as fast as he could. This was dangerous. Stupid. Insane.

And he wanted it. So badly. Just one night. One more time with Millie.

'All right, Scary. I agree.'

'Even without knowing what you're getting into?'

'I think I can handle it.'

'Funny,' she murmured. 'That's what I thought when I first met you. Boy, was I wrong.'

She set her wine glass back down on the work top and walked past him towards the living room. 'Where you going, Scary?'

She glanced over her shoulder. 'To the bedroom, of course.'

Adrenalin pumped through him. 'That's kind of quick.'

'The only part of the evening that will be.'

Good Lord. Chase closed his eyes. This was the stuff of fantasies, of his dreams, for the last three months. He followed her into the bedroom.

The shades were drawn against the night, the king-sized bed covered with a pale-blue duvet that matched the curtains and carpet. The room was as tastefully boring as the rest of the apartment, but with Millie standing in the middle of it—her hands planted on her hips; one long, lovely leg thrust out as her gaze roved over him—it felt like the most erotic chamber he'd ever entered.

He shut the door behind him and leaned against it. 'Well?'

'Take off your clothes.'

He heard the slightest tremble in her voice and knew she wasn't quite the confident seductress she'd first seemed to be. Somehow that made him glad.

'Will do,' he drawled, and tugged off his tie. Millie watched him, her gaze dark and hot as he undid the studs of his shirt and cummerbund and tossed both on the floor. He raised his eyebrows. 'Well?'

'The trousers too, hotshot.'

He slid out of his trousers and kicked them off; his boxers and socks followed. He was naked and fully aroused while Millie was still in her clothes, even her high heels.

She looked him up and down and then lifted her honest, open gaze to his. 'I missed you, Chase.'

Chase didn't say anything. She was investing this night with emotion, emotion he felt. This was so dangerous. And exciting. He couldn't have walked away even if he'd wanted to. She nodded towards the bed. 'Get on there.'

Smiling a little, he stretched out on the bed just as she once had, hands behind his head, the image of someone totally at ease. Tension still raced through him. He didn't know what Millie planned, but he knew it was something. He could tell by the set of her shoulders, that glint in her eyes, the sense of expectation that pulsed in the room.

What was she going to do to him?

In one fluid movements Millie unzipped her dress and stepped out of it.

'I see you've bought some sexy lingerie since we last saw each other,' Chase said, and had to clear his throat.

Millie smiled. She was wearing a black satin bra and matching thong, and those suspenders. Sheer black stockings encased her lovely legs. She put one foot on the bed and slowly, languorously, rolled the stocking down her calf. Chase watched, mesmerised. Then she did the same with the other leg and stood up, the stockings held in her hand, the black lace suspenders discarded.

'Is this some kind of striptease thing? Because I like it.'

'I'm so glad,' she purred, and then leaned over him. Chase was so distracted by the close-up of her high, firm breasts encased in black satin that he didn't realise what she was doing with those sheer stockings. And when he did realise, it was too late.

'You tied me up.' One hand to each bed post.

'That's right.'

Chase pulled one hand, tested the weight of the bind. She'd tied a good knot, but he could still break out pretty easily. He wasn't going to, though. He was too intrigued by what Millie intended to do.

She ran one fingertip down the length of his chest, across his hip, and then down his inner thigh. His reaction to that little touch was, in his rather exposed and vulnerable state, completely obvious.

She stood up, hands on her hips, and Chase arched his eyebrows. 'What now, Scary?'

'You'll see.' She reached behind her for something long and silky. 'Or, actually, you won't.'

She was blindfolding him. Chase remained passive as she tied the scarf around his eyes, still too curious to stop this little game. 'You didn't ask if this was OK with me, you know. You're not being very PC about this.'

'I didn't want to ask,' Millie replied. 'There's no getting out of this, Chase.'

For the first time actual unease prickled between his shoulder blades. He kept his tone light. 'What are you going to do to me, Millie?'

'Make you tell the truth.'

Chase stiffened. 'The truth?' he repeated neutrally, because suddenly this didn't seem like such a sexy little game anymore.

'Yes, the truth.' He could tell by the sound of her voice that she was walking around the bed, and he felt more exposed than ever. 'Because it's taken me this long to realise you weren't telling me the truth when you said how you didn't want me to go through all the heartache of losing someone again, blah, blah, blah. Yawn, yawn, yawn.'

He managed a smile. 'You are reducing my heartfelt sensitivity to something rather trite.'

'It wasn't trite,' Millie said, and he knew she'd come closer. 'It was a lie.'

And Chase couldn't think to respond for a moment because she'd straddled his hips, lowered herself onto his thighs. He could feel the damp heat of her and she brushed against him so he actually moaned.

'You're torturing me here, Millie.'

'That's the idea.'

She moved again, so her body brushed against his in the most agonisingly exquisite and intimate of sensations. Chase scrambled to think of something coherent.

'Why do you think I was lying?'

'Maybe,' Millie said thoughtfully, 'you didn't realise you were lying. You'd convinced yourself you didn't want to hurt me.'

She leaned forward so her breasts brushed his chest, trailed a few lingering kisses along his shoulder. Thinking anything sensible was nearly impossible.

'I didn't want to hurt you,' he managed, his voice strangled. 'I still don't.'

'No, Chase,' she said softly, and her breath fanned against

his bare skin. 'You didn't want to hurt yourself. You still don't.'

For the first time Chase considered freeing himself, ending this farce. What the hell was she talking about? Then he heard the tear of foil and felt her slowly roll a condom onto him. His breath came out in a shudder as she lowered herself onto him.

'Millie—'

'I didn't see it at first,' she said, setting a slow pace that had him arching instinctively upwards. 'How you needed to lose control as much as I did.'

Somehow he found the strength to speak. 'I think I'm seconds from losing control right now.'

'Not that kind of control.' He heard amusement in her voice and she slowed the pace, rocking her hips just a little. 'But I want to spin this out a bit longer, so bear with me.'

Chase cursed. Millie laughed softly. 'Now, now, Chase.'

'Do you know what you're doing to me?'

She rocked her hips again. 'I sort of think I do.'

'What do you want, Millie?'

'I told you—the truth.'

'I gave you the truth.'

'No. The truth, Chase, is that you aren't afraid of leaving me alone. You're afraid of *being* alone. You're afraid I wouldn't be able to hack it and I'd walk away, leave you to suffer by yourself. Break your heart.' As she spoke she'd started moving again, setting a faster and faster rhythm so her voice was soft and breathless and Chase couldn't speak at all.

He could only listen, which he knew was exactly what she wanted.

'Hurting you just like your mother hurt you by dying when you were only a boy. Like your father, by never forgiving you and disinheriting you. Like your brothers, by not caring enough even to ask what's going on in your life. You gave me all the pieces of the puzzle, Chase, but I was so wrapped up in my own pain that it took me too long to fit it all together.'

Feeling blazed through him. Too much feeling. He was on the brink of the most intense orgasm he'd thought he'd ever had even as his heart started to splinter. *Shatter*.

Because she was right.

'Millie!' he gasped, her name torn from him.

She leaned over him, freed his hands and took off his blindfold. Chase blinked back sudden tears as she cradled her face in his hands, her expression so tender and fierce and loving. 'I'm sorry for not getting it sooner. I'm sorry I waited so long.' She kissed him long and deep. 'I'm not going to leave you, Chase. I'm not going to leave you even if you're sick and scared and dying. We have something special, something amazing, and I'll fight for it for the rest of my life.'

Then she kissed him again, still moving on top of him, and with a shudder of joy he came, his arms around her, drawing her even closer to him.

He was never going to let her go.

Some time later, after more love-making and honest words, Millie lay in his arms as Chase stared up at the ceiling. His mind and body still buzzed with everything that had happened. 'You know,' he said, running his hand up and down her arm, 'that was so not the deal we made.'

'It was better,' she murmured, and snuggled closer.

And Chase had to agree. This deal was much better. In fact, it was perfect.

EPILOGUE

Four years later.

MILLIE gazed out at the tranquil aquamarine sea and gave a sigh of pure contentment. She could hear Chase in the kitchen of the villa, humming as he made dinner for the two of them.

They'd come to St Julian's to celebrate the fifth anniversary of his diagnosis, a red-letter day, because his doctor had declared him officially in remission. As of now, he had the same life expectancy as a person without CML, which was to say, who knew how long? Who knew how long anyone had?

There was just this moment. This happiness. And enjoying what they'd been given for as long as they'd been given it.

The last four years hadn't been without some fear and heartache. Right after their wedding, his symptoms had played up and his doctor had prescribed a drug that was still in clinical trials. Thankfully, it had seemed to work.

Chase had told his brothers about his condition, and several years ago they'd had a reckoning, a reunion. Millie would never forget the wonder and gratitude she'd seen in Chase's eyes when he'd embraced the brothers who had rallied around him even though he'd secretly feared they wouldn't.

'It's almost ready,' Chase called, and Millie smiled, her hand resting against her still-flat tummy.

She had something else to be happy about, something secret and precious and scary too. Something she hadn't yet told Chase about, because she hadn't even been sure how she felt about it. It had taken four years to get to this moment, this willingness to risk so much again.

She felt ready now; being with Chase had given her the strength, the courage, to try, even while knowing that there were no guarantees. Life was scary, uncertain and full of pain. But it was also full of hope—glorious, prevailing, strong.

'Sweetheart?' Chase called and, smiling, ready to tell her secret, Millic rose from the sand and went to her husband.

* * * * *

THE WEDDING
PLANNER'S BIG DAY

CARA COLTER

To all those readers who have made the last
30 years such an incredible journey.

CHAPTER ONE

"No."

A paper fluttered down on her temporary desk, slowly floating past Becky English's sunburned nose. She looked up, and tried not to let her reaction to what she saw—or rather, whom she saw—show on her face.

The rich and utterly sexy timbre of the voice should have prepared her, but it hadn't. The man was gorgeous. Bristling with bad humor, but gorgeous, nonetheless.

He stood at least six feet tall, and his casual dress, a dark green sports shirt and pressed sand-colored shorts, showed off a beautifully made male body. He had the rugged look of a man who spent a great deal of time out of doors. There was no sunburn on his perfectly shaped nose!

He had a deep chest, a flat stomach and the narrow hips of a gunslinger. His limbs, relaxed, were sleekly muscled and hinted at easy strength.

The stranger's face was mesmerizing. His hair, dark brown and curling, touched the collar of his shirt. His eyes were as blue as the Caribbean Sea that Becky could just glimpse out the open patio door over the incredible broadness of his shoulder.

Unlike that sea, his eyes did not look warm and inviting. In fact, there was that hint of a gunslinger, again, something cool and formidable in his uncompromising gaze. The look in his eyes did not detract, not in the least, from the fact that his features were astoundingly perfect.

"And no," he said.

Another piece of paper drifted down onto her desk, this one landing on the keyboard of her laptop.

"And to this one?" he said. "Especially no."

And then a final sheet glided down, hit the lip of the desk, forcing her to grab it before it slid to the floor.

Becky stared at him, rather than the paper in her hand. A bead of sweat trickled down from his temple and followed the line of his face, slowly, slowly, slowly down to the slope of a perfect jaw, where he swiped at it impatiently.

It was hot here on the small, privately owned Caribbean island of Sainte Simone. Becky resisted a temptation to swipe at her own sweaty brow with the back of her arm.

She found her voice. "Excuse me? And you are?"

He raised an arrogant eyebrow at her, which made her rush to answer for him.

"You must be one of Allie's Hollywood friends," Becky decided.

It seemed to her that only people in Allie's field of work, acting on the big screen, achieved the physical beauty and perfection of the man in front of her. Only they seemed to be able to carry off that rather unsettling I-own-the-earth confidence that mere mortals had no hope of achieving. Besides, it was more than evident how the camera would love the gorgeous planes of his face, the line of his nose, the fullness of his lips...

"Are you?" she asked.

This was exactly why she had needed a guest list, but no, Allie had been adamant about that. She was looking after the guest list herself, and she did not want a single soul—up to and including her event planner, apparently—knowing the names of all the famous people who would be attending her wedding.

The man before Becky actually snorted in disgust, which was no kind of answer. Snorted. How could that possibly sound sexy?

"Of course, you are very early," Becky told him, trying for a stern note. Why was her heart beating like that, as if she had just run a sprint? "The wedding isn't for two weeks."

It was probably exactly what she should be expecting. People with too much money and too much time on their hands were just going to start showing up on Sainte Simone whenever they pleased.

"I'm Drew Jordan."

She must have looked as blank as she felt.

"The head carpenter for this circus."

Drew. Jordan. Of course! How could she not have registered that? She was actually expecting him. He was the brother of Joe, the groom.

Well, he might be the head carpenter, but she was the ringmaster, and she was going to have to establish that fact, and fast.

"Please do not refer to Allie Ambrosia's wedding as a circus," the ringmaster said sternly. Becky was under strict orders word of the wedding was not to get out. She was not even sure that was possible, with two hundred guests, but if it did get out, she did not want it being referred to as a circus by the hired help. The paparazzi would pounce on that little morsel of insider information just a little too gleefully.

There was that utterly sexy snort again.

"It is," she continued, just as sternly, "going to be the event of the century."

She was quoting the bride-to-be, Hollywood's latest "it" girl, Allie Ambrosia. She tried not to show that she, Becky English, small-town nobody, was just a little intimidated that she had been chosen to pull off that event of the century.

She now remembered Allie warning her about this very man who stood in front of her.

Allie had said, *My future brother-in-law is going to head up construction. He's a bit of a stick-in-the-mud. He's a few years older than Joe, but he acts, like, seventy-five. I find him quite cranky. He's the bear-with-the-sore-bottom type. Which explains why* he *isn't married.*

So, this was the future brother-in-law, standing in front of Becky, looking nothing at all like a stick-in-the-mud, or like a seventy-five-year-old. The bear-with-the-sore-bottom part was debatable.

With all those facts in hand, why was the one that stood out the fact that Drew Jordan was not married? And why would Becky care about that, at all?

Becky had learned there was an unexpected perk of being a wedding planner. She had named her company, with a touch of whimsy and a whole lot of wistfulness, Happily-Ever-After. However, her career choice had quickly killed what shreds of her romantic illusions had remained after the bitter end to her long engagement. She would be the first to admit she'd had far too many fairy-tale fantasies way back when she had been very young and hopelessly naive.

Flustered—here was a man who made a woman want to believe, all over again, in happy endings—but certainly not wanting to show it, Becky picked up the last paper Drew Jordan had cast down in front of her, the *especially no* one.

It was her own handiwork that had been cast so dismissively in front of her. Her careful, if somewhat rudimentary, drawing had a big black X right through the whole thing.

"But this is the pavilion!" she said. "Where are we supposed to seat two hundred guests for dinner?"

"The location is fine."

Was she supposed to thank him for that? Somehow words, even sarcastic ones, were lost to her. She sputtered ineffectually.

"You can still have dinner at the same place, on the front lawn in front of this monstrosity. Just no pavilion."

"This monstrosity is a castle," Becky said firmly. Okay, she, too, had thought when she had first stepped off the private plane that had whisked her here that the medieval stone structure looked strangely out of place amidst the palms and tropical flowers. But over the past few days, it had been growing on her. The thick walls kept it deliciously cool inside and every room she had peeked in had the luxurious feel of a five-star hotel.

Besides, the monstrosity was big enough to host two hundred guests for the weeklong extravaganza that Allie wanted for her wedding, and monstrosities like that were very hard, indeed, to find.

With the exception of an on-site carpenter, the island getaway came completely staffed with people who were accustomed to hosting remarkable events. The owner was record mogul Bart Lung, and many a musical extravaganza had been held here. The very famous fund-raising documentary *We Are the Globe*, with its huge cast of musical royalty, had been completely filmed and recorded here.

But apparently all those people had eaten in the very expansive castle dining room, which Allie had said with a sniff would not do. She had her heart set on alfresco for her wedding feast.

"Are you saying you can't build me a pavilion?" Becky tried for an intimidating, you-can-be-replaced tone of voice.

"Not can't. Won't. You have two weeks to get ready for the circus, not two years."

He was not the least intimidated by her, and she suspected it was not just because he was the groom's brother. She suspected it would take a great deal to intimidate Drew Jordan. He had that don't-mess-with-me look about his eyes, a set to his admittedly sexy mouth that said he was far more accustomed to giving orders than to taking them.

She debated asking him, again, not to call it a circus, but that went right along with not being able to intimidate him. Becky could tell by the stubborn set of his jaw that she might as well save her breath. She decided levelheaded reason would win the day.

"It's a temporary structure," she explained, the epitome of calm, "and it's imperative. What if we get inclement weather that day?"

Drew tilted his head at her and studied her for long enough that it was disconcerting.

"What?" she demanded.

"I'm trying to figure out if you're part of her Cinderella group or not."

Becky lifted her chin. Okay, so she wasn't Hollywood gorgeous like Allie was, and today—sweaty, casual and sporting a sunburned nose—might not be her
best day ever, but why would it be debatable whether
she was part of Allie's Cinderella group or not?

She didn't even know what that was. Why did she
want to belong to it, or at least seem as if she could?

"What's a Cinderella group?" she asked.

"Total disconnect from reality," he said, nodding at
the plan in her hand. "You can't build a pavilion that
seats two hundred on an island where supplies have to
be barged in. Not in two weeks, probably not even in
two years."

"It's temporary," she protested. "It's creating an illusion, like a movie set."

"You're not one of her group," he decided firmly,
even though Becky had just clearly demonstrated her
expertise about movie sets.

"How do you know?"

"Imperative," he said. *"Inclement."* His lips twitched,
and she was aware it was her use of the language that
both amused him and told him she was not part of
Allie's regular set. Really? She should not be relieved
that it was vocabulary and not her looks that had set
her apart from Allie's gang.

"Anyway, *inclement* weather—"

Was he making fun of her?

"—is highly unlikely. I Googled it."

She glanced at her laptop screen, which was already
open on Google.

"This side of this island gets three days of rain per
year," he told her. "In the last forty-two years of record-

keeping, would you care to guess how often it has rained on the Big Day, June the third?"

The way he said *Big Day* was in no way preferable to *circus*.

Becky glared at him to make it look as if she was annoyed that he had beat her to the facts. She drew her computer to her, as if she had no intention of taking his word for it, as if she needed to check the details of the June third weather report herself.

Her fingers, acting entirely on their own volition, without any kind of approval from her mind, typed in D-r-e-w J-o-r-d-a-n.

CHAPTER TWO

DREW REGARDED BECKY ENGLISH thoughtfully. He had expected a high-powered and sophisticated West Coast event specialist. Instead, the woman before him, with her sunburned nose and pulled-back hair, barely looked as if she was legal age.

In fact, she looked like an athletic teenager getting ready to go to practice with the high school cheer squad. Since she so obviously was not the image of the professional woman he'd expected, his first impression had been that she must be a young Hollywood hanger-on, being rewarded for loyalty to Allie Ambrosia with a job she was probably not qualified to do.

But no, the woman in front of him had nothing of slick Hollywood about her. The vocabulary threw his initial assessment. The way she talked—with the earnestness of a student preparing for the Scripps National Spelling Bee—made him think that the bookworm geeky girl had been crossed with the high school cheerleader. Who would have expected that to be such an intriguing combination?

Becky's hair was a sandy shade of brown that looked virgin, as if it had never been touched by dye or blond highlights. It looked as if she had spent about thirty seconds on it this morning, scraping it back from her face and capturing it in an elastic band. It was a rather nondescript shade of brown, yet so glossy with good health, Drew felt a startling desire to touch it.

Her eyes were plain old brown, without a drop of makeup around them to make them appear larger, or wider, or darker, or greener. Her skin was pale, which would have been considered unfashionable in the land of endless summer that he came from. Even after only a few days in the tropics, most of which he suspected had been spent inside, the tip of her nose and her cheeks were glowing pink, and she was showing signs of freckling. There was a bit of a sunburn on her slender shoulders.

Her teeth were a touch crooked, one of the front ones ever so slightly overlapping the other one. It was oddly endearing. He couldn't help but notice, as men do, that she was as flat as a board.

Drew Jordan's developments were mostly in Los Angeles. People there—especially people who could afford to buy in his subdivisions—were about the furthest thing from *real* that he could think of.

The women he dealt with had the tiny noses and fat lips, the fake tans and the unwrinkled foreheads. They had every shade of blond hair and the astonishingly inflated breast lines. Their eyes were widened into a look of surgically induced perpetual surprise and their teeth were so white you needed sunglasses on to protect you from smiles.

Drew was not sure when he had become used to it all, but suddenly it seemed very evident to him why he had. There was something about all that fakeness that was *safe* to a dyed-in-the-wool bachelor such as himself.

The cheerleader bookworm girl behind the desk radiated something that was oddly threatening. In a world that seemed to celebrate phony everything, she seemed as if she was 100 percent real.

She was wearing a plain white tank top, and if he leaned forward just a little bit he could see cutoff shorts. Peeking out from under the desk was a pair of sneakers with startling pink laces in them.

"How did you get mixed up with Allie?" he asked. "You do not look the way I would expect a high-profile Hollywood event planner to look."

"How would you expect one to look?" she countered, insulted.

"Not, um, wholesome."

She frowned.

"Take it as a compliment," he suggested.

She looked uncertain about that, but marshaled herself.

"I've run a very successful event planning company for several years," she said with a proud toss of her head.

"In Los Angeles," he said with flat disbelief.

"Well, no, not exactly."

He waited.

She looked flustered, which he enjoyed way more than he should have. She glared at him. "My company serves Moose Run and the surrounding areas."

Was she kidding? It sounded like a name Hollywood would invent to conjure visions of a quaintly rural and charming America that hardly existed anymore. But, no, she had that cute and geeky earnestness about her.

Still, he had to ask. "Moose Run? Seriously?"

"Look it up on Google," she snapped.

"Where is it? The mountains of Appalachia?"

"I said look it up on Google."

But when he crossed his arms over his chest and raised an eyebrow at her, she caved.

"Michigan," she said tersely. "It's a farm community in Michigan. It has a population of about fourteen thousand. Of course, my company serves the surrounding areas, as well."

"Ah. Of course."

"Don't say *ah* like that!"

"Like what?" he said, genuinely baffled.

"Like *that explains everything.*"

"It does. It explains everything about you."

"It does not explain everything about me!" she said. "In fact, it says very little about me."

There were little pink spots appearing on her cheeks, above the sunburned spots.

"Okay," he said, and put up his hands in mock surrender. Really, he should have left it there. He should keep it all business, let her know what she could and couldn't do construction wise with severe time restraints, and that was it. His job done.

But Drew was enjoying flustering her, and the little pink spots on her cheeks.

"How old are you?" he asked.

She folded her arms over her own chest—battle stations—and squinted at him. "That is an inappropriate question. How old are you?" she snapped back.

"I'm thirty-one," he said easily. "I only asked because you look sixteen, but not even Allie would be ridiculous enough to hire a sixteen-year-old to put together this cir—event—would she?"

"I'm twenty-three and Allie is not ridiculous!"

"She isn't?"

His brother's future wife had managed to arrange her very busy schedule—she was shooting a movie in Spain—to grant Drew an audience, once, on a brief return to LA, shortly after Joe had phoned and told him with shy and breathless excitement he was getting married.

Drew had not been happy about the announcement. His brother was twenty-one. To date, Joe hadn't made many major decisions without consulting Drew, though Drew had been opposed to the movie-set building and Joe had gone ahead anyway.

And look where that had led. Because, in a hushed tone of complete reverence, Joe had told Drew *who* he was marrying.

Drew's unhappiness had deepened. He had shared it with Joe. His normally easygoing, amenable brother had yelled at him.

Quit trying to control me. Can't you just be happy for me?

And then Joe, who was usually happy-go-lucky and sunny in nature, had hung up on him. Their conversations since then had been brief and clipped.

Drew had agreed to meet Joe here and help with a few construction projects for the wedding, but he had a secret agenda. He needed to spend time with his brother. Face-to-face time. If he managed to talk some sense into him, all the better.

"I don't suppose Joe is here yet?" he asked Becky with elaborate casualness.

"No." She consulted a thick agenda book. "I have him arriving tomorrow morning, first thing. And Allie arriving the day of the wedding."

Perfect. If he could get Joe away from Allie's influence, his mission—to stop the wedding, or at least reschedule it until cooler heads prevailed—seemed to have a better chance of succeeding.

Drew liked to think he could read people—the woman in front of him being a case in point. But he had come away from his meeting with Allie Ambrosia feeling a disconcerting sense of not being able to read her at all.

Where's my brother? Drew had demanded.

Allie Ambrosia had blinked at him. *No need to make it sound like a kidnapping.*

Which, of course, was exactly what Drew had been feeling it was, and that Allie Ambrosia was solely responsible for the new Joe, who could hang up on his brother and then ignore all his attempts to get in touch with him.

"Allie Ambrosia is sensitive and brilliant and sweet."

Drew watched Becky with interest as the blaze of color deepened over her sunburn. She was going to rise to defend someone she perceived as the underdog, and that told him almost as much about her as the fact that she hailed from Moose Run, Michigan.

Drew was just not sure who would think of Allie Ambrosia as the underdog. He may have been frustrated about his inability to read his future sister-in-law, but neither *sensitive* nor *sweet* would have made his short list of descriptive adjectives. Though they probably would have for Becky, even after such a short acquaintance.

Allie? Brilliant, maybe. Though if she was it had not shown in her vocabulary. Still, he'd been aware of the possibility of great cunning. She had seemed to Drew to be able to play whatever role she wanted, the real person, whoever and whatever that was, hidden behind eyes so astonishingly emerald he'd wondered if she enhanced the color with contact lenses.

He'd come away from Allie frustrated. He had agreed to build some things for the damn wedding, hoping, he supposed, that this seeming capitulation to his brother's plans would open the door to communication between them and he could talk some sense into Joe.

He'd have his chance tomorrow. Today, he could unabashedly probe the secrets of the woman his brother had decided to marry.

"And you would know Allie is sensitive and brilliant and sweet, why?" he asked Becky, trying not to let on just how pleased he was to have found someone who actually seemed to know Allie.

"We went to school together."

Better still. Someone who knew Allie *before* she'd caught her big break playing Peggy in a sleeper of a movie called *Apple Mountain*.

"Allie Ambrosia grew up in Moose Run, Michigan?" He prodded her along. "That is not in the official biography."

He thought Becky was going to clam up, careful about saying anything about her boss and old school chum, but her need to defend won out.

"Her Moose Run memories may not be her fondest ones," Becky offered, a bit reluctantly.

"I must say Allie has come a long way from Moose Run," he said.

"How do you know? How well do you know Allie?"

"I admit I'm assuming, since I hardly know her at all," Drew said. "This is what I know. She's had a whirlwind relationship with my little brother, who is building a set on one of her movies. They've known each other weeks, not months. And suddenly they are getting married. It can't last, and this is an awful lot of money and time and trouble to go to for something that can't last."

"You're cynical," she said, as if that was a bad thing.

"We can't all come from Moose Run, Michigan."

She squinted at him, not rising to defend herself, but staying focused on him, which made him very uncomfortable. "You are really upset that they are getting married."

He wasn't sure he liked that amount of perception. He didn't say anything.

"Actually, I think you don't like weddings, period."

"What is this, a party trick? You can read my mind?" He intended it to sound funny, but he could hear a certain amount of defensiveness in his tone.

"So, it's true then."

"Big deal. Lots of men don't like weddings."

"Why is that?"

He frowned at her. He wanted to ferret out some facts about Allie, or talk about construction. He was comfortable talking about construction, even on an ill-conceived project like this. He was a problem solver. He was not comfortable discussing feelings, which an aversion to weddings came dangerously close to.

"They just don't like them," he said stubbornly. "Okay, I don't like them."

"I'm curious about who made you your brother's keeper," she said. "Shouldn't your parents be talking to him about this?"

"Our parents are dead."

When something softened in her face, he deliberately hardened himself against it.

"Oh," Becky said quietly, "I'm so sorry. So you, as older brother, are concerned, and at the same time have volunteered to help out. That's very sweet."

"Let's get something straight right now. There is nothing sweet about me."

"So why did you agree to help at all?"

He shrugged. "Brothers help each other."

Joe's really upset by your reaction to our wedding, Allie had told him. *If you agreed to head up the construction, he would see it was just an initial reaction of surprise and that of course you want what is best for your own brother.*

Oh, he wanted what was best for Joe, all right. Something must have flashed across Drew's face, because Becky's brow lowered.

"Are you going to try to stop the wedding?" she asked suspiciously.

Had he telegraphed his intention to Allie, as well? "Joe's all grown up, and capable of making up his own mind. But so am I. And it seems like a crazy, impulsive decision he's made."

"You didn't answer the question."

"You'd think he would have asked me what I thought," Drew offered grimly.

A certain measure of pain escaped in that statement, and so he frowned at Becky, daring her to give him sympathy.

Thankfully, she did not even try. "Is this why I can't have the pavilion? Are you trying to sabotage the whole thing?"

"No," he said curtly. "I'll do what I can to give my brother and his beloved a perfect day. If he comes to his senses before then——" He lifted a shoulder.

"If he changes his mind, that would be a great deal of time and money down the tubes," Becky said.

Drew lifted his shoulder again. "I'm sure you would still get paid."

"That's hardly the point!"

"It's the whole point of running a business." He glanced at her and sighed. "Please don't tell me you do it for love."

Love.

Except for what he felt for his brother, his world was comfortably devoid of that pesky emotion. He was sorry he'd even mentioned the word in front of Becky English.

CHAPTER THREE

"Since you brought it up," Becky said solemnly, "I got the impression from Allie that she and your brother are head over heels in love with one another."

"Humph." There was no question his brother was over the moon, way past the point where he could be counted on to make a rational decision. Allie was more difficult to interpret. Allie was an actress. She pretended for a living. It seemed to Drew his brother's odds of getting hurt were pretty good.

"Joe could have done worse," Becky said, quietly. "She's a beautiful, successful woman."

"Yeah, there's that."

"There's that cynicism again."

Cynical. Yes, that described Drew Jordan to an absolute T. And he liked being around people who were as hard-edged as him. Didn't he?

"Look, my brother is twenty-one years old. That's a little young to be making this kind of decision."

"You know, despite your barely contained scorn for Moose Run, Michigan, it's a traditional place where they love nothing more than a wedding. I've planned dozens of them."

Drew had to bite his tongue to keep from crushing her with a sarcastic *Dozens?*

"I've been around this for a while," she continued. "Take it from me. Age is no guarantee of whether a marriage is going to work out."

"He's known her about eight weeks, as far as I can tell!" He was confiding his doubts to a complete stranger, which was not like him. It was even more unlike him to be hoping this wet-behind-the-ears country girl from Moose Run, Michigan, might be able to shed some light on his brother's mysterious, flawed decision-making process. This was why he liked being around people as *not* sweet as himself. There was no probing of the secrets of life.

"That doesn't seem to reflect on how the marriage is going to work out, either."

"Well, what does then?"

"When I figure it out, I'm going to bottle it and sell it," she said. There was that earnestness again. "But I've planned the weddings of lots of young people who are still together. Young people have big dreams and lots of energy. You need that to buy your first house and have your first baby, and juggle three jobs and—"

"Baby?" Drew said, horrified. "Is she pregnant?" That would explain his brother's rush to the altar of love.

"I don't think so," Becky said.

"But you don't know for certain."

"It's none of my business. Or yours. But even if she is, lots of those kinds of marriages make it, too. I've planned weddings for people who have known each other for weeks, and weddings for people who have known each other for years. I planned one wedding for a couple who had lived together for sixteen years. They were getting a divorce six months later. But I've seen lots of marriages that work."

"And how long has your business been running?"

"Two years," she said.

For some reason, Drew was careful not to be quite as sarcastic as he wanted to be. "So, you've seen lots that work for two years. Two years is hardly a testament to a solid relationship."

"You can tell," she said stubbornly. "Some people are going to be in love forever."

Her tone sounded faintly wistful. Something uncomfortable shivered along his spine. He had a feeling he was looking at one of those forever kinds of girls. The kind who were not safe to be around at all.

Though it would take more than a sweet girl from Moose Run to penetrate the armor around his hard heart. He felt impatient with himself for the direction of his thoughts. Wasn't it proof that she was already penetrating something since they were having this discussion that had nothing to do with her unrealistic building plans?

Drew shook off the feeling and fixed Becky with a particularly hard look.

"Sheesh, maybe you are a member of the Cinderella club, after all."

"Despite the fact I run a company called Happily-Ever-After—"

He closed his eyes. "That's as bad as Moose Run."

"It is a great name for an event planning company."

"I think I'm getting a headache."

"But despite my company name, I have long since given up on fairy tales."

He opened his eyes and looked at her. "Uh-huh," he said, loading those two syllables with doubt.

"I have!"

"Lady, even before I heard the name of your company, I could tell that you have 'I'm waiting for my prince to come' written all over you."

"I do not."

"You've had a heartbreak."

"I haven't," she said. She was a terrible liar.

"Maybe it wasn't quite a heartbreak. A romantic disappointment."

"Now who is playing the mind reader?"

"Aha! I was right, then."

She glared at him.

"You'll get over it. And then you'll be in the prince market all over again."

"I won't."

"I'm not him, by the way."

"Not who?"

"Your prince."

"Of all the audacious, egotistical, ridiculous—"

"Just saying. I'm not anybody's prince."

"You know what? It is more than evident you could not be mistaken for Prince Charming even if you had a crown on your head and tights and golden slippers!"

Now that he'd established some boundaries, he felt he could tease her just a little. "Please tell me you don't like men who wear tights."

"What kind of man I like is none of your business!"

"Correct. It's just that we will be working in close proximity. My shirt has been known to come off. It has been known to make women swoon." He smiled.

He was enjoying this way more than he had a right

to, but it was having the desired effect, putting up a nice big wall between them, and he hadn't even had to barge in the construction material to do it.

"I'm not just *getting* a headache," she said. "I've had one since you marched through my door."

"Oh, great," he said. "There's nothing I like as much as a little competition. Let's see who can give who a bigger headache."

"The only way I could give you a bigger headache than the one you are giving me is if I smashed this lamp over your head."

Her hand actually came to rest on a rather heavy-looking brass lamp on the corner of her desk. It was evident to him that she would have loved to do just that if she wasn't such a prim-and-proper type.

"I'm bringing out the worst in you," he said with satisfaction. She looked at her hand, resting on the lamp, and looked so appalled with herself that Drew did the thing he least wanted to do. He laughed.

Becky snatched her hand back from the brass lamp, annoyed with herself, miffed that she was providing amusement for the very cocky Mr. Drew Jordan. She was not the type who smashed people over the head with lamps. Previously, she had not even been the type who would have ever thought about such a thing. She had dealt with some of the world's—or at least Michigan's—worst Bridezillas, and never once had she laid hand to lamp. It was one of the things she prided herself in. She kept her cool.

But Drew Jordan had that look of a man who could turn a girl inside out before she even knew what had hit her. He could make a woman who trusted her cool suddenly aware that fingers of heat were licking away inside her, begging for release. And it was disturbing that he knew it!

He was laughing at her. It was super annoying that instead of being properly indignant, steeling herself against attractions that he was as aware of as she was, she could not help but notice how cute he was when he laughed—that sternness stripped from his face, an almost boyish mischievousness lurking underneath.

She frowned at her computer screen, pretending she was getting down to business and that she had called up the weather to double-check his facts. Instead, she learned her head of construction was also the head of a multimillion-dollar Los Angeles development company.

The bride's future brother-in-law was not an out-of-work tradesman that Becky could threaten to fire. He ran a huge development company in California. No wonder he seemed to be impatient at being pressed into the service of his very famous soon-to-be sister-in-law.

No wonder he'd been professional enough to Google the weather. Becky wondered why she hadn't thought of doing that. It was nearly the first thing she did for every event.

It was probably because she was being snowed under by Allie's never-ending requests. Just now she was trying to find a way to honor Allie's casually thrown-out email, received that morning, which requested freshly planted lavender tulips—picture attached—to line the outdoor aisle she would walk down toward her husband-to-be.

Google, that knowledge reservoir of all things, told

Becky she could not have lavender tulips—or any kind of tulip for that matter—in the tropics in June.

What Google confirmed for her now was not the upcoming weather forecast or the impossibility of lavender tulips, but that Drew Jordan was used to million-dollar budgets.

Becky, on the other hand, had started shaking when she had opened the promised deposit check from Allie. Up until then, it had seemed to her that maybe she was being made the butt of a joke. But that check—made out to Happily-Ever-After—had been for more money than she had ever seen in her life.

With trembling fingers she had dialed the private cell number Allie had provided.

"Is this the budget?"

"No, silly, just the deposit."

"What exactly is your budget?" Becky had asked. Her voice had been shaking as badly as her fingers.

"Limitless," Allie had said casually. "And I fully intend to exceed it. You don't think I'm going to be outdone by Roland Strump's daughter, do you?"

"Allie, maybe you should hire whoever did the Strump wedding, I—"

"Nonsense. Have fun with it, for Pete's sake. Haven't you ever had fun? I hope you and Drew don't manage to bring down the mood of the whole wedding. Sourpusses."

Sourpuss? She was studious to be sure, but sour? Becky had put down the phone contemplating that. Had she ever had fun? Even at Happily-Ever-After, planning fun events for other people was very serious business, indeed.

Well, now she knew who Drew was. And Allie had

been right when it came to him. He could definitely be a sourpuss! It was more worrying that he planned to take off his shirt. She had to get back to business.

"Mr. Jordan—"

"Drew is fine. And what should I call you?"

Barnum. "Becky is fine. We can't just throw a bunch of tables out on the front lawn as if this were the church picnic."

"We're back to that headache." His lips twitched. "I'm afraid my experience with church picnics has been limited."

Yes, it was evident he was all devilish charm and dark seduction, while it was written all over her that that was what she came from: church picnics and 4-H clubs, a place where the Fourth of July fireworks were *the* event of the year.

She shifted her attention to the second *no.* "And we absolutely need some sort of dance floor. Have you ever tried to dance on grass? Or sand?"

"I'm afraid," Drew said, "that falls outside of the realm of my experience, too. And you?"

"Oh, you know," she said. "We like to dust up our heels after the church picnic."

He nodded, as if that was more than evident to him and he had missed her sarcasm completely.

She focused on his third veto. She looked at her clumsy drawing of a small gazebo on the beach. She had envisioned Allie and Joe saying their vows under it, while their guests sat in beautiful lightweight chairs looking at them and the sea beyond them.

"And what's your complaint with this one?"

"I'll forgive you this oversight because of where you are from."

"Oversight?"

"I wouldn't really expect a girl from Michigan to have foreseen this. The *wedding*—" he managed to fill that single word with a great deal of contempt "—according to my notes, is supposed to take place at 4:00 p.m. on June third."

"Correct."

"If you Google the tide chart for that day, you'll see that your gazebo would have water lapping up to the third stair. I'm not really given to omens, but I would probably see that as one."

She was feeling very tired of Google, except in the context of learning about him. It seemed to her he was the kind of man who brought out the weakness in a woman, even one who had been made as cynical as she had been. Because she felt she could ogle him all day long. And he knew it, she reminded herself.

"So," she said, a little more sharply than intended, "what do you suggest?"

"If we scratch the pavilion for two hundred—"

"I can get more people to help you."

He went on as if she hadn't spoken. "I can probably build you a rudimentary gazebo at a different location."

"What about the dance floor?"

"I'll think about it."

He said that as if he were the boss, not her. From what she had glimpsed about him on the internet he was very used to being in charge. And he obviously knew his stuff, and was good with details. He had spotted the weather and the tides, after all. Really, she should be grateful. What if her bride had marched down her tulip-lined aisle—or whatever the aisle ended up being lined with—to a wedding gazebo that was slowly being swallowed by water?

It bothered her to even think it, but Drew Jordan was right. That would have been a terrible omen.

Still, gratitude was not what Becky felt. Not at all.

"You are winning the headache contest by a country mile," she told him.

"I'm no kind of expert on the country," he said, without regret, "but I am competitive."

"What did Allie tell you? Are you in charge of construction?"

"Absolutely."

He said it too quickly and with that self-assured smile of a man way too used to having his own way, particularly with the opposite sex.

"I'm going to have to call Allie and see what that means," Becky said, steeling herself against that smile. "I'm happy to leave construction to you, but I think I should have the final word on what we are putting up and where."

"I'm okay with that. As long as it's reasonable."

"I'm sure we define that differently."

He flashed his teeth at her again. "I'm sure we do."

"Would it help you do your job if I brought more people on-site? Carpenters and such?"

"That's a great idea, but I don't work with strangers. Joe and I have worked together a lot. He'll be here tomorrow."

"That wouldn't be very romantic, him building the stuff for his own wedding."

"Or you could see it as him putting an investment and some effort into his own wedding."

She sighed. "You want him here so you can try to bully him out of getting married."

"I resent the implication I would bully him."

But Becky was stunned to see doubt flash across those self-confident features. "He isn't talking to you, is he?" Becky guessed softly.

She could tell Drew was not accustomed to this level of perception. He didn't like it one little bit.

"I have one of my teams arriving soon. And Joe. I'm here a day early to do some initial assessments. What I need is for you to pick the site for the exchange of vows so that I can put together a plan. We don't have as much time as you think."

Which was truly frightening, because she did not think they had any time at all. Becky looked at her desk: flowers to be ordered, ceremony details to be finalized, accommodations to be organized, boat schedules, food, not just for the wedding feast, but for the week to follow, and enough staff to pull off pampering two hundred people.

"And don't forget fireworks," she added.

"Excuse me?"

"Nothing," she muttered. She did not want to be thinking of fireworks around a man like Drew Jordan. Her eyes drifted to his lips. If she were ever to kiss someone like that, it would be the proverbial fireworks. And he knew it, too. That was why he was smiling evilly at her!

Suddenly, it felt like nothing in the world would be better than to get outside away from this desk—and from him—and see this beautiful island. So far, she had mostly experienced it by looking out her office window.

The sun would be going down soon. She could find a place to hold the wedding and watch the sun go down.

"Okay," she said. "I'll find a new site. I'll let you know as soon as I've got it."

"Let's do it together. That might save us some grief."

She was not sure that doing anything with him was going to save her some grief. She needed to get away from him…and the thoughts of fireworks he had caused.

CHAPTER FOUR

"I'D PREFER TO do it on my own," Becky said, even though it seemed ungracious to say so. She felt a need to establish who was running the cir—show.

"But here's the problem," Drew said with annoying and elaborate patience.

"Yes?"

"You'll pick a site on your own, and then I'll go look at it and say no, and so then you'll pick another site on your own, and I'll go look at it and say no."

She scowled at him. "You're being unnecessarily negative."

He shrugged. "I'm just making the point that we could, potentially, go on like that endlessly, and there is a bit of a time crunch here."

"I think you just like using the word *no*," she said grumpily.

"Yes," he said, deadpan, as if he was not being deliberately argumentative now.

She should argue that she was quite capable of picking the site by herself and that she had no doubt her next selection would be fine, but her first choice was not exactly proof of that. And besides, then who would be the argumentative one?

"It's too late today," Drew decided. "Joe's coming in on the first flight. Why don't we pick him up and the three of us will pick a site that works for the gazebo?"

"Yes, that would be fine," she said, aware her voice was snapping with ill grace. Really, it was an opportunity. Tomorrow morning she would not scrape her hair back into a careless ponytail. She would apply makeup to hide how her fair skin, fresh out of a Michigan winter, was already blotchy from the sun.

Should she wear her meet-the-potential-client suit, a cream-colored linen by a famous designer? That would certainly make a better impression than shorty-shorts and a sleeveless tank that could be mistaken for underwear!

But the following morning it was already hot, and there was no dry cleaner on the island to take a sweat-drenched dress to.

Aware she was putting way too much effort into her appearance, Becky donned white shorts and a sleeveless sun-yellow shirt. She put on makeup and left her hair down. And then she headed out of her room.

She met Drew on the staircase.

He looked unreasonably gorgeous!

"Good morning," she said. She was stupidly pleased by how his eyes trailed to her hair and her faintly glossed lips.

He returned her greeting gruffly and then went down the stairs in front of her, taking them two at a time. But he stopped and held open the main door for her. They were hit by a wall of heat.

"It's going to be even hotter in two weeks," Drew

told her, when he watched her pause and draw in her breath on the top stair of the castle.

"Must you be so negative?"

"Pragmatic," he insisted. "Plus…"

"Don't tell me. I already know. You looked it up. That's how you know it will be even hotter in two weeks."

He nodded, pleased with himself.

"Keep it up," she warned him, "and you'll have to present me with the prize. A king-size bottle of headache relief."

They stood at the main door to the castle, huge half circles of granite forming a staircase down to a sparkling expanse of emerald lawn. The lawn was edged with a row of beautifully swaying palm trees, and beyond that was a crescent of powdery white sand beach.

"That beach looks so much less magical now that I know it's going to be underwater at four o'clock on June the third."

Drew glanced at Becky. She looked older and more sophisticated with her hair down and makeup on. She had gone from cute to attractive.

It occurred to Drew that Becky was the kind of woman who brought out things in a man that he would prefer to think he didn't have. Around a woman like this a man could find himself wanting to protect himself—and her—from disappointments. That's all he wanted for Joe, too, not to bully him but to protect him.

He'd hated that question, the one he hadn't answered. Had he bullied his brother? He hoped not. But the sad truth was Joe had been seven when Drew, seventeen, was appointed his guardian. Drew had floundered, in way over his head, and he'd resorted to doing whatever needed to be done to get his little brother through childhood.

No wonder his brother was so hungry for love that he'd marry the first beautiful woman who blinked sideways at him.

Unless he could talk some sense into him. He cocked his head. He was pretty sure he could hear the plane coming.

"How hot is it supposed to be on June third?" she asked. He could hear the reluctance to even ask in her voice.

"You know that expression? Hotter than Hades—"

"Never mind. I get it. All the more reason that we really need the pavilion," she said. "We'll need protection from the sun. I planned to have the tables running this way, so everyone could just turn their heads and see the ocean as the sun is going down. The head table could be there, at the bottom of the stairs. Imagine the bride and groom coming down that staircase to join their guests."

Her voice had become quite dreamy. Had she really tried to tell him she was not a romantic? He knew he'd pegged it. She'd had some kind of setback in the romance department, but inside her was still a giddy girl with unrealistic dreams about her prince coming. He had to make sure she knew that was not him.

"Well, I already told you, you can't have that," he said gruffly. He did not enjoy puncturing her dream as much as he wanted to. He did not enjoy being mean as much as he would have liked. He told himself it was for her own good.

He was good at doing things for other people's own

good. You could ask Joe, though his clumsy attempts at parenting were no doubt part of why his brother was running off half-cocked to get married.

"I'm sure we can figure out something," Becky said of her pavilion dream.

"We? No, *we* can't."

This was better. They were going to talk about practicalities, as dream-puncturing as those could be!

The plane was circling now, and they moved toward the airstrip.

He continued, "What you're talking about is an open, expansive structure with huge unsupported spans. You'd need an architect and an engineer."

"I have a tent company I use at home," Becky said sadly, "but they are booked nearly a year in advance. I've tried a few others. Same story. Plus, the planes that can land here aren't big enough to carry that much canvas, and you have to book the supply barge. There's only one with a flat enough bottom to dock here. An unlimited budget can't get you what you might think."

"Unlimited?" He heard the horror in his voice.

She ignored him. "Are you sure I'd need an architect and an engineer, even for something so temporary?"

He slid her a look. She looked quite deflated by all this.

"Especially for something so temporary," he told her. "I'm sure the last thing Allie wants is to be making the news for the collapse of her wedding pavilion. I can almost see the headlines now. 'Three dead, one hundred and eighty-seven injured, event planner and building contractor missing.'"

He heard her little gasp and glanced at her. She was blushing profusely.

"Not missing like *that*," he said.

"Like what?" she choked.

"Like whatever thought is making you blush like that."

"I'm not blushing. The sun has this effect on me."

"Sheesh," he said, as if she had not denied the blush at all. "It's not as if I said that while catastrophe unfolded all around them, the event planner and the contractor went missing *together*."

"I said I wasn't blushing! I never would have thought about us together in any way." Her blush deepened.

He watched her. "You aren't quite the actress that your employer is."

"I am not thinking of us together," she insisted. Her voice was just a little shrill. He realized he quite enjoyed teasing her.

"No?" he said, silkily. "You and I seeking shelter under a palm frond while disaster unfolds all around us?"

Her eyes moved skittishly to his lips and then away. He took advantage of her looking away to study her lips in profile. They were plump little plums, ripe for picking. He was almost sorry he had started this. Almost.

"You're right. You are not a prince. You are evil," she decided, looking back at him. There was a bit of reluctant laughter lurking in her eyes.

He twirled an imaginary moustache. "Yes, I am. Just waiting for an innocent from Moose Run, Michigan, to cross my path so that in the event of a tropical storm, and a building collapse, I will still be entertained."

A little smile tugged at the lips he had just noticed were quite luscious. He was playing a dangerous game.

"Seriously," she said, and he had a feeling she was

the type who did not indulge in lighthearted banter for long, "Allie doesn't want any of this making the news. I'm sure she told you the whole wedding is top secret. She does not want helicopters buzzing her special day."

Drew felt a bit cynical about that. Anyone who wanted a top secret wedding did not invite two hundred people to it. Still, he decided, now might not be the best time to tell Becky a helicopter buzzing might be the least of her worries. When he'd left the States yesterday, all the entertainment shows had been buzzing with the rumors of Allie's engagement.

Was the famous actress using his brother—and everyone else, including small-town Becky English—to ensure Allie Ambrosia was front and center in the news just as her new movie was coming out?

Even though it went somewhat against his blunt nature, the thought that Becky might be being played made Drew soften his bad news a bit. "This close to the equator it's fully dark by six o'clock. The chance of heatstroke for your two hundred guests should be minimized by that."

They took a path through some dense vegetation. On the other side was the airstrip.

"Great," she said testily, though she was obviously relieved they were going to discuss benign things like the weather. "Maybe I can create a kind of 'room' feeling if I circle the area with torches and dress up the tables with linens and candles and flowers and hope for the best."

"Um, about the torches? And candles?" He squinted at the plane touching down on the runway.

"What?"

"According to Google, the trade winds seem to pick

up in the late afternoon. And early evening. Without any kind of structure to protect from the wind, I think they'll just blow out. Or worse."

"So, first you tell me I can't have a structure, and then you tell me all the problems I can expect because I don't have a structure?"

He shrugged. "One thing does tend to lead to another."

"If the wind is strong enough to blow out the candles, we could have other problems with it, too."

"Oh, yeah, absolutely. Tablecloths flying off tables. Women's dresses blowing up over their heads. Napkins catching fire. Flower arrangements being smashed. There's really a whole lot of things people should think about before planning their wedding on a remote island in the tropics."

Becky glared at him. "You know what? I barely know you and I hate you already."

He nodded. "I have that effect on a lot of people."

He watched the plane taxi toward them and grind to a halt in front of them.

"I'm sure you do," she said snippily.

"Does this mean our date under the palm frond is off?"

"It was never on!"

"You should think about it—the building collapsed, the tablecloths on fire, women's dresses blowing over their heads as they run shrieking…"

"Please stop."

But he couldn't. He could tell he very nearly had her where he wanted her. Why did he feel so driven to make little Miss Becky English angry? But also to make her laugh?

"And you and me under a palm frond, licking wedding cake off each other's fingers."

At first she looked appalled. But then a smile tickled her lips. And then she giggled. And then she was laughing. In a split second, every single thing about her seemed transformed. She went from plain to pretty.

Very pretty.

This was exactly what he had wanted: to glimpse what the cool Miss English would look like if she let go of control.

It was more dangerous than Drew had anticipated. It made him want to take it a step further, to make her laugh harder or to take those little lips underneath his and…

He reminded himself she was not the type of girl he usually invited out to play. Despite the fact she was being relied on to put on a very sophisticated event, there didn't seem to be any sophistication about her.

He had already figured out there was a heartbreak in her past. That was the only reason a girl as apple pie as her claimed to be jaundiced about romance. He could tell it wasn't just dealing with people's wedding insanity that had made her want to be cynical, even as it was all too evident she was not. He had seen the truth in the dreamy look when she had started talking about how she wanted it all to go.

He could tell by looking at her exactly what she needed, and it wasn't a job putting together other people's fantasies.

It was a husband who adored her. And three children. And a little house where she could sew curtains for the windows and tuck bright annuals into the flower beds every year.

It was whatever the perfect life in Moose Run, Michigan, looked like.

Drew knew he could never give her those things. Never. He'd experienced too much loss and too much responsibility in his life.

Still, there was one thing a guy as jaundiced as him did not want or need. To be stuck on a deserted island with a female whose laughter could turn her from a plain old garden-variety girl next door into a goddess in the blink of an eye.

He turned from her quickly and watched as the door of the plane opened. The crew got off, opened the cargo hold and began unloading stuff beside the runway.

He frowned. No Joe.

He took his phone out of his pocket and stabbed in a text message. He pushed Send, but the island did not have great service in all places. The message to his brother did not go through.

Becky was searching his face, which he carefully schooled not to show his disappointment.

"I guess we'll have to find that spot ourselves. Joe will probably come on the afternoon flight. Let's see what we can find this way."

Instead of following the lawn to where it dropped down to the beach, he followed it north to a line of palm trees. A nice wide trail dipped into them, and he took it.

"It's like jungle in here," she said.

"Think of the possibilities. Joe could swing down from a vine. In a loincloth. Allie could be waiting for him in a tree house, right here."

"No, no and especially no," she said.

He glanced behind him. She had stopped to look at

a bright red hibiscus. She plucked it off and tucked it behind her ear.

"In the tropics," he told her, "when you wear a flower behind your ear like that, it means you are available. You wouldn't want the cook getting the wrong idea."

She glared at him, plucked the flower out and put it behind her other ear.

"Now it means you're married."

"There's no winning, is there?" she asked lightly.

No, there wasn't. The flower looked very exotic in her hair. It made him very aware, again, of the enchantment of tropical islands. He turned quickly from her and made his way down the path.

After about five minutes in the deep shade of the jungle, they came out to another beach. It was exposed to the wind, which played in the petals of the flower above her ear, lifted her bangs from her face and pressed her shirt to her.

"Oh," she called, "it's beautiful."

She had to shout because unlike the beach the castle overlooked, this one was not in a protected cove.

It was a beautiful beach. A surfer would probably love it, but it would have to be a good surfer. There were rocky outcrops stretching into the water that looked like they would be painful to hit and hard to avoid.

"It's too loud," he said over the crashing of the waves. "They'd be shouting their vows."

He turned and went back into the shaded jungle. For some reason, he thought she would just follow him, and it took him a few minutes to realize he was alone.

He turned and looked. The delectable Miss Becky English was nowhere to be seen. He went back along the path, annoyed. Hadn't he made it perfectly clear they had time constraints?

When he got back out to the beach, his heart went into his throat. She had climbed up onto one of the rocky outcrops. She was standing there, bright as the sun in that yellow shirt, as a wave smashed on the rock just beneath her. Her hands were held out and her face lifted to the spray of white foam it created. With the flower in her hair, she looked more like a goddess than ever, performing some ritual to the sea.

Did she know nothing of the ocean? Of course she didn't. They had already established that. That, coming from Moose Run, there were things she could not know about.

"Get down from there," he shouted. "Becky, get down right now."

He could see the second wave building, bigger than the first that had hit the rock. The waves would come in sets. And the last wave in the set would be the biggest.

The wind swallowed his voice, though she turned and looked at him. She smiled and waved. He could see the surf rising behind her alarmingly. The second wave hit the rock. She turned away from him, and hugged herself in delight as the spray fell like thick mist all around her.

"Get away from there," he shouted. She turned and gave him a puzzled look. He started to run.

Becky had her back to the third wave when it hit. It hit the backs of her legs. Drew saw her mouth form a surprised O, and then her arms were flailing as she tried to regain her balance. The wave began pulling back, with at least as much force as it had come in with. It yanked her off the rock as if she were a rag doll.

CHAPTER FIVE

BECKY FELT THE shocked helplessness as her feet were jerked out from under her and she was swept off the rock. The water closed over her head and filled her mouth and nose. She popped back up like a cork, but her swimming skills were rudimentary, and she was not sure they would have helped her against the fury of the sea. She was being pulled out into what seemed to be an endless abyss. She tried frantically to swim back in toward shore. In seconds she was as exhausted as she had ever been.

I'm going to drown, she thought, stunned, choking on water and fear. How had this happened? One moment life had seemed so pleasant and beautiful and then...it was over.

Her life was going to be over. She waited, helplessly, for it to flash before her eyes. Instead, she found herself thinking that Drew had been right. It hadn't been a heartbreak. It had been a romantic disappointment. Ridiculous to think that right now, but on the other hand, right now seemed as good a time as any to be acutely and sadly aware of things she had missed.

"Hey!" His voice carried over the crashing of the sea. "Hang on."

Becky caught a glimpse of the rock she had fallen off. Drew was up there. And then she went under the water again.

When she surfaced, Drew was in the water, slashing through the roll of the waves toward her. "Don't panic," he called over the roar of the water pounding the rock outcropping.

She wanted to tell him it was too late for that. She was already panicked.

"Tread," he yelled. "Don't try to swim. Not yet. Look at my face. Nowhere else. Look at me."

Her eyes fastened on his face. There was strength and calm in his features, as if he did this every day. He was close to her now.

"I'm going to come to you," he shouted, "but you have to be calm first. If you panic, you will kill us both."

It seemed his words, and the utter strength and determination in his face, poured a honey of calm over her, despite the fact she was still bobbing like a cork in a ravaged sea. He seemed to see or sense the moment she stopped panicking, and he moved in close.

She nearly sobbed with relief when Drew reached out and touched her, then folded his arms around her and pulled her in tight to him. He was strong in the water—she suspected, abstractly, he was strong everywhere in his life—and she rested into his embrace, surrendering to his warmth. She could feel the power of him in his arms and where she was pressed into the wet slickness of his chest.

"Just let it carry you," he said. "Don't fight it anymore"

It seemed as if he could be talking about way more than water. It could be a message about life.

It seemed the water carried them out forever, but eventually it dumped them in a calmer place, just beyond where the waves began to crest. Becky could feel the water lose its grip on her, even as he refused to.

She never took her eyes off his face. Her mind seemed to grow calmer and calmer, even amused. If this was the last thing she would see, it told her, that wasn't so bad.

"Okay," he said, "can you swim?"

"Dog paddle." The water was not cold, but her voice was shaking.

"That will do. Swim that way. Do your best. I've got you if you get tired." He released her.

That way was not directly to the shore. He was asking her to swim parallel to the shore instead of in. But she tried to do as he asked. She was soon floundering, so tired she could not lift her arms.

"Roll over on your back," he said, and she did so willingly. His hand cupped her chin and she was being pulled through the water. He was an enormously strong swimmer.

"Okay, this is a good spot." He released her again and she came upright and treaded water. "Go toward shore. I've got you, I'm right with you."

She was scared to go back into the waves. It was too much. She was exhausted. But she glanced at his face once more and found her own courage there.

"Get on your tummy, flat as a board, watch for the next wave and ride it in. Watch for those rocks on the side."

She did as she was told. She knew she had no choice. She had to trust him completely. She felt the wave lift her up and drive her toward the shore at a stunning speed. And then it spit her out. She was lying in shallow water, but she could already feel the wave pulling at her, trying to drag her back in. She used what little strength she had left to scramble to her knees and crawl through the sugar pebbles of the sand.

Drew came and scooped her out of the water, lifted her to his chest and struggled out of the surf.

On the beach, above the foaming line of the ocean, he set her down on her back in the sun-warmed sand. For a moment she looked at the clear and endless blue of the sky. It was the very same sky it had been twenty minutes ago, but everything felt changed, some awareness sharp as glass within her. She rolled over onto her stomach and rested her head on her forearms. He flung himself onto the sand beside her, breathing hard.

"Did you just save my life?" she whispered. Her voice was hoarse. Her throat hurt from swallowing salt water. She felt drowsy and extraordinarily peaceful.

"You'll want to make sure this beach is posted before guests start arriving," he finally said, when he spoke.

"You didn't answer the question," she said, taking a peek at him over her folded arm. "Is that a habit with you?"

Drew didn't answer. She looked at him, feeling as if she was drinking him in, as if she could never get enough of looking at him. It was probably natural to feel that way after someone had just saved your life, and she did not try to make herself stop.

She was in a state of altered awareness. She could see the water beading on his eyelashes, and the sun streaming through his wet hair. She could see through his soaked shirt where it was plastered to his body.

"Did you just save my life?" she asked again.

"I think you Michigan girls should stay away from the ocean."

"Do you ever just answer a question, Drew Jordan? Did you save my life?"

He was silent again.

"You did," she finally answered for him.

She could not believe the gratitude she felt. To be alive. It was as if the life force was zinging inside her, making her every cell quiver.

"You risked yourself for me. I'm nearly a complete stranger."

"No, you're not. Winning the headache competition, by the way."

"By a country mile?"

"Oh, yeah."

"That was incredibly heroic." She was not going let him brush it off, though he was determined to.

"Don't make it something it wasn't. I'm nobody's hero."

Just like he had insisted earlier he was nobody's prince.

"Well," she insisted, "you're mine."

He snorted, that sexy, cynical sound he made that was all his own and she found, right now, lying here in the sand, alive, so aware of herself and him, that she liked that sound very much, despite herself.

"I've been around the ocean my whole life," he told her grimly. "I grew up surfing some pretty rough water. I knew what I was doing. Unlike you. That was incredibly stupid."

In her altered state, she was aware that he thought he could break the bond that had been cementing itself into place between them since the moment he had entered the water to rescue her.

"Life can change in a blink," he said sternly. "It can be over in a blink."

He was lecturing her. She suddenly *needed* him to know she could not let him brush it off like that. She needed him to know that the life force was flowing through her. She had an incredible sense of being alive.

"You were right," she said, softly.

There was that snort again. "Of course I'm right. You don't go climbing up on rocks when the surf is that high."

"Not about that. I mean, okay, about that, too, but I wasn't talking about that."

"What were you talking about?"

"It wasn't a heartbreak," Becky said. "It was a romantic disappointment."

"Huh?"

"That's what I thought of when I went into the water. I thought my whole life would flash before my eyes, but instead I thought of Jerry."

"Look, you're obviously in shock and we need to—"

"He was my high school sweetheart. We'd been together since I was seventeen. I'd always assumed we were going to get married. Everybody in the whole town thought we would get married. They called us Salt and Pepper."

"You know what? This will keep. I have to—"

"It won't keep. It's important. I have to say it before I forget it. Before this moment passes."

"Oh, sheesh," he said, his tone indicating he wanted nothing more than for this moment to pass.

"I wanted that. I wanted to be Salt and Pepper, *for-*

ever. My parents had split up the year before. It was awful. My dad owned a hardware store. One of his clerks. And him."

"Look, Becky, you are obviously rattled. You don't have to tell me this."

She could no more have stopped herself from telling him than she could have stopped those waves from pounding on the shore.

"They had a baby together. Suddenly, they were the family we had always been. That we were supposed to be. It was horrible, seeing them all over town, looking at each other. Pushing a baby carriage. I wanted it back. I wanted that feeling of being part of something back. Of belonging."

"Aw, Becky," he said softly. "That sucks. Really it does, but—"

But she had to tell all of it, was compelled to. "Jerry went away to school. My mom didn't have the money for college, and it seemed my dad had new priorities.

"I could see what the community needed, so I started my event company."

"Happily-Ever-After," he said. "Even though you had plenty of evidence of the exact opposite."

"It was way more successful than I had thought it could be. It was way more successful than Jerry thought it could be, too. The more successful I became, the less he liked me."

"Okay. Well. Some guys are like that."

"He broke up with me."

"Yeah, sorry, but now is not the time—"

"This is the reason it's important for me to say it right now. I understand something I didn't understand before. I thought my heart was broken. It is a terrible thing to suffer the humiliation of being ditched in a small town. It was a double humiliation for me. First my dad, and then this. But out there in the water, I felt glad. I felt if I had married him, I would have missed something. Something essential."

"Okay, um—"

"A grand passion."

He said a word under his breath that they disapproved of in Moose Run, Michigan.

"Salt and pepper?" She did a pretty good imitation of his snort. "Why settle for boring old salt and pepper when the world is full of so many glorious flavors?"

"Look, I think you've had a pretty bad shake-up. I don't have a clue what you are talking about, so—"

She knew she was making Drew Jordan wildly uncomfortable, but she didn't care. She planned to make him more uncomfortable yet. She leaned toward him. He stopped talking and watched her warily.

She needed to know if the life force was as intense in him right now as it was in her. She needed to take advantage of this second chance to be alive, to really live.

She touched Drew's back through the wetness of his shirt, and felt the sinewy strength there. The strength that had saved her.

She leaned closer yet. She touched her forehead to his, as if she could make him *feel* what was going on inside her, since words could not express it. He had a chance to move away from her. He did not. He was as caught in what was unfolding as she had been in the wave.

And then, she touched her lips to his, delicately, *needing* the connection to intensify.

His lips tasted of salt and strength and something

more powerful and more timeless than the ocean. That desire that people had within them, not just to live, but to go on.

For a moment, Drew was clearly stunned to find her lips on his. But then, he seemed to get whatever she was trying to tell him, in this primal language that seemed the only thing that could express the celebration of all that lived within her.

His lips answered hers. His tongue chased the ridges of her teeth, and then probed, gently, ever so gently...

It was Becky's turn to be stunned. It was everything she had hoped for. It was everything she had missed.

No, it was *more* than what she had hoped for, and more than what she could have ever imagined. A kiss was not simply a brushing of lips. No! It was a journey, it was a ride on pure energy, it was a connection, it was a discovery, it was an intertwining of the deepest parts of two people, of their souls.

Drew stopped kissing her with such abruptness that she felt forlorn, like a blanket had been jerked from her on a freezing night. He said Moose Run's most disap-proved-of word again.

She *liked* the way he said that word, all naughty and nasty.

He found his feet and leaped up, staring down at her. He raked a hand through his hair, and water droplets scattered off his crumpled hair, sparkling like diamonds in the tropical heat. His shirt, crusted in golden sand, was clinging to his chest.

"Geez," he said. "What was that about?"

"I don't know," she said honestly. *But I liked it.*

"A girl like you does not kiss a guy like me!"

She could ask what he meant by a girl like her, but

she already knew that he thought she was small town and naive and hopelessly out of her depth, and not just in the ocean, either. What she wanted to know was what the last half of that sentence meant.

"What do you mean a guy like you?" she asked. Her voice was husky from the salt and from something else. Desire. Desire was burning like a white-hot coal in her belly. It was brand-new, it was embarrassing and it was wonderful.

"Look, Becky, I'm the kind of guy your mother used to warn you about."

Woo-hoo, she thought, but she didn't dare say it. Instead, she said, "The kind who would jump in the water without a thought for his own safety to save someone else?"

"Not that kind!"

She could point out to him that he obviously *was* that kind, and that the facts spoke for themselves, but she probed the deeper part of what was going on.

"What kind of guy then?" she asked, gently curious.

"Self-centered. Commitment-phobic. Good-time Charlie. Confirmed bachelor. They write whole articles about guys like me in your bridal magazines. And not about how to catch me, either. How to give a guy like me a wide berth."

"Just in case you didn't listen to your mother's warnings," she clarified.

He glanced at her. She bit her lip and his gaze rested there, hot with memory, until he seemed to make himself look away.

"I wouldn't have pictured you as any kind of expert about the content of bridal magazines," she said.

"That is not the point!"

"It was just a kiss," she pointed out mildly, "not a posting of the banns."

"You're in shock," he said.

If she was, she hoped she could experience it again, and soon!

CHAPTER SIX

DREW LOOKED AT Becky English. Sprawled out, belly
down in the sand, she looked like a drowned rat, her
hair plastered to her head, her yellow shirt plastered
to her lithe body, both her shirt and her white shorts
transparent in their wetness. For a drowned rat, and for
a girl from Moose Run, Michigan, she had on surprisingly sexy underwear.

She looked like a drowned rat, and she was a small-
town girl, but she sure as hell did not kiss like either
one of those things. There had been nothing sweet or
shy about that kiss!

It had been hungry enough to devour him.

But, Drew told himself sternly, she was exceedingly
vulnerable. She was obviously stunned from what had
just happened to her out there at the mercy of the ocean.
It was possible she had banged her head riding that final
wave in. The blow might have removed the filter from
her brain that let her know what was, and what wasn't,
appropriate.

But good grief, that kiss. He had to make sure nothing like that ever happened again! How was he going
to be able to look at her without recalling the sweet,
salty taste of her mouth? Without recalling the sweet

welcome? Without recalling the flash of passion, the pull of which was at least as powerful as those waves?

"Becky," he said sternly, "don't make me your hero. I've been cast in that role before, and I stunk at it."

Drew had been seventeen when he became a parent to his brother. He had a sense of having grown up too fast and with too heavy a load. He was not interested in getting himself back into a situation where he was responsible for someone else's happiness and well-being. He didn't feel the evidence showed he had been that good at it.

"It was just a kiss," she said again, a bit too dreamily.

It wasn't just a kiss. If it had been just a kiss he would feel nothing, the same as he always did when he had just a kiss. He wouldn't be feeling this need to set her straight.

"When were you cast in that role before? How come you stank at it?" she asked softly. He noticed that, impossibly, the flower had survived in her hair. Its bright red petals were drooping sadly, kissing the tender flesh of her temple.

"This is not the time or the place," he said curtly before, in this weakened moment, in this contrived atmosphere of closeness, he threw himself down beside her, and let her save him, the way he had just saved her.

"Are you hurt?" he asked, cold and clinical. "Any bumps or bruises? Did you hit your head?"

Thankfully, she was distracted, and considered his question with an almost comical furrowing of her brow.

"I don't think I hit my head, but my leg hurts," she decided. "I think I scraped it on a rock coming in."

She rolled onto her back and then struggled to sit up. He peered over her shoulder. There was six inches of scrapes on the inside of her thigh, one of the marks looked quite deep and there was blood clumping in the sand that clung to it.

What was wrong with him? The first thing he should have done was check for injuries.

He stripped off his wet shirt and got down beside her. This was what was wrong with him. He was way too aware of her. The scent of the sea was clinging to her body, a body he was way too familiar with after having dragged her from the ocean and then accepted the invitation of her lips.

Becky was right. There was something exhilarating about snatching life back out of the jaws of death. That's why he was so aware of her on every level, not thinking with his customary pragmatism.

He brushed the sand away from her wound. He should have known touching the inner thigh of a girl like Becky English was going to be nothing like a man might have expected.

"Ow," she said, and her fingers dug into his shoulder and then lingered there. "Oh, my," she breathed. "You did warn me what would happen if you took your shirt off."

"I was kidding," he said tersely.

"No, you weren't. You were warning me off."

"How's that working for you, Drew?" he muttered to himself. He cleaned the sand away from her wound as best he could, then wrapped it in his soaked shirt.

She sighed with satisfaction like the geeky girl who had just gotten all the words right at the spelling bee. "Women adore you."

"Not ones as smart as you," he said. "Can you stand? We have to find a first aid kit. I think that's just a superficial scrape, but it's bleeding quite a lot and we need to get it looked after."

He helped her to her feet, still way too aware, steeling himself against the silky resilience of her skin. She swayed against him. Her wet curves were pressed into him, and her chin was pressed sharply into his chest as she looked up at him with huge, unblinking eyes.

Had he thought, just an hour ago, her eyes were ordinary brown? They weren't. They were like melted milk chocolate, deep and rich and inviting.

"You were right." She giggled. "I'm swooning."

"Let's hope it's not from blood loss. Can you walk?"

"Of course."

She didn't move.

He sighed and scooped her up, cradling her to his chest, one arm under her knees, the other across her back. She was lighter than he could have believed, and her softness pressed into him was making him way more vulnerable than the embraces of women he'd known who had far more in the curvy department.

"You're very masterful," she said, snuggling into him.

"In this day and age how can that be a good thing?"

"It's a secret longing."

He did not want to hear about her secret longings!

"If you don't believe me, read—"

"Stop it," he said grimly.

"I owe you my life."

"I said stop it."

"You are not the boss over me."

"That's what I was afraid of."

He carried her back along the path. She was small and light and it took no effort at all. At the castle, he found the kitchen, an enormous room that looked like the kind of well-appointed facility one would expect to find in a five-star hotel.

"Have you got a first aid attendant here?" Drew asked one of the kitchen staff, who went and fetched the chef.

The chef showed him through to an office adjoining the kitchen, and Drew settled Becky in a chair. The chef sent in a young man with a first aid kit. He was slender and golden-skinned with dark, dark hair and almond-shaped eyes that matched.

"I am Tandu," he said. "I am the medical man." His accent made it sound as if he had said *medicine man*.

Relived that he could back off from more physical contact with the delectable Miss Becky, Drew motioned to where she sat.

Tandu set down his first aid kit and crouched down in front of her. He carefully unwrapped Drew's wet shirt from her leg. He stared at Becky's injury for a moment, scrambled to his feet, picked up the first aid kit and thrust it at Drew.

"I do not do blood."

"What kind of first aid attendant doesn't—?"

But Tandu had already fled.

Drew, even more aware of her now that he had nearly escaped, went and found a pan of warm water, and then cleaned and dressed her wound, steeling himself to be as professional as possible.

Becky stared down at the dark head of the man kneeling at her feet. He pressed a warm, wet cloth against the tender skin of her inner thigh, and she gasped at the sensation that jolted through her like an electric shock.

He glanced up at her, then looked back to his task quickly. "Sorry," he muttered. "I will try to make this as painless as possible."

Despite the fact his touch was incredibly tender—or maybe because of it—it was one of the most deliciously painful experiences of Becky's life. He carefully cleaned the scrapes, dabbed an ointment on them and then wound clean gauze around her leg.

She could feel a quiver within her building. There was going to be an earthquake if he didn't finish soon! She longed to reach out and touch his hair, to brush the salt and sand from it. She reached out.

A pan dropped in the kitchen, and she felt reality crashing back in around her. She snatched her hand back, just as Drew glanced up.

"Are you okay?"

"Sure," she said shakily, but she really wasn't. What she felt like was a girl who had been very drunk, and who had done all kinds of uninhibited and crazy things, and was now coming to her senses.

She had kissed Drew Jordan shamelessly. She had shared all her secrets with him. She had blabbered that he was masterful, as if she enjoyed such a thing! Now she had nearly touched his hair, as if they were lovers instead of near strangers!

Okay, his hand upon her thigh was obviously creating confusion in the more primal cortexes of her brain, but she had to pull herself together.

"There," he said, rocking back on his heels and studying the bandage around her thigh, "I think—"

She didn't let him finish. She shot to her feet, gazed down at her bandaged thigh instead of at him. "Yes, yes, perfect," she said. She sounded like a German engineer approving a mechanical drawing. Her thigh was tingling unmercifully, and she was pretty sure it was from his touch and not from the injury.

"I have to get to work," she said in a strangled voice.

He stood up. "You aren't going to work. You're going to rest for the afternoon."

"But I can't. I—"

"I'm telling you, you need to rest."

She thought, again, of telling him he was masterful. Good grief, she could feel the blush rising up her cheeks. She had probably created a monster.

In him and in herself.

"Go to bed," he said. Drew's voice was as caressing as his hand had been, and just as seductive. "Just for what is left of the afternoon. You'll be glad you did."

You did not discuss bed with a man like this! And especially not after he had just performed intimate rituals on your thigh! Particularly not after you had noticed his voice was seduction itself, all deep and warm and caressing.

You did not discuss bed with a man like this once you had come to your senses. She opened her mouth to tell him she would decide for herself what needed to be done. It would not involve the word *bed*. But before she could speak, he did.

"I'll go scout a spot for the wedding. Joe will be here in a while. By the time you wake up, we'll have it all taken care of."

All her resolve to take back the reins of her own life dissolved, instantly, like sugar into hot tea.

It felt as if she was going to start crying. When was the last time anything had been taken care of for her? After her father had left, her poor shattered mother had absconded on parenting. It felt as if Becky had been the one who looked after everything. Jerry had seemed to like her devoting herself to organizing his life. Even her career took advantage of the fact that Becky English was the one who looked after things, who tried valiantly to fix all and to achieve perfection. She took it all on... until the weight of it nearly crushed her.

Where had that thought come from? She *loved* her job. Putting together joyous and memorable occasions for others had soothed the pain of her father's abandonment, and had, thankfully, been enough to fill her world ever since the defection of Jerry from her personal landscape.

Or had been enough until less than twenty-four hours ago, when Drew Jordan had showed up in her life and showed her there was still such a thing as a hero.

She turned and fled before she did something really foolish. Like kissing him again.

Becky found that as much as she would have liked to rebel against his advice, she had no choice but to take it. Clear of the kitchen, her limbs felt like jelly, heavy and nearly shaking with exhaustion and delayed reaction to all the unexpected adventures of the day. It took every bit of remaining energy she had to climb the stone staircase that led to the wing of the castle with her room in it.

She went into its cool sanctuary and peeled off her wet clothes. It felt like too much effort to even find something else to put on. She left the clothes in a heap and crept under the cool sheets of the welcoming bed. Within seconds she was fast asleep.

She dreamed that someone was knocking on her door, and when she went to answer it, Drew Jordan was on the other side of it, a smile of pure welcome on his face. He reached for her, he pulled her close, his mouth dropped over hers...

Becky started awake. She was not sure what time it was, though the light suggested early evening, which meant she had frittered away a whole precious afternoon sleeping.

She wanted to leap from bed, but her body would not let her. She felt, again, like the girl who had had too much to drink. She tested each of her limbs. It was official. Her whole body hurt. Her head hurt. Her mouth and throat felt raw and dry. But mostly, she felt deeply ashamed. She had lost control, and she hated that.

Her door squeaked open.

"How you doing?"

She shot up in bed, pulled the sheet more tightly around herself. "What are you doing here?"

"I knocked. When there was no answer, I thought I'd better check on you. You slept a long time."

Drew Jordan looked just as he had in the dream—gorgeous. Though in real life there was no expression of tender welcome on his face. It did not look like he was thinking about sweeping her into his big strong arms.

In fact, he slipped into the room, but rested himself against the far wall—as far away from her as possible—those big, strong arms folded firmly across his chest. He was wearing a snowy-white T-shirt that showed off the sun-bronzed color of his arms, and khaki shorts that showed off the long, hard muscle of equally sun-bronzed legs.

"A long time?" She found her cell phone on the bedside table. "It's only five. That's not so bad."

"Um, maybe you should have a look at the date on there."

She frowned down at her phone. Her mouth fell open. "What? I slept an entire day? But I couldn't have! That's impossible."

She started to throw back the covers, then remembered she had slipped in between the sheets naked. She yanked them up around her chin.

"It was probably the best thing you could do. Your body knows what it needs."

She looked up at him. Her body, treacherous thing, did indeed know what it needed! And all of it involved him.

"If you would excuse me," she said, "I really need—"

Now her brain, treacherous thing, silently screamed *you*.

"Are you okay?"

No! It simply was not okay to be this aware of him, to yearn for his touch and his taste.

"I'm fine. Did your brother come?" she asked, desperate to distract him from her discomfort, and from the possibility of him discerning what was causing it.

"Nope. I can't seem to reach him on my phone, either."

"Oh, Drew," she said softly.

Her tone seemed to annoy him. "You don't really look fine," he decided.

"Okay, I'm not fine. I don't have time to sleep away a whole day. Despite all that rest, I feel as if I've been through the spin cycle of a giant washing machine. I hurt everywhere, worse than the worst hangover ever."

"You've had a hangover?" He said this with insulting incredulousness.

"Of course I have. Living in Moose Run isn't like taking vows to become a nun, you know."

"You would be wasted as a nun," he said, and his gaze went to her lips before he looked sharply away.

"Let's talk about that," she said.

"About you being wasted as a nun?" he asked, looking back at her, surprised.

"About the fact you think you would know such a thing about me. I don't normally act like that. I would never, under ordinary circumstances, kiss a person the way I kissed you. Naturally, I'm mortified."

He lifted an eyebrow.

"There was no need to throw myself at you, no matter how grateful and discombobulated I was."

His lips twitched.

"It's not funny," she told him sternly. "It's embarrassing."

"It's not your wanton and very un-nun-like behavior I was smiling about."

"Wanton?" she squeaked.

"It was the fact you used *discombobulated* in a sentence. I can't say as I've ever heard that before."

"Wanton?" she squeaked again.

"Sorry. Wanton is probably overstating it."

"Probably?"

"We don't all have your gift for picking exactly the right word," he said. He lifted a shoulder. "People do weird things when they are in shock. Let's move past it, okay?"

Actually, she would have preferred to find out exactly what he meant by wanton—it had been a little kiss really, it didn't even merit the humiliation she was feeling about it—but she didn't want to look like she was unwilling to move past it.

"Okay," she said grudgingly. "Though just for the

record, I want you to know I don't like masterful men. At all."

"No secret longing?"

He was teasing her! There was a residue of weakness in her, because she liked it, but it would be a mistake to let him know her weaknesses.

"As you have pointed out," Becky said coolly, "I was in shock. I said and did things that were completely alien to my nature. Now, let's move past it."

Something smoky happened to his eyes. His gaze stopped on her lips. She had the feeling he would dearly like to prove to her that some things were not as alien to her nature as she wanted them both to believe.

But he fended off the temptation, with apparent ease, pushing himself away from the wall and heading back for the door. "You have one less thing to worry about. I think I have the pavilion figured out."

"Really?" She would have leaped up and gave him a hug, except she was naked underneath the sheet, he already thought she was wanton enough, and she was not exposing anything to him, least of all not her longing to let other people look after things for a change. And to feel his embrace once more, his hard, hot muscles against her naked flesh.

"You do?" she squeaked, trying to find a place to put her gaze, anywhere but his hard, hot muscles.

"I thought about what you said, about creating an illusion. I started thinking about driving some posts, and suspending fabric from them. Something like a canopy bed."

She squinted at him. That urge to hold him, to feel him, to touch him, was there again, stronger. It was because he was looking after things, taking on a part of the burden without being asked. It was because he had listened to her.

Becky English, lying there in her bed, naked, with her sheet pulled up around her chin, studied her ceiling, so awfully aware that a woman could fall for a guy like him before she even knew what had happened to her.

CHAPTER SEVEN

THANKFULLY FOR BECKY, Drew Jordan had already warned her about guys like him.

"What does a confirmed bachelor know about canopy beds?" she said, keeping her gaze on the ceiling and her tone deliberately light. "No, never mind. I don't want to know. I think I'm still slightly discombobulated."

"Admit it."

She glanced over at him just as he grinned. His teeth were white and straight. He looked way too handsome. She returned her gaze to the ceiling. "I just did. I'm still slightly discombobulated."

"Not that! Admit it's brilliant."

She couldn't help but smile. And look at him again. "It is. It's brilliant. It will create that illusion of a room, and possibly provide some protection from the sun if we use fabric as a kind of ceiling. It has the potential to be exceedingly romantic, too. Which is why I'm surprised you came up with it."

"Hey, nobody is more surprised than me. Sadly, after traipsing all over the island this afternoon, I still haven't found a good site for the ceremony. But you might as well come see what's going on with the pavilion."

She should not appear too eager. But really? Pretending just felt like way too much effort. She would have to chalk it up to her near drowning and the other rattling events of the day. "Absolutely. Give me five minutes."

"Sure. I'll meet you on the front stairs."

Of course, it took Becky longer than five minutes. She had to shower off the remains of her adventure. She had sand in places she did not know sand could go. Her hair was destroyed. Her leg was a mess and she had to rewrap it after she was done. She had faint bruising appearing in the most unlikely places all over her body.

She put on her only pair of long pants—as uninspiring as they were in a lightweight grey tweed—and a long-sleeved shirt in a shade of hot pink that matched some of the flowers that bloomed in such abundance on this island. Her outfit covered the worst of the damage to her poor battered body, but there was nothing she could do about the emotional battering she was receiving. And it wasn't his fault. Drew Jordan was completely oblivious to the effect he was having on her.

Or accustomed to it!

Becky dabbed on a bit of makeup to try to hide the crescent moons from under her eyes. She looked exhausted. How was that possible after nearly twenty-four hours of sleep? At the last minute, she just touched a bit of gloss to her lips. It wasn't wrong to want him to look at them, but she hoped she would not be discombobulated enough to offer them to him again anytime in the near future.

"Or any future!" she told herself firmly.

She had pictured Drew waiting impatiently for her, but when she arrived at the front step, he had out a can of spray paint and was marking big X's on the grassy lawn in front of the castle.

Just when she was trying not to think of kisses anymore. What was this clumsy artwork on the lawn all about? An invitation? A declaration of love? A late Valentine?

"Marking where the posts should go," he told her, glancing toward her and then looking back at what he was doing. "Can you come stand right here and hold the tape measure?"

So much for a declaration of love! Good grief. She had always harbored this secret and very unrealistic side. She thought Jerry had cured her of her more fantastic romantic notions, but no, some were like little seeds inside her, waiting for the first hint of water and sun to sprout into full-fledged fairy tales. Being rescued from certain death by a very good-looking and extremely competent man who had so willingly put his own life on the line for her had obviously triggered her most fanciful longings.

She just needed to swat herself up the side of the head with the facts. She and Drew Jordan barely knew one another, and before she was swept off the rock they had been destined to butt heads.

She had to amend that: she barely knew Drew Jordan, but he knew her better than he should because she had blurted out her whole life story in a moment of terrible weakness. It was just more evidence that she must have hit her head somewhere in that debacle. Except for the fact she was useful for holding the tape measure, he hardly seemed aware that she was there.

Finally, he rolled up the tape measure. "What do you think?"

His X's formed a large rectangle. She could picture it already with a silken canopy and the posts swathed in fabric. She could picture the tables and the candles, and music and a beautiful bride and groom.

"I think it's going to be perfect," she breathed. And for the first time since she had taken on this job, she felt like maybe it would be.

How much of that had to do with the man who was, however reluctantly, helping her make it happen?

"Don't get your hopes up too high," he said. "Perfection is harder to achieve than you think. And we still have the evening tropical breezes to contend with. And I haven't found a ceremony site. It could go sideways yet."

"Especially if you talk to your brother?"

He rolled his shoulders. "There doesn't seem to be much chance of that happening. But there are a lot of things that could go sideways before the big day."

Yes, she had seen in recent history how quickly things could go sideways. In fact, when she looked at him, she was pretty sure Drew Jordan was the kind of man who could make your whole life go sideways with no effort on his part at all.

"Let's go see if we can find a place for the ceremony."

She *had* to go with him. It was her job. But tropical breezes seemed to be the least of her problems at the moment.

"I should be getting danger pay," she muttered to herself.

"Don't worry, I won't be letting you anywhere near any rocks."

No sense clarifying with him that was not where the danger she was worried about was coming from. Not at all.

They were almost at the edge of the lawn when a voice stopped them.

"Miss Becky. Mr. Drew."

They turned to see Tandu struggling across the lawn with a huge wicker basket. "So sorry, no good with blood. Take you to place for wedding vow now."

"Oh, did you tell him we were looking for a new ceremony site?" Becky asked. "That was smart."

"Naturally, I would like to take credit for being smart, but I didn't tell him. They must do weddings here all the time. He's used to this."

"Follow, follow," Tandu ordered.

They fell into step behind him, leaving the lawn and entering the deep, vibrant green of the jungle forest. Birds chattered and the breeze lifting huge leaves made a sound, too.

"Actually, the owner of the island told me they had hosted some huge events here, but never a wedding," Becky told Drew. "He's the music mogul, Bart Lung. He's a friend of Allie's. He's away on business but he'll be back for the wedding. He's very excited about it."

"Are you excited about meeting him?"

"I guess I hadn't really thought about it. We better catch up to Tandu, he's way ahead of us."

Drew contemplated what had just happened with a trace of self-loathing.

Are you excited about meeting him? As bad as asking the question was how much he had liked her answer. She genuinely seemed not to have given a thought to meeting Bart Lung.

But what had motivated Drew to ask such a question? Surely he hadn't been feeling a bit threatened about

Becky meeting the famously single and fabulously wealthy record broker? He couldn't possibly have felt the faintest little prickle of...jealousy.

He never felt jealous. He'd had women he had dated who had tried to make him jealous, and he'd been annoyed by how juvenile that felt. But at the heart of it, he knew they had wanted him to show what he couldn't: that he cared.

But he'd known from the moment she had instigated that kiss that Becky English was different from what his brother liked to call the rotating door of women in his life. The chemistry between them had been unexpected, but Drew had had chemistry before. He wasn't sure exactly what it was about the cheerleader-turned-event-planner that intrigued him, but he knew he had to get away from it.

Which was exactly why he had marched up to her room. He had two reasons, and two reasons only, to interact with her: the pavilion and the ceremony site. He'd promised his brother and Becky his help, and once the planning for his assigned tasks was solidly in place, he could minimize his interactions with her. He was about to get very busy with construction. That would leave much less time for contemplating the lovely Miss English.

"I hate to say it," he told Becky, looking at Tandu's back disappearing down a twisting path in front of them, "but I've already been over this stretch of the island. There is no—"

"This way, please." Tandu had stopped and was holding back thick jungle fronds. "Path overgrown a bit. I will tell gardening staff. Important for all to be ready for big day, eh?"

It was just a short walk, and the path opened onto a beautiful crescent of beach. Drew studied it from a construction point of view. He could see the high tide line, and it would be perfect for building a small pavilion and setting up chairs for the two hundred guests. Three large palms grew out of the center of the beach, their huge leathery leaves shading almost the entire area.

Becky, he could see, was looking at it from a far less practical standpoint than he was. She turned to look at him. Her eyes were shiny with delight, and those little plump lips were curved upward in the nicest smile.

Task completed! Drew told himself sternly. Pavilion, check. Wedding location, check. Missing brother...well, that had nothing to do with her. He had to get away from her—and her plump little lips—and *stay* away from her.

"It's perfect," he said. "Do you agree?"

She turned those shining eyes to him. "Agree?" she said softly. "Have you ever seen such a magical place in your whole life?"

He looked around with magic in mind rather than construction. He was not much of a magic kind of person, but he supposed he had not seen a place quite like this before. The whole beach was ringed with thick shrubs with dark green foliage. Tucked in amongst the foliage was an abundance of pale yellow and white flowers the size of cantaloupes. The flowers seemed to be emitting a perfume that was sweet and spicy at the same time. Unfortunately, that made him think of her lips again.

He glared at the sand, which was pure white and finer than sugar. They were in a cove of a small bay, and the water was striped in aqua shades of turquoise, all the way out to a reef, where the water turned dark navy blue, and the waves broke, white-capped, over rocks.

"Well," he said, "I'll just head back."

"Do you ever just answer a question?"

"Sit, sit," Tandu said from behind them.

Drew swung around to look at him. While he had been looking out toward the sea, Tandu had emptied the wicker basket he carried. There was a blanket set up in the sand, and laid out on it was a bottle of wine, beaded with sweat, two wineglasses and two plates. There was a platter of blackened chicken, fresh fruit and golden, steaming croissants.

"What the hell?" Drew asked.

"Sit, sit—amens…amens."

"I'm not following," Drew said. He saw that Becky had had no trouble whatsoever plopping herself down on the blanket. Had she forgotten she'd lost a whole day? She had to be seriously behind schedule.

"I make amens," Tandu said quietly, "for not doing first aid."

"Oh, *amends*," Drew said uncomfortably. "Really, it's not necessary at all. I have a ton of stuff to do. I'm not very hungry." This was a complete lie, though he had not realized quite how hungry he was until the food had *magically* appeared.

Tandu looked dejected that his offer was being refused.

"You very irritated with me," Tandu said sadly.

Becky caught his eye, lifted her shoulder—*come on, be a sport*—and patted the blanket. With a resigned shake of his head, Drew lowered himself onto the blanket. He bet if he ate one bite of this food that had been set out the spell would be complete.

"Look, I wasn't exactly irritated." This was as much a lie as the one about how he wasn't hungry, and he had a feeling Tandu was not easily fooled. "I was just a little surprised by a first aid man who doesn't like blood."

"Oh, yes," Tandu said happily. "Sit, sit, I fix."

"I am sitting. There's to nothing to fix." Except that Sainte Simone needed a new first aid attendant—before two hundred people descended on it would be good— but Drew found he did not have the heart to tell Tandu that.

Maybe the place was as magical as it looked, because he found himself unable to resist sitting beside Becky on the picnic blanket, though he told himself he had complied only because he did not want to disappoint Tandu, who had obviously misinterpreted his level of annoyance.

"I am not a first aid man," Tandu said. "Uh, how you say, medicine man? My family are healers. We see things."

"See things?" Drew asked. "I'm not following."

"Like a seer or a shaman?" Becky asked. She sounded thrilled.

Drew shot her a look. *Don't encourage him.* She ignored him. "Like what kind of things? Like the future?"

Drew groaned.

"Well, how did he know we needed a wedding site?" she challenged him.

"Because two hundred people are descending on this little piece of paradise for a marriage?"

She actually stuck one of her pointy little elbows in his ribs as if it was rude of him to point out the obvious.

"Yes, yes, like future," Tandu said, very pleased,

missing or ignoring Drew's skepticism and not seeing Becky's dig in his ribs. "See things."

"So what do you see for the wedding?" Becky asked eagerly, leaning forward, as if she was going to put a great deal of stock in the answer.

Tandu looked off into the distance. He suddenly did not look like a smiling servant in a white shirt. Not at all. His expression was intense, and when he turned his gaze back to them, his liquid brown eyes did not seem soft or merry anymore.

"Unexpected things," he said softly. "Lots of surprises. Very happy, very happy wedding. Everybody happy. Babies. Many, many babies in the future."

Becky clapped her hands with delight. "Drew, you're going to be an uncle."

"How very terrifying," he said drily. "Since you can see things, Tandu, when is my brother arriving?"

"Not when you expect," Tandu said, without hesitation.

"Thanks. Tell me something I don't know."

Tandu appeared to take that as a challenge. He gazed off into the distance again. Finally he spoke.

"Broken hearts mended," Tandu said with satisfaction.

"Whose broken hearts?" Becky asked, her eyes wide. "The bride? The groom?"

"For Pete's sake," Drew snapped.

Tandu did not look at him, but gazed steadily and silently at Becky.

"Oh," Becky said, embarrassed. "I don't have a broken heart."

Tandu cocked his head, considering. Drew found himself listening with uncomfortable intentness.

"You left your brokenness in the water," Tandu told Becky. "What you thought was true never was."

She gasped softly, then turned faintly accusing eyes to Drew. "Did you tell him what I said about Jerry?"

He was amazed how much it stung that she thought he would break her confidence. That accusing look in her eyes should be a good thing—it might cool the sparks that had leaped up between them.

But he couldn't leave well enough alone. "Of course not," he said.

"Well, then how did he know?"

"He's a seer," Drew reminded her with a certain amount of satisfaction.

Tandu seemed to have not heard one word of this conversation.

"But you need to swim," he told Becky. "Not be afraid of water. Water here very, very good swimming. Safe. Best swimming beach right here."

"Oh, that's a good idea," she said, turning her head to look at the inviting water, "but I'm not prepared."

"Prepared?" Tandu said, surprised. "What to prepare?"

"I don't have a swimming suit," Becky told him.

"At all?" Drew asked, despite himself. "Who comes to the Caribbean without a swimming suit?"

"I'm not here to play," she said with a stern toss of her head.

"God forbid," he said, but he could not help but feel she was a woman who seemed to take life way too seriously. Which, of course, was not his problem.

"I don't actually own a swimming suit," she said. "The nearest pool is a long way from Moose Run. We aren't close to a lake."

"Ha. Born with swimming suit," Tandu told her seriously. "Skin waterproof."

Drew watched with deep pleasure as the crimson crept up her neck to her cheeks. "Ha-ha," he said in an undertone, "that's what you get for encouraging him."

"You swim," Tandu told her. "Eat first, then swim. Mr. Drew help you."

"Naked swimming," Drew said. "Happy to help when I can. Tandu, do you see skinny-dipping in my future?"

There was that pointy little elbow in his ribs again, quite a bit harder than it had been the last time.

But before he could enjoy Becky's discomfort too much, suddenly Drew found himself pinned in Tandu's intense gaze. "The heart that is broken is yours, Mr. Drew?"

CHAPTER EIGHT

DREW JORDAN ORDERED himself to say no. No to magic. No to the light in Becky's eyes. And especially no to Tandu's highly invasive question. But instead of saying no, he found he couldn't speak at all, as if his throat was closing and his tongue was stuck to the roof of his mouth.

"They say a man is not given more than he can take, eh?" Tandu said.

If there was an expression on the face of the earth that Drew hated with his whole heart and soul it was that one, but he still found he could say nothing.

"But you were," Tandu said softly. "You were given more than you could take. You are a strong man. But not that strong, eh, Mr. Drew?"

His chest felt heavy. His throat felt as if it was closing. There was a weird stinging behind his eyes, as if he was allergic to the overwhelming scent of those flowers.

Without warning, he was back there.

He was seventeen years old. He was standing at the door of his house. It was the middle of the night. His feet and chest were bare and he had on pajama bottoms. He was blinking away sleep, trying to comprehend the

*stranger at the door of his house. The policeman said,
"I'm sorry, son." And then Drew found out he wasn't
anyone's son, not anymore.*

Drew shook his head and looked at Tandu, fiercely.

"You heal now," Tandu said, not intimidated, as if
it was an order. "You heal." And then suddenly Tandu
was himself again, the easygoing grin on his face, his
teeth impossibly perfect and white against the golden
brown of his skin. His eyes were gentle and warm. "Eat,
eat. Then swim. Then sunset."

And then he was gone.

"What was that about?" Becky asked him.

"I don't have a clue," he said. His voice sounded
strange to him, choked and hoarse. "Creepy weirdness."

Becky was watching him as if she knew it was a lie.
When had he become such a liar? He'd better give it
up, he was terrible at it. He poured two glasses of wine,
handed her one and tossed back the other. He set down
the glass carefully.

"There. I've toasted the wedding spot. I'm going to
go now." He didn't move.

"Have you?" she asked.

"Have I what? Toasted the wedding spot?"

"Had a heartbreak?" she asked softly, with concern.

And he felt, suddenly, as alone with his burdens as he
had ever felt. He felt as if he could lay it all at her feet.
He looked at the warmth and loveliness of her brushed-
suede eyes. *You heal now.*

He reeled back from the invitation in her eyes. He
was the most pragmatic of men. He was not under the
enchantment of this beach, or Tandu's words, or her.

Not yet, an inner voice informed him cheerfully.

Not ever, he informed the inner voice with no cheer

at all. He was not touching that food with its potential to weaken him even further. And no more wine.

"People like me," he said, forcing a cavalier ease into his voice.

She leaned toward him.

"We don't have hearts to break. I'm leaving now." Still, he did not move.

She looked as if she wanted to argue with that, but she took one look at his face and very wisely turned her attention to the chicken. "Is this burned?" she asked, poking one of the pieces gingerly with her fingertip.

"I think it's jerked, a very famous way of cooking on these islands." It felt like a relief to focus on the chicken instead of what was going on inside himself.

She took a piece and nibbled it. Her expression changed to one of complete awe. "You have to try it," she insisted. "You have to try it and tell me if it isn't the best thing you have ever tasted. Just one bite before you go."

Despite knowing this food probably had a spell woven right into it, he threw caution to the wind, picked up a leg of chicken and chomped into it. Just a few hours ago it definitely would have been the best thing he had ever tasted. But now that he was under a spell, he saw things differently.

Because the blackened jerk chicken quite possibly might have been the best thing he'd ever tasted, if he hadn't very foolishly sampled her lips when she had offered them yesterday afternoon.

"You might as well stay and eat," she said. She reached over and refilled his empty wineglass. "It would be a shame to let it go to waste."

He was not staying here, eating enchanted food in

an enchanted cove with a woman who was clearly putting a spell on him. On the other hand, she was right. It would be a shame to let the food go to waste.

There was no such thing as spells, anyway. He picked up his second piece of chicken. He watched her delicately lick her fingertips.

"We don't have this kind of food in Moose Run," she said. "More's the pity."

"What kind of food do you have?" He was just being polite, he told himself, before he left her. He frowned. That second glass of wine could not be gone.

"We have two restaurants. We have the Main Street Diner which specializes in half-pound hamburgers and claims to have the best chocolate milk shake in all of Michigan."

"Claims?"

"I haven't tried all the chocolate milk shakes in Michigan," she said. "But believe me, I'm working on it."

He felt something relax within him. He should not be relaxing. He needed to keep his guard up. Still, he laughed at her earnest expression.

"And then we have Mr. Wang's All-You-Can-Eat Spectacular Smorgasbord."

"So, two restaurants. What else do you do for fun?"

She looked uncomfortable. It was none of his business, he told himself firmly. Why did he care if it was just as he'd suspected? She did not have nearly enough fun going on in her life. Not that it was any concern of his.

"Is there a movie theater?" he coaxed her.

"Yes. And don't forget the church picnic."

"And dancing on the grass," he supplied.

"I'm not much for the church socials, actually. I don't really like dancing."

"So what do you like?"

She hesitated, and then met his eyes. "I'm sure you are going to think I am the world's most boring person, but you know what I really do for fun?"

He felt as if he was holding his breath for some reason. Crazy to hope the answer was going to involve kissing. Not that anyone would consider that boring, would they? Was his wineglass full again? He took a sip.

"I read," she said, in a hushed whisper, as if she was in a confessional. She sighed. "I love to read."

What a relief! Reading, not kissing! It should have seemed faintly pathetic, but somehow, just like the rest of her, it seemed real. In an amusement park world where everyone was demanding to be entertained constantly, by bigger things and better amusements and wilder rides and greater spectacles, by things that stretched the bounds of what humans were intended to do, it seemed lovely that Becky had her own way of being in the world, and that something so simple as opening a book could make someone contented.

She was bracing herself, as if she expected him to be scornful. It made him wonder if the ex-beau had been one of those put-down kind of guys.

"I can actually picture you out in a hammock on a sunny afternoon," he said. "It sounds surprisingly nice."

"At this time of year, it's a favorite chair. On my front porch. We still have front porches in Moose Run."

He could picture a deeply shaded porch, and a sleepy street, and hear the sound of birds. This, too, struck him as deliciously simple in a complicated world. "What's your favorite book?" he asked.

"I have to pick one?" she asked with mock horror.

"Let me put it differently. If you had to recommend a book to someone who hardly ever reads, which one would it be?"

And somehow it was that easy. The food was disappearing and so was the wine, and she was telling him about her favorite books and authors, and he was telling her about surfing the big waves and riding his motorbike on the Pacific Coast Highway between LA and San Francisco.

The fight seemed to ease out of him, and the wariness. The urgent need to be somewhere else seemed silly. Drew felt himself relaxing. Why not enjoy it? It was no big deal. Tomorrow his crew would be here. He would immerse himself in his work. He could enjoy this last evening with Becky before that happened, couldn't he?

Who would have ever guessed it would be so easy to be with a man like this? Becky thought. The conversation was comfortable between them. There was so much work that needed to be done on Allie's wedding, and she had already lost a precious day. Still, she had never felt less inclined to do work.

But as comfortable as it all was, she could feel a little nudge of disappointment. How could they go from that electrifying kiss, to this?

Not that she wanted the danger of that kiss again, but she certainly didn't want him to think she was a dull small-town girl whose idea of an exciting evening was sitting out on her front porch reading until the fireflies came out.

Dinner was done. The wine bottle was lying on its

side, empty. All that was left of the chicken was bones,
and all that was left of the croissants were a few golden
crumbs. As she watched, Drew picked one of those up
on his fingertip and popped it in his mouth.

How could such a small thing be so darned sexy?

In her long pants and long-sleeved shirt, Becky was
suddenly aware of feeling way too warm. And over-
dressed. She was aware of being caught in the enchantment of Sainte Simone and this beautiful beach. She
longed to be free of encumbrances.

Like clothing? she asked herself, appalled, but not
appalled enough to stop the next words that came out
of her mouth.

"Let's go for that swim after all," she said. She tried
to sound casual, but her heart felt as if she had just finished running a marathon.

"I really need to go." He said it without any kind of
conviction. "Are you going to swim in nature's bathing suit?"

"Don't be a pervert!"

"I'm not. Tandu suggested it. One-hundred-percent
waterproof."

"Don't look," she said.

"Sure. I'll stop breathing while I'm at it."

What was she doing? she asked herself.

For once in her life, she was acting on a whim, that's
what she was doing. For once in her life she was being
bold, that's what she was doing. For once in her life, she
was throwing convention to the wind, she was doing
what she wanted to do. She was not leaving him with
the impression she was a dull small-town girl who had
spent her whole life with her nose buried in a book.
Even if she had been!

She didn't want that to be the whole truth about her anymore, and not just because of him, either. Because the incident in the water yesterday, that moment when she had looked her own death in the face and somehow been spared, had left her with a longing for second chances.

She stood up and turned her back to him. Becky took a deep breath and peeled her shirt over her head, then unbuckled her slacks and stepped out of them. She had on her luxurious Rembrandt's Drawing brand underwear. The underwear was a matching set, a deep shade of turquoise not that different from the water. It was as fashionable as most bathing suits, and certainly more expensive.

She glanced over her shoulder, and his expression—stunned, appreciative, approving—made her run for the water. She splashed in up to her knees, and then threw herself in. The water closed over her head, and unlike yesterday afternoon, it felt wonderful in the heat of the early evening, cool and silky as a caress on her nearly naked skin.

She surfaced, then paddled out and found her footing when she was up to her neck in water, her underwear hidden from him. She turned to look at where he was still sitting on the blanket. Even from here, she could see the heat in his eyes.

Oh, girlfriend, she thought, *you do not know what you are playing with.* But the thing about letting a bolder side out was that it was very hard to stuff it back in, like trying to get a jack-in-the-box back in its container.

"Come in," she called. "It's glorious."

He stood up slowly and peeled his shirt off. She held

her breath. It was her turn to be stunned, appreciative and approving.

She had seen him without his shirt already when he had sacrificed it to doctor her leg. But this was different. She wasn't in shock, or in pain, or bleeding all over the place.

Becky was aware, as she had been when she had first laid eyes on him, that he was the most beautifully made of men. Broad shouldered and deep chested, muscular without being muscle-bound. He could be an actor or a model, because he had that mysterious something that made her—and probably every other woman on earth— feel as if she could look at him endlessly, drink in his masculine perfection as if he was a long, cool drink of water and she was dying of thirst.

Was he going to take off his shorts? She was aware she was holding her breath. But no, he kicked off his shoes and, with the khaki shorts safely in place, ran toward the water. Like she had done, he ran in up to about his thighs and then she watched as he dived beneath the surface.

"I didn't peg you for shy," she told him when he surfaced close to her.

He lifted an eyebrow at her.

"I've seen men's underwear before. I'm from Moose Run, not the convent."

"You've mentioned you weren't a nun once before," he said. "What's with the fascination with nuns?"

"You just seem to think because I'm small town I'm prim and proper. You didn't have to get your shorts all wet to save my sensibilities."

"I don't wear underwear."

Her mouth fell open. She could feel herself turning crimson. He laughed, delighted at her discomfort.

"How are your sensibilities doing now?" he asked her.

"Fine," she squeaked. But they both knew it was a lie, and he laughed.

"Come on," he said, shaking the droplets of water from his hair. "I'll race you to those rocks."

"That's ridiculous. I don't have a hope of winning."

"I know," he said fiendishly.

"I get a head start."

"All right."

"A big one."

"Okay, you tell me when I can go."

She paddled her way toward the rocks. When it seemed there was no chance he could catch her, she called, "Okay, go."

She could hear him coming up behind her. She paddled harder. He grabbed her foot!

"Hey!" She went under the water. He let go of her foot, and when she surfaced, he had surged by her and was touching the rock.

"You cheater," she said indignantly.

"You're the cheater. What kind of head start was that?"

"Watch who you are calling a cheater." She reached back her arm and splashed him, hard. He splashed her back. The war was on.

Tandu had been so right. She needed to leave whatever fear she had remaining in the water.

And looking at Drew's face, she realized, her fear was not about drowning. It was about caring for someone else, as if pain was an inherent ingredient to that.

Becky could see that if she had not let go enough in

life, neither had he. Seeing him like this, playful, his face alight with laugher and mischief, she realized he did carry some burden, like a weight, just as Tandu had suggested. Drew had put down his burden for a bit, out here in the water, and she was glad she had encouraged him to come swim with her.

She wondered what his terrible burden was. Could he really have been given more than he thought he could handle? He seemed so unbelievably strong. But then again, wasn't that what made strength, being challenged to your outer limits? She wondered if he would ever confide in her, but then he splashed her in the face and took off away from her, and she took chase, and the serious thoughts were gone.

A half hour later, exhausted, they dragged themselves up on the beach. Just as he had promised, the trades came up, and it was surprisingly chilly on her wet skin and underwear. She tried to pull her clothes over her wet underwear, but it was more difficult than she thought. Finally, with her clothes clinging to her uncomfortably, she turned to him.

He had pulled his shirt back on over his wet chest and was putting the picnic things back in the basket.

"We have to go," she said. "I feel guilty."

"Tut-tut," he said. "There's that nun thing again. But I have to go, too. My crew is arriving first thing in the morning. I'd like to have things set up so we can get right to work. You're a terrible influence on me, Sister English."

"Sister Simone, to you."

He didn't appear to be leaving, and neither did she.

"I am so far behind in what I need to get done," Becky said. "I didn't expect to be here this long. If I go to work right now, I can still make a few phone calls. What time do you think it is in New York?"

"Look what I just found."

Did he ever just answer the question?

He had been rummaging in the picnic basket and he held up two small mason jars that looked as if they were filled with whipped cream and strawberries.

"What is that?" Knowing the time in New York suddenly didn't seem important at all.

"I think it's dessert."

She licked her lips. He stared at them, before looking away.

"I guess a little dessert wouldn't hurt," she said. Her voice sounded funny, low and seductive, as if she had said something faintly naughty.

"Just sit in the sand," he suggested. "We'll wrap the picnic blanket over our shoulders. We might as well eat dessert and watch the sun go down. What's another half hour now?"

They were going to sit shoulder to shoulder under a blanket eating dessert and watching the sun go down? It was better than any book she had ever read! The time in New York—and all her other responsibilities—did a slow fade-out, as if it was the end of a movie.

CHAPTER NINE

BECKY PLUNKED HERSELF down like a dog at obedience class who was eager for a treat. Drew picked up the blanket and placed it carefully over her shoulders, then sat down in the sand beside her and pulled part of the blanket over his own shoulders. His shoulder felt warm and strong where her skin was touching it. The chill left her almost instantly.

He pried the lid off one of the jars and handed it to her with a spoon.

"Have you ever been to Hawaii?" He took the lid off the other jar.

"No, I'm sorry to say I haven't been. Have you?"

"I've done jobs there. It's very much like this, the climate, the foliage, the breathtaking beauty. Everything stops at sunset. Even if you're still working against an impossible deadline, you just stop and face the sun. It's like every single person stops and every single thing stops. This stillness comes over everything. It's like the deepest form of gratitude I've ever experienced. It's this thank-you to life."

"I feel that right now," she said, with soft reverence. "Maybe because I nearly drowned, I feel so intensely alive and so intensely grateful."

No need to mention sharing this evening with him might have something to do with feeling so intensely alive.

"Me, too," he said softly.

Was it because of her he felt this way? She could feel the heat of his shoulder where it was touching hers. She desperately wanted to kiss him again. She gobbled up strawberries and cream instead. It just made her long, even more intensely, for the sweetness of his lips.

"I am going to hell in a handbasket," she muttered, but still she snuggled under the blanket and looked at where the sun, now a huge orb of gold, was hovering over the ocean.

He shot her a look. "Why would you say that?"

Because she was enjoying him so much, when she, of all people, was so well versed in all the dangers of romance.

"Because I am sitting here watching the sun go down when I should be getting to work," she clarified with a half-truth. "I knew Allie's faith in me was misplaced."

"Why would you say that?"

"I'm just an unlikely choice for such a huge undertaking."

"So, why did she pick you, then?"

"I hadn't seen her, or even had a note from her, since she moved away from Moose Run." Becky sighed and pulled the blanket tighter around her shoulders. "Everyone in Moose Run claims to have been friends with Allison Anderson *before* she became Allie Ambrosia the movie star, but really they weren't. Allison was lonely and different, and many of those people who now claim to have been friends with her were actually exceptionally intolerant of her eccentricities.

"Her mom must have been one of the first internet daters. She came to Moose Run and moved in with Pierce Clemens, which anybody could have told her was a bad bet. Allie, with her body piercings and colorful hair and hippie skirts, was just way too exotic for Moose Run. She only lived there for two years, and she and I only had a nodding acquaintance for most of that time. We were in the same grade, but I was in advanced classes."

"That's a surprise," he teased drily.

"You could have knocked me over with a feather when I got an out-of-the-blue phone call from her a couple of weeks ago and she outlined her ambitious plans. She told me she was putting together a guest list of two hundred people and that she wanted it to be so much more than a wedding. She wants her guests to have an *experience*. The island was hers for an entire week after the wedding, and she wanted all the guests to stay and have fun, either relaxing or joining in on organized activities.

"You know what she suggested for activities? Volleyball tournaments and wienie roasts around a campfire at night, maybe fireworks! You're from there. Does that strike you as Hollywood?"

"No," he said. "Not at all. Hollywood would be Jet Skis during the day and designer dresses at night. It would be entertainment by Cirque and Shania and wine tasting and spa treatments on the beach."

"That's what I thought. But she was adamant about what she wanted. I couldn't help but think that Allie's ideas of fun, despite this exotic island setting, are those of a girl who had been largely excluded from the teen cliques who went together to the Fourth of July activities. She seems, talking to her, to be more in sync with the small-town tastes of Moose Run than with lifestyles of the rich and famous."

"It actually makes me like her more," he said reluctantly.

"I asked her if what she wanted was like summer camp for adults, to make sure I was getting it right. She said—" Becky imitated the famous actress's voice "—'Exactly! I knew I could count on you to get it right.'"

Drew chuckled at Becky's imitation of Allie, which encouraged her to be even more foolish. She did both voices, as if she was reading for several parts in a play.

"Allie, I'm not sure I'm up to this. My event company has become the go-to company for local weddings and anniversaries, but— 'Of course you are up to it, do you think I don't do my homework? You did that great party for the lawyer's kid. Ponies!'

"She said *ponies* with the same enthusiasm she said *fireworks* with," Becky told Drew ruefully. "I think she actually wanted ponies. So I said, 'Um…it would be hard to get ponies to an island—and how did you know that? About the party for Mr. Williams's son?' And she said, 'I do my research. I'm not quite as flaky as the roles I get might make you think.' Of course, I told her I never thought she was flaky, but she cut me off and told me she was sending a deposit. I tried to talk her out of it. I said a six-week timeline was way too short to throw together a wedding for two hundred people. I told her I would have to delegate all my current contracts to take it on. She just insisted. She said she would make it worth my while. I told her I just wasn't sure, and she said she was, and that I was perfect for the job."

"You were trying to get out of the opportunity of a lifetime?" Drew weighed in, amused.

"Was I ever. But then her lighthearted delivery kind of changed and she said I was the only reason she survived Moose Run at all. She asked me if I remembered the day we became friends."

"Did you?"

"Pretty hard to forget. A nasty group of boys had her backed into the corner in that horrid place at the high school where we used to all go to smoke.

"I mean, I didn't go there to smoke. I was Moose Run High's official Goody Two-shoes."

"No kidding," he said drily. "Do not elbow my ribs again. They are seriously bruised."

They sat there in companionable silence for a few minutes. The sun demanded their stillness and their silence. The sunset was at its most glorious now, painting the sky around it in shades of orange and pink that were reflecting on a band on the ocean, that seemed to lead a pathway of light right to them. Then the sun was gone, leaving only an amazing pastel palette staining the sky.

"Go on," he said.

Becky thought she was talking too much. Had they really drunk that whole bottle of wine between the two of them? Still, it felt nice to have someone to talk to, someone to listen.

"I was taking a shortcut to the library—"

"Naturally," he said with dry amusement.

"And I came across Bram Butler and his gang tormenting poor Allie. I told them to cut it out.

"Allie remembers me really giving it to them. She told me that for a long time she has always thought of me as having the spirit of a gladiator."

"I'll attest to that," he said. "I have the bruises on my ribs to prove it." And then his tone grew more serious. "And you never gave up in the water yesterday, either."

"That was because of you. Believe me, I am the little bookworm I told you I was earlier. I do not have the spirit of a gladiator."

Though she did have some kind of unexpected spirit of boldness that had made her, very uncharacteristically, rip off her clothes and go into the water.

"How many guys were there?"

"Hmm, it was years ago, but I think maybe four. No, five."

"What were they doing?"

"They kind of had her backed up against a wall. She was quite frightened. I think that stupid Bram was trying to kiss her. He's always been a jerk. He's my second cousin."

"And you just waded right in there, with five high school guys being jerks? That seems brave."

She could not allow herself to bask in his admiration, particularly since it was undeserved.

"I didn't exactly wade right in there. I used the Moose Run magic words."

"Which were?"

"Bram Butler, you stop it right now or I'll tell your mother."

He burst out laughing, and then so did she. She noticed that it had gotten quite dark. The wind had died. Already stars were rising in the sky.

"Allie and I hung out a bit after that," she said. "She was really interesting. At that time, she wanted to be a clothing designer. We used to hole up in my room and draw dresses."

"What kind of dresses?"

"Oh, you know. Prom. Evening. That kind of thing. Allie and her mom moved away shortly after that. She said we would keep in touch—that she would send me her new address and phone number—but she never did."

"You and Allie drew wedding dresses, didn't you?"

"What would make you say that?" Becky could feel a blush rising, but why should she have to apologize for her younger self?

"I'm trying to figure out if she has some kind of wedding fantasy that my brother just happened into."

"Lots of young women have romantic fantasies. And then someone comes along to disillusion them."

"Like your Jerry," he said. "Tell me about that."

"So little to tell," she said wryly. "We lived down the street from one another, we started the first grade together. When we were seventeen he asked me to go to the Fourth of July celebrations with him. He held my hand. We kissed. And there you have it, my whole future mapped out for me. We were just together after that. I wanted exactly what I grew up with, until my dad left. Up until then my family had been one of those solid, dull families that makes the world feel so, so safe.

"An illusion," she said sadly. "It all ended up being such an illusion, but I felt determined to prove it could be real. Jerry went away to college and I started my own business, and it just unraveled, bit by bit. It's quite humiliating to have a major breakup in a small town."

"I bet."

"When I think about it, the humiliation actually might have been a lot harder to handle than the fact that I was not going to share my life with Jerry. It was like a second blow. I had just barely gotten over being on the receiving end of the pitying looks over my dad's scandal."

"Are you okay with your dad's relationship now?"

"I wish I was. But they still live in Moose Run, and I have an adorable little sister who I am pathetically jealous of. They seem so happy. My mom is still a mess. Aside from working in the hardware store, she'd never even had a job."

"And you rushed in to become the family breadwinner," he said.

"It's not a bad thing, is it?"

"An admirable thing. And kind of sad."

His hand found hers and he gave it a squeeze. He didn't let go again.

"Were you thinking of Jerry when you were drawing those dresses?" he finally asked softly.

"No," she said slowly, "I don't think I was."

She suddenly remembered one dress in particular that Allie had drawn. *This is your wedding dress*, she had proclaimed, giving it to Becky.

It had been a confection, sweetheart neckline, fitted bodice, layers and layers and layers of filmy fabric flowing out in that full skirt with an impossible train. The dress had been the epitome of her every romantic notion. Becky had been able to picture herself in that dress, swirling in front of a mirror, giggling. But she had never, not even once, pictured herself in that dress walking down an aisle toward Jerry.

When Jerry had broken it to her that her "business was changing her"—in other words, he could not handle her success—and he wanted his ring back, she had never taken that drawing from where it was tucked in the back of one of her dresser drawers.

"I've talked too much," she said. "It must have been the wine."

"I don't think you talked too much."

"I usually don't confide in people so readily." She suddenly felt embarrassed. "Your name should be a clue."

"To?"

"You *drew* my secrets right out of me."

"Ah."

"We have to go now," she said.

"Yes, we do," he said.

"Before something happens," she said softly.

"Especially before that," he agreed just as softly.

Her hand was still in his. Their shoulders were touching. The breeze was lifting the leathery fronds of the palm trees and they were whispering songs without words. The sky was now almost completely black, and finding their way back was not going to be easy.

"Really," Becky said. "We need to go."

"Really," he agreed. "We do.

Neither of them moved.

CHAPTER TEN

DREW ORDERED HIMSELF to get up and leave this beach. But it was one of those completely irresistible moments: the stars winking on in the sky, their shoulders touching, the taste of strawberries and cream on his lips, the gentle lap of the waves against the shore, her small hand resting within the sanctuary of his larger one.

He turned slightly to look at her. She was turning to look at him.

It seemed like the most natural thing in the world to drop his head over hers, to taste her lips again.

Her arms came up and twined around his neck. Her lips were soft and pliant and welcoming.

He could taste everything she was in that kiss. She was bookish. And she was bold. She was simple, and she was complex. She was, above all else, a forever kind of girl.

It was that knowledge that made him untangle her hands from around his neck, to force his lips away from the soft promise of hers.

You heal now.

He swore under his breath, scrambled to his feet. "I'm sorry," he said.

"Are you?"

Well, not really. "Look, Becky, we have known each other for a shockingly short period of time. Obviously circumstances have made us feel things about each other a little too quickly."

She looked unconvinced.

"I mean, in Moose Run, you probably have a date or two before you kiss like that."

"What about in LA?"

He thought about how fast things could go in Los Angeles and how superficial that was, and how he was probably never going to be satisfied with it again. Less than forty-eight hours, and Becky English, bookworm, was changing everything in his world.

What was his world going to look like in two weeks if this kept up?

The answer was obvious. This could not keep up.

"Look, Becky, I obviously like you. And find you extremely attractive."

Did she look pleased? He did not want her to look pleased!

"There is obviously some kind of chemistry going on between us."

She looked even more pleased.

"But both of us have jobs to do. We have very little time to do those jobs in. We can't afford a, um, complication like this."

She stared at him, uncomprehending.

"It's not professional, Becky," he said gruffly. "Kissing on the job is not professional."

She looked as if he had slapped her. And then she just looked crushed.

"Oh," she stammered. "Of course, you're right."

He felt a terrible kind of self-loathing that she was taking it on, as if it were her fault.

She pulled herself together and jumped up, doing what he suspected she always did. Trying to fix the whole world. Her clothes were still wet. Her pink blouse looked as though red roses were blooming on it where it was clinging to that delectable set of underwear that he should never have seen, and was probably never going to be able to get out of his mind.

"I don't know what's gotten into me. It must still be the aftereffects of this afternoon. And the wine. I want you to know I don't usually rip my clothes off around men. In fact, that's extremely uncharacteristic. And I'm usually not such a blabbermouth. Not at all."

Her voice was wobbling terribly.

"No, it's not you," he rushed to tell her. "It's not. It's me, I—"

"I've given you the impression I'm—what did you call it earlier—wanton!"

"I told you at the time I was overstating it. I told you that was the wrong word."

She held up her hand, stopping him. "No, I take responsibility. You don't know how sorry I am."

And then she rushed by him, found the path through the darkened jungle and disappeared.

Perfect, he thought. He'd gotten rid of her before things got dangerously out of control. But it didn't feel perfect. He felt like a bigger jerk than the chicken they had eaten for supper.

She had fled up that path—away from him—with extreme haste, probably hoping to keep the truth from him. That she was crying.

But that's what I am, Drew told himself. He was a

jerk. Just ask his brother, who not only wasn't arriving on the island, but who also was not taking his phone calls.

The truth was, Drew Jordan sucked at relationships. It was good Becky had run off like that, for her own protection, and his. It would have been better if he could have thought of a way to make her believe it was his fault instead of hers, though.

Sitting there, alone, in the sand, nearly choking on his own self-loathing, Drew thought of his mother. He could picture her: the smile, the way she had made him feel, that way she had of cocking her head and listening so intently when he was telling her something. He realized the scent he had detected earlier had reminded him of her perfume.

The truth was, he was shocked to be thinking of her. Since that day he had become both parents to his younger brother, he had tried not to think of his mom and dad. It was just too painful. Losing them—everything, really, his whole world—was what life had given him that was too much to bear.

But the tears in Becky's eyes that she had been holding back so valiantly, and the scent in the air, made him think of his mother. Only in his mind, his mother wasn't cocking her head, listening intently to him with that soft look of wonder that only a mother can have for her offspring.

No, it felt as if his mother was somehow near him, but that her hands were on her hips and she was looking at him with total exasperation.

His mother, he knew, would never have approved of the fact he had made that decent, wholesome young woman from Moose Run, Michigan, cry. She would be really angry with him if he excused his behavior by saying, *But it was for her own good.* His mother, if she was here, would remind him of all the hurt that Becky had already suffered at the hands of men.

She would show him Becky, trying to keep her head up as her father pushed a stroller down the main street of Moose Run, as news got out that the wedding planner's own wedding was a bust.

Sitting there in the sand with the stars coming out over him, Drew felt he was facing some hard truths about himself. Would his mother even approve of the man he had become? Work-obsessed, so emotionally unavailable he had driven his brother right out of his life and into the first pair of soft arms that offered comfort. His mother wouldn't like it one bit that not only was he failing to protect his brother from certain disaster, his brother would not even talk to him.

"So," he asked out loud, "what would you have me do?"

Be a better man.

It wasn't her voice. It was just the gentle breeze stirring the palm fronds. It was just the waves lapping onshore. It was just the call of the night birds.

But is that what her voice had become? Everything? Was his mother's grace and goodness now in everything? Including him?

Drew scrambled out of the sand. He picked up the picnic basket and the blanket and began to run.

"Becky! Becky!"

When he caught up with her, he was breathless. She was walking fast, her head down.

"Becky," he said, and then softly, "Please."

She spun around. She stuck her chin up in the air.

But she could not hide the fact that he was right. She had been crying.

"I didn't mean to hurt your feelings," he said. "I'm the one in the wrong here, not you."

"Thank you," she said icily. "That is very chivalrous of you. However the facts speak for themselves."

Chivalrous. Who used that in a sentence? And why did it make him feel as if he wanted to set down the picnic basket, gather her in his arms and hold her hard?

"Facts?"

"Yes, facts," she said in that clipped tone of voice. "They speak for themselves."

"They do?"

She nodded earnestly. "It seems to me I've just dragged you along with my *wanton* behavior, kissing you, tearing off my clothes. You were correct. It is not professional. And it won't be happening again."

He knew that it not happening again was a good thing, so why did he feel such a sense of loss?

"Becky, I handled that badly."

"There's a good way to handle 'keep your lips off me'?"

He had made her feel rejected. He had done to her what every other man in her life had done to her: given her the message that somehow she didn't measure up, she wasn't good enough.

He rushed to try to repair the damage.

"It's not that I don't want your lips on me," he said. "I do. I mean I don't. I mean we can't. I mean I won't."

She cocked her head, and looked askance at him.

"Do I sound like an idiot?" he said.

"Yes," she said, unforgivingly.

"What I'm trying to say, Becky, is I'm not used to women like you."

"What kind of women are you used to?"

"Guess," he said in a low voice.

She did not appear to want to guess.

He raked his hand through his hair, trying desperately to think of a way to make her get it that would somehow erase those tearstains from her cheeks.

"I'm scared I'll hurt you," he said, his voice gravelly in his own ears. "I don't think it's a good idea to move this fast. Let's back up a step or two. Let's just be friends. First."

He had no idea where that *first* had come from. It implied there would be something following the friendship. But really, that was impossible. And he just had to get through what remained of two weeks without hurting her any more than he already had. He could play at being the better man for eleven damn days. He was almost sure of it.

"Do you ever answer a question?" she asked. "What kind of women are you used to?"

"Ones who are as shallow as me," he said.

"You aren't shallow!"

"You don't know that about me."

"I do," she said firmly.

He sucked in his breath and tried again. Why was she insisting on seeing him as a better man when he did not deserve that? "Ones who don't expect happily-ever-after."

"Oh."

"You see, Becky, my parents died when I was seventeen." *Shut up*, he ordered himself. *Stop it.* "It broke something in me. The sense of loss was just as Tandu said this afternoon. It was too great to bear. When I've had relationships, and it's true, I have, they have been deliberately superficial."

Becky went very still. Her eyes looked wide and beautiful in the starlight that filtered through the thick leaves of the jungle. She took a step toward him. And she reached up and laid the palm of her hand on his cheek.

Her touch was extraordinary. He had to shut his eyes against his reaction to the tenderness in it. In some ways it was more intimate than the kisses they had shared.

"Because you cannot handle one more loss," she guessed softly.

Drew opened his eyes and stared at Becky. It felt as if she could see his soul and was not the least frightened by what she saw there.

This was going sideways! He was not going to answer that. He could not. If he answered that, he would want to lay his head on her shoulder and feel her hand in his hair. He would want to suck up her tenderness like a dry sponge sucking up moisture. If he answered that he would become weak, instead of what he needed to be most.

He needed to be strong. Since he'd been seventeen years old, he had needed to be strong. And it wasn't until just this minute he was seeing that as a burden he wanted to lay down.

"I agree," she said softly, dropping her hand away from his cheek. "We just need to be friends."

His relief was abject. She got it. He was too damaged to be any good for a girl like her.

Only then she went and spoiled his relief by standing on her tiptoes and kissing him on the cheek where her hand had lay with such tender healing. She whispered something in his ear.

And he was pretty sure it was the word *first*.

And then she turned and scampered across the moon-lit lawn to the castle door and disappeared inside it.

And he had to struggle not to touch his cheek, where the tenderness of her kiss lingered like a promise.

You heal now.

But he couldn't. He knew that. He could do his best to honor the man his mother had raised him to be, to not cause Becky any more harm, but he knew that his own salvation was beyond what he could hope for.

Because really in the end, for a man like him, wasn't hope the most dangerous thing of all?

CHAPTER ELEVEN

BECKY LISTENED TO the sound of hammers, the steady *ratta-tat-tat* riding the breeze through the open window of her office. When had that sound become like music to her?

She told herself, sternly, she could not give in to the temptation, but it was useless. It was as if a cord circled her waist and tugged her toward the window.

This morning, Drew's crew had arrived, but not his brother. They had arrived ready to work, and in hours the wedding pavilion was taking shape on the emerald green expanse of the front lawn. They'd dug holes and poured the cement they had mixed by hand out of bags. Then they had set the posts—which had arrived by helicopter—into those holes.

She had heard helicopters delivering supplies all morning. It sounded like a MASH unit around here.

Now she peeped out the window. In all that activity, her eyes sought him. Her heart went to her throat. Drew, facing the ocean, was straddling a beam. He had to be fifteen feet off the ground, his legs hanging into nothingness. He had a baseball cap on backward and his shirt off.

His skin was sun-kissed and perfect, his back broad

and powerful. He was a picture of male strength and confidence.

She could barely breathe he was so amazing to look at. It was also wonderful to be able to look at him without his being aware of it! She could study the sleek lines of his naked back at her leisure.

"You have work to do," she told herself. Drew, as if he sensed someone watching, turned and glanced over his shoulder, directly at her window. She drew back into the shadows, embarrassed, and pleased, too. Was he looking to glimpse her? Did it fill him with this same sense of delight? Anticipation? Longing?

Reluctantly, she turned her back to the scene, but only long enough to try to drag her desk over to the window. She could multitask. The desk was very heavy. She grunted with exertion.

"Miss Becky?" Tandu was standing in the doorway with a tray. "Why you miss lunch?"

"Oh, I—" For some reason she had felt shy about lunch, knowing that Drew and his crew would be eating in the dining room. Despite their agreement last night to be friends, her heart raced out of control when she thought of his rescue of her, and eating dinner with him on the picnic blanket last night, and swimming with him. But mostly, she thought of how their lips had met. Twice.

How was she going to choke down a sandwich around him? How was she going to behave appropriately with his crew looking on? Anybody with a heartbeat would take one look at her—them—and know that something primal was sizzling in the air between them.

This was what she had missed by being with Jerry

for so long. She had missed all the years when she
should have been learning the delicate nuances of how
to conduct a relationship with a member of the opposite sex.

Not that it was going to be a relationship. A friendship. She thought of Drew's lips. She wondered how a
friendship was going to be possible.

There must be a happy medium between wanton and
so shy she couldn't even eat lunch with him!

"What you doing?" Tandu asked, looking at the desk
she had managed to move about three feet across the
room.

"The breeze!" she said, too emphatically. "I thought
I might get a better breeze if I moved the desk."

Tandu set down the lunch tray. With his help it was
easier to wrestle the big piece of furniture into its new
location.

He looked out the window. "Nice view," he said with
wicked amusement. "Eat lunch, enjoy the view. Then
you are needed at helicopter pad. Cargo arriving. Many,
many boxes."

"I have a checklist. I'll be down shortly. And Tandu,
could you think of a few places for wedding photographs? I mean, the beaches are lovely, but if I could
preview a few places for the photographer, that would
be wonderful."

"Know exactly the place," he said delightedly. "Waterfall."

"Yes!" she said.

"I'll draw you a map."

"Thank you. A waterfall!"

"Now eat. Enjoy the view."

She did eat, and she did enjoy the view. It was actually much easier to get to work when she could just glance up and watch Drew, rather than making a special trip away from her desk and to the window.

Later that afternoon, she headed down to the helicopter loading dock with her checklist and began sorting through the boxes and muttering to herself.

"Candles? Check. Centerpieces? Check."

"Hi there." She swung around.

Drew was watching her, a little smile playing across his handsome features.

"Hello." Oh, God, did she have to sound so formal and geeky?

"Do you always catch your tongue between your teeth like that when you are lost in thought?"

She hadn't been aware she was doing it, and pulled her tongue back into her mouth. He laughed. She blushed.

"The pavilion is looking great," she said, trying to think of something—anything—to say. She was as tongue-tied as if she were a teenager meeting her secret crush unexpectedly at the supermarket!

"Yeah, my guys are pretty amazing, aren't they?"

She had not really spared a glance to any of the other guys. "Amazing," she agreed.

"I just thought I'd check and see if the fabric for draping the pavilion has arrived. I need to come up with a method for hanging it."

"I'll look."

But he was already sorting through boxes, tossing them with easy strength. "This might be it. It's from a fabric store. There's quite a few boxes here." He took a box cutter out of his shirt pocket and slit open one of the boxes. "Come see."

She sidled over to him. She could feel the heat radiating off him as they stood side by side.

"Yes, that's it."

He hefted up one of the boxes onto his shoulder. "I'll send one of the guys over for the rest."

She stood there. That was going to be the whole encounter. *Very professional*, she congratulated herself.

"You want to come weigh in on how to put it up?" he called over his shoulder.

And she threw professionalism to the wind and scampered after him like a puppy who had been given a second chance at affection.

"Hey, guys," he called. "Team meeting. Fabric's here."

His guys, four of them, gathered around.

"Becky, Jared, Jason, Josh and Jimmy."

"The J series," one of them announced. "Brothers. I'm the good-looking one, Josh." He gave a little bow.

"But I'm the strong one," Jimmy announced.

"And I'm the smart one."

"I'm the romantic," Jared said, and stepped forward, picked up her hand and kissed it, to groans from his brothers. "You are a beauty, me lady. Do you happen to be available? I see no rings, so—"

"That's enough," Drew said.

His tone had no snap to it, at all, only firmness, but Becky did not miss how quickly Jared stepped back from her, or the surprised looks exchanged between the brothers.

She liked seeing Drew in this environment. It was obvious his crew of brothers didn't just respect him, they adored him. She soon saw why.

"Let's see what we have here," Drew said. He opened

a box and yards and yards of filmy white material spilled out onto the ground.

He was a natural leader, listening to all the brothers' suggestions about how to attach and drape the fabric to the pavilion poles they had worked all morning installing.

"How about you, Becky?" Drew asked her.

She was flattered that her opinion mattered, too. "I think you should put some kind of bar on those side beams. Long bars, like towel bars, and then thread the fabric through them."

"We have a winner," one of the guys shouted, and they all clapped and went back to work.

"I'll hang the first piece and you can see if it works," Drew said.

With amazing ingenuity he had fabricated a bar in no time. And then he shinnied up a ladder that was leaning on a post and attached the first bar to the beam. And then he did the same on the other side.

"The moment of truth," he called from up on the wall.

She opened the box and he leaned way down to take the fabric from her outstretched hand. Once he had it, he threaded it through the first bar, then came down from the ladder, trailing a line of wide fabric behind him. He went up the ladder on the other side of what would soon look like a pavilion, and threaded the fabric through there. The panel was about three feet wide and dozens of feet long. He came down to the ground and passed her the fabric end.

"You do it," he said.

She tugged on it until the fabric lifted toward the sky, and then began to tighten. Finally, the first panel was in place. The light, filmy, pure-white fabric formed a dreamy roof above them, floating walls on either side of them. Only it was better than walls and a roof because of the way the light was diffused through it, and the way it moved like a living thing in the most gentle of breezes.

"Just like a canopy bed," he told her with satisfaction.

"You know way too much about that," she teased him.

"Actually," he said, frowning at the fabric, "come to think of it, it doesn't really look like a canopy bed. It looks like—"

He snatched up the hem of fabric and draped it over his shoulder. "It looks like a toga."

She burst out laughing.

He struck a pose. "'To be or not to be…'" he said.

"I don't want to be a geek…" she began.

"Oh, go ahead—be a geek. It comes naturally to you."

That stung, but even with it stinging, she couldn't let *To be or not to be* go unchallenged. "'To be or not to be' is Shakespeare," she told him. "Not Nero."

"Well, hell," he said, "that's what makes it really hard for a dumb carpenter to go out with a smart girl."

She stared at him. "Are we going out?" she whispered.

"No! I just was pointing out more evidence of our incompatibility."

That stung even worse than being called a geek. "At least you got part of it right," she told him.

"Which part? The geek part?"

"I am not a geek!"

He shook his head sadly.

"That line? 'To be or not to be.' It's from a soliloquy in the play *Hamlet*. It's from a scene in the nunnery."

"The nunnery?" he said with satisfaction. "Don't *you* have a fascination?"

"No! You *think* I have a fascination. You are incorrect, just as you are incorrect about me being a geek."

"Yes, and being able to quote Shakespeare, chapter and verse, certainly made that point."

She giggled, and unraveled the fabric from around him.

"Hey! Give me back my toga. I already told you I don't wear underwear!

But it was her turn to play with the gauzy fabric. She inserted herself in the middle of it and twirled until she had made it into a long dress. Then she swathed some around her head, until only her eyes showed. Throwing inhibition to the wind, she swiveled her hips and did some things with her hands.

"Guess who I am?" she purred.

He frowned at her. "A bride?"

The thing he liked least!

"No, I'm not a bride," she snapped.

"A hula girl!"

"No."

"I give up. Stop doing that."

"I'm Mata Hari."

"Who? I asked you to stop."

"Why?"

"It's a little too sexy for the job site."

"A perfect imitation of Mata Hari, then," she said with glee. And she did not stop doing it. She was rather enjoying the look on his face.

"Who?"

"She was a spy. And a dancer."

He burst out laughing as if that was the most improbable thing he had ever heard. "How well versed was she in her Shakespeare?"

"She didn't have to be." Becky began to do a slow writhe with her hips. He didn't seem to think it was funny anymore.

In fact, the ease they had been enjoying—that sense of being a team and working together—evaporated.

He stepped back from her, as if he thought she was going to try kissing him again. She blushed.

"I have so much to do," she squeaked, suddenly feeling silly, and at the very same time, not silly at all.

"Me, too," he said.

But neither of them moved.

"Uh, boss, is this a bad time?"

Mata Hari dropped her veil with a little shriek of embarrassment.

"The guys were thinking maybe we could have a break? It's f—"

Drew stopped his worker with a look.

"It's flipping hot out here. We thought maybe we could go swimming and start again when it's not so hot out."

"Great idea," Drew said. "We all need cooling off, particularly Mata Hari here. You coming swimming, Becky?"

She knew she should say no. She had to say no. She didn't even have a proper bathing suit. Instead she unraveled herself from the yards of fabric, called, "Race you," ran down to the water and flung herself in completely clothed.

Drew's crew crashed into the water around her,

following her lead and just jumping in in shorts and T-shirts. They played a raucous game of tag in the water, and she was fully included, though she was very aware of Drew sending out a silent warning that no lines were to be crossed. And none were. It was like having five brothers.

And wouldn't that be the safest thing? Wasn't that what she and Drew had vowed they were going to do? Hadn't they both agreed they were going to retreat into a platonic relationship after the crazy-making sensation of those shared kisses?

What had she been thinking, playing Mata Hari? What kind of craziness was it that she wanted him to not see her exactly as she was: not a spy and dancer who could coax secrets out of unsuspecting men, but a book-loving girl from a small town in America?

After that frolic in the water, the J brothers included her as one of them. Over the next few days, whenever they broke from work to go swimming, one of them came and pounded on her office door and invited her to come.

Today, Josh knocked on the door.

"Swim time," he said.

"I just can't. I have to tie bows on two hundred chairs. And find a cool place to store three thousand potted lavender plants. And—"

Without a word, Josh came in, picked her up and tossed her over his shoulder like a sack of potatoes.

"Stop it. This is my good dress!" She pounded on his back, but of course, with her laughing so hard, he did not take her seriously. She was carried, kicking and screaming and pounding on his back, to the water, where she was unceremoniously dumped in.

"Hey, what the hell are you doing?" Drew demanded, arriving at the water's edge and fishing her out.

The fact that she was screaming with laughter had softened the protective look on his face.

Josh had lifted a big shoulder. "Boss, you said don't take no for an answer."

"No means no, boss," she inserted, barely able to breathe she was laughing so hard.

Drew gave them both an exasperated look, and turned away. Then he turned back, picked her up, raced out into the surf and dumped her again!

She rose from the water sputtering, still holding on to his neck, both their bodies sleek with salt water, her good dress completely ruined.

Gazing into the mischief-filled face of Drew Jordan, Becky was not certain she had ever felt so completely happy.

CHAPTER TWELVE

AFTER THAT BECKY was "in." She and the J's and Drew became a family. They took their meals together and they played together. Becky soon discovered this crew worked hard, and they played harder.

At every break and after work, the football came out. Or the Frisbee. Both games were played with rough-and-tumble delight at the water's edge. She wasn't sure how they could have any energy left, but they did.

The first few times she played, the brothers howled hysterically at both her efforts to throw and catch balls and Frisbees. They good-naturedly nicknamed her Barnside.

"Barnside?" she protested. "That's awful. I demand a new nickname. That is not flattering!"

"You have to earn a new nickname," Jimmy informed her seriously.

"Time to go back to work," Drew told them, after one coffee-break Frisbee session when poor Josh had to climb a palm tree to retrieve a Frisbee she'd thrown. He caught her arm as she turned to leave. "Not you."

"What?" she said.

"Have you heard anything from Allie recently?" he asked.

"The last I heard from her was a few days ago, when she okayed potted lavender instead of tulips." She scanned his face. "You still haven't heard from Joe?"

He shrugged. "It's no big deal."

But she could tell it was. "I'm sorry."

He obviously did not want to talk about his distress over his brother. Becky was aware that she felt disappointed. He was okay with their relationship—with being "friends" on a very light level.

Did he not trust her with his deeper issues?

Apparently not. Drew said, "It's time you learned how to throw a Frisbee. I consider it an essential life skill."

"How could I have missed that?" she asked drily. As much as she wanted to talk to him about his brother, having fun with him was just too tempting. Besides, maybe the lighthearted friendship growing between them would develop some depth, and some trust on his part, if she just gave it time.

"I'm not sure how you could have missed this important life skill," he said, "but it's time to lose 'Barnside.' They are calling you that because you could not hit the side of a barn with a Frisbee at twenty feet."

"At twenty feet? I could!"

"No," Drew informed her with a sad shake of his head, "you couldn't. You've now tossed two Frisbees out to sea, and Josh risked his life to rescue the other one out of the palm tree today. We can't be running out of Frisbees."

"That would be a crisis," she agreed, deadpan.

"I'm glad you understand the seriousness of it. Now, come here."

He placed her in front of him. He gave her a Frisbee. "Don't throw it. Not yet."

He wrapped his arms around her from behind, drawing her back into the powerful support of his chest. He laid his arm along her arm. "It's in the wrist, not the arm. Flick it, don't pitch it." He guided her throw.

Becky actually cackled with delight when it flew true, instead of her normal flub. Soon, he released her to try on her own, and then set up targets for her to throw at. The troubled look that had been on his face since he mentioned his brother evaporated.

Finally, he high-fived her, gave her a little kiss on the nose and headed back to his crew. She watched him go and then looked at the Frisbee in her hand.

How could such a small thing make it feel as if a whole new world was opening up to her? Of course, it wasn't the Frisbee, it was him.

It was being with him and being with his crew.

It occurred to Becky she felt the sense of belonging she had craved since the disintegration of her own family. They were all becoming a team. Drew and his crew were a building machine. The pavilion went up, and they designed and began to build the dance floor. And Becky loved the moments when she and Drew found themselves alone. It was so easy to talk to each other.

The conversation flowed between them so easily. And the laughter.

The hands-off policy had been a good one, even if it was making the tension build almost unbearably between them. It was like going on a diet that had an end date. Not that they had named an end date, but some kind of anticipation was building between them.

And meanwhile, her admiration for him did nothing but grow. He was a natural leader. He was funny. He was smart. She found herself making all kinds of excuses to be around him. She was pretty sure he was doing the same thing to be around her.

The days flew by until there were only three days until the wedding. The details were falling into place seamlessly, not just for the wedding but for the week following. The pagoda and dance floor were done, the wedding gazebo was almost completed, though it still had to be painted.

Usually when she did an event, as the day grew closer her excitement grew, too. But this time she had mixed feelings. In a way, Becky wished the wedding would never come. She had never loved her life as much as she did right now.

Today she was at the helipad looking at the latest shipment of goods. Again, there was a sense of things falling into place: candles in a large box, glass vases for the centerpieces made up of single white roses. She made a note as she instructed the staff member who had been assigned to help her where to put the boxes. Candles would need to be unwrapped and put in candle holders, glass vases cleaned to sparkling. The flowers—accompanied by their own florist—would arrive the evening before the wedding to guarantee freshness.

Then one large, rectangular box with a designer name on it caught her eye. It was the wedding dress. She had not been expecting it. She had assumed it would arrive with Allie.

And yet it made sense that it would need to be hung.

Becky plucked it from all the other boxes and, with some last-minute instructions, walked back to the castle with it. She brought it up to the suite that Allie would inhabit by herself the day before the wedding, and with her new husband after that.

The suite was amazing, so softly romantic it took Becky's breath away. She had a checklist for this room, too. It would be fully supplied with very expensive toiletries, plus fresh flowers would abound. She had chosen the linens from the castle supply room herself.

Becky set the box on the bed. A sticker in red caught her eye. They were instructions stating that the dress should be unpacked, taken out of its plastic protective bag and hung immediately upon arrival. And so Becky opened the box and lifted it out. She unzipped the bag, and carefully lifted the dress out.

Her hands gathered up a sea of white foam. The fabric was silk, so sensuous under her fingertips that Becky could feel the enchantment sewn right into the dress. There was a tall coatrack next to the mirror, and Becky hung the silk-wrapped hanger on a peg and stood back from it.

She could not believe what she was seeing. That long-ago dress that Allie had drawn and given to her, that drawing still living in the back of Becky's dresser drawer, had been brought to life.

The moment was enough to make a girl who had given up on magic believe in it all over again.

Except that's not what it did. Looking at the dress made Becky feel as though she was being stabbed with the shards of her own broken dreams. The dress shimmered with a future she had been robbed of. In every winking pearl, there seemed to be a promise: of someone to share life with, of laughter, of companionship, of passion, of "many babies," fat babies chortling and clapping their hands with glee.

Becky shook herself, as if she was trying to break free of the spell the dress was weaving around her. She wanted to tell herself that she was wrong. That this was not the dress that Allie had drawn on that afternoon of girlish delight all those years ago, not the drawing she had handed to her and said, *This is your wedding dress.*

But she still had that drawing. She had studied it too often now not to know every line of that breathtakingly romantic dress. She had dreamed of herself walking down the aisle in that dress one too many times. There was simply no mistaking which dress it was. Surely, Allie was not being deliberately cruel?

No, Allie had not kept a drawing of the dress. She had given the only existing drawing to Becky. Allie must have remembered it at a subliminal level. Why wouldn't she? The dress was exactly what every single girl dreamed of having one day.

But Becky still felt the tiniest niggle of doubt. What if Drew's cynicism was not misplaced? What if his brother was making a mistake? What if this whole wedding was some kind of publicity stunt orchestrated by Allie? The timing was perfect: Allie was just finishing filming one movie, and another was going to be released in theaters within weeks.

With trembling hands, Becky touched the fabric of the dress one more time. Then she turned and scurried from the room. She felt as if she was going to burst into tears, as if her every secret hope and dream had been shoved into her face and mocked. And then she bumped right into Drew and did what she least wanted to do. She burst into tears.

"Hey!" Drew eased Becky away from him. She was crying! If there was something worse than her laughing and being joyful and carefree, it was this. "What's the matter?"

"Nothing," she said. "I'm just tired. There's so much to do and—"

But he could tell she wasn't just tired. And from working with her for the past week, he could tell there was hardly anything she liked more than having a lot to do. Her strength was organizing, putting her formidable mind to problems that needed to be solved. No, something had upset her. How had he come to be able to read Becky English so accurately?

She was swiping at those tears, lifting her chin to him with fierce pride, backing away from a shoulder to cry on.

The wisest thing would be to let her. Let her go her own way and have a good cry about whatever, and not involve himself any more than he already had.

Who was he kidding? Just himself. He'd noticed his crew sending him sideways looks every time she was around. He'd noticed Tandu putting them together. He was already involved. Spending the past days with her had cemented that.

"You want to be upset together?" he asked her.

"I told you I'm not upset."

"Uh-huh."

"What are you upset about?"

He lifted a shoulder. "You're not telling, I'm not telling."

"Fine."

"Tandu asked me to give you this."

"How could Tandu have possibly known you were going to bump into me?" Becky asked, taking the paper from him.

"I don't know. The man's spooky. He seems to know things."

Becky squinted at the paper. "Sheesh."

"What?"

"It's a map. He promised it to me over a week ago. Apparently there's a waterfall that would make a great backdrop for wedding pictures. Can you figure out this drawing?"

She handed the map back to him. It looked like a child's map for a pirate's treasure. Drew looked at a big arrow, and the words, *Be careful this rock. Do not fall in water, please.*

"I'll come with you," he decided.

"Thank you," she said. "That's unnecessary." She snatched the map back and looked at it. "Which way is north?"

"I'll come."

The fight went out of her. "Do you ever get tired of being the big brother?"

He thought of how tired he was of leaving Joe messages to call him. He looked at her lips. He thought of how tired he was getting of this friendship between them.

"Suck it up, buttercup," he muttered to himself.

She sighed heavily. "If you have a fault, do you know what it is?"

"Please don't break it to me that I have a fault. Not right now."

"What happened?"

"I said I'm not talking about it, if you're not talking about it."

"Your fault is that you don't answer questions."

"Your fault is—" What was he going to say? Her

fault was that she made him think the kind of thoughts he had vowed he was never going to think? "Never mind. Let's go find that waterfall."

"I don't know," Becky said dubiously, after they had been walking twenty minutes. "This seems like kind of a tough walk at any time. I'm in a T-shirt and shorts and I'm overheating. What would it be like in a wedding dress?"

Drew glanced at her. Had she flinched when she said *wedding dress*?

"Maybe her royal highness, the princess Allie is expecting to be delivered to her photo op on a litter carried by two manservants," Drew grumbled. "I hope I'm not going to be one of them."

Becky laughed and took the hand he held back to her to help her scramble over a large boulder.

"Technically, that would be a sedan chair," she said, puffing.

"Huh?"

"A seat that two manservants can carry is sedan chair. Anything bigger is a litter."

He contemplated her. "How do you know this stuff?" he asked.

"That's what a lifetime of reading gets you, a brain teeming with useless information." She contemplated the rock. "Maybe we should just stop here. There's no way Allie can scramble over this rock in a wedding dress."

He contemplated the map. "I think it's only a few more steps. I'm pretty sure I can hear the falls. We might as well see it, even if Allie never will."

And he was right. Only a few steps more and they

pushed their way through a gateway of heavy leaves, as big and as wrinkled as elephant ears, and stood in an enchanted grotto.

"Oh, my," Becky breathed.

A frothing fountain of water poured over a twenty-foot cliff and dropped into a pool of pure green water. The pond was surrounded on all sides by lush green ferns and flowers. A large flat rock jutted out into the middle of it, like a platform.

"Perfect for pictures," she thought out loud. "But how are we going to get them here?"

"Wow," Drew said, apparently not the least bit interested in pictures. In a blink, he had stripped off his shirt and dived into the pond. He surfaced and shook his head. Diamonds of water flew. "It's wonderful," he called over the roar of the falls. "Get in."

Once again, there was the small problem of not having bathing attire.

And once again, she was caught in the spell of the island. She didn't care that she didn't have a bathing suit. She wanted to be unencumbered, not just by clothing, but by every single thought that had ever held her prisoner.

CHAPTER THIRTEEN

So AWARE OF the look on Drew's face as he watched her, Becky undid the buttons of her blouse, shrugged it off and then stepped out of her skirt.

When she saw the look on Drew's face, she congratulated herself on her investment in the ultra-sexy and exclusive Rembrandt's Drawing brand underwear. Today, her matching bra and panties were white with tiny red hearts all over them.

And then she stepped into the water. She wanted to dive like him, but because she was not that great a swimmer, she waded in up to her ankles first. The rocks were slipperier than she had expected. Her arms began to windmill.

And she fell, with a wonderful splash, into where he was waiting to catch her.

"The water is fantastic," Becky said, blinking up at him.

"Yes, it is."

She knew neither of them were talking about the water. He set her, it seemed with just a bit of reluctance, on her feet. She splashed him.

"Is that any way to thank me for rescuing you?"

"That is to let you know I did not need to be rescued!"

"Oh," he said. "You planned to fall in the water."

She giggled. "Yes, I did."

"Don't take up poker."

She splashed him again. He got a look on his face. She giggled and bolted away. He was after her in a flash. Soon the grotto was filled with the magic of their splashing and laughter. The days of playing with him—of feeling that sense of belonging—all seemed to have been leading to this. Becky had never felt so free, so wondrous, so aware as she did then.

Finally, exhausted, they hauled themselves out onto the warmth of the large, flat rock, and lay there on their stomachs, side-by-side, panting to catch their breaths.

"I'm indecent," she decided, without a touch of remorse.

"I prefer to think of it as wanton."

She laughed. The sun was coming through the greenery, dappled on his face. His eyelashes were tangled with water. She laid her hand—wantonly—on the firmness of his naked back. She could feel the warmth of him seeping into her hand. He closed his eyes, as if her touch had soothed something in him. His breathing slowed and deepened.

And then so did hers.

When she awoke, her hand was still on his back. He stirred and opened his eyes, looked at her and smiled.

She shivered with a longing so primal it shook her to the core. Drew's smile disappeared, and he found his feet in one catlike motion. As she sat up and hugged herself, chilled now, he retrieved his T-shirt. He came back and slid it over her head. Then he sat behind her, pulled her between the wedge of his legs and wrapped his arms around her until she stopped shivering.

The light was changing in the grotto and the magic deepened all around them.

"What were you upset about earlier?" he asked softly.

She sighed. "I unpacked Allie's wedding dress."

He sucked in his breath. "And what? You wished it was yours?"

"It was mine," she whispered. "It was the dress she drew for me one of those afternoons all those years ago."

"What? The very same dress? Maybe you're just re-membering it wrong."

Was there any way to tell him she had kept that pic-ture without seeming hopelessly pathetic?

"No," she said firmly. "It was that dress."

"Representing all your hopes and dreams," he said. "No wonder you were crying."

She felt a surge of tenderness for him that there was no mockery in his tone, but instead, a lovely empathy.

"It was just a shock. I am hoping it is just a weird coincidence. But I'm worried. I didn't know Allie that well when we were teenagers. I don't know her at all now. What if it's all some gigantic game? What if she's playing with everyone?"

"Exactly the same thing I was upset about," Drew confessed to her. "My brother was supposed to be here. He's not. I've called him twice a day, every day, since I got here to find out why. He won't return my calls. That isn't like him."

"Tell me what *is* like him," Becky said gently.

And suddenly he just wanted to unburden himself. He felt as if he had carried it all alone for so long, and he was not sure he could go one more step with the weight of it all. It felt as if it was crushing him.

He was not sure he had ever felt this relaxed or this at ease with another person. Drew had a deep sense of being able to trust this woman in front of him. It felt as if every day before this one—all those laughter-filled days of getting to know one another, of splashing and playing, and throwing Frisbees—had been leading to this.

He needed to think about that: that this wholesome woman, with her girl-next-door look, was really a Mata Hari, a temptress who could pull secrets from an unwilling man. But he didn't heed the warning that was flashing in the back of his brain like a red light telling of a train coming.

Drew just started to talk, and it felt as if a rock had been removed from a dam that had held back tons of water for years. Now it was all flowing toward that opening, trying to get out.

"When my parents died, I was seventeen. I wasn't even a mature seventeen. I was a superficial surfer dude, riding a wave through life."

Something happened to Becky's face. A softness came to it that was so real it almost stole the breath out of his chest. It was so different than the puffy-lipped coos of sympathy that he had received from women in the past when he'd made the mistake of sharing even small parts of his story.

This felt as if he could go lay his head on Becky's slender, naked shoulder, and rest there for a long, long time.

"I'm so sorry," she said quietly, "about the death of your parents. Both of them died at the same time?"

"It was a car accident." He could stop right there, but no, he just kept going. All those words he had never spoken felt as if they were now rushing to escape a building on fire, jostling with each other in their eagerness to be out.

"They had gone out to celebrate the anniversary of some friends. They never came home. A policeman arrived at the door and told me what had happened. Not their fault at all, a drunk driver..."

"Drew," she breathed softly. Somehow her hand found his, and the dam within him was even more compromised.

"You have never met a person more totally unqualified for the job of raising a seven-year-old brother than the seventeen-year-old me."

She squeezed his hand, as if she believed in the younger him, making him want to go on, to somehow dissuade this faith in him.

He cleared his throat. "It was me or foster care, so—" He rolled his shoulders.

"I think that's the bravest thing I ever heard," she said.

"No, it wasn't," he said fiercely. "Brave is when you have a choice. I didn't have any choice."

"You did," she insisted, as fierce as him. "You did have a choice and you chose love."

That word inserted into any conversation between them should have stopped it cold. But it didn't. In fact, it felt as if more of the wall around everything he held inside crumbled, as if her words were a wrecking ball seeking the weakest point in that dam.

"I love my brother," he said. "I just don't know if he knows how much I do."

"He can't be that big a fool," Becky said.

"I managed to finish out my year in high school and

then I found a job on a construction crew. I was tired all the time. And I never seemed to be able to make enough money. Joe sure wasn't wearing the designer clothes the rest of the kids had. I got mad if he asked. That's why he probably doesn't have a clue how I feel about him."

Becky's hand was squeezing his with unbelievable strength. It was as if her strength—who could have ever guessed this tiny woman beside him held so much strength?—was passing between them, right through the skin of her hand into his, entering his bloodstream.

"I put one foot in front of the other," Drew told her. "I did my best to raise my brother. But I was so scared of messing up that I think I was way too strict with him. I thought if I let him know how much I cared about him he would perceive it as weakness and I would lose control. Of him. Of life.

"I'd already seen what happened when I was not in control."

"Did you feel responsible for the death of your parents?" she asked. He could hear that she was startled by the question.

"I guess I asked myself, over and over, what I could have done. And the answer seemed to be, 'Never let anyone you love out of your sight. Never let go.' Most days, I felt as if I was hanging on by a thread.

"When he was a teen? I was not affectionate. I was like Genghis Khan, riding roughshod over the troops. The default answer to almost everything he wanted to do was *no*. When I did loosen the reins a bit, he had to check in with me. He had a curfew. I sucked, and he let me know it."

"Sucked?" she said, indignant.

"Yeah, we both agreed on that. Not that I let him know I agreed with him in the you-suck department."

"Then you were both wrong. What you did was noble," she said quietly. "The fact that you think you did it imperfectly does not make it less noble."

"Noble!" he snapped, wanting to show only annoyance and not vulnerability. "There's nothing noble about acting on necessity."

But she was having none of it. "It's even noble that you saw it as a necessity, not a choice."

"Whatever," he said. He suddenly disliked himself. He felt as if he was a small dog yapping and yapping and yapping at the postman. He sat up. She sat up, too. He folded his arms over his chest, a shield.

"Given that early struggle, you seem to have done well for yourself."

"A man I worked for gave me a break," Drew admitted, even though he had ordered himself to stop talking. "He was a developer. He told me I could have a lot in one of his subdivisions and put up a house on spec. I didn't have to pay for the lot until the house sold. It was the beginning of an amazing journey, but looking back, I think my drive to succeed also made me emotionally unavailable to my brother."

"You feel totally responsible for him, still."

Drew sighed, dragged a hand through his sun-dried hair. "I'm sure it's because of how I raised him that we are in this predicament we're in now, him marrying a girl I know nothing about, who may be using him. And you. And all of us."

"I don't see that as your fault."

"If I worked my ass off, I could feed him," he heard himself volunteering. "I could keep the roof over his head. I could get his books for school. I even managed to get him through college. But—"

"But what?"

"I could not teach him about finding a good relationship." Drew's voice dropped to a hoarse whisper. It felt as if every single word he had said had been circling around this essential truth.

"I missed them so much, my mom and dad. They could have showed him what he should be looking for. They were so stable. My mom was a teacher, my dad was a postal worker. Ordinary people, and yet they elevated the ordinary.

"I didn't know what I had when I had it. I didn't know what it was to wake up to my dad downstairs, making coffee for my mom, delivering it to her every morning. He sang a song while he delivered it. An old Irish folk song. They were always laughing and teasing each other. We were never rich but our house was full. The smell of cookies, the sound of them arguing good-naturedly about where to put the Christmas tree, my mom reading stories. I loved those stories way after I was too old for them. I used to find some excuse to hang out when she was reading to Joe at night. How could I hope to give any of that kind of love to my poor orphaned baby brother? When even thinking about all we had lost felt as if it would undermine the little bit of control that I was holding over my world? Instead, the environment I raised Joe in was so devoid of affection that he's gotten involved with Allie out of his sheer desperation to be loved."

"Maybe he longs for your family as much as you do."

"It's not that I didn't love him," Drew admitted gruffly. "I just didn't know how to say that to him."

"Maybe that's the area where he's going to teach you," she said softly.

Something shivered up and down Drew's spine, a tingle of pure warning, like a man might feel seconds before the cougar pounced from behind, or the plane began to lose altitude, or the earth began to shake. The remainder of the dam wall felt as if it tumbled down inside him.

"You can say that, even after finding the dress? When neither of us is sure about Allie or what her true motives are?"

"I'm going to make a decision to believe love is going to win. No matter what."

He stared at her. There should have been a choice involved here. There should have been a choice to get up and run.

But if there was that choice? He was helpless to make it.

Instead he went into her open arms like a warrior who had fought too many battles, like a warrior who had thought he would never see the lights of familiar fires again. He laid his head upon her breast and felt her hand, tender, on the nape of his neck.

He sighed against her, like a warrior who unexpectedly found himself in the place he had given up on. That place was home.

"You did your best," she said softly. "You can forgive yourself if you weren't perfect."

She began to hum softly. And then she began to sing. Her voice was clear and beautiful and it raised the hair on the back of his neck. It was as if it affirmed that love was the greatest force of all, and that it survived everything, even death.

Because of the millions of songs in the world, how was it possible Becky was gently singing this one, in her soft, true voice?

It was the same song his father had sung to his mother, every day as he brought her coffee.

Drew's surrender was complete. He had thought his story spilling out of him, like water out of a dam that had been compromised, would make him feel weak, and as though he had lost control.

Instead, he felt connected to Becky in a way he had not allowed himself to feel connected to another human being in a long, long time.

Instead, he realized how alone he had been in the world, and how good it felt not to be alone.

Instead, listening to her voice soar above the roar of the waterfall and feeling it tingle along his spine, it felt as though the ice was melting from around his heart. He felt the way he had felt diving into the water to save her all those days ago. He felt brave. Only this time, he felt as if he might be saving himself.

Drew realized he felt as brave as he ever had. He contemplated the irony that a complete surrender would make him feel the depth of his own courage.

You heal now.

And impossibly, beautifully, he was.

CHAPTER FOURTEEN

NIGHT HAD FALLEN by the time they left the waterfall and found their way back to the castle grounds. He left her with his T-shirt and walked beside her bare-chested, happy to give her the small protection of his clothing. He walked her to her bedroom door, and they stood there, looking at each other, drinking each other in like people who had been dying of thirst and had found a spring.

He touched the plumpness of her lip with his thumb, and her tongue darted out and tasted him.

She sighed her surrender, and he made a guttural, groaning sound of pure need. He did what he had been wanting to do all this time.

He planted his hands, tenderly, on either side of her head, and dropped his lips over hers. He kissed her thoroughly, exploring the tenderness of her lips with his own lips, and his tongue, probing the cool grotto of her mouth.

He had thought Becky, his little bookworm, would be shy, but she had always had that surprising side, and she surprised him now.

That gentle kiss of recognition, of welcome, that sigh of surrender, deepened quickly into something else.

It was need and it was desire. It was passion and it

was hunger. It was nature singing its ancient song of wanting life to have victory over the cycle of death.

That was what was in this kiss: everything it was to be human. Instinct and intuition, power and surrender, pleasure that bordered on pain it was so intense. He dragged his lips from hers and anointed her earlobes and her eyelids, her cheeks and the tip of her nose. He kissed the hollow of her throat, and then she pulled him back to her lips.

Her hands were all over him, touching, exploring, celebrating the hard strength in the muscles that gloried at the touch of her questing fingertips.

Finally, rational thought pushed through his primal reaction to her, calling a stern *no*. But it took every ounce of Drew's substantial strength to peel back from her. She stood there, quivering with need, panting, her eyes wide on his face.

His rational mind was gaining a foothold now that he had managed to step back from her. She had never looked more beautiful, even though her hair was a mess, and any makeup she had been wearing had washed off long ago. She had never looked more beautiful, even though she was standing there in a T-shirt that was way too large for her.

But nothing could hide the light shining from her. It was the purity of that light that reminded Drew that Becky was not the kind of girl you tangled with lightly. She required his intentions to be very clear.

In the past few days, he had felt his mother's spirit around him in a way he had not experienced since her death. It was the kind of idea he might have scoffed at two short weeks ago.

And yet this island, with its magic, and Becky with

her own enchantment, made things that had seemed impossible before feel entirely possible now.

Drew knew his mother would be expecting him to be a decent man, expecting him to rise to what she would have wanted him to be if she had lived.

She knew what he had forgotten about himself: that he was a man of courage and decency. Drew took another step back from Becky. He saw the sense of loss and confusion in her face.

"I have to go," he said, his voice hoarse.

"Please, don't."

Her voice was hoarse, too, and she stepped toward him. She took the waistband of his shorts and pulled her to him with surprising strength.

"Don't go," she said fiercely.

"You don't know what you're asking."

"Yes, I do."

For a moment he was so torn, but then his need to be decent won out. If things were going to go places with this girl—and he knew they were—it would require him to be a better man than he had been with women in the past.

It would require him to do the honorable thing.

"I have to make a phone call tonight, before it's too late." It was a poor excuse, but it was the only one he could think of. With great reluctance, he untangled her hands from where they held him, and once again stepped back from her.

If she asked again, he was not going to be able to refuse. A man's strengths had limits, after all.

But she accepted his decision. She raked a hand through her hair and looked disgruntled, but pulled herself together and tilted her chin at him.

"I have a phone call to make, too," she said. She was, just like that, his little bookworm spelling-bee contestant again, prim and sensible, and pulling back from the wild side she had just shown him.

She took a step back from him.

Go, he ordered himself. But he didn't. He stepped back toward her. He kissed her again, quickly, and then he tore himself away from her and went to his own quarters.

Rattled by what he was feeling, he took a deep breath. He wandered to the window and looked at the moon, and listened to the lap of the water on the beach. He felt as alive as he had ever felt.

He glanced at the time, swore softly, took out his cell phone and stabbed in Joe's number.

There was, predictably, no answer. He needed to tell Joe what he had learned of love tonight. It might save Joe from imminent disaster. But, of course, there was no answer, and you could hardly leave a message saying somehow you had stumbled on the secret of life and you needed to share that *right now.*

Joe would think his coolheaded, hard-hearted brother had lost his mind. So, that conversation would have to wait until tomorrow.

According to the information Becky had, Joe and Allie were supposed to arrive only on the morning of the wedding day. This was apparently to slip under the radar of the press.

Tomorrow, the guests would begin arriving, in a co-ordinated effort that involved planes and boats landing on Sainte Simone all day.

Two hundred people. It was going to be controlled chaos. And then Joe and Allie would arrive the next day, just hours before the wedding. How was he going to get Joe alone? Drew was aware that he *had* to get his brother alone, that he *had* to figure out what the hell was really going on between him and Allie.

And he was aware that he absolutely *had* to protect Becky. He thought of her tears over that dress that Allie had had specially made, and he felt fury building in him. In fact, all the fury of his powerlessness over Joe's situation seemed to be coming to a head.

"Look, Joe," he said, after that annoying beep that made him want to pick up the chair beside his bed and throw it against the wall, "I don't know what your fiancée is up to, but you give her a message from me. You tell your betrothed if she does anything to hurt Becky English—anything—I will not rest until I've tracked her to the ends of the earth and dealt with it. You know me well enough to know I mean it. I'm done begging you to call me. But I don't think you have a clue what you're getting mixed up in."

Drew disconnected the call, annoyed with himself. He had lost control, and probably reduced his chances of getting his brother to meet with him alone.

Becky went to her room and shut the door, leaning against it. Her knees felt wobbly. She felt breathless. She touched her lips, as if she could still feel the warmth of his fire claiming her. She hugged herself. She could not believe she had invited Drew Jordan into her room. She was not that kind of girl!

Thank goodness his good sense had prevailed, but what did that mean? That he was not feeling things quite as intensely as she was?

She sank down on her bed. It was as if the world had

gone completely silent, and into that silence flowed a frightening truth.

She had fallen for Drew Jordan. She loved him. She had never felt anything like what she was feeling right now: tingling with aliveness, excited about the future, aware that life had the potential to hold the most miraculous surprises. She, Becky English, who had sworn off it, had still fallen under its spell. She was in love. It wasn't just the seduction of this wildly romantic setting. It wasn't.

She loved him so much.

It didn't make any sense. It was too quick, wasn't it?

But, in retrospect, her relationship with Jerry had made perfect sense, and had unfolded with respectable slowness.

And there had been nothing real about it. She had been chasing security. She had settled for safety. Salt and pepper. Good grief, she had almost made herself a prisoner of a dull and ordinary life.

But now she knew how life was supposed to feel. And she felt so alive and grateful and on fire with all the potential the days ahead held. They didn't feel safe at all. They felt like they were loaded with unpredictable forces and choices. It felt as if she was plunging into the great unknown, and she was astonished to find she *loved* how the great adventure that was life and love was making her feel.

And following on the heels of her awareness of how much she loved Drew, and how much that love was going to make her life change, Becky felt a sudden fury with his brother. How could he treat Drew like this? Surely Joe was not so stupid that he could not see his brother had sacrificed everything for him?

Drew's whole life had become about making a life for his brother, about holding everything together. He had tried so hard and done so much, and now Joe would not even return his phone calls?

It was wrong. It was just plain old wrong.

Becky's fingers were shaking when she dialed Allie's number. She didn't care that it was late in Spain. She didn't care at all. Of course, after six rings she got Allie's voice commanding her to leave a message.

"Allie, it's Becky English. I need you to get an urgent message to Joe. He needs to call his brother. He needs to call Drew right now. Tomorrow morning at the latest." There, that was good enough. But her voice went on, shaking with emotion. "It's unconscionable that he would be ignoring Drew's attempts to call him after all Drew has done for him. I know you will both be arriving here early on the morning of the wedding, but he needs to talk to Drew before that. As soon as you get this message he needs to call."

There. She didn't need to say one other thing. And yet somehow she was still talking.

"You tell him if he doesn't call his brother immediately he'll be…" She thought and then said, "Dealing with me!"

She disconnected her phone. Then snickered. She had just used a terrible, demanding tone of voice on the most prosperous client she had ever had. She didn't care. What was so funny was her saying Drew's brother would be dealing with her, as if that was any kind of threat.

And yet she felt more powerful right now than she had ever felt in her entire life. It did feel as if she could whip that disrespectful young pup into shape!

That's what love did, she supposed. It didn't take away power, it gave it.

Becky allowed herself to feel the shock of that. She had somehow, someway, fallen in love with Drew Jordan. And not just a little bit in love: irrevocably, crazily, impossibly, feverishly in love.

It was nothing at all like what she had thought was love with Jerry. Nothing. That had felt safe and solid and secure, even though it had turned out to be none of those things. This was the most exciting thing that she had ever felt. It felt as if she was on the very crest of the world's highest roller coaster, waiting for that stomach-dropping swoop downward, her heart in her throat, both terrified and exhilarated by the pathway ahead. And just like that roller coaster, it felt as if somehow she had fully committed before she knew exactly where it was all leading. It felt like now she had no choice but to hang on tight and enjoy the wildest ride of her life.

In a trance of delight at the unexpected turn in her life, Becky pulled off Drew's T-shirt and put on her pajamas. And then she rolled up the T-shirt, and even though it was still slightly damp, she used it as her pillow and drifted off to sleep with the scent of him lulling her like a boat rocking on gentle waves.

She awoke the next morning to the steady *wop-wop-wop* of helicopter blades slicing the air. At first, she lay in bed, hugging Drew's T-shirt, listening and feeling content. Waking up to the sound of helicopters was not unusual on Sainte Simone. It was the primary way that supplies were delivered, and with the wedding just one day away, all kinds of things would be arriving today. Fresh flowers. The cake. The photographer.

Two hundred people would also be arriving over

the course of the day, on boats and by small commercial jets.

There was no time for lollygagging, Becky told herself sternly. She cast back the covers, gave the T-shirt one final hug before putting it under her pillow and then got up and went to the window.

One day, she thought, looking at the helicopters buzzing above her. She had to focus. She had to shake off this dazed, delicious feeling that she was in love and that was all that mattered.

And then it slowly penetrated her bliss that something was amiss. Her mouth fell open. She should have realized from the noise levels that something was dreadfully wrong, but she had not.

There was not one helicopter in the skies above Sainte Simone. From her place at the window, she could count half a dozen. It looked like an invasion force, but with none of the helicopters even attempting to land. They were hovering and dipping and swooping.

She could see a cameraman leaning precariously out one open door! There were so many helicopters in the tiny patch of sky above the island that it was amazing they were managing not to crash into each other.

As she watched, one of the aircraft swooped down over the pavilion. The beautiful white gauze panels began to whip around as though they had been caught in a hurricane. One ripped away, and was swept on air currents out to the ocean, where it floated down in the water, looking for all the world like a bridal veil.

A man—Josh, she thought—raced out into the surf and grabbed the fabric, then shook his fist at the helicopter. The helicopter swooped toward him, the cameraman leaning way out to get that shot.

Becky turned from the window, got dressed quickly and hurried down the stairs and out the main door onto the lawn. The staff were all out there—even the chef in his tall hat—staring in amazement at the frenzied sky dance above them.

Josh came and thrust the wet ball of fabric at her.

"Sorry," he muttered. Tandu turned and looked at her sadly. "It's on the news this morning. That the wedding is here, tomorrow. I have satellite. It's on every single channel."

She felt Drew's presence before she saw him. She felt him walk up beside her and she turned to him, and scanned his familiar face, wanting him to show her how to handle this and what to do.

He put his hand on her shoulder, and she nestled into the weight of it. This is what it meant to not be alone. Life could throw things at you, but you didn't have to handle it all by yourself. The weight of the catastrophe could be divided between them.

Couldn't it? She turned to him. "What are we going to do?"

He looked at her blankly, and she realized he was trying to read her lips. There was no way he could have heard her. She repeated her question, louder.

"I don't know," he said.

He didn't know? She felt a faint shiver of disappointment.

"How could we hold a wedding under these circumstances?" she shouted. "No one will be able to hear anything. The fabric is already tearing away from the pavilion. What about Allie's dress? And veil? What about dinner and candles and…" Her voice fell away.

"I don't think there's going to be a wedding," he said.

Her sense of her whole world shifting intensified. He could not save the day. Believing that he could would only lead to disillusionment. Believing in another person could only lead to heartache.

How on earth had she been so swept away that she had forgotten that?

She shot him a look. He sounded sorry, but was there something else in his voice? She studied Drew more carefully. He had his handsome head tilted to look at the helicopters, his arms folded over his chest.

Did he look grimly satisfied that there was a very good possibility that there was going to be no wedding?

CHAPTER FIFTEEN

BECKY FELT HER heart plummet, and it was not totally because the wedding she had worked so hard on now seemed to be in serious danger of being canceled.

Who, more than any other person on the face of the earth, did not want this wedding to happen?

Drew took his eyes from the sky and looked at her. He frowned. "Why are you looking at me like that?"

"I was just wondering about that phone call you were all fired up to make last night," she said. She could hear the stiffness in her own voice, and she saw that her tone registered with him.

"I recall being all fired up," he said, "but not about a phone call."

How dare he throw that in her face right now? That she had invited him in. He saw it as being all fired up. She saw, foolishly, that she had put her absolute trust in him.

"Is this why you didn't come in?" she said, trying to keep her tone low and be heard above the helicopters at the same time.

"Say what?"

"You didn't give in to my wanton invitation because you already knew you were planning this, didn't you?"

"Planning this?" he echoed, his brow furrowing. "Planning what, exactly?"

Becky sucked in a deep breath. "You let it out, didn't you?"

"What?"

"Don't play the innocent with me! You let it out on purpose, to stop the wedding. To stop your brother and Allie from getting married, to buy yourself a little more time to convince him not to do it."

He didn't deny it. Something glittered in his eyes, hard and cold, that she had never seen before. She reminded herself, bitterly, that there were many things about him she had never seen before. She had only known him two weeks. How could she, who of all people should be well versed in the treachery of the human heart, have let her guard down?

"That's why you had to rush to the phone last night," she decided. "Maybe you even thought you were protecting me. I should have never told you about the wedding dress."

"There are a lot of things we should have never told each other," he bit out.

She stared at him and realized the awful truth. It had all happened too fast between them. It was a reminder to her that they didn't know each other at all. She had been susceptible to the whole notion of love. Because the island was so romantic, because of that dress, because of those crazy moments when she had wanted to feel unencumbered, she had thrown herself on the altar of love with reckless abandon.

She'd been unencumbered all right! Every ounce of good sense she'd possessed had fled her!

But really, hadn't she known this all along? That love

was that roller coaster ride, thrilling and dangerous? And that every now and then it went right off the tracks?

She shot him an accusing look. He met her gaze unflinchingly.

A plane circled overhead and began to prepare to land through the minefield of helicopters. Over his shoulder, she could see a passenger barge plowing through seas made rough by the wind coming off those blades.

"Guess what?" she said wearily. "That will be the first of the guests arriving. All those people are expecting a wedding."

He lifted a shoulder negligently. What all those people were expecting didn't matter one iota to him. And neither did all her hard work. Or what this disaster could mean to her career. He didn't care about her at all.

But if he thought she was going to take this lying down, he was mistaken.

"I'm going to call Allie's publicity people," she said, with fierce determination. "Maybe they can make this disaster stop. Maybe they can call off the hounds if they are offered something in exchange."

"Good luck with that," Drew said coolly. "My experience with hounds, limited as it might be, is once they've caught the scent, there is no calling them off."

"I'm sure if Allie offers to do a photo shoot just for them, after the wedding, they will stop this. I'm sure of it!"

Of course, she was no such thing.

He gazed at her. "Forever hopeful," he said. She heard the coldness in his tone, as if being hopeful was a bad thing.

And it was! She had allowed herself to hope she could love this man. And now she saw it was impossible. Now, when it was too late. When she could have none of the glory and all of the pain.

Drew could not let Becky see how her words hit him, like a sword cleaving him in two. Last night he had taken the biggest chance he had ever taken. He had trusted her with everything. He had been wide-open.

Love.

Sheesh. He, of all people, should know better than that. Joe had not called him back. That's what love really was. Leaving yourself wide-open, all right, wide-open to pain. And rejection. Leaving yourself open to the fact that the people you loved most of all could misinterpret everything you did, run it through their own filter and come to their own conclusions, as wrong as those might be. He, of all people, should know that better than anyone else.

How could she think that he would do this to her? How could she trust him so little? He felt furious with her, and fury felt safe. Because when his fury with Becky died down, he knew what would remain. What always remained when love was gone. Pain. An emptiness so vast it felt as though it could swallow a man whole.

And he, knowing that truth as intimately as any man could know it, had still left himself wide-open to revisiting that pain. What did that mean?

"That I'm stupid," he told himself nastily. "Just plain old garden-variety stupid."

Becky felt as if she was in a trance. Numb. But it didn't matter what she was feeling. She'd agreed to do a job, and right now her job was welcoming the first of the wedding guests to the island and trying to hide it from them all that the wedding of the century was quickly turning into the fiasco of the century.

She stood with a smile fixed on her face as the door of the plane opened and the first passenger stepped down onto the steps.

In a large purple hat, and a larger purple dress, was Mrs. Barchkin, her now retired high school social sciences teacher.

"Why, Becky English!" Mrs. Barchkin said cheerily. "What on earth are you doing here?"

Her orders had been to keep the wedding secret. She had not told one person in her small town she was coming here.

Her smile clenched in place, she said, "No, what on earth are you doing here?"

Mrs. Barchkin was clutching a rumpled card in a sweaty hand. She passed it to Becky. Despite the fact people were piling up behind Mrs. Barchkin, Becky smoothed out the card and read, "In appreciation of your kindness, I ask you to be my guest at a celebration of love." There were all the details promising a limousine pickup and the adventure of a lifetime.

"Pack for a week and plan to have fun!" And all this was followed with Allie Ambrosia's flowing signature, both the small *i*'s dotted with hearts.

"Isn't this all too exciting?" Mrs. Barchkin said.

"Too exciting," Becky agreed woodenly. "If you just go over there, that golf cart will take you to your accommodations. Don't worry about your luggage."

Don't worry. Such good advice. But Becky's sense of worry grew as she greeted the rest of the guests coming down the steps of the plane. There was a poor-looking young woman in a cheaply made dress, holding a baby who looked ill. There was a man and a wife and their three kids chattering about the excitement of their first plane ride. There was a minister. At least he *might* be here to conduct the ceremony.

Not a single passenger who got off that plane was what you would expect of Hollywood's A-list. And neither, Becky realized an hour later, was anyone who got off the passenger barge. In fact, most everyone seemed to be the most ordinary of people, people who would have fit right in on Main Street in Moose Run.

They were all awed by the island and the unexpected delight of an invitation to the wedding of one of the most famous people in the world. But none of them—not a single person of the dozens that were now descending on the island—actually seem to know Allie Ambrosia or Joe Jordan.

Becky had a deepening conviction that somehow they were all pawns in Allie's big game. Maybe, just maybe, Drew had not been so wrong in doing everything he could to stop the wedding.

But why had he played with her? Why had he made it seem as if he was going along with getting a wedding ready if he was going to sabotage it? Probably, this— the never-ending storm of helicopters hovering overhead—had been a last-ditch effort to stop things when his every effort to reach his brother had been frustrated.

Still, the fact was she had trusted him. She was not going to make excuses for him! She was determined to not even think about him.

As each boat and plane delivered its guests and departed, Becky's unease grew. Her increasingly frantic texts and messages to Allie and members of Allie's staff were not being answered. In fact, Allie's voice mailbox was now full.

Becky crawled into bed that night, exhausted. The wedding was less than twenty-four hours away. If they were going to cancel it, they needed to do that now.

Though one good thing about all the excitement was that she had not had time to give a thought to Drew. But now she did.

And lying there in her bed, staring at the ceiling, she burst into tears. And the next morning she was thankful she had used up every one of her tears, because a private jet landed at precisely 7:00 a.m.

The door opened.

And absolutely nothing happened. Eventually, the crew got off. A steward told her, cheerfully, they were going to layover here. He showed her the same invitation she had seen at least a dozen times. The one that read, "In appreciation of your kindness, I ask you to be my guest at a celebration of love."

Becky had to resist the impulse to tear that invitation from his hands and rip it into a million pieces. Because now she knew the plane was empty. And Allie and Joe had not gotten off it.

Of course, it could be part of the elaborate subterfuge that was necessary to avoid the paparazzi, but the helicopters overhead were plenty of evidence they had already failed at that.

How could she, Becky asked herself with a shake of her head, still hope? How could she still hope they were coming, and still hope that love really was worth celebrating?

She quit resisting the impulse. She took the invitation from the crew member, tore it into a dozen pieces and threw them to the wind. Despite the surprised looks she received, it felt amazingly good to do that!

She turned and walked away. No more hoping. No more trying to fill in the blanks with optimistic fiction. She was going to have to find Tandu and cancel everything. She was going to have to figure out the logistics of how to get all those disappointed people back out of here.

Her head hurt thinking about it.

So Drew had won the headache competition after all. And by a country mile at that.

CHAPTER SIXTEEN

DREW PULLED HIMSELF from the ocean and flung himself onto the beach. His crew had just finished the gazebo and had departed, sending him looks that let him know he'd had been way too hard on them. He'd had them up at dawn, putting the final touches of paint on the gazebo, making sure the dance floor was ready.

What did they expect? There was supposed to be a wedding here in a few hours. Of course he had been hard on them.

Maybe a little too hard, since it now seemed almost everyone on the island, except maybe the happy guests, had figured out the bride and groom were missing.

Drew knew his foul mood had nothing to do with the missing bride and groom, or the possibility, growing more real by the second, that there wasn't going to be a wedding. He had driven his crew to perfection anyway, unreasonably.

He had tried to swim it off, but now, lying in the sand, he was aware he had not. The helicopter that buzzed him to see if he was anyone interesting did not help his extremely foul mood.

How could Becky possibly think he had called the

press? After all they had shared together, how could she not know who he really was?

It penetrated his morose that his phone, lying underneath his shirt, up the beach, was ringing. And then he froze. The ring tone was the one he had assigned for Joe!

He got up and sprinted across the sand.

"Hello?"

"Hi, bro."

It felt like a shock to hear his brother's voice. Even in those two small syllables, Drew was sure he detected something. Sheepishness?

"How are you, Drew?"

"Cut the crap."

Silence. He thought Joe might have hung up on him, but he heard him breathing.

"Where the hell have you been? Why haven't you been answering my calls? Are you on your way here?"

"Drew, I have something to tell you."

Drew was aware he was holding his breath.

"Allie and I got married an hour ago."

"What?"

"The whole island thing was just a ruse. Allie leaked it to the press yesterday morning that we were going to get married there to divert them away from where we really are."

"You lied to me?" He could hear the disbelief and disappointment in his own voice.

"I feel terrible about that. I'm sorry."

"But why?"

Inside he was thinking, *How could you get married without me to stand beside you? I might have made mistakes, but I'm the one who has your back. Who has always had your back.*

"It's complicated," Joe said.

"Let me get this straight. You aren't coming here at all?"

"No."

Poor Allie, Drew thought.

"We got married an hour ago, just Allie and me and a justice of the peace. We're in Topeka, Kansas. Who would ever think to look there, huh?"

"Topeka, Kansas," he repeated dully.

His brother took it as a question. "You don't have to be a resident of the state to get married here. There's a three-day waiting period for the license, but I went down and applied for it a month ago."

"You've been planning this for a month?" Drew felt the pain of it. He had been excluded from one of the most important events of his brother's life. And it was his own fault.

"I'm sorry," he said.

"For what?" Joe sounded astounded.

"That I could never tell you what you needed to hear."

"I'm not following."

"That I loved you and cared about you and would have fought alligators for you."

"Drew! You think I don't know that?"

"I guess if you know it, I don't understand any of this."

"It's kind of all part of a larger plan. I'll fill you in soon. I promise. Meanwhile, Allie's got her people on it right now. In a few hours the press will know we aren't there, and whatever's going on there will die down. They'll leave you guys alone."

"Leave us alone? You think I'm going to stay here?"

"Why not? It's a party. That's all the invitations ever said. That it was a party to celebrate love."

"Who are all these people arriving here?"

And when Joe told him, Drew could feel himself, ever so reluctantly, letting go of the anger.

Even his anger at Becky felt as if it was dissipating.

He understood, suddenly, exactly why she had jumped at the first opportunity to see him in a bad light. That girl was terrified of love. She'd been betrayed by it at too many turns. She was terrified of what she was feeling for him.

"Joe? Tell Allie not to call Becky about the wedding not happening. I'll look after it. I'll tell her myself."

There was a long silence. And then Joe said softly, "All part of a larger plan."

"Yeah, whatever." He wanted to tell his brother congratulations, but somehow he couldn't. Who was this woman that Joe had married? It seemed as if she was just playing with all their strings as if they were her puppets.

Drew threw on his shirt and took the now familiar path back toward the castle. What remained of his anger at Becky for not trusting him was completely gone.

All he wanted to do was protect her from one more devastating betrayal. He understood, suddenly, what love was. With startling clarity he saw that it was the ability to see that it was not all about him. To be able to put her needs ahead of his own and not be a baby because his feelings had been hurt.

As he got closer to the castle, he could see there were awestruck people everywhere prowling the grounds. He spotted Tandu in the crowd, talking to a tall, distinguished-looking man in a casual white suit and bare feet.

"Mr. Drew Jordan, have you met Mr. Lung?" Tandu asked him.

"Pleasure," Drew said absently. "Tandu, can I talk to you for a minute?"

Tandu stepped to the side with him. "Have you seen Becky?" he asked, with some urgency.

"A few minutes ago. She told me to cancel everything."

So, she already knew, or thought she did. She was carrying the burden of it by herself.

"Impossible to cancel," Tandu said. "The wedding must go on!"

"Tandu, there is not going to be a wedding. I just spoke to my brother."

"Ah," he said. "Oh, well, we celebrate love anyway, hmm?" And then he gave Drew a look that was particularly piercing, and disappeared into the crowd.

"How are you enjoying my island?" Bart Lung was on his elbow.

"It's a beautiful place," Drew said, scanning the crowd for Becky. "Uh, look, Mr. Lung—"

"Bart, please."

"Bart, I think you need to have a qualified first aid person on the island to host this many guests."

"I have an excellent first aid attendant. That was him who just introduced us. Don't be fooled by the tray of canapés."

"Look, Tandu is a nice guy. Stellar. I just don't think being afraid of blood is a great trait for a first aid attendant."

"Tandu? Afraid of blood? Who told you that?"

Before Drew could answer that Tandu himself had told him that, Bart went on.

"Tandu is from this island, but don't be fooled by that island boy accent or the white shirt or the tray of canapés. He's a medical student at Oxford. He comes back in the summers to help out." Bart chortled. "Afraid of blood! I saw him once when he was the first responder to a shark attack. I have never seen so much blood and I have never seen such cool under pressure."

Drew felt a shiver run up and down the whole length of his spine.

And then he saw Becky. She was talking to someone who was obviously a member of the flight crew, and she was waving her arms around expressively.

"Excuse me. I have an urgent matter I need to take care of."

"Of course."

"Becky!"

She turned and looked at him, and for a moment, everything she felt was naked in her face.

And everything she was.

Drew realized fully that her lack of trust was a legacy from her past, and that to be the man she needed, the man worthy of her love, he needed to not hurt her more, but to understand her fears and vulnerabilities and to help her heal them.

Just as she had, without even knowing that was what she was doing, helped him heal his own fears and vulnerabilities.

"We need to talk," he said. "In private."

She looked at him, and then looked away. "Now? I don't see that there is any way they are coming. I was just asking about the chances of getting some flight schedules changed."

Despite the fact she *knew* Allie and Joe weren't com-

ing, despite the fact that she had asked Tandu about can-
celing, despite the fact that she was trying to figure out
how to get rid of all these people, he saw it, just for a
second, wink behind her bright eyes.

Hope.

Against all odds, his beautiful, funny, bookish,
spunky Becky was still hoping for a happy ending.

"We need to talk," Drew told her.

She hesitated, scanned the sky for an incoming jet
and then sighed. "Yes, all right," she said.

He led her away from the crowded front lawn and
front terrace.

"I just talked to Joe," he said in a low voice.

"And? Is everything okay? Between you?"

This was who she really was: despite it all, despite
thinking that he had betrayed her trust, she was worried about him and his troubled relationship with his
brother, first. And the wedding second.

"I guess time will tell."

"You didn't patch things up," she said sadly.

"He didn't phone to patch things up. Becky, he gave
me some bad news."

"Is he all right?" There it was again, a boundless
compassion for others. "What?" she whispered.

"There isn't going to be a wedding."

It was then that he knew she had been holding her
breath, waiting for a miracle, because the air whooshed
out of her and her shoulders sagged.

"Because of the press finding out?" she said.

"No, Becky, there was never going to be a wedding."

She looked at him with disbelief.

"Apparently this whole thing—" he swept his arm
to indicate the whole thing "—was just a giant ruse

planned out in every detail by Allie. She sent the press here, yesterday morning, on a wild-goose chase."

"It wasn't you," she whispered. Her skin turned so pale he wondered if she was going to faint.

"Of course it wasn't me."

She began to tremble. "But how are you ever going to forgive me for thinking it was you?"

"I don't believe," he said softly, "that you ever did believe that. Not in your heart."

"Why did she do that?" Becky wailed.

"So that she and my brother could sneak away and get married in peace. Which they did. An hour ago. In Topeka, Kansas, of all places."

Her hand was on his arm. She was looking at him searchingly. "Your brother got married without you?"

He lifted a shoulder.

"Oh! That is absolutely unforgivable!"

"It's not your problem."

"Oh, my God! Here I am saying what is unforgivable in other people, and what I did was unforgivable. I accused you of alerting the press!"

"Is it possible," he asked her softly, "that you wanted to be mad at me? Is it possible it was just one last-ditch effort to protect yourself from falling in love with me?"

She was doing now what she had not done when he told her there would be no wedding. She was crying.

"I'm so sorry," she said.

"Is it true then? Are you in love with me?"

"Yes, I'm afraid it is. It's true."

"It's true for me, too. I'm in love with you, Becky. I am so in love with you. And I'm as terrified as you are. I'm afraid of loving. I'm afraid of loss. I'm afraid I can't be the man you need me to be. I'm afraid…"

She stopped him with her lips. She stopped him by twining her hands around his neck and pulling him close to her.

And when she did that, he wasn't afraid of anything anymore.

mouth,

CHAPTER SEVENTEEN

"WHY DID SHE do all this?" Becky asked.

"Joe told me that she never told any of these people they were coming to a wedding."

"She didn't! That's true. She told them in appreciation for their kindness they were being invited to a celebration of love. I saw some of the invitations today. It doesn't really answer *why* she did all this, does it? All this tremendous expense for a ruse? There are a million things that would have been easier and cheaper to send the press in the wrong direction so they could get married in private."

"Joe told me why she did it."

"And?"

"Joe told me that people would look at her humble beginnings and share personal stories about themselves. And so she sent invitations to the ones with the most compelling personal stories, a comeback from cancer, a bankruptcy, surviving the death of a child.

"Joe says she has thought of nothing else for months—that she did her homework. That she chose the ones who rose above their personal circumstances and still gave back to others.

"He said those are the ones they want to celebrate

love with them. He said Allie wants her story to bring
hope to lives where too many bad things had occurred.
He says she's determined to make miracles happen."

"Wow," Becky said softly. "It almost makes me not
want to be mad at her."

"Regretfully, me, too."

They laughed softly together.

"It's quite beautiful, isn't it?" Becky said quietly.

He wanted to harrumph it. He wanted to say it was
impossibly naive and downright dumb. He wanted to
say his future sister-in-law—no, make that his current
sister-in-law—was showing signs of being extraordinarily clever about manipulating others.

He wanted to say all that, but somehow he couldn't.

Because here he was, the beneficiary of one of the
miracles that Allie Ambrosia had been so determined
to make happen.

You heal now, Tandu had said to him. And somehow
his poor wounded heart had healed, just enough to let
this woman beside him past his defenses. Now, he found
himself hoping they would have the rest of their lives
to heal each other, to get better and better.

"You know, Becky, all those people are expecting
a wedding. Tandu said it's impossible to put a hold on
the food now."

"It's harder to reschedule those exit flights than you
might think."

"The minister is already here. And so is the photographer."

"What of it?"

"I think any wedding that is a true expression of love
will honor why we are all here."

"What are you suggesting?"

"I don't think she ever had that dress made to hurt you."

"Oh, my God." Becky's fist flew to her mouth, and tears shone behind her eyes.

"And I've been thinking about this. There is no way my brother would ever get married without me. Not unless he thought it was for my own good."

"They put us together deliberately!"

"I'm afraid that's what I'm thinking."

"It's maddening."

"Yes."

"It's a terrible manipulation."

"Yes."

"It's like a blind date on steroids."

"Yes."

"Are you angry?"

"No."

"Me, neither."

"Because it worked. If they would have just introduced us over dinner somewhere, it would have never worked out like this."

"I know. You would have seen me as a girl from Moose Run, one breath away from becoming a nun."

"You would have seen me as superficial and arrogant and easily bored."

"You would have never given me a second chance."

"You wouldn't have wanted one."

They were silent for a long time, contemplating how things could have gone, and how they did.

"What time is the wedding?" he asked her.

"It's supposed to be at three."

"That means you have one hour and fifteen minutes to make up your mind."

"I've made up my mind," Becky whispered.

"You should put on that dress and we should go to that gazebo I built, and in the incredible energy of two hundred people who have been hand-chosen for the bigness of their hearts, we should get married."

"It won't be real," she whispered. "I mean, not legal. It will be like we're playing roles."

"Well, I won't be playing a role, and I don't think you're capable of it. We'll go to Kansas when it's all over. In three days we'll have a license."

"Are you asking me to marry you? For real? Not as part of Allie's amazing pretend world?"

"Absolutely, 100 percent for real."

She stared at him. She began to laugh, and then cry. She threw her arms around his neck. "Yes! Yes! Yes!" she said.

All the helicopters had gone away. The world was perfect and silent and sacred.

Despite the fact they were using up a great deal of that one hour and fifteen minutes, they talked. They talked about children. And where they would live. And what they would do. They talked about how Tandu seemed as if he was a bit of a matchmaker, too, leaving Drew to doctor Becky's leg when he had been more than capable of doing it himself, of delivering them to the best and most romantic places on the island, of "seeing" the future.

Finally, as the clock ticked down, they parted ways with a kiss.

Tandu was waiting for her when she arrived back at the castle. He took in her radiant face with satisfaction.

"You need my help to be best bride ever?"

"How do you know these things?" she asked him.

"I see."

"I know you're a medical student at Oxford."

He chuckled happily. "That is when *seeing* is the most helpful."

Tandu accompanied her up the stairs, but when she went to go to her room, Tandu nudged her in a different direction. "Take the bridal suite."

Becky stared at him suspiciously. "Have you been in on this all along?"

He smiled. "Allie has been to Sainte Simone before. I count her as my friend. I will go let the guests know there has been a slight change in plan and arrange some helpers. I will look after everything."

She could not argue with him. All her life she had never been able to accept good things happening to her, but she was willing to change. She was willing to embrace each gift as it was delivered.

Had she not been delivered a husband out of a storybook? Why not believe? She went to the bridal suite, and stood before the dress that she had hung up days before. She touched it, and it felt not unlike she had been a princess sleeping, who was now waking up.

Tandu had assembled some lovely women helpers and she was treated like a princess. Given that the time until the wedding was so brief, Becky was pampered shamelessly. Her hair was done, her makeup was applied.

And then the beautiful dress was delivered to her. She closed her eyes. Becky let her old self drop away with each stich of her clothing. The dress, and every dream that had been sewn right into the incredible fabric, skimmed over her naked skin. She heard the zipper whisper up.

"Look now," one of her shy helpers instructed.

Becky opened her eyes. Her mouth fell open. The most beautiful princess stood in front of her, her hair piled up on top of her head, with little tendrils kissing the sides of her face. Her eyes, expertly made-up, looked wide and gorgeous. Her cheekbones looked unbelievable. Her lips, pink glossed and slightly turned up in an almost secretive smile, looked sensual.

Her eyes strayed down the elegant curve of her neck to the full enchantment of the dress. The vision in the mirror wobbled like a mirage as her eyes filled with tears.

The dress was a confection, with its sweetheart neckline and fitted bodice, and layers and layers and layers of filmy fabric flowing out in that full skirt with an impossible train. It made her waist look as if a man could span it with his two hands.

Shoes were brought to her, and they looked, fantastically, like the glass slippers in fairy tales.

All those years ago this dress had been the epitome of her every romantic notion. Becky had been able to picture herself in it, but she had never been able to picture it being Jerry that she walked toward.

Because she had never felt like she felt in this moment.

She was so aware that the bride's beauty was not created by the dress. The dress only accentuated what was going on inside, that bubbling fountain of life that love had built within her.

"No crying! You'll ruin your makeup."

But everyone else in the room was crying, all of them feeling the absolute sanctity of this moment, when someone who has been a girl realizes she is ready to be a woman. When someone who has never known the reality of love steps fully into its light.

A beautiful bouquet of island flowers was placed in her hands.

"This way."

Still in a dream, she moved down the castle stairs and out the door. The grounds that had been such a beehive of activity were strangely deserted. A golf cart waited for her and it whisked her silently down the wide path, through the lushness of the tropical growth, to the beach.

She walked down that narrow green-shaded trail to where it opened at the beach. The chairs were all full. If anyone was disappointed that it was not Allie who appeared at the edge of the jungle, it did not show on a single face.

If she had to choose one word to explain the spirit she walked in and toward it would be *joy*.

Bart Lung bowed to her and offered her his arm. She kicked off the glass slippers and felt her feet sink into the sand. She was so aware that she felt as if she could feel every single grain squish up between her toes.

A four-piece ensemble began to play the traditional wedding march.

She dared to look at the gazebo. If this weren't true, this was the part where she would wake up. In her nightmares the gazebo would be empty.

But it was not empty. The minister that she had welcomed on the first plane stood there in purple cleric's robes, beaming at her.

And then Drew turned around.

Becky's breath caught in her throat. She faltered, but the light that burned in his eyes picked her up and made her strong. She moved across the space between them unerringly, her eyes never leaving his, her sense of wonder making it hard to breathe.

She was marrying this man. She was marrying this strong, funny, thrillingly handsome man who would protect those he loved with his life. She was the luckiest woman in the world and she knew it.

Bart let go of her arm at the bottom of the stairs, and Becky went to Drew like an arrow aimed straight for his heart.

She went to him like someone who had been lost in the wilderness catching sight of the way home.

She went to him with his children already being born inside her.

She repeated the vows, those age-old vows, feeling as if each word had a deep meaning she had missed before.

And then came these words:

"I now pronounce you husband and wife."

And before the minister could say anything more, Becky turned and cast her beautiful bouquet at the gathering and went into his arms and claimed his lips.

And then he picked her up and carried her down the steps and out into the ocean, and with the crowd cheering madly, he kissed her again, before he wrapped his arms tightly around her and they both collapsed into the embrace of a turquoise sea.

When they came up for air, they were laughing and sputtering, her perfect hair was ruined, her makeup was running down her face and her dress was clinging to her in wet ribbons.

"This has been the best day of my entire life," she told him. "There will never be another day as good as this one."

And Drew said to her, "No, that's not quite right. This day is just the beginning of the best days of our lives."

And he kissed her again, and the crowd went wild, but her world felt like a grotto of silence and peace, a place cut out of a busy world, just for them. A place created by love.

EPILOGUE

"Who agreed to this insanity?" Drew demanded of his wife.

"You did," Becky told him. She handed him a crying baby and scooped the other one out of the car seat that had been deposited on their living room floor.

Drew frowned at the baby and held it at arm's length. "Does he stink?"

"Probably. I don't think that's he. I think it's she. Pink ribbon in hair."

Drew squinted at the pink ribbon. It would not be beyond his brother to put the ribbon in Sam's hair instead of Sally's.

"I've changed my mind," Drew declared over the howling of the smelly baby. "I am not ready for this. I am not even close to being ready for this."

"Well, it's too late. Your brother and Allie are gone to Sainte Simone. They never had a honeymoon, and if ever a couple needed one, they do."

"I'm not responsible for their choices," he groused, but he was aware it was good-naturedly. His sister-in-law, Allie, was exasperating. And flaky. She was completely out of touch with reality, and her career choice of pretending to be other people had made that quality even more aggravating in her. She believed, with a childlike enthusiasm, in the fairy tales she acted out, and was a huge proponent of happily-ever-after.

And yet…and yet, could you ask for anyone more genuinely good-hearted than her? Or generous? Or kind? Or devoted to her family in general, and his brother in particular?

There was no arguing that Joe, his sweet, shy brother, had blossomed into a confident and happy man under the influence of his choice of a life partner.

In that Hollywood world where a marriage could be gone up in smoke in weeks, Allie and Joe seemed imminently solid. They had found what they both longed for most: that place called home. And they were not throwing it away.

"Mommy gone? Daddy gone?"

Drew juggled the baby, and stared down at one more little face looking up at him. It occurred to him now would be a bad time to let his panic show.

"Yes, Andrew," he said quietly, "You're staying with Uncle Drew and Aunt Becky for a few days."

"Don't want to," Andrew announced.

That makes two of us.

Joe and Allie had adopted Andrew from an orphanage in Brazil not six months after they had married. The fact that the little boy was missing a leg only seemed to make them love him more. He'd only been home with them for about a month when they had found out they were pregnant. The fact that they had been pregnant with twins had been a surprise until just a few weeks before Sam and Sally had been born.

But the young couple had handled it with aplomb. Drew could see what he had never seen before: that

Joe longed for that sense of family they had both lost even more than he himself had. Joe had chosen Allie, out of some instinct that Drew did not completely understand, as the woman who could give him what he longed for.

So, Joe and Allie were celebrating their second anniversary with a honeymoon away from their three children.

And Drew and Becky would celebrate their second anniversary, one day behind Joe and Allie, with a pack of children, because Allie had announced they were the only people she would trust with her precious offspring.

"I wish I had considered the smell when I agreed to this," he said. "How are we going to have a romantic anniversary now?"

"Ah, we'll think of something," Becky said with that little wink of hers that could turn his blood to liquid lava. "They have to sleep sometime."

"Are you sure?"

"It will be good practice for us," she said. She said it very casually. Too casually. She shot him a look over the tousled dandelion-fluff hair of the baby she was holding.

He went very still. He moved the baby from the crook of one arm to the crook of the other. He stared at his wife, and took in the radiant smile on her face as she looked away from him and gazed at the baby in her arms.

"Good practice for us?"

Andrew punched him in the leg. "I hate you," he decided. "Where's my daddy?"

Becky threw back her head and laughed.

And he saw it then. He wondered how he had missed

it, he who thought he knew every single nuance of his wife's looks and personality and moods.

He saw that she was different. Becky was absolutely glowing, softly and beautifully radiant.

"Yes," she said softly. "Good practice for us."

Andrew kicked him again. Drew looked down at him. Soon, sooner than he could ever have prepared for, he was going to have a little boy like this. A boy who would miss him terribly when he went somewhere. Who would look to him for guidance and direction. Who would think he got up early in the morning and put out the sun for him.

Or maybe he would have a little girl like the one in his arms, howling and stinky, and so, so precious it could steal a man's breath away. A little girl who would need him to show her how to throw a baseball so that the boys wouldn't make her think less of herself. And who would one day, God forbid, need him to sort through all the boys who wanted to date her to find one that might be suitable.

How could a man be ready for that?

He looked again into his wife's face. She was watching him with a soft, knowing smile playing across the fullness of her lips.

That's how he could be ready.

Because love made a man what he could never hope to be on his own. Once, because of the loss of those he had loved the most, he'd thought it was the force that could take a man's strength completely.

Now he saw that all love wove itself into the person a man eventually became. His parents were with him. Becky's love shaped him every day.

And made him ready for whatever was going to happen next.

Andrew punched him again. Juggling the baby, he bent down and scooped Andrew up in his other arm.

"I know," he said. "I know you miss your daddy."

Andrew wailed his assent and buried his head in Drew's neck. The stinky baby started to cry. Becky laughed again. He leaned over and kissed her nose.

And it felt as if in a life full of perfect moments, none had been more perfect than this one.

Daddy. He was going to be a daddy.

It was just as he had said to her the day they had gotten married. It wasn't the best day of their lives. All that was best was still in front of him, in a future that shone bright in the light of love. That love flowed over him from the look in her eyes. It flowed over him and drenched him and all of those days that were yet to come in its shimmering light.

* * * * *

FOREVER A STALLION

DEBORAH FLETCHER MELLO

To Wes 'Third' Woody,

You are a source of sheer inspiration.

Your bright smile absolutely moves my spirit.

Please know that you are much loved.

Chapter 1

Mason Boudreaux extended a large hand toward the president and chief executive officer of Stallion Enterprises. John Stallion shook it heartily, cementing his company's five-billion-dollar acquisition of the Boudreaux hotel chain.

"Congratulations!" Mason intoned as John's brother, Matthew Stallion, popped the cork on a vintage bottle of Veuve Clicquot Brut champagne.

John nodded. "And congratulations to you, as well, sir. I'm sure this means that you will be wearing retirement quite well."

"I don't know about retirement." Mason let out a deep chuckle. "But I imagine I'm going to have a hell of a time with whatever my next business venture might be."

Matthew passed each man a crystal flute filled with drink. "Well, Mason, if your next adventure is as profitable as this one was, you'll be doing exceptionally well for yourself, my friend."

Mason nodded his agreement as he lifted his champagne glass in salute, celebrating the sale of his hotel-owning company to the Stallion family. At his age of thirty-seven, selling the forty-five hundred hotels that constituted Boudreaux International Hotels and Resorts was a testament to his hard work and dedication. The multibillion-dollar payment was an acknowledgment of his success.

"And now that Boudreaux International is under the Stallion umbrella, I can only hope and pray that we will continue to build on all of your accomplishments," John said, grinning broadly, "which is why I'm happy that we could convince you to stay on board in a consulting capacity. I'm certain that we'll need to draw on your knowledge and experience."

Mason took a sip of his drink. "It's going to be a great partnership and I'm glad we're keeping it in the family," he said as he gestured in Matthew's direction.

Matthew laughed. "I appreciate that, brother-in-law. More than you know."

"Oh, I know!" Mason said, laughing with him. "I know my sister. I'm sure Katrina has just about worked your last nerve offering her advice about this deal. I've lost count of the number of times she's wrangled me to give her opinion."

"You know it!" Matthew said, thinking of his beautiful new wife. Mason's sister Katrina and he had married a few weeks earlier. His whirlwind relationship with the district court judge had taken them both by surprise and now the couple was anxiously awaiting

the arrival of their first child together. "And those preg-
nancy hormones have not helped."

The third oldest Stallion brother, Mark, chimed
in as he stepped through the conference room door.
His baby daughter was clutched to his chest, the six-
month-old little girl looking around in wide-eyed wonder. "Well, the wives are headed upstairs. Good news
traveled fast."

"I swear, it's like they all have radar." John laughed
and shook his head. He leaned to nuzzle his niece's
chubby cheek.

"I heard that, John Stallion," his wife, Marah, said
as she led the way into the oversize room.

John laughed as the beautiful woman moved to his
side. He leaned to kiss her lips, wrapping his arms
tightly around her small frame. "I didn't say anything,
baby!"

Marah rolled her eyes as she kissed him back. "Uh-
huh. Sure you didn't!"

Mark's wife, Michelle Stallion, waved her hand in
greeting as she brought up the rear. "Hey, everyone,"
she said brightly as she reached to take her daughter
from her husband's arms. Mark wrapped them both in
a deep bear hug.

"Congratulations!" Katrina shouted. She moved to
kiss her brother's cheek first and then her husband's.
"This is so exciting!" she said as she nestled close
against Matthew's chest.

Matthew caressed the bulge of new baby that pro-
truded from her abdomen, his fingers lingering where
the baby kicked once, and then a second time. "Yes,
it is!"

With the arrival of the women, the chatter in the

room rose exponentially. Mason was feeling right at home as he looked around at the gleaming faces. Family—the best cheerleaders any man could wish for. He and his sister Katrina came from a large family, so this felt very much like home to them both. He grinned widely as he noted the endearing gestures she and her husband exchanged.

He couldn't help being in awe of the wealth of love that filled the room. With Matthew and Katrina; John and his wife, Marah; and Mark, his wife, Michelle, and their new baby girl, Irene, the room overflowed with love.

Mason was suddenly introspective as he imagined what it might be like to have someone of his own to love. He had mastered professional success to the detriment of his personal life. Although he'd enjoyed the many beautiful women who had gone hand in hand with his lifestyle, he'd grown weary of the endless workweeks and his playboy lifestyle. Mason found himself not only ready for a change, but actively searching for the comforts family and stability would afford him. Selling his business could not have come at a more opportune time. He could feel himself grinning at the prospects.

His thoughts were interrupted by the persistent chatter. He shifted forward in his seat as he drew his focus back to the conversation.

"Where's Luke?" Katrina was asking. "And Joanne? I thought they'd be here."

John shook his head. "Last-minute wedding chores. They had to have their final session of couple's counseling with Reverend Barnes, and this was the only time he could fit them in. They'll catch up with us all later."

"Speaking of chores," Marah interjected. "We ladies have a very long list of things to get done. Between the rodeo and the wedding, we'll be running from one event to the next through the end of the month, and that takes some preparing for. Each one of us is going to need a few new outfits to wear. Isn't that right?" she said as Michelle and Katrina nodded in agreement.

Mark winked toward his brothers, shaking his head. "I told Luke to elope but no, you women had to throw in your two cents. He and Joanne could have been married by now. Done and finished. Then none of you would need to do any shopping at all!"

John laughed. "Do not get these women started, please."

Marah tapped John against the chest. "You've got some nerve."

"Don't pay either one of them any attention," Katrina said, rolling her eyes skyward. "Matthew will tell you that he enjoyed every second of our wedding. Didn't you, honey?"

Matthew leaned to kiss her cheek. "That's right, my darling! Walking down the aisle with you was the best thing I ever did," he said, winking at the men.

Mason chuckled. "It sounds to me like you guys have your hands full."

Matthew's head bobbed up and down. "Oh, no, not at all," he said, his eyes widening mischievously as Katrina punched him playfully in the arm.

Mason grinned broadly as he watched his sister and brother-in-law, the two teasing each other playfully. It had been a long time since he'd seen Katrina so happy.

Joy shimmered out of her dark eyes, everything between her and her husband exemplifying the dynamic relationship they shared. An unexpected hint of jealousy flooded Mason's spirit. As if reading his mind, Katrina moved to her big brother's side, wrapping her arm around his broad shoulders.

"There will be a lot of beautiful, successful women for you to meet while you're here in Dallas, Mason," she said casually.

Mason smiled. "Really?" he questioned, crossing his arms over his chest.

Katrina nodded. "You might even find us a new sister-in-law if you play your cards right, big brother!"

Tossing his head back, Mason laughed heartily. Saying nothing aloud, he leaned to kiss his sister's cheek. *From your mouth to God's ears,* he thought to himself, his smile brightening even more. *From your mouth to God's ears!*

Chapter 2

Phaedra Parrish closed and locked the front door of her family home after bidding a member from her mother's church goodbye. People had been popping in to check on her since the funeral, and with the day being her twenty-eighth birthday, there had been a revolving door of family and friends coming to give her support. It had been a long day and an even longer month, and she was glad for the wealth of silence that quickly enveloped the room. She sighed deeply as she dropped down onto the cushioned sofa that sat opposite her mother's favorite rocking chair.

As she stared at the empty seat, Phaedra's tears clouded her dark eyes. It didn't feel as if a whole month had passed since her mother, Arneta Parrish, had last rocked in that chair, everything seemingly well. Then without warning, a pulmonary embolism had taken her away. Their family doctor had reasoned that she'd probably been experiencing symptoms days earlier, the blood clot traveling from her leg to her lung. But Phaedra had not been there to know, and now her mother was gone from her.

Swiping at the tears that fell down her cheeks, Phaedra closed her eyes and inhaled, filling her lungs with a deep breath. She couldn't help wishing that she'd come home as originally scheduled instead of extending her photography assignment those additional days. Had she been home, then just maybe her beloved mother would still be there with her.

Even as the thought crossed her mind, Phaedra could hear her mother admonishing her, the woman's deep alto voice echoing in her thoughts. *"You're wasting time, little girl! Focus on what you need to do and get your narrow behind to doin' somethin' worthwhile."* And just as the thought crossed her mind, she felt a warm breeze blow through the room and a gust of wind gently caressing her cheeks.

Phaedra rose to her feet, wrapping her arms tightly around her torso. Across the room she imagined that her mother's chair was rocking, the movement ever so slight, and she couldn't help smiling, sensing that Miss Arneta was still there, still watching over her, still intent on keeping her on the straight and narrow. She shook her head from side to side as she laughed. "Yes, ma'am," she said out loud, chuckling softly.

Moving through the modest home, Phaedra checked that the lower level was secure, ensuring that all the doors and windows were locked. Leaving the one light on in the hallway, she headed up the stairs, hesitating for a brief moment in front of her mother's bedroom door. She'd known that at some point she would have to sort through her mother's things, and although it wasn't a task Phaedra had looked forward to, she knew it had to be done.

Pushing the door open, Phaedra flicked the light switch on the wall as she moved inside the small room. Dropping down against the full-size mattress, she drew her hands across the handmade quilt that decorated the bed. She missed her mother with a vengeance. Her grief was so consuming that she couldn't imagine how she was going to survive. She let out a deep sigh.

As she moved to stand back up, Phaedra's heel brushed against a large shoe box protruding from beneath the bed. Reaching down, she drew her hand against the exterior surface, pausing as she thought about its contents. She'd found the container while searching for her mother's favorite black heels to take to the undertaker. As she'd scanned the documents inside, none of it had made any sense to her. Refusing to acknowledge what she'd discovered, she'd tossed it to the floor, kicking it back beneath the bed. She'd known that she would eventually have to revisit it all and she'd chosen to ignore it until there was nothing else on her plate to deal with.

Slipping her tank top over her head and stepping out of her shorts, she dropped the garments to the floor. Pulling back the covers, she crawled into her mother's bed, drawing the comforter around her small frame. The box rested against the bed beside her, and her hand shook ever so slightly as she tossed the container's cover to the floor. Pulling the documents into her lap, Phaedra took a deep breath and then a second.

If anyone had asked her about her mother having secrets, Phaedra would have sworn on her own life that there wasn't anything about Arneta Parrish that she didn't know. But Arneta had carried the biggest secret of her life to her grave, never disclosing the bombshell that would soon be her only daughter's life.

Arneta's collection of diaries rested on top. Pulling the leather-bound journals into her hands, Phaedra pulled at a black-and-white photo that served as a page holder for the most recent entry. The image was of her mother and a man Phaedra didn't know, the couple caught in a deep embrace. Her mother was smiling, joy shining in her expression. The handsome man's smile was not as bright, something in his eyes telling a very different story. But he had a kind face and it was obvious that his presence was making her mother very happy.

Flipping the photo over, Phaedra read the name on the back side. James David Stallion. The photo was dated a year before Phaedra was born. Resting the photo back inside the book, she continued to flip through other papers on James Stallion's life.

There was a letter dated just a few short months after the photo, Mr. Stallion apologizing for a quick departure, wishing his dear friend Arneta a bright and successful future. The ink had faded in spots, drops of moisture having dampened the paper. It was obvious her mother had cried over that letter, remnants of her tearstains having marred some of the words.

Tucked in the envelope with that single letter was a yellowed newspaper article that had been folded closed. It was the obituary that carried the news of James Stallion's death. The man had died in a fiery car accident with his beloved wife, Irene, the couple leaving behind four young sons.

Four sons. Four boys who'd grown to be four very successful men. Phaedra's mother had kept tabs on the Stallion kin, collecting articles of their many accomplishments. Flipping through the articles, Phaedra couldn't help being impressed. But she didn't understand her mother's reasons for caring, the woman having never mentioned the family to her daughter. Phaedra had to wonder why.

Adjusting the pillows beneath her head, Phaedra flipped through the diaries until she found the one dated the year before her birth. She opened the journal to the first page, pulling her knees upright as she rested the book against her thighs. She was suddenly anxious to know her mother's secret and the story that she'd never been told. And she was anxious to read them in her mother's own words.

One week later flight number 1267 from New Orleans, Louisiana, to Dallas, Texas, departed, leaving Phaedra with one hour and thirty-five minutes to rethink what she was planning to do before touching down. Her stomach knotted, feeling as if her sugared beignet and chicory coffee breakfast was not going to sit well. Phaedra knew it was only nerves, anxiety pretending to be her new best friend since she'd read her mother's journals, opening a chapter into her own life that she'd not been prepared for.

Phaedra drew her manicured fingers against her Coach bag, two of her mother's journals and some supporting documents secured in a side pocket. It hadn't taken any time at all for her to go through her mother's papers and discover that there had been much about the woman that she hadn't known. The writings had read

like a bestselling romance novel, detailing the highs of
her mother's relationship with James David Stallion.
And then the lows, James David Stallion disappearing from Arneta's life like a dream lost too soon to a
morning sunrise. James leaving before ever learning
about the child Arneta would eventually raise alone.

James David Stallion. Phaedra's biological father.
The secret her mother had never wanted her to know.
Phaedra shook her head for the umpteenth time since
finding out, her eyes lifting to stare out the airplane
window. An endless bright blue sky marred by an oc-
casional tuft of cloud brought a slight smile to her face.
The view was magical, soothing the inner turmoil that
threatened Phaedra's peace of mind.

All of her life Phaedra had believed that Daniel Parrish had been her father. Daniel Parrish had only been
married to her mother for short two years before disappearing into the Louisiana penal system. Reading her
mother's story, Phaedra discovered Arneta had already
been pregnant when she'd met and married Daniel.

After many years of therapy Phaedra had come to
terms with having an absentee father who preferred a
life of crime over his loving wife and daughter. Her
mother had often used her own life as an example of
what happened when a woman made bad choices over
men who were not deserving of her. She'd been apolo-
getic for not having served Phaedra better.

When Daniel had died, still locked behind prison
walls, Phaedra had mourned the loving father she had
wanted him to be, not the apathetic parent he had actually been. And through it all, her mother had never
once considered that Phaedra needed to know the truth
of her paternity. But reading her mother's words, Phae-

dra had come to understand that her mother had wanted only to protect both her daughter and James Stallion, the only man she'd apparently ever loved. Holding the truth close to her heart had been Arneta's way of shielding all of them from heartbreak. But Arneta had been wrong because her heart had been broken, and now Phaedra's heart was broken, too.

Heading to Dallas, Phaedra was now hoping for an opportunity to meet the siblings who shared her bloodline. Hoping against all odds to connect with her father's family, the family that was also her own.

Chapter 3

"**W**ow!" Mason called out, his eyes widening as they settled down against the bleachers to watch the annual Wild West rodeo show that was about to begin. The entire morning had been a whirlwind of events, one happening right after the other. Mason would never have imagined the magnitude of the Briscoe-Stallion Annual Rodeo, it being the most attended community event in Dallas each year.

Briscoe Ranch was well over eight hundred acres of working cattle ranch, an equestrian center and an entertainment complex that specialized in corporate and private client services. With the property being central to Austin, Houston, Dallas and Fort Worth, Briscoe Ranch had made quite a name for itself.

Back in the day, Edward Briscoe, the ranch's original owner, had been one of the original black cowboys. Not long after the birth of his three daughters, Eden and the twins, Marla and Marah, he and his first wife had expanded their Texas longhorn operation, adding two twenty-thousand-square-feet event barns and a country bed-and-breakfast.

After Marah Briscoe's marriage to business tycoon John Stallion, Edward had given the property to his daughter and new son-in-law, her love for a Stallion ending the conflict that had brought the couple together in the first place. Under the Stallion family umbrella, Briscoe Ranch was growing steadily and now a point of consideration for a number of government programs to assist children and families in need. The ranch was home to them all, and the pride and joy of both families.

"This is something!" Mason said, tipping his head toward John and Matthew, who'd settled down beside him.

John laughed. "Marah's father, Edward, has been hosting this event since forever. Every year we're amazed at just how big it's gotten."

Matthew nodded his concurrence. "At the rate we're growing, I'm afraid we might run out of land to accommodate everyone," he said jokingly.

John and Mason both laughed with him.

"So, what then?" Mason queried. "Will you buy the state of Texas?"

John grinned broadly. "Maybe Mexico, too, especially if we keep allowing these women to be in charge!" he mused.

Laughter rang out among them, the three men clearly having a good time.

From a safe distance across the way, Phaedra adjusted the lens on her camera, focusing her sight on the two brothers seated beside each other. She snapped a photo and then a second one before letting the camera rest back against her chest, hanging from a secure leather strap around her neck.

The rodeo event had been a stroke of luck for her. Access to the ranch and the Stallion men had come with minimal difficulty. From the moment Phaedra had stepped onto the property, the brothers had been front and center, taking their hosting responsibilities seriously. Without needing to ask, Phaedra had been able to identify the four of them almost instantly.

From the back pocket of her denim jeans, Phaedra pulled out the photograph she'd found in her mother's possessions, glancing from them to it and back again. There was no mistaking the Stallion lineage detailed in their facial features, each son the spitting image of his father, and hers. Their resemblance to her was even more startling. From the warm coloration of their black-coffee complexions, chiseled jawlines, plush pillows for lips and warm, endearing smiles, Phaedra saw hints of her own reflection. She had their eyes, the same nose, high cheekbones and mouth. Had she inherited her father's dark complexion instead of her mother's milk-chocolate tone, she would easily have passed for a Stallion twin. Phaedra took a deep breath as she suddenly fought not to cry.

Lifting her camera back to her eyes, she peered through the lens, once again pointing it toward where the brothers sat. She focused her gaze on one and then the other. She watched as the brother on the end leaned over to exchange conversation with a man who sat on his sibling's other side. Phaedra shifted her camera and refocused it, zooming in on the stranger. There was something about the handsome man that suddenly had her curious. She couldn't help wondering who he was, his brilliant smile warm and magnanimous.

Whoever the man was, he was quite good-looking, Phaedra thought as she spun the lens into focus, snapping a quick shot and then a second. The trio seemed quite friendly with one another, clearly enjoying the events playing out in the center of the arena. And then, as if his radar had sounded an alarm, the man suddenly looked up, his gaze shifting directly toward her as if he knew she was staring at him. Phaedra lowered her camera abruptly, feeling as if she'd gotten caught with both hands in the cookie jar, her palms overflowing with her favorite oatmeal-raisin treats. She pulled her hands through the length of her hair. The moment was slightly unnerving.

From the ground below, Phaedra suddenly heard her name being called, the sound of it startling her from her thoughts.

"Phaedra? Is that you? Phaedra Parrish!"

Glancing below, she caught sight of the red-haired white man waving wildly for her attention. His own cameras hung down against his side as he struggled not to drop them. Phaedra's eyes widened brightly, the familiar face warming her spirit.

"Hooper!" Phaedra squealed, waving back. She eased her way down from the bleachers to move to the man's side.

With his mane of fire-engine-red hair and the pipe that hung from his mouth like an appendage, Hooper Mars was a welcome sight, looking more like a lumberjack right out of the thick of a deep forest than the award-winning photographer that he was. Hooper's brilliant smile put Phaedra instantly at ease. As she stepped off the last plank, the man wrapped her in a deep bear hug.

Her mentor in art school, Hooper was single-handedly responsible for Phaedra changing her major from creative writing to photography. The two had become fast friends, he challenging her creative spirit and she excelling beyond his expectations. Phaedra's successful career had only been rivaled by his.

"Watch the camera!" Phaedra laughed, lifting the device above her head as she hugged him tightly.

"Nice equipment," Hooper responded, eyeing her Canon 5D Mark II full-frame camera with its long telephoto lens.

Phaedra adjusted her Lowepro camera backpack against her shoulder. "Thanks. What are you doing here?" she asked, surprise still ringing in her tone.

"Working. You?"

"Not working!" Phaedra said with a smile.

"So, what brings you all the way to Dallas and to here of all places?"

Phaedra hesitated, her shoulders shrugging skyward. "I was just passing through town before I head to my next gig in Thailand and I heard about the rodeo. Thought I'd stop by to check it out. See what I might be able to shoot," she said, hoping she sounded believable.

Her friend nodded his understanding. "I was really sorry to hear about your mother, Phaedra. She was a really sweet lady."

Phaedra took a deep breath and forced her mouth into a slight smile. "Thanks, Hooper. And thank you for the flowers! I really appreciated you thinking of me."

"Hey, what are friends for?" the man said. There

was a sudden rush of noise behind them as the audience cheered something going on in the center of the arena. Both Phaedra and Hooper both turned to stare as a horse and rider went through their paces.

"I should be shooting this," Phaedra said absently, her gaze shifting for a split second toward the stands and the men who were still sitting in observation.

"Speaking of shoot, I loved that LeBron James layout you did for *Sports Illustrated*. Creative, challenging, technically proficient. That was some nice work, woman. That shot where you had him hanging upside down from the basketball hoop was seriously dope!"

Phaedra turned her attention back to her friend. "Thank you! It was fun to do and LeBron was a dream client. So, what are you working on here?"

"I'm here to shoot the wedding."

Phaedra eyed him curiously. "What wedding?"

"The Stallion wedding. I'm the wedding photographer."

Phaedra laughed. "I didn't know you did weddings."

Hooper shrugged. "I usually don't, not in a good long time, but I bend the rules for my very special friends. The bride," he said, lifting his eyebrows, "is Joanne Lake. We were roomies for a short time back in Cali when she was going to art school and I was aspiring to make movies."

"I didn't know you made movies."

Hooper laughed. "It was a very short porn career because I was very short."

Phaedra shook her head, laughing with him. "So, this Joanne Lake is getting married to one of the Stallions?"

"Yep!" Hooper nodded. "The youngest brother, Luke Stallion. Great guy! They make a nice couple."

Phaedra felt her heart skip a quick beat. Knowing where she fell in the lineup of Stallion offspring had been a point of angst for her mother. During their short tryst, James Stallion had been married, the truth of that coming as a complete surprise. Although he'd been separated from his wife during the time they were together, the revelation of his marital connection had not sat well with the matriarch. James returning to his wife and three older sons had been earth-shattering, completely devastating Arneta's world. Now here Phaedra was, discovering that her younger brother was about to be married. She took a deep breath, holding it for a brief moment before blowing the air out slowly.

"Hey," Hooper said suddenly. "What are you doing tonight? You interested in working?"

Phaedra lifted her eyebrows questioningly. "What do you need?"

"I have an assistant who will be helping me, but I could always use another photographer. You interested in working? I mean, since you already have your equipment with you."

"At the wedding?"

"The wedding and the reception. You game?"

Taking another quick glance toward where the Stallion men were seated, Phaedra suddenly saw opportunity where none had existed before. Unable to resist, she took note of the handsome stranger one last time, then without a second thought nodded, her answer emphatic. "Yes!"

Joanne Lake stood in the center of the room, a hand fanning in front of her face as she tried to catch her breath.

"I swear," she said, breathing heavily, "I'm so nervous that I can't breathe!"

Marah laughed, moving to the young woman's side. "I felt the same way when John and I were married," she said, remembering the moment as if it had just happened. "Just take a deep breath, hold it and relax. Everything is going to be perfect."

"Absolutely," Joanne's mother, Lillian Taylor, echoed as she slowly laced the back of her only daughter's wedding gown. "Everything will be beautiful, *ma fille chéri,*" the woman said, the warm lilt of her deep French accent comforting.

Tears misted in Joanne's eyes as she took in her image in the mirror. The gown she'd designed for herself accentuated every ounce of her curvaceous frame. She was an absolutely stunning bride in the silk-and-organza creation and she couldn't wait for Luke to see her coming down the aisle that very first time. She took in a deep breath, fighting to ease the rise of nervous energy.

There was a low knock at the door and Marah's older sister, Eden, moved to see who was waiting on the other side. When Eden pulled the entrance open, Phaedra was smiling brightly, waving her camera in greeting.

"Hi, I've come to take some preliminary shots of the bride, if that's okay?" Phaedra said, meeting Eden's questioning gaze.

"Oh, yes, definitely," the woman responded as she reached for Phaedra's hand and pulled her into the room. "Your timing is perfect."

Phaedra nodded as she entered the space, the women inside all turning to stare in her direction. Joanne's bright smile eased the moment.

"Hi, I'm Joanne. Hooper said you'd be coming. It's such a pleasure to meet you," she said excitedly.

"It's nice to meet you, too. My name's Phaedra. Phaedra Parrish," she said, pausing momentarily as if she hoped there might be some recognition that she was family, too. "Congratulations!"

"Thank you," Joanne intoned. "Thank you so much. Well, just tell us where you want us."

Phaedra smiled back. "I just want you to finish getting dressed. Just interact the way you were doing before I arrived and pretend I'm not even here. The best shots are those where you're most natural, so just be yourself."

Joanne nodded as her mother moved back to lacing the last few ties on her gown. As she did, Phaedra lifted her camera and took a quick shot. She began to slowly move around the room, snapping photo after photo of Joanne and her bridal party as they completed the finishing touches on their makeup and hair. It was an extravaganza of ivory-colored lace, chocolate charmeuse and tan chiffon.

"This is so exciting!" Katrina commented, smoothing the front of her own gown across her pregnant belly.

"This family has definitely had its fair share of weddings and baby showers!" an elderly woman intoned. "It's been a blessing!" She swiped at a tear that pressed anxiously at the edge of her eye.

Phaedra paused to look where the voice had come from. Seated on the couch was a woman close to her mother's age. She looked quite smart in a two-piece dress suit the color of sweet tea. She smiled when she saw Phaedra staring. Phaedra smiled back as she lifted her camera and took a snapshot of the woman's smiling face.

"Don't you start crying, Aunt Juanita," someone scolded. "If you start you'll have us all crying up in here."

The women all laughed, the warmth of it echoing around the room.

"Y'all know I'm gonna cry," the woman named Juanita said. "The last of my babies is getting married," she said with a loud sniffle. A blanket of silence dropped down against the room as they all stopped to take in her comment.

Phaedra's gaze danced from face to face as she took them all in. Juanita caught her staring and Phaedra fiddled with her camera as the woman stared back.

"Are you from around here?" Juanita asked, her question directed at Phaedra.

The young woman met the matriarch's curious gaze. "No, ma'am. I'm from New Orleans," she said softly.

Juanita smiled, still staring. "You look like you could be related to the family," she said, "like one of the cousins. Doesn't she?" Juanita queried, moving the rest of them to turn and stare a second time.

Joanne glanced in Phaedra's direction. "You really do," she said with a slight giggle.

Phaedra only smiled, resuming her picture-taking.

Marah interrupted the moment. "It's time, ladies. This wedding will start on time," she said, her tone commanding as she shifted into wedding planner mode.

There were nods of agreement as each woman paused to take one last look at her reflection in the wall of mirrors that decorated the space.

The woman they called Aunt Juanita stood up, moving to the center of the room toward the bride, who suddenly looked as if she'd turned two shades of green.

"Everyone join hands," Juanita said as she gestured for them to move into a circle around Joanne.

Phaedra moved back against the wall, mindful not to intrude upon the moment. She listened intently as the woman began to speak, her camera at eye level as she captured the moment on film.

"This family is a beautiful thing to behold," Juanita said. "I have watched John, Matthew, Mark and Luke grow into wonderful men. I know that if their parents were here today they would be very proud. Each of them has chosen an amazing, wonderful woman to carry the Stallion name and be with them by their sides. They got that from their daddy because their mother, Irene, was an amazing woman and the best friend I could ever have had."

Juanita paused to press a lace hankie to her eye. Her gaze paused on each face as she called out their names. "Marah, Michelle, Katrina and now Joanne, each of you is the most important thing in your husband's life and the lifelines that will continue this family. Don't you ever forget it and don't ever let anyone tell you otherwise.

"Marah, business is important to John, but it will never be more important than you are. Mitch," she said, calling Michelle by her family nickname, "I never thought there would be anyone who could tame that wild Stallion, but you did, and Mark's love for you and that baby girl of yours has no limits.

"Katrina, you told me on your wedding day that Matthew seduced you, but you're the one who actually swept Matthew off his feet. I have never seen him happier." Juanita reached for Joanne's hand, squeezing the woman's fingers beneath her own. "And now our baby boy is getting married. Joanne, you and Luke were both lost until you found each other's arms for support. He is a better man because of you and I couldn't be more proud.

"So, baby girl, you enjoy every minute of this very special day. May you and Luke grow in your love for each other and may you both find joy and happiness for the rest of your days. Welcome to our family. We love you and we couldn't be happier for you both."

"Amen to that," Marah chimed, everyone echoing those sentiments.

Joanne fanned her hands in front of her face, fighting not to bawl like a newborn baby. "Thank you," she said, fighting back the tears. "I love you all so much," she said as her mother wrapped her in a warm embrace.

Juanita moved toward the door. "Well, let's go get you married!" she said, the rest of them following behind her.

And as they moved out of the room, in the direction of the family chapel, Phaedra swiped the tears from her own eyes, snapping one more photo for the Stallion wedding album.

Chapter 4

Mason Boudreaux was all partied out as he moved from the tented reception area back toward the Stallion family home. Guests were still enjoying the Stallion hospitality as they moved from the banquet tables laden with a surplus of food to the dance floor and back again.

Outside, the sun was in the final moments of its descent, the backdrop of a darkening sky heightening the rise of an almost full moon. Small white lights twinkled from the trees that lined the property, casting a seductive glow over the landscape. Looking out over the magnificent view, he couldn't help being touched by the magnitude of it all. He took a deep breath, filling his lungs with the warm evening air.

As he slowly strolled in the direction of the family's home he couldn't help noticing the beautiful woman who stood with her camera in hand snapping photographs. He had noticed her earlier in the day as she'd taken photographs of the crowd at the rodeo and he'd noticed her during the wedding ceremony and again at the reception. In fact, so in awe of her, he'd spent a good deal of time noticing her, almost forgetting why he was there in the first place.

The exquisite woman was casually dressed in black slacks, a white button-down dress shirt and red Durango cowboy boots. The slacks were cut low against the curve of her round hips and she had the tiniest waist of any woman he had ever seen. Having more leg than torso, she appeared model-tall despite her petite stature. The lengthy appendages gave her the lean, lanky look of a gazelle, and the curvature of her full bustline showed that she clearly had more than a handful. Her flawless complexion was milk chocolate, so rich and decadent that with her distinct features he could easily see her posing on the other side of any camera.

He wasn't quite sure what she was focused on as she stared out in the distance, but with the large telephoto lens and the light that flashed with each snap he was intrigued, curious to discover who she was and what she might be up to.

He casually strolled to her side, his movements so stealthlike that Phaedra didn't notice him until he was standing directly behind her. She jumped, suddenly taken by surprise as the man stepped into her space.

"Good evening," Mason said, a bright smile warming the curvature of his face.

"You scared me," Phaedra gasped, pressing a hand to her chest.

Mason's smile brightened. "My apologies! I didn't mean to frighten you."

"That's what usually happens when you sneak up on a person," she said, her heart still racing.

"I wasn't sneaking," Mason said casually. "You were just distracted. What are you photographing?" he asked as he looked off toward where she'd been staring.

Phaedra was still eyeing him with reservation. When he cut his eye at her and back toward the landscape, a wave of heat suddenly coursed up the length of her spine. He cut his eye at her a second time, a wry smile pulling at his full lips as he waited for her reply.

Phaedra tilted her camera so that he could see the LCD display, depressing the display button so that he could view the images she'd just taken. "Foxes," she said nonchalantly. "There was a family of red foxes scurrying along the fence line."

The man nodded as he met her gaze. "Interesting," he said, his deep voice echoing through the evening air. He extended his hand. "I'm Mason Boudreaux," he said as he wrapped Phaedra's fingers beneath his own.

"Phaedra," she answered, the heat he radiated causing her to take a swift breath. "Phaedra Parrish."

"It's very nice to meet you, Phaedra Parrish."

Phaedra smiled, hoping he wouldn't notice the blush that heated her cheeks. "The pleasure is all mine, Mason Boudreaux."

"You have a very distinct accent," Mason said, noting her deep Southern dialect with its hint of French Creole syntax. "Where are you from in Louisiana?"

"Good ear," she said, smiling sweetly. "New Orleans. Born and raised."

He chuckled softly. "Me, too, although I live in Arizona now."

"I don't hear any accent," Phaedra said, eyeing him with a raised brow.

Mason laughed, shifting into the familiar phonology. "Y'all headed up da house o' ova back da fields?"

Phaedra laughed with him, the warmth of the sound teasing. "So, why Arizona?"

Mason became pensive, hesitating in reflection for a brief moment. "My family was displaced after Hurricane Katrina," he finally said, noting the 2005 category-five storm that had been one of the worst natural disasters on record. "I'd already had a house there and my parents decided to stay when their home was destroyed."

"They didn't want to go back?" Phaedra questioned.

Mason shrugged. "They did and actually, they're back and forth as it suits them. We're still rebuilding the family home, but it's been slow going. That storm really broke their spirits for a bit. And it didn't help that my sister shared its name," he said with slight chuckle. "For whatever reasons, they haven't been in any rush."

Phaedra nodded her understanding. "My mother refused to leave. I was traveling so much for business that she couldn't imagine herself being able to adjust anywhere else. It took everything we both had to repair the damage after the storm, but it was worth it. New Orleans was her home and she was determined to live out the rest of her life where she was happiest. She passed away a few weeks ago," Phaedra said, her voice catching in her throat as she thought about her mother.

"My condolences," Mason said, taking a step in her direction. He drew his hand against the length of her arm. "I'm very sorry for your loss."

Phaedra nodded ever so slightly. His touch was so

powerful that her mind suddenly turned to mush. Phaedra couldn't begin to fathom why she was reacting so
intensely. She took a deep breath as she took a step
back, suddenly needing to put some distance between
them.

Feeling the same thing, Mason crossed his arms
over his broad chest, locking his hands beneath his
armpits. He hadn't meant to be so forward. There was
a brief pause as both pondered how to move past the
awkwardness of the moment.

"So, did you enjoy the wedding?" Phaedra asked,
wanting to move the conversation in another direction.

"I did. How about you?"

She nodded. "They throw quite a shindig around
here."

Mason laughed. "Yes, they do."

"Are you family?" Phaedra asked, curiosity tint-
ing her words.

"By marriage. My sister Katrina is married to Matthew Stallion."

Phaedra's head bobbed against her thin neck a second time. "Your sister, she's pregnant."

"You've met?"

"Not formally. She was with the bride when I took
photographs earlier and I noticed."

The man nodded. "This will be her second child,
their first baby together. We're all very excited. So,
are you related to the Stallions?" Mason asked, having
noted a resemblance between Phaedra and the brothers.

There was an awkward pause as Phaedra turned to
stare out into the distance. She suddenly wished there
was someone with whom she could share her story.
Mason appeared to have a compassionate spirit, the

breadth of it tempting Phaedra to drop her guard and spill her secret. But Mason's connection to the Stallions made him a highly unlikely ally. After a pause, Phaedra gave a deep sigh and said nothing at all, pretending as though she'd not even heard the question. She lifted her camera, aimed it directly at Mason and snapped the shot, once, twice and then a third time.

Mason found himself smiling, not expecting to suddenly be the center of attention. He shook his head as Phaedra smiled back at him. After a quick moment of silence, Mason spoke. "Well, you look busy, so I'll get out of your way. This was fun, Phaedra Parrish," he concluded, moving as if to leave her side.

Phaedra smiled, meeting his gaze. "Perhaps we'll run into each other again in N'Orleans," she said brightly.

Mason grinned as he lifted his hand in a slight wave. Then as if a lightbulb had gone off in his head, he spun back toward her. "Phaedra, are you doing anything tomorrow?" he questioned.

Phaedra met his gaze. "What did you have in mind?"

"I was thinking breakfast, sightseeing, lunch, maybe even dinner. I haven't had an opportunity to explore Dallas yet, so we can make a day of it if you don't have any plans."

She hesitated only briefly, then nodded, excitement painting her expression. "That sounds like it would be a lot of fun. I'd like that a lot."

"Where are you staying?" Mason asked.

"The Four Seasons."

"I'll pick you up in the morning. Will eight o'clock work for you?"

"I'll be ready at eight," Phaedra answered.

Mason tossed her a quick wink of his eye. "See you tomorrow, Phaedra Parrish!"

Her eyes widening in delight, Phaedra watched as Mason eased his way in the direction of the large homestead. He paused briefly on the front porch to toss her one last wave before he disappeared inside. Lifting her eyes to stare at the moon, Phaedra bubbled with excitement. She suddenly couldn't wait for tomorrow to happen.

Chapter 5

Phaedra was only slightly taken aback when the luxury limousine pulled up in front of the Four Seasons Hotel, the driver beckoning for her attention. She was a bit perturbed when there was no sign of Mason Boudreaux, only instructions for her to be delivered to where he was. Granted, she didn't date often, but when she did she was accustomed to the man actually picking her up. She considered casting one strike against him but hesitated, deciding to at least wait to see where he was waiting for her before she put him on her short list.

When the vehicle pulled into the circular drive of Briscoe Ranch, Phaedra's stomach suddenly did backflips. She hadn't anticipated returning to the Stallion family home so soon and definitely not as the guest of a man she'd just met. Nervous tension creased the lines of her forehead. Since the wedding and the close proximity of the brothers, Phaedra had been in turmoil trying to decide if, when and how she might be able to tell them who she was and what she'd recently learned about her paternity.

As the driver came to a halt in front of the family home, Mason stood at the foot of the stairwell, anxiously awaiting Phaedra's arrival. He'd tossed and turned most of the night thinking about the beautiful woman who'd captured his attention, and he'd been overly anxious to see Phaedra again. He brushed the driver aside as he leaned to open the limo door.

"Good morning," Mason said eagerly, reaching for her hand.

"Good morning to you," Phaedra answered as she stepped out of the vehicle, clasping Mason's hand for support. She gave him a hesitant smile. "I wasn't expecting all this," she said, gesturing at the car, the driver and their surroundings.

Mason laughed warmly, a chuckle rising from deep in his midsection. "Neither was I. But it seems I was expected at the family breakfast this morning and although I tried to get out of it, the family wouldn't let me. So it just made sense for me to send the car for you to join us while my sister lectured me on what I should and shouldn't do on our date today."

Phaedra laughed with him. "Instructions! So you don't date often, I take it."

"Apparently, to hear my sister tell it, not the right way!" the man answered as he cupped his hand beneath her elbow and guided her up the deep steps to the front door.

"Are you sure I won't be intruding?" Phaedra asked, anxiety spinning in the air around her.

Mason shook his head. "Not at all. In fact—" he started just as the front door was thrown open, Marah and Katrina stepping outside to interrupt.

"Good morning!" both women said simultaneously.

"Good morning," Phaedra answered, her eyes widening.

Katrina leaned to give her a warm hug. "Welcome! I'm Katrina Stallion, Mason's sister, and I'm so excited to see you. We didn't get a chance to officially meet yesterday."

"I'm Phaedra," she responded, tossing Mason a quick glance.

The man shook his head. "Be careful," he cautioned, his tone suddenly serious. "If you stand still too long, I'm told, these two will have you married and pregnant before you realize it."

Katrina rolled her eyes skyward. "Ignore my brother, please. Not that it would hurt him to be married and pregnant," she said as she cradled her bulging belly. "We're just excited to see him with a woman our parents would approve of."

Marah laughed. "And Phaedra's not running yet, so there's still hope we haven't scared her off!" she said teasingly.

Phaedra laughed with them. "I don't scare that easily," she quipped as they welcomed her inside the large home.

"That's good," Katrina said, "because we enjoy giving Mason a hard time. But really, we're delighted you could join us for breakfast, although I admit it's not like we gave you much of a choice."

Mason shook his head as he instinctively reached

for Phaedra's hand, clasping her fingers between his own. Her comfort level rose exponentially.

"I appreciate you including me," Phaedra said, squeezing his fingers ever so slightly.

Both Katrina and Marah were grinning broadly as they led the way into the oversize kitchen and family room. There was a crowd of family who greeted them as they made their way inside.

"Let me introduce you to everyone," Marah said as she pulled Phaedra from Mason's grasp. "Everyone, this is Mason's new friend, Phaedra Parrish," she said. "Phaedra, this is the family." Marah gestured around the large oak table. "This is my father, Edward Briscoe, and his wife, Juanita. And that handsome guy right there is my husband, John Stallion."

Phaedra stared as John came to his feet and shook her hand, his smile warm and inviting. Marah continued down the line.

"That woman over there who looks like me, but not as cute, is my twin sister, Marla, her husband, Michael, and that cutie pie in her lap is their son, Michael Jr."

"Hi," the toddler said, eagerly waving both hands in Phaedra's direction.

"Hi," Phaedra said, grinning brightly as she waved back at him. "Aren't you an absolute doll!"

The little boy laughed happily.

Marah chuckled softly. "And this is John's brother Matthew."

"He's mine," Katrina said as she eased her pregnant body into the seat beside her husband, reaching to kiss his lips as she did.

Marah shook her head as she went on. "The big guy

holding that baby girl there is Mark, and his daughter's name is Irene."

Mark lifted a hand and gave Phaedra a slight wave. "Nice to meet you!"

"And you probably remember Mark's wife, Michelle, from the wedding yesterday."

"Everyone calls me Mitch," Michelle said as she adjusted a spit towel over her husband's shoulder, moving him to lift their baby to his shoulder to burp the air from her tummy.

"Hi," Phaedra said softly. "She's a beautiful baby!"

Mark grinned. "Thank you. Takes after her daddy!" he said with a wink of his eye.

Everyone shook their head. Marah continued down the line. "And of course, you remember the bride and groom from yesterday, Luke and Joanne."

"Thank you again for everything," Joanne said as she looped her arm through her new husband's, leaning her head against his shoulder. "You and Hooper did a great job!"

Phaedra nodded. "Hooper's a thrill to work with. I'm glad I was available to assist him."

"Well, he certainly speaks very highly of you," Luke added. "Your reputation preceded you."

"Thank you," Phaedra said.

"And last but definitely not least," Marah concluded, gesturing toward the end of the table, "this is Vanessa Long, a dear family friend, and her baby boy, Vaughan."

"Hey, hey, hey!" Vanessa said, her baby boy clutched awkwardly beneath her arm as she maneuvered a plate in one hand and a bottle in the other.

"I declare," Juanita intoned, moving swiftly to take

the baby from Vanessa's hold. "Girl, you gon' drop that baby holding him like that!"

The family laughed, heads shaking.

"Y'all gon' make my boy soft the way you keep coddling him," Vanessa said. "I need to keep him on his toes. If he bounces once or twice, it'll toughen him up."

Juanita gave the woman a swift slap to the back of her head.

"Ouch, Aunt Juanita!" Vanessa yelled. "That hurt."

"Love tap!" the brothers chorused, everyone breaking out into laughter.

Wide-eyed, Phaedra was suddenly aware of the large hand pressing gently against her lower back, Mason standing comfortably beside her.

"You look overwhelmed!" he said teasingly. "You don't have any siblings, do you?"

She hesitated, her gaze moving along the row of eyes that were staring back at her. Stammering slightly, she shrugged. "I was raised as an only child," she said, "so this is very different for me."

Michelle nodded. "You get used to it," she said. "I was an only child, too."

"So was I," Joanne echoed.

"Please, have a seat," John said, gesturing toward the two empty place settings across from him and Matthew.

"Thank you," Phaedra said as Mason guided her to a chair, pulling it out as she took a seat. He dropped into the chair beside her.

"Ignore this bunch," John said, meeting Phaedra's gaze. "They always get out of hand at family breakfast." His smile was warm and welcoming.

"You all do this often?" Phaedra questioned, her curiosity piqued.

"Every Sunday," John answered. "Once our business went public, Aunt Juanita insisted on it. She felt like we were losing touch with each other."

"It was the only way to get them to relax over a meal," Juanita said, still rocking Vanessa's baby in the cradle of her arms.

"We have two rules for family breakfast," Marah said. "Everyone must show up unless they're out of town. And there is no business discussed. Ever."

"Wow," Phaedra said, impressed. "And everyone always complies?"

John nodded. "It's kept us grounded. Spending a few hours together just being brothers with our families has kept us from taking ourselves too seriously."

"So, where are you from, Phaedra?" Luke asked, resting his chin in his hands as he leaned on the table.

"N'Orleans," Phaedra answered. She twisted a napkin nervously in her lap.

"So are we!" Katrina said excitedly. "Or at least that's where our parents are from. Our father was active army, so we were military brats and traveled around, but the older kids, Mason, Donovan, Kendrick and Kamaya, were all born in New Orleans. I was born in Germany but I can't tell you where the rest of them were born."

Phaedra glanced toward Mason. "How many brothers and sisters do you have?"

Mason laughed. "There are nine of us." He cut an eye at his sister. "Our family meals are quite a bit bigger," he said, his sister nodding her agreement.

Phaedra shook her head and laughed, totally in awe of it all.

Food suddenly appeared out of nowhere, platters of every breakfast item imaginable being passed around the table. Between the food and the fellowship, it was an overabundance of everything. So much so that Phaedra felt as if she were on sensory overload.

She pushed at the eggs on her plate, her stomach still doing flips as she realized she was actually having breakfast with her brothers. Her brothers. John, Matthew, Mark and Luke. The only family she had left. She closed her eyes and took a deep breath and then a second before opening them to find John staring at her curiously. She gave him a slight smile, unnerved by the look he was giving her.

A lanky teenager suddenly entered the room, waving his hand sheepishly at everyone around the table. "Good morning," he said as he reached for an empty plate. Greetings rang back in his direction.

"Collin Broomes, you're late," Katrina chastised, her eyebrows raised as she massaged a hand over her swollen stomach.

"Sorry, Mom," the man-child named Collin answered. "I was helping them muck the stables. It took longer than I expected."

"I hope you took a shower," his mother said, her tone questioning.

Collin rolled his eyes. "Yes, ma'am. That's why I'm late." He moved to an empty chair at the kitchen counter, his plate now filled with bacon and toast.

Matthew chuckled. "I wasn't expecting you to do that before breakfast, son," he said, pride gleaming from his eyes.

The teen nodded. "I know, sir, but I wanted to get it out of the way so that I could ride after breakfast. If that's okay?"

"That's definitely okay," Matthew said. He nodded in Phaedra's direction. "Phaedra, this is our son, Collin. Collin, this is Miss Parrish, your uncle Mason's friend."

Collin tossed his hand hello, his mouth stuffed with food.

"Please, call me Phaedra," she said, waving back.

"Nice to meet you, Miss Phaedra," Collin answered after swallowing. He pointed a finger in Mason's direction, winked at his uncle and grinned.

Mason shook his head as he cut a quick glance at Phaedra.

"Y'all are funny," Phaedra said, lifting her eyes to meet his gaze. She laughed, dropping her manicured hand against his thigh as she leaned her shoulder into his. A jolt of electricity shot through his body and he felt himself quiver from the sensation.

Mason was enjoying every ounce of the moment, conversation flowing with ease. Phaedra didn't seem at all bothered by the family gathering. He understood that this was not at all what she'd been expecting and he was impressed by her sportsmanship, his charming companion seeming very much at ease with their additional breakfast companions.

"So, Phaedra, do you have family in New Orleans?" John suddenly asked.

Phaedra shook her head. "No," she said, her voice catching deep in her throat.

Mason noticed her discomfort at the question. He intervened on her behalf. "Phaedra's mother just passed away a few weeks ago," he said softly.

"Oh, we're so sorry," Marah interjected, everyone turning to stare at the young woman.

"We're very sorry for your loss," Matthew added.

Phaedra nodded, biting down against her bottom lip. She suddenly missed her mother more than she had imagined possible.

"We lost our parents many years ago," John said as he reached a large hand across the table to brush his fingers against the back of her hand. "I know it's not easy."

Phaedra met his stare, holding it ever so briefly, before she pulled her hand from his, clutching her palms together in her lap. She turned to meet Mason's intense gaze, then dropped her stare into her lap with her hands. Tears suddenly pressed hot behind her eyelids. She felt her body begin to shake and she was grateful for the chair beneath her bottom, which kept her from falling to the floor. She swiped at her eyes with the backs of her hands, heat rising to her cheeks as she fought to contain the rise of emotion that was threatening to spill out of her.

"What about your father?" Katrina asked softly. "Is he still alive?"

Everyone in the room was suddenly taken aback when Phaedra suddenly began to sob, her body quivering out of control. Concern wafted thickly around the space.

"Phaedra? What's wrong?" Mason questioned, wrapping an arm around the back of her chair as he leaned in to whisper in her ear. He pressed a napkin to her cheek to stall the flow of saline that rained over her cheeks.

"I'm sorry," Phaedra apologized. "I am so sorry. I

didn't mean…" she gasped, trying to catch her breath as the sobs racked her body.

Mason gently caressed her back, his large hands stroking the width of her shoulders. He was without words, not having a clue what he could say to soothe her. His gaze met John's, the man's stare acknowledging the same sentiment, both lost when it came to a woman's tears.

Juanita was suddenly at her side, a box of tissues in hand. The older woman brushed a warm hand against Phaedra's shoulder. "It's okay, baby. You cry if you want to," she said as she lifted Phaedra's chin with her fingers, brushing the young woman's tears away. She suddenly hesitated, staring deeply. "I declare, child, you look just like Luke when you cry. He gets the ugly face, too," she said, shaking her head.

John laughed. "I was just thinking the same thing," he said, hoping to diffuse the seriousness of the moment. "But your ugly face is definitely prettier than Luke's is," he added.

Luke rolled his eyes. "First off, I don't cry, and when I do, I don't get the ugly face."

"Yeah, you do," Mark chimed in. "And you used to boo-hoo like a baby back in the day. Right up to your sixteenth birthday you'd cry if someone looked at you funny."

Sixteen years old himself, Collin laughed heartily at the thought.

"That is so not true," Luke said.

Phaedra suddenly came to her feet, the napkin in her lap dropping to the floor. She turned her attention to Juanita, who was still trying to console her, something in the woman's stare seeming to acknowledge more than she'd spoken. "Did you by chance know my mother, Miss Juanita? Her name was Arneta Parrish."

Juanita paused, the name spinning through her thoughts. Her eyes suddenly widened, her body tensing. She took a swift breath. "Your mother was Arneta Parrish?"

Phaedra nodded, her gaze still locked with Juanita's.

"Why don't you and I go fix your face?" Juanita said, her hand pressing against Phaedra's arm. "We can talk where it's quiet."

"You know, don't you?" Phaedra questioned suddenly.

"Know what?" John asked curiously, noting the rise of tension that had suddenly filled the space between the two women.

Both turned to stare in his direction. Juanita's gaze moved back to Phaedra, her body starting to shake with nervousness. Phaedra was still staring at John, her gaze moving from his face, to Matthew's, then to Mark and Luke before she locked eyes with him one last time, his stare still questioning.

Phaedra's next words came like lead weights dropping heavily against a wooden floor. "Your father, James David Stallion, was my father, too."

Chapter 6

Phaedra was visibly shaken as she maneuvered her way down the front steps of the family home. Not having a clue how to access the driver and car who'd brought her there, she began to walk as fast as she could, wanting to be as far from all of them as she could possibly manage.

Nothing that had happened in the past ten minutes had been as she'd imagined. After dropping the bombshell that she was James Stallion's only daughter, she'd spewed every detail of what she knew, the words spilling out of her mouth like water from a faucet. She couldn't even remember taking a breath as she'd told them all how James and her mother had had an affair resulting in her conception.

Phaedra hadn't known what to expect, but she'd not been at all prepared for the wave of hostility that had suddenly engulfed her. Mark had been the most vocal, insisting there was no way possible for them to share a bloodline. But it was John and his wealth of silence that had been the most unnerving. And when she'd been done, having no other information to share, John had stormed out of the room, brushing past her with a rage that left her feeling completely annihilated, his anguished stare cutting through her like ice.

"She's lying," Mark said as he paced the floor in the home's library. "There is no way she's our sister. We don't have a sister. We can't have a sister."

John stood staring out the large picture window to the fields in the distance. Matthew stared where he stared as Luke drummed his fingers against the oak-topped desk.

"Would Dad have cheated on our mom?" Luke questioned, looking from one brother to the other. He'd only been two years old when his parents had died, and the thought discredited everything he'd ever been told about them.

"No," Mark answered, still pacing, his footsteps heavy against the polished wood floors. "Never!" he said emphatically.

"We really don't know that," Matthew stated, meeting Mark's intense glare. "We would hope not, but anything is possible. Besides, she looks just like us," he noted, turning to face his brothers. "Maybe Dad did step outside of his marriage."

"I know you're not buying that load of horse crap," Mark scoffed. "Are you, John?"

They all turned to John for a reaction, the man still staring out into space. Their big brother hadn't said anything at all since Phaedra's pronouncement. The sting of her words had stunned him into silence and all he had been able to do in that moment was leave the room before he said something he would later regret. He'd left and Matthew, Mark and Luke had followed closely on his heels.

Now he was thinking about their father and their mother, having idolized the two since forever. Their father had always called their mother "Sug," short for "Sugar," his sweet and honey, he used to say. John remembered wanting what his mom and dad had when he grew up and found a wife, their love so magnanimous that he and his brothers use to look on them with awe. He'd wanted to love his woman as hard as he remembered James having loved Irene, and he did, his heart so full for his wife, Marah, that he couldn't ever imagine life without the phenomenal woman.

John also couldn't fathom the thought of being unfaithful to Marah and he couldn't begin to rationalize his father having committed such a crime against his mother. There had been little the couple hadn't shared or done together. John had vivid memories of the two bowling together, camping together and just enjoying the beauty of each other's company. They'd been the perfect complement to each other. His father had been stern and commanding, with only one weakness, his wife. Irene Stallion had been the epitome of virtue, a woman with a huge heart of pure gold. She'd been the most giving person John had ever known, devoting her time and energy to more causes than any of them could ever begin to count. But not once did she sacrifice her children or her family, the Stallion boys always front and center in her mind and her heart.

John smiled as he remembered the many kisses and

hugs and secret touches of affection that had passed between his parents when neither thought anyone was paying attention. The two had shown so much love for each other that to now discover that maybe their relationship hadn't been so perfect was truly challenging his spirit.

Hearing his name being called pulled him back to the moment.

"John, what do you think?" Matthew was questioning, echoing Mark's query.

John turned to face them, his dejected expression causing each of them concern. He shrugged his shoulders, one teardrop escaping past his thick lashes. "I don't know. I don't know anything anymore. Right now Aunt Juanita seems to know more than any one of us ever did."

"Lord, have mercy, this cannot be happening," Juanita whispered loudly as she moved to clear the dishes from the table.

Marah pressed her hand against the woman's arm. "Aunt Juanita, what is this all about?"

Juanita met Marah's gaze. She gently tapped the back of Marah's hand, not saying anything else at all, then continued with the dishes.

"Marah," Edward said, noting his wife's distress. "We'll all talk about it later. Let Juanita be, please."

"I think we need to talk about it now, Daddy," Marah said defiantly, her hand falling to her hip. "Did you see my husband's face? I've never seen John so devastated."

"And Mark was so mad he was ready to spit nails,"

Michelle added as she cradled baby Irene close to her chest. "Mark never gets mad about anything."

Juanita was still shaking her head.

"Is that girl really their sister?" Collin asked, his innocent gaze skating from one adult to the next. "I mean, she does look like them!"

"Collin, why don't you go down to the stables and ride, please," Katrina suggested.

"But, why do—" Collin started.

"Now, Collin," Katrina ordered, her stern tone silencing his question.

Collin mumbled his way out of the room, visibly annoyed that he was always being sent someplace else when it was the adults messing up. When he messed up, it was adult central with all of them coming to toss in two cents. He could sense that things were about to get interesting and he was irritated that he might miss the really good stuff.

"Did you know about this?" Katrina mouthed in her brother's direction, her eyes widened with surprise. Mason had shaken his head at his sister, shrugging in astonishment. It had all happened so fast that he was just as stunned by the turn of events as the rest of them.

As the brothers had left the room in one direction, Phaedra had rushed out in the other. The ensuing commotion from the other women had been a complete distraction. When Mason had turned back to her, Phaedra was gone. Ignoring the questions the women were suddenly hammering him with, he raced to catch up with her.

Outside, Phaedra was doing a run-walk thing up the expansive driveway, her high heels impeding her from breaking out into a full sprint. As he paused at the top of the steps, he stared off in her direction.

Bounding down the steps, Mason raced to catch up to her, calling her name. "Phaedra! Please stop!" he shouted. "Please!"

With Mason suddenly on her heels, Phaedra found herself wishing for a deep hole to drop down into. If there was any way possible for the day to go from bad to worse, having to face Mason Boudreaux had to be it. She picked up her pace, wrapping her arms tightly around her torso. She was still sobbing, her eyes swollen red, and all she wanted was for Mason to go away and not see her in such a state of distress.

Catching up to her, Mason clasped his hand beneath her elbow, gently spinning her around to face him. His heart suddenly cracked, pierced by the pain that shimmered in the woman's dark eyes. Before he realized what he was doing, he pulled her to him and wrapped his arms around her. When Phaedra didn't pull away, allowing herself to give in to the embrace, he tightened his hold as he leaned to whisper in her ear, "I've got you, Phaedra. I've got you. Everything is going to be just fine. I won't let anything hurt you. I promise."

From the family porch Vanessa Long stood staring out at the couple hugging in the middle of the driveway. Her son slept comfortably against her shoulder, the baby oblivious of the excitement around him. Vanessa took a deep breath and then a second as she looked from the papers that Phaedra had dropped, out toward the couple and back again.

Friends with the Stallion sons for as long as any of them could remember, Vanessa was family to them,

the only "sister" they had ever known. She'd been best
friends with brother Mark first, the two allies on the
playground. Vanessa was all tomboy, her daredevil
antics rivaling most males and giving each of them a
run for his money. For a brief moment, Mark and the
woman had been boyfriend and girlfriend, the rest of
the family thinking the two would end up head over
heels in love with each other. College changed the dy-
namics of their relationship when Vanessa admitted her
predilection for women. Each of the Stallion men had
been only slightly disturbed when their family friend
had finally come out about her sexuality. But over time
they had all found their balance, Vanessa acting as if
she were just one of the boys and the brothers treating
her so. Then she'd had a baby with the help of a sperm
donor and the brothers had each stepped in to be the
best uncles baby Vaughan would ever know.

And now Vanessa understood better than anyone
that this news had twisted everything the four men
had ever believed into a tight knot that might not come
undone. Each of the brothers had exalted his father,
believing the man had never, in his whole life, done
one thing wrong. John, especially, had emulated everything about his father, defining himself as a true
alpha male with a rock-solid confidence that radiated
from the inside out.

Since his parents' deaths when John was eighteen,
every decision he had made for himself and his brothers had been based on the ideologies his father had in-
stilled in him. And each of the brothers had followed
suit. Without realizing it, Phaedra had tarnished the
gold that was James Stallion, and Vanessa knew that

his sons might not ever be the same because of this revelation.

Vanessa turned to face the front door just as John and Matthew stepped out onto the porch. She gave them both a quick smile and a wink as Matthew reached to take baby Vaughan from her arms.

Noticing the papers in her hand, John asked, "Is there anything there that supports what she says?" He stared out to where she stared, Mason and Phaedra still clinging to each other.

"Nothing concrete. I think it's all pure conjecture right now. I can do some digging to see what I can come up with, though," Vanessa said, falling into her private investigator mode.

John nodded. "Do you know where Aunt Juanita disappeared to?"

"She and Mr. Edward took off a few minutes ago. Those women in there were giving her a pretty rough time. He decided they needed to go for a ride before he and Marah got into it."

"My wife can be a little hard on her stepmother."

"Your wife is worried about you guys. So am I."

John cut his eye at Vanessa.

Matthew chuckled softly, nuzzling Vanessa's baby beneath his chin. "Your buddy Mark is about to have a seizure, he's so worked up. Mitch put him on diaper duty for the rest of the day to give him something else to think about."

Vanessa smiled. "Maybe I should add Vaughan to Mark's list, too."

"What list is that?" Mark asked, hearing his name called as he joined them on the porch. Luke followed closely on his heels.

"Your diaper list," Vanessa said with a slight giggle. "I hear you're the go-to man today."

Mark rolled his eyes. "You and my wife need to recognize that I've got skills when it comes to these kids. I'm the go-to man every day!" he said as he dropped into a cushioned rocking chair.

"So, what's next?" Luke asked as he took a seat on the top step and leaned back against the rails. "What are we going to do about her?" He turned to stare up at John.

Mark and Matthew both turned to look at their older brother, anxious for him to answer.

John took a deep breath, filling his lungs with the warm morning air. His gaze was still focused on the young woman standing off in the distance, fighting to regain her composure.

"If what she says is true and she is our sister, then a DNA test will confirm it," John finally said.

Matthew nodded. "I'll call and make the arrangements."

"And then?" Vanessa asked.

John hesitated, his thoughts feeling fractured as they spun through his head. He shrugged. "I haven't gotten that far yet."

Phaedra didn't know why she'd allowed Mason to convince her to go back to the house to continue the conversation with John and his brothers. But she had and now she was sitting in the home's wood-paneled library staring at them as hard as they were staring back at her.

Other than Matthew, who'd been talking into his cell phone, no one had said anything, waiting for what,

Phaedra wasn't sure. The tension in the room was so intense that the young woman imagined they might all self-combust if such a thing were possible.

Seated beside her, Mason had a tight grip on her hand, having promised to not let it, or her, go until she was safe and secure back in her hotel room. She couldn't help wondering what he had to be thinking of her and the drama she'd rained down on them all. So much for their first date, she thought as she stole a glance in his direction, careful not to catch his eye.

Seeming to read her thoughts, Mason drew his hand down the length of her back, an easy caress that helped to calm her nerves. His concern for her well-being was sincere, warming her spirit and affording her a level of comfort she hadn't felt since the last time she'd spent with her mother.

As Matthew seemed to be concluding his telephone call, John came to his feet, reaching for the door. As he pulled it open, Marah, Vanessa and Joanne fell into the entrance, catching themselves before hitting the floor. Mark and Luke both burst out laughing, the chortles gut-deep. Mason grinned, shaking his head. Behind the three women, Katrina stood with a hand pressed over her mouth, her eyes widened, as she tried not to laugh.

John crossed his arms over his chest, eyeing his wife with a raised eyebrow. "I swear," he said, shaking his head. "If I didn't know better I'd declare this whole damn family was crazy."

"Talk about yourself," Vanessa said, her hands gliding down the front of her shirt as if she needed to brush her clothes back into place.

"Sorry," Marah said, embarrassed, her cheeks turning a bright shade of crimson red. "We were..." she started as she shrugged.

"You were being nosy," John finished for her. He extended his arms as Marah stepped into them, easing up on her toes to kiss his cheek.

"Yes, we were," she said.

Luke pointed a finger at his new wife. "Joanne, we leave for our honeymoon in just a few hours. Please do not let these women corrupt you before we do. Please, baby!"

Joanne laughed. "Yes, dear," she said sheepishly.

John chuckled. "I like that. You need to take some pointers from Joanne, Marah. Brush up on your 'yes, dears.' See how nicely she did that? Yes, dear!" he said, mimicking his new sister-in-law.

Marah shook her head. "We just wanted you to know that we'll be in the family room if you need us for anything."

"Anything," Vanessa echoed, pushing a closed fist into her open palm. "We got your back!"

Shaking his head, John closed the door behind them. As he moved back to his seat, he met Phaedra's stare, the woman watching him closely. "They can be a handful sometimes," he said, his full lips bending into a slight smile.

Phaedra smiled back, the bend to her own mouth just as slight.

John cleared his throat as Matthew laid his iPhone on the desktop and sat down, closing the circle of siblings. He leaned forward in his seat, his elbows dropping to his thighs as he rested his chin over his hands.

"Phaedra, first, I want to apologize for anything we may have said or done this morning that may have offended or hurt you. I think I speak for all of us when I say that you really knocked us off guard and I'm embarrassed that we…that I…reacted so horribly."

Phaedra nodded as Mason squeezed her fingers. She continued to listen as John went on.

"I have no doubts that you honestly believe that our father is your father, but I hope that you will understand and not hold it against us if we have some doubts."

"And we have some doubts," Mark chimed in, his body tense as he postured in his seat.

John tossed his brother a look.

Phaedra nodded again. "I was as surprised as you were," she said, her soft voice just shy of being a loud whisper. "And I didn't mean for it to come out the way it did. I just…well…" She paused, looking to Mason and then John as she searched for the words to explain.

John smiled warmly. "I don't think there was any perfect way to say something like that."

Mason shifted in his seat. "Obviously, there is only one way for you all to know the truth," he said, looking from John to Matthew and back.

Matthew nodded. "We've already got that covered," he said. "Phaedra, if you're in agreement, I've arranged for all of us to be DNA-tested tomorrow afternoon. We have a two o'clock appointment at the genetics center in Houston."

"Everyone except me, that is," Luke interjected.

"Everyone except Luke," Matthew acknowledged. "Luke will be in South Africa on his honeymoon."

"But I'm sure if you're related to the rest of these mugs, then you'll be related to me, too," Luke said, winking an eye in Phaedra's direction.

"I wouldn't be so sure of that," Matthew countered.

"We keep telling him that he was found on our doorstep. We don't know where he came from!"

"Ha, ha, ha," Luke said. "I hope you inherited a better sense of humor, Phaedra!"

Phaedra's smile widened. "Thank you," she said.

Mark rolled his eyes. "This is ridiculous," he said. "I don't know why we're wasting the time."

An uneasy quiet fell over the room. Phaedra's gaze skated from one brother to the other, resting on Mark, who was glaring in her direction.

"You know everything I know," she said, her comments directed at Mark. "And after tomorrow we'll know even more. And I understand if you aren't interested in our being family, but if the tests show that we are related, I hope that you'll at least try to get to know me. We might never be friends, but I hope that we won't be enemies."

Mark took a deep breath, brushing his palms against his thighs. He didn't bother to respond as John and Matthew both shook their heads in his direction. "I hear my daughter crying," he said finally. "I need to go change a diaper or something." He stood abruptly and crossed to the other side of the room. He paused in the doorway, his hand clutching tightly to the doorknob. He took a quick glance over his shoulder, his gaze meeting Phaedra's. "I won't be your enemy," he said, his eyes locking with hers.

Phaedra met his stare evenly, tears swelling again in her eyes. She nodded and then he turned and exited the room.

"He'll come around," Luke said softly.

As the others rose to their feet to follow, John extended his hand to shake Mason's. "Thank you," he said. "I appreciate you keeping an eye on our new friend here." He gave the young woman an easy smile.

Mason locked eyes with Phaedra, his own smile widening across his face as she met his gaze and held it. He nodded. "Not to worry. I don't plan to let her out of my sight."

Chapter 7

There was an awkward silence as Mason closed the hotel room door behind them. Phaedra crossed over to the sitting area, dropping her purse to the wooden desk against the wall as she kicked off her high-heeled pumps. Mason stood at the entrance, his gaze following every move. Dropping down into a wingback chair, Phaedra extended her legs in front of her, both hands bearing down against the seat cushion as she twisted her ankles from side to side. She lifted her gaze to study the man who was watching her so intently.

Mason Boudreaux was just shy of being six feet tall. With his hands locked behind his back, his feet shoulder width apart, he was quite the male specimen. His chest was broad, flanked by wide shoulders and thick arms that were indicative of his daily workouts with a very good trainer. His legs were long, the khaki slacks he wore nicely complementing the hard, full, basketball-like curves of his behind. His chocolate-syrup complexion stretched nicely over tight, toned muscles, complementing his closely cropped head of silver-and-black peppered curls. The man was delectable and a seriously pleasant diversion.

She smiled, her lips stretching wide and full over her Colgate smile. "You can come in and have a seat," she said, gesturing for him to join her. "I promise no more hysterical sobbing."

Mason smiled back. "The sobbing didn't bother me."

Phaedra lifted her eyes, a smirk crossing her face.

Mason laughed. "Really, the tears didn't bother me at all," he said as he made his way to the chair beside her and sat down.

"I don't know if I believe you, Mr. Boudreaux, but it's very sweet of you to say so."

He nodded. "I don't know why you wouldn't believe me. I'm usually so convincing," he said teasingly.

Phaedra giggled softly. "I believe that."

Mason laughed with her and then the awkward silence stepped back into the room.

Phaedra closed her eyes for a brief second, wiping her palms across her thighs. Reopening her eyes, she cut her gaze in Mason's direction, the man seeming to be lost in very deep thought.

Phaedra couldn't remember the last time she'd been in such close proximity to such a beautiful man, and Mason Boudreaux was one beautiful specimen of maleness. He exuded strength, his self-confidence, compassionate spirit and obvious integrity like a banner of honor wrapped around him. There was something clearly special about him, and Phaedra found herself wanting to know about everything that made him so.

With her mother dying, then discovering that she had family she knew nothing about, and with one of the biggest photo assignments of her career now on her plate, Phaedra was surprised that she was even thinking about men. But Mason wasn't your average guy next door. Mason Boudreaux was a man a woman couldn't help thinking about.

She lifted her eyes to his. When Mason smiled sweetly, Phaedra smiled back.

"I want to thank you for everything you did for me today," she said softly, "and I want to apologize."

"Apologize for what?"

"For spoiling our first date," Phaedra said, her smile coy.

Mason nodded. "Apology accepted as long as you're willing to give me another chance to impress you," he said with a wry smile back.

Phaedra nodded. "Well, I'm already impressed, but I was thinking that dinner might be a nice idea. My treat, of course, so that I can make up for all the crying."

"I think dinner would be a great idea," Mason answered, meeting her gaze.

And Phaedra couldn't help noticing that there was something she was really starting to like shimmering deep in his eyes.

Collin Broomes rode the large black stallion with an air of confidence. He made two slow laps around the paddock grinning widely from ear to ear. Matthew stood with Mason and John outside the fenced closure, the men all nodding their approval.

"He's a natural," Mason said.

Matthew nodded in agreement. "Collin is exceptionally skilled. I admire the fact that he's allowed himself to learn and he doesn't mind being critiqued. He's come a long way. I am really proud of his maturity."

"We all appreciate the time you've invested in him, Matthew," Mason said. "Collin needed a strong male presence in his life, and you being willing to step up to the plate has been admirable."

Matthew grinned. "I love your sister. How could I not love that big-headed son of hers!" he said with deep chuckle.

John leaned on the fence beside them, taking in the conversation. He didn't say so, but he was as proud of his brother as his brother was proud of the youngster. None of them could have predicted that young Collin stealing Matthew's car months earlier would have ended with Matthew married to the woman of his dreams and about to welcome his own child into the world. It never ceased to amaze him how life could turn on the flip of a dime. He suddenly thought about his own father and Phaedra.

"How was Phaedra when you left her?" John asked, shifting his attention toward Mason.

His friend nodded. "Better. This was a difficult day for her and I don't think she was prepared for it."

"I know we didn't help the situation."

"This isn't easy for any of you," Mason said. "I know Phaedra regrets that it came out the way it did, but ultimately it needed to come out."

Matthew nodded in agreement. "So, tell me," he said curiously. "You and Phaedra seem to have gotten quite close, quite fast. What's up with you two?"

Mason laughed. "What, my sister put you up to asking?"

Matthew laughed with him. "You know she did and you know if I didn't ask I will never hear the end of it."

John's head waved from side to side. "Just to toss in another two cents, Marah made a point of saying you two make a very nice couple."

"Was that before Phaedra dropped her bombshell or after?" Mason questioned.

"Before—" John paused, his eyebrows raised "—and after. Actually, they all really seem to like Phaedra."

Matthew laughed out loud. "It was on the tip of my tongue to say, 'what's not to like?' because the woman is absolutely stunning, but now that she might actually be our sister, that seems kind of weird."

John laughed with him, shaking his head. "You're right! In fact, now that I think about it, if she is our sister, we're going to have to start screening all of her dates. You're lucky, Mason. You've already passed inspection," he joked.

Mason grinned. "I appreciate that!"

"You should," Matthew added, "because I assure you if it turns out that we're related, it's not me or John you'd have to impress. I bet my last dollar Mark is going to be the most overprotective. Phaedra doesn't have a clue what she'll be in for."

John smiled. "I was thinking the same thing. He's playing hard, but Mark is as soft as they come."

"I may be wrong, but I really don't think Phaedra will mind," Mason noted as the three men fell into reflection.

Minutes later Collin lapped the paddock for the umpteenth time and Matthew gestured for the young man's attention. Collin brought the horse to a halt in front of his stepfather and uncles. He leaned forward, his hand gliding down the horse's thick neck. "Isn't he great? He makes it so easy for me to ride."

The horse nuzzled his muzzle against Matthew's hand. "Yeah! He's a good boy. Ride him into the barn. One of the hands will help you unsaddle him. He needs to cool down and be brushed. Then you're going to put him into the stall you mucked earlier. Make sure he has fresh feed before you leave. Understand?"

"Yes, sir."

Collin paused, neither he nor the horse moving.

"Is something wrong, son?" Matthew asked.

"Aren't you going to watch me?"

Matthew shook his head. "No. I trust you'll do what I expect."

Collin raised a questioning eyebrow. "You trust me?"

Matthew smiled. "If I didn't you wouldn't be riding my favorite horse."

With a nod of his head, and a grin as wide as a canyon, Collin galloped the horse toward the barn. John met his brother's gaze, both he and Mason enjoying the moment.

"You're getting pretty good at that father thing," John said, chuckling softly.

Matthew laughed. "I learned from the best, big brother," he said as he bumped shoulders and fists with the man. "I learned from the best."

Juanita was hiding out in the kitchen when John made his way back into the family home. As he stood watching her stir a pot that was bubbling on the stove, he sensed that she was no more interested in having a conversation with him than the man in the moon. But they were going to have to talk because he had questions and she seemed to have all the answers. He called her name, startling her from her thoughts.

"John!" Juanita gasped, pressing a hand to her heart as she spun in his direction.

"I'm sorry, Aunt Juanita. I didn't mean to startle you, but we need to talk."

Juanita sighed. Resting the spoon in her hand on the counter, she bit down against her bottom lip, taking another breath and blowing it out. She gestured for John to follow her to a seat at the counter. "Do you want something to drink, baby?" she asked as he settled himself comfortably on a cushioned stool.

John shook his head no. "But thank you for asking."

Juanita nodded as she took the seat beside him. She'd been regretting this conversation, and no matter how much she wished she could avoid it, she knew John would never consider letting it go. She looked him in the eye as he waited for her to start the conversation.

"Is it true?" John finally asked. "Is it possible that Phaedra is our sister?"

Juanita blew another deep breath. His mother, Irene Stallion, had been her dearest friend in the whole wide world. The two had grown up together, best friends since they'd both been singing in the children's choir of the Baptist church they'd been raised in. They'd gone through every imaginable trial and tribulation with each other, from bad hair to bad boy days. There wasn't a secret Juanita hadn't shared with Irene or Irene with her. And Irene had shared one secret that Juanita had hoped to take to her grave.

John interrupted her thoughts. "I really need the

truth, Aunt Juanita. Was our father unfaithful? Did he cheat on our mother?"

Juanita hesitated, pausing as she took a deep breath. "Yes," she said, meeting his gaze evenly. "But it's not what you think."

"I don't know what to think," John said, cutting to the chase. "But I want facts, not assumptions, so if you can give me that I would really appreciate it. I just need the truth, Aunt Juanita."

Juanita nodded. "You all were just babies. You were five, maybe six. Matthew was three or four, and Mark was just beginning to walk good. That was the first summer that Irene let you boys go to your uncle Joseph's to spend time with Travis."

John nodded. There had been many summers when they'd gone to visit his favorite cousin. He had no memory of that very first summer.

Juanita continued. "Your parents were going through a lot that summer. Your dad had just started his refrigeration repair business. He was working in the factory at nights and running the repair shop during the day. Your mom was also working two jobs and it put a lot of stress on their relationship. The only reason Irene let you boys go was so she could take the time to try to get her marriage back on track."

"And Dad helped her do that by cheating on her?"

"It's more complicated than that. Your mother was lonely. She didn't get to spend a lot of time with James and it was a big issue between them. And then she met this man."

John suddenly slammed his fist against the countertop. Heat flushed his face, rage seeming to rise out of nowhere. Juanita jumped, rattled by the brash display of emotion. John's fists were clenched tight as he processed what he thought she was trying to tell him. Juanita held up both her hands in pause.

"Nothing happened, I swear. Your mother loved your father, but this man could see that she was vulnerable and he preyed on that. The only mistake your mother made was to let this man get into her ear and put doubt into her heart. Your father saw what was happening and it was a nasty blowup, but I swear, nothing ever happened between your mother and that man. Nothing!

"But your father didn't know that. James thought the absolute worst because it looked that way. God knows it looked bad," Juanita said, her head shaking frantically. "James thought he'd lost her. Anyway, that summer your father had gotten the Amana appliance contract to be their regional representative here in Texas and he had to go to New Orleans for a training seminar. He was still thinking that your mother wanted to be with this other man and he just wanted her to be happy, so he left believing that Irene had done him dirty and their marriage was done and finished."

John nodded. "And that's when he met Arneta Parrish?"

"Yes. James was gone for almost two months. When Irene finally realized what had happened, she followed James there and brought him back home. Your father told her about Arneta and it was rough for them for a long time, but they eventually found their way back to each other. No two people have ever loved each other as much as James and Irene loved each other."

"Did he know about Phaedra?"

"No, I don't think so," Juanita said. "If he had, your

father would have acknowledged her and your mother would have supported his decision to do so. James would never have abandoned any child of his. Never! You know better than anyone that your father was not that kind of man."

John's gaze drifted to the view outside the large picture window. He did know. He had always known what kind of man his father was. He had worked all of his life to be at least half that man, emulating the best of who he'd known his dad to be. He was suddenly overcome with emotion, fighting not to break down. Outside, it had begun to rain, dark clouds crying a fine mist of warm water in sympathy.

Relationships were complicated. What John now understood was that whatever challenges his parents might have had to face, and clearly they had gone through some things, when communication broke down between them, they'd been lost. Somehow, though, they'd been able to find their way back to each other and John remembered them only at their very best. All he had ever seen between them had been a wealth of love, that summer of reckoning not even the shimmer of a memory in his mind.

Rising from his seat, John leaned to wrap Juanita in a big bear hug. He kissed her wrinkled cheek, held the gaze she gave him for a brief second, then went in search of his wife. He needed to find sanctuary in what he trusted most, wanting only to hold Marah tight in his arms and to tell her how much she was loved.

Chapter 8

"I owned a hotel-owning company that I just sold to the Stallions."

Phaedra looked slightly confused. "And what exactly is a hotel-owning company?"

Mason smiled. "Mine was an entity that owned, managed, leased or franchised, through various subsidiaries, over four thousand hotels and more than six hundred and fifty thousand guest rooms in one hundred countries and territories around the world."

"Sweet!" Phaedra said. "That's pretty impressive."

Mason shrugged. "It had moments," he said nonchalantly.

The duo had been talking nonstop, the restaurant having closed its doors around them. Bribing the manager, Mason had convinced the man to let them stay, the staff pretending they were not even there. With the exception of their waiter, who would periodically check to see if they needed anything, they hadn't seen anyone else for hours.

Phaedra leaned back in her chair, crossing her legs out in front of her, her hands resting in her lap. "So, what's next for Mason Boudreaux? What's your next business adventure?"

Mason lifted his elbows to the table, resting his chin against the backs of his hands. "I'm not sure. I'm going to take a short sabbatical for a few weeks to wind down and then I'm going to pretend to help your brothers for a few months, although they really don't need my help. Then we'll see. Who knows what might come up?"

Phaedra sighed as she lifted her glass of pinot grigio and took a sip. "My brothers... That sounds so strange," she said, shaking her head.

"I'm sure it's only a matter of time before it will be the most natural thing in the world for you to hear," Mason countered.

"I wish I was as certain as you," she replied with a slight shrug.

Mason shifted his large body in his chair. "So, Ms. Parrish, how long are you planning to be in Dallas?"

"Not long at all actually. I'll stay for the DNA tests tomorrow and then I have to leave for Thailand the day after. I have a photo assignment that I'm contractually obligated to do. I can't get out of it."

"Thailand!" Mason shouted. "You're going to love it! Thailand is beautiful."

"You've been to Thailand?"

Mason nodded. "I've spent a lot of time in Thailand. I used to have a hotel there," he said, smiling, "and I still own some property off the coast of Phuket."

Phaedra looked intrigued. "What kind of property?"

Smiling, Mason leaned forward, moving Phaedra to lean toward him as if he were about to share a deep secret with her. "It's a private island called Koh Rang Yai, one of the most beautiful pieces of property that you could ever experience."

His tone was low and deep and sent a shiver of electricity through Phaedra's core. Phaedra shifted her body back as though she'd been burned. Her eyes widened at the sensation.

"It sounds very special," Phaedra said, her own voice coming in a deep whisper.

Mason smiled. "I'd love to show it to you someday."

"I'd love to see it," Phaedra responded, so lost in the intense look he was giving her that she wasn't sure she'd ever be able to find her way back.

"How about the day after tomorrow?" Mason asked.

"Excuse me?"

"Let me go to Thailand with you and when you're done working I can show you my private island."

Phaedra laughed, tossing her head back against her shoulders. "You're kidding me, right?"

Mason eased himself even closer, dropping a hand against her knee. "I don't kid about things that are important to me," he said.

His seductive tone was just too distracting to be any good for anyone, Phaedra thought suddenly. She took a deep breath, dropped her hand against the back of his and gently pushed his palm away from her leg.

"I am not that kind of girl, Mr. Boudreaux," she said teasingly.

This time Mason laughed, the sound coming from deep in his midsection. He shook his head. "I assure

you, Miss Parrish, my intentions are strictly aboveboard."

Phaedra still eyed him with reservation. "So, why
would you want to go to Thailand with me?"

Mason smiled, the look so spectacular that Phaedra
found herself holding her breath at the sight of him.
When he responded she melted into a puddle of over-
stimulated hormones, every nerve ending in her body
feeling as if it were about to combust.

"Because you are the most exquisite woman I have
ever met and if following you to Thailand will allow
me more time to get to know you, then I'm following
you to Thailand."

Phaedra paused as she took in his comment. Then
she smiled back. "Understand, Mr. Boudreaux, nothing and no one gets in my way when I'm working. So
understand there will be no private anything, island
or otherwise, between us until after my photo shoot.
Is that clear?"

Mason grinned, his head bobbing eagerly. "Crystal."

She nodded. "So, tell me more about your island."

Too fast. Phaedra's words echoed through Mason's
thoughts. *You move too fast.* He smiled as he reflected
on her. She was obstinate when he'd insisted on them
flying his private jet to Bangkok. Phaedra had resisted,
reasoning that she had a perfectly good airline ticket
courtesy of the company that had hired her to photograph their new line of women's shoes.

It had been Phaedra's suggestion that they shoot in
the tropical paradise. Adding her opinion and creative
vision to the advertising presentation had helped her

beat out fifty other photographers for the job. Her first-class travel expenses had been one of the many perks she'd negotiated for herself and she saw no reason for it to go to waste. But Mason had insisted and she had come kicking, steadfast in her pronouncement that he was moving way too fast for his own good.

Mason smiled as he brushed the backs of his fingers along the profile of her face. She shifted ever so slightly beneath his light touch. He slowly drew back his hand, mindful about not disturbing her rest. She'd been sleeping soundly in the leather seat beside him since they'd stopped to refuel in Tokyo. They'd been in the air for twelve-plus hours and it had taken most of that time for her to finally calm down and relax.

It had been a long and tedious twenty-four hours for them both. Mason had taken Phaedra to Houston for her DNA test, meeting the brothers on-site. And despite their best efforts, just as they had been the day before, John had been reserved, his quiet stance unnerving her. Mark had still been resentful, unreasonably cold and annoyed by the inconvenience of it all. And Matthew had been in full lawyer mode, mindful that there was an appropriate and legal chain of custody to ensure that there would be no tampering with the results.

All of them had to be properly identified and their DNA samples collected with a documented paper trail, and everyone involved, from the specimen collector to the DNA analyst, needed to guarantee that they had no interest in the outcome of the test. It had been an emotional roller coaster for them all.

Mason had held Phaedra's hand through all of it, sensing that she desperately needed a shoulder to lean on. She fought not to show it, but losing her mother and finding brothers while trying to pretend life was normal had shaken her foundation. Mason was determined to keep her upright and moving until she regained her sense of balance. The circumstances of their coming together were well out of the norm, but he was certain that given enough time, normalcy together would be exactly what the two could find. And if he were really moving fast, it was only because he really wanted to know her and he really wanted her to know him.

Mason's laugh was like pure honey, Phaedra thought to herself as she lay with her eyes closed tight, pretending to be asleep. It had to be the thickest, richest, sweetest sound that she'd ever heard. And he enjoyed laughing, easily moving her to laugh with him.

The flight attendant was flirting with him shamelessly, the statuesque woman whispering loudly as she tried to impress him. Phaedra was clearly entertained as Mason struggled to be polite all the while avoiding the overt innuendos the woman was throwing his way. He was cool as a cucumber, but she could hear in his voice that Mason would have liked to be anywhere but in the midst of that conversation with her sitting so close to his side.

She took a deep breath and exhaled loudly, stretching her body against the length of her seat. She sat up as she rubbed her eyes, yawning as if to pull herself from the pretend slumber. Mason smiled excitedly as the flight attendant turned away in a huff, retreating to the plane's galley.

Mason smiled down at Phaedra, his grin spread

from ear to ear. "Hey, sleepyhead! Are you feeling better?"

Phaedra nodded. "Much. I needed a good nap," she answered. "How about you?"

"I feel good. Ready to be back on the ground, though."

"What time is it? Are we close?"

"Yes," Mason said. "In fact, the stewardess was just saying that the pilot will probably be preparing us for landing in the next thirty minutes."

"And what else was she saying?" Phaedra asked, one eyebrow raised as she stared in his direction.

Mason laughed, that syrupy sound caressing her eardrums. "Whatever do you mean?"

"You know exactly what I mean. The way she was tossing her sugar cookies at you, it sounded like she had some serious plans for you two," Phaedra whispered, tossing a glance in the direction of the galley.

"Were you eavesdropping, Ms. Parrish?"

Phaedra nodded. "I most certainly was, and from what I heard, she had plans and you weren't going along willingly."

Mason shook his head, grinning widely. "No, I wasn't," he said, a smirk painted across his expression. "Were you jealous?"

Phaedra laughed. "Do I look like I was jealous?"

"You look a little jealous," he teased.

She leaned closer to him, her smile titillating every nerve ending in his body. "I don't do jealous, Mr. Boudreaux."

Mason leaned in, as well. "Good, because no one has my attention right now except you. You have no reason to be jealous."

Phaedra's smiled brightened as she shook her head. "You are such a man," she said, laughing.

Mason laughed with her. "Woman, you just don't know!"

Chapter 9

Lying in the heart of Southeast Asia, roughly equidistant between India and China, Thailand is distinguished by its breathtaking scenery, featuring spectacular green mountains, white tropical beaches and sparkling blue seas. Within twenty-four hours of her arrival in the capital of Bangkok, Phaedra was so in awe of the culture and her surroundings that she had changed the venue for her shoot, hired new models and was completely immersed in the job she'd been hired to do. She was moving nonstop, barely pausing to rest her eyes.

Like a fly on a wall, Mason disappeared into the background, in awe of her commanding presence. Phaedra knew what she wanted to capture for posterity and what she needed to do to make that happen. Neither the creative director for the project nor the client representative was happy with her, but it was clear that Phaedra was going to give them far more than they'd even begun to imagine.

Mason had taken control that first day, helping Phaedra to acclimate to her new environment. Within hours of arriving he had treated her to a Thai massage at Madara Spa to alleviate the stress of the lengthy trip. Afterward Phaedra had insisted on a quick excursion to Wang Lang Market to try the street food. She'd not been satisfied until she'd had her fill of *muu daeng yan,* a spicy roasted Thai pork with a plateful of springy wheat noodles peppered with chopped scallions. Her meal had been complete when she'd polished off a serving of *kanom krok,* tiny Thai cupcakes baked in a hot metal mold, and more of the crispy tacolike wafers, *kanom buang maprow,* filled with meringue and sweet coconut, than he'd been able to count.

"You have a healthy appetite," Mason said as he passed her a napkin, in awe of the amount of food she'd managed to consume.

"I do like to eat," she said, "and I make no apologies for it."

"I like a woman with a healthy appetite. But as tiny as you are, I'm just trying to figure out where you're putting all that food." Mason laughed.

"That just sounds like another pastry moment to me!" Phaedra said with a wink as she downed her umpteenth wafer dessert.

By the second day Mason was pasted on that wall, an observer in a world that was completely ruled by Phaedra Parrish. The only thing he was allowed to suggest was a ride in a *tuk-tuk,* a rickshaw taxi, that skirted them from one point to another as Phaedra finalized the plans for her assignment.

On day three he followed her to northern Thailand and the Red Karen Village where an indigenous tribe of people known as the Padaung thrived. The Padaung women were renowned for the brass coils they wore around their necks, elongating them for a giraffelike appearance. The extra-long neck was considered a sign of great beauty and wealth and it was thought that such would enable them to better attract a husband.

Women of the tribe identified themselves by their different forms of dress: white robes for single women seeking partners and the brighter colors for married women. Phaedra had been enamored after their guide had explained the coiling process, the brass rings first applied to young girls when they were as young as five years old. As the girls matured, each coil was replaced with a longer coil, the weight of the brass pushing the collarbone down and compressing the rib cage. The illusion of their stretched necks was created by the deformation of their clavicles.

With help from an interpreter, their guide and the permission of a village elder, Phaedra secured the village for her photo shoot. Against the backdrop of a rising sun, the lush greenery of the paddy fields and twelve Padaung girls and teens, Phaedra captured the beauty of high-priced European stilettos, the likes of which had never been done before. When she was finished, no one was more in awe of her than Mason.

Their fourth day in Thailand, after the CEO of that shoe company himself called to express his gratitude for her outstanding work, Phaedra laid her head down on a plush pillow in the luxury suite of their five-star hotel and slept for eighteen straight hours.

* * *

Mason tapped lightly on the door between their adjoining bedrooms. When he got no answer he opened the door slowly and let himself inside. "Rise and shine," Mason said as he tapped the covers atop Phaedra's comatose body. "Time to get up, sleepyhead!"

Phaedra jumped, startled from a very pleasant dream. For a brief moment she had no recollection of where she was or who was talking. Recognition came slowly as Mason stood at the foot of the bed, smiling down at her.

"You're missing all the sunshine," Mason said softly, his hand gently caressing her foot.

Phaedra yawned, stretching her body against the too-comfortable mattress. As she did, the soft covers caressing her skin, she realized that she was naked beneath the sheets. Her eyes widened as she suddenly clutched the covers beneath her chin. "What time is it?" she asked.

"A better question would be, what day is it?" Mason said with a hearty chuckle.

"Have I been asleep that long?"

Mason nodded. "You've missed a whole day. And I've missed you," he added.

Heat suddenly radiated from Phaedra's core, searing everything that made her feminine. She was suddenly feeling very exposed.

"Well," Phaedra said softly, Mason still staring.

He laughed as he winked his eye at her. "I'll give you some privacy," he said. He pointed to a collection of plates resting against the table in the center of the room. "Breakfast is there. It's fresh fruit, coffee, juice, those pastry things you liked and a few traditional Thai dishes. If you want something different just let me know," he said as he moved in the direction of the door.

Phaedra nodded. "So, are we headed to your island today?" she asked, curiosity pulling at her.

Mason shrugged his broad shoulders as he exited the room. "Maybe," he said as he tossed her one last look, "and then again, maybe not!"

"So, what should I wear?" she called after him.

Mason laughed. "I like what you have on now," he answered, the door closing behind him.

Phaedra lifted the edge of the comforter and peered beneath it. What had he seen? Phaedra pondered. She shook her head as she tossed back the covers and slid her body from the bed. She tried to convince herself that he couldn't possibly have seen anything at all.

She paused to savor the assortment of goodies laid out for her to eat, pouring herself a large glass of orange juice and popping a fruit tart into her month, taking note that Mason had started the day nicely.

As she stepped into the glass shower, a warm spray of water raining down over her head and shoulders, she thought about the man, reminiscing about the time they'd shared since meeting at the wedding.

Mason had been solid as a rock. He was intelligent, magnetic, charming and unpretentious. He'd been sweet and caring, sensitive to her needs and most important, he made her laugh. Making her laugh when she couldn't begin to think of anything to even smile about had been the surest way to win her over, and Phaedra was feeling as if she'd struck gold in a landfill. She suddenly realized she was grinning like the Cheshire cat as she rinsed lavender-scented suds from her arms and back. She liked Mason. She liked him a lot and the thought brought more smiles to her face.

Two hours later a private biplane transported them from Bangkok to the coast of Phuket. Mason had teased her, saying that they would be meeting one of his favorite friends, and there she was, moored to the docks at Chalong Bay. His favorite friend was a private sailing yacht, some ninety-one feet long with a striking polished mahogany hull and the most dazzling royal-blue sails that Phaedra had ever seen. The sailboat was named *My Mistress* and she was elegant, a thing of sheer beauty. Reaching for the camera hanging around her neck, Phaedra couldn't resist taking a few photos.

"She's a beauty, isn't she?" Mason said, a hint of pride in his tone.

"Incredible," Phaedra said in agreement. "Is it yours?"

Mason smiled, a slight shrug to his shoulders his only response. He gestured for one of the crew members to come collect their belongings and guided her aboard.

"So, you named her *My Mistress?*" Phaedra questioned, her eyebrows raised.

He laughed heartily. "I was married to my business and when I could sneak away for some necessary R & R, I liked to go sailing. It seemed appropriate at the time."

Phaedra laughed with him. "That's so funny," she said as he led her on a quick tour of the luxury accommodations, a glass of champagne in hand.

Later, when Phaedra stepped out on deck in a pale yellow bikini that complemented the warm tones of her complexion, Mason had to fight not to stare. With her hair piled into a loose chignon atop her head, the woman was stunning, her hourglass figure stirring a low fire deep in him. The sudden rush of excitement threw him completely off guard, the muscles in his body reacting with a mind of their own. Mason guzzled the last of his drink, thinking that he might have to dive ocean-deep to stall the rise of wanting that would give his desire away. He took a seat, dropping swiftly into a deck chair as he crossed a leg over his lap.

As if she could sense his discomfort, Phaedra tossed him a wink, slowly adjusted the line of her bikini bottom, draped a towel beneath her and stretched the length of her frame across the deck chair beside him. She laughed softly as she took a slow sip of her own drink.

Mason didn't miss the crew eyeing her with appreciation and him with envy. Even the captain gave him two thumbs-up as Phaedra made herself comfortable, clearly relishing the cool ocean breeze and the bright midday sun. Before the afternoon was through they set sail, shadowing the Thai shoreline on a course to paradise. As they skimmed the crystal-blue waters in the direction of several islands off the coast of Thailand near the Malaysian sea border, Mason and Phaedra became deadly serious about doing absolutely nothing.

"I could get used to this," Phaedra said, tossing a hand over her eyes to block the sunlight blinding her view. She sat up to stare in Mason's direction.

"Then you should do it as often as you can," Mason answered, opening one eye to meet her gaze.

Phaedra reached for her champagne glass and took another sip. "So, explain to me again why it might take as long as two weeks to get the results back from the DNA tests."

"Two weeks is the maximum amount of time that it should take," Mason responded as he spun his legs off the side of the lounger and sat upright. "According to John, the results should actually be back within the week. But they've requested a full DNA profile be done on all of you, and that takes some time."

"And DNA profiling is where they identify the DNA markers for accurate genetic identity or something like that, right?"

"Yes. Your markers are the short DNA sequences that make up who you are. You get two copies, one inherited from your mother and one inherited from your father. Every person inherits a unique combination of genetic markers from his biological parents. Thus the DNA profile can serve as a permanent biological record of your identity. They have to identify and ensure that you have the same paternal markers they have, which will prove you all have the same father. The techniques and statistical calculations they will use to calculate the probability of your biological relationship just takes time."

"Technology at its finest," Phaedra said facetiously. "What would we do without it?"

"John will call as soon as they know, so stop worrying about it."

"We're on a boat. I don't see too many phone lines floating on that water."

Mason laughed. "John will call," he repeated. "You need to relax."

Phaedra blew a deep sigh.

Mason sat staring at her, the woman struggling not

to meet his gaze. He smiled, the seductive gesture moving Phaedra to squirm ever so slightly in her seat. The electricity between them seemed to give the boat more speed as it glided through the glassy waters.

"Don't look at me like that," she said suddenly.

"Like what?"

"Like the way you're looking at me. I feel naked."

He laughed again. "I'm looking at you because you're so beautiful and if I'm honest, I wish you were naked," he said casually.

"Aren't you the pervert?" Phaedra responded as she rolled her eyes.

"Come here," Mason said, a crooked index finger waving her toward him.

"What?"

"Come here," Mason said, his voice dropping low, the seductive tone like a sweet caress against Phaedra's ears.

Intrigued, Phaedra rose from her seat, the string bikini she wore, more string than bikini, looking like wet paint against her toned form. As she moved to his side, Mason lifted his legs to straddle the cushioned lounger he was seated on. He patted the seat between his legs.

"Sit here," he said, holding up a hand to guide her down to the seat.

Turning her back to his chest Phaedra sat down between his legs, stretching the length of her own legs outward. Mason wrapped his arms around her waist and pulled her against him, nestling the round of her buttocks against his pelvis. Phaedra inhaled swiftly, the warmth of his touch startling. He gently pressed his fingers against the back of her neck, slowly kneading the soft flesh beneath his fingertips.

Without realizing it Phaedra gave in to the sensations sweeping through her body. She was loving the feeling of sitting so close to him. She dropped her chin down toward her chest and leaned forward to allow him better access to the muscles that had tightened through her neck and across her shoulder blades. Heat radiated from his palms, pleasure burning deep into her core.

Mason loved how his touch was affecting her. Phaedra's legs relaxed, then flexed, her body beginning to quiver. Her hands tightened as she clutched them in tight fists. Her eyes were closed and her breathing started to come in short gasps as she subconsciously licked her lips. When she moaned, the sound like a soft purr, he chuckled softly, causing Phaedra to jump out of the reverie. Taken aback, she leaped from her seat, skirting far from Mason's touch.

"What's wrong?" Mason asked, his grin disarming her sensibilities.

"You…you…you shouldn't have been doing that!" Phaedra stammered, her breathing heavy.

"Doing what?"

"That… What you were doing!"

He laughed, his head waving. "I was only giving you a massage."

"That wasn't just a massage."

"But you liked what I was doing and you liked how I was doing it," he said matter-of-factly.

Heat flushed her face and her complexion tinted a deep red at the truth of his statement. She had enjoyed it and if she were honest she had wanted him to do much more. "That's beside the point," Phaedra said, crossing her arms over her chest.

Mason laughed loudly. "Fine," he said, "instead of giving you a massage myself I'll call for someone on the island to come ease the tension out of your muscles. Will that be better?"

Phaedra rolled her eyes. "You think you're cute."

Mason smiled brightly. "Yes, I do!"

Two days later Phaedra couldn't imagine their time together getting any better. The captain had guided the boat into a channel cradled between the islands. They were wined and dined on deck, the tantalizing meals unending. Mason's personal chef overwhelmed them with fresh fish chowders, amazing salads, vine-ripened fruits and sumptuous Thai cuisine. When they weren't dozing deckside, falling asleep to the sound of small waves slapping against the hull, they were snorkeling above exquisite coral gardens. They awoke to the beauty of the rising sun in the mornings, and in the evenings, the sunsets seemed spiritual, each one more soothing and poignant than the last.

Through it all Mason remained the perfect gentleman. He had called in a professional masseuse for them both, the woman arriving by dinghy to join the crew. More times than not she caught him staring, the looks he gave her like daggers of piercing heat. There was no mistaking the waves of desire that danced between the two of them. But Phaedra wasn't ready to move their newfound friendship in a more intimate direction. And despite having the best spa services at their disposal, Phaedra couldn't stop herself from thinking of Mason and the way he had touched her, wishing him to do it all over again.

Phaedra couldn't begin to imagine why she was so restless. She and Mason had spent most of the night deckside in deep conversation, sharing everything they could possibly think to share with each other. She'd heard stories about his family and had talked about her relationship with her mother. They'd confided details of her first kiss, his first sexual encounter, their most embarrassing moments, biggest fears and greatest hopes. They had discovered things about each other that no one else knew, and no topic had been off-limits.

When they'd parted ways, she going to her cabin and he to his, both had wished for a few more minutes, neither wanting to let the other go. Then Phaedra had tossed and turned in her bed, unable to explain the wealth of emotion she was feeling. She blew a deep sigh as she sat upright in the bed, tossing her legs over the side.

The heat from the morning sun had awakened her, making her cabin too warm to sleep in. Rising, she slipped into a one-piece bathing suit and wrapped a brightly colored sarong around her hips, then maneuvered herself topside to look around. Mason was already sitting comfortably beneath the bright blue sky, a glass of fresh-squeezed juice in his hand.

"Good morning," the man said.

"Good morning."

"Did you sleep well?"

Phaedra nodded. "I slept okay, not great," she said as she reached for the glass of juice he was passing to her.

He nodded his understanding, knowing full well what she was describing. He hadn't slept well, either, the night spent thinking of her and nothing else.

She took the seat beside him. "So, what's on the agenda today?" she asked casually, both hands wrapped around the crystal glass. "Will I get to see that island of yours sometime soon?"

Mason nodded as he met her stare. He pointed a finger to the landscape behind her back. Turning to stare past the boat's stern, Phaedra eyed the white-sand beach that ran along the side of the boat, kissing the dazzling turquoise channel beneath them. A dense jungle fronted the entire length of the beach, a formidable barrier to the naked eye. The place seemed divinely empty, unspoiled and promising a peaceful quiet to anyone willing to brave the terrain.

Jutting out of the water on stilts were four thatched-roof, overwater bungalows, each featuring a glass-bottomed floor that allowed stunning views of the marine life below. With private decks, each with steps down into the lagoon for easy access to the water, the simplicity of the accommodations was breathtaking.

A lone figure dotted the beachside, a fisherman who waved excitedly in their direction. In the waters that surrounded the land, clouds of tropical fish shimmered and danced in erratic synchronized displays. Puffer fish, angelfish and sea urchins hid in coral passages. A manta ray glided lazily along the bottom as he headed out to sea. Phaedra stole a quick glance toward Mason, a look of sheer enchantment crossing her face.

"Welcome to my home," Mason said as he moved against her back, wrapping his arms around her torso and nuzzling his face into her hair.

Taking a deep breath of warm ocean air, Phaedra relaxed against him, allowing herself to savor the sweet sensation of being in his arms.

Chapter 10

They were having dinner in Phuket, an outrigger canoe scheduled to pick them up and carry them to their destination. After their arrival on the island, Mason had given Phaedra a quick tour of her hut before disappearing to his own. Knowing that the beautiful woman had only bought casual clothes for her trip, he arranged for a selection of formal clothing to be delivered to her room.

Phaedra had sent him a text message when the rack of garments had arrived, her appreciation evident in the words on his smartphone screen. Mason smiled, moving to the window to stare toward her hut. Phaedra stood in the open entrance of her own space and waved in gratitude. The two paused, staring intently at each other. Then Phaedra moved back inside, disappearing to get dressed.

Dropping down onto the king-size bed in his room,

Mason closed his eyes and took a deep breath. There was something brewing between him and Phaedra, like nothing he had ever experienced before. It was exciting and special and it had seeped deep beneath his skin to spread like wildfire into his system. It was something he'd been searching for since forever, never imagining that it would feel quite as magnanimous as this.

An hour or so later Mason waited on the dock as Phaedra made her way toward him. She'd chosen a simple Monique Lhuillier black lace cocktail dress with mile-high Christian Louboutin stilettos. Her lush curls had been straightened, hanging down to her shoulders. The entire ensemble flattered the petite lines of her frame, the strapless styling absolutely stunning on her. Mason couldn't find words.

"Is this okay?" Phaedra asked, doing a pivot turn in front of him.

Mason smiled, nodding sheepishly. "Wow," he said, his gaze skirting the lines of her body, racing from the tip of her head to the bottoms of her feet. "Wow!"

Phaedra smiled back. "I'll take that as a yes."

"Yes," Mason said. "You look amazing!"

Phaedra glanced toward the skipper of the canoe, who was waiting patiently for them to board.

Mason followed her gaze. "Your chariot awaits, madame!"

She nodded as she eased around him, stepping gently to keep from falling into the water. As she stepped into his space, Mason inhaled the scent of her perfume, a light floral fragrance wafting beneath his nose. Before he realized what he was doing, he clutched her arm, pulling her to him. He hesitated for only a moment, Phaedra meeting his intense stare with a look of her own. Her breath caught deep in her chest, her heart racing unexpectedly.

Without a second thought Mason leaned in to kiss her, allowing his lips to lightly graze hers. His breath was hot with wanting, his full lips quivering in anticipation. He pulled away and stared into her eyes a second time and then he dropped his mouth to hers, meeting Phaedra's lips in a deep, soul-searing kiss.

Time seemed to come to a standstill. Phaedra felt as if the world had rotated her into the stratosphere, everything spinning around her. Mason held her tightly, his hands burning hot against the bare skin of her arms and shoulders. His body melded tight to hers and both were in awe of the sensations, feeling as if they were melting—one into the other. When he finally pulled back he knew beyond any doubt that he had absolutely fallen in love with Phaedra and Phaedra was falling in love with him.

They had dinner reservations at Da Maurizio Bar Ristorante, located on Patong Beach. Da Maurizio was considered the finest contemporary Italian restaurant in the south of Thailand and had won numerous awards. With the granite boulder-strewn beach below the alfresco dining room, it counted Mother Nature as part of the decor. The white linen tablecloths, colorful bar and brick floors served to complement the classic Italian styling. It was clearly one of the most beautiful dining venues in Phuket, stylish, impressive, memorable and unpretentious.

A light Italian ballad played in the background as Mason and Phaedra stepped inside, her hand entwined with his, both still floating from the kiss they'd shared.

The hostess greeted him by name, quickly escorting them to one of their best tables, and the impeccably clad waitstaff hovered at the ready to do his bidding. For a brief moment Phaedra regretted not bringing her camera to capture the eclectic mix of diners who had come from all over the globe to enjoy the constant background flow of the Andaman Sea, which helped the restaurant's atmosphere remain true to Thailand's laid-back reputation.

Mason ordered dinner for them, starting with a gourmet appetizer treat of foie gras and candied walnuts atop cubed green apples on a crisp homemade raisin bread and port wine reduction and fresh al dente fettuccine with marinated and lightly seared yellowfin tuna, capers, Gaeta olives and anchovies. They had just begun their meal when Phaedra saw the woman enter the room.

Phaedra saw her before Mason did, the stunning beauty catching the attention of everyone in the room. She was tall and slender, her figure more androgynous than feminine, as she sported a leopard-print jumpsuit with matching high-heeled shoes. Her jet-black hair was closely cropped around the back, and she had long sweeping bangs streaked with vibrant gold highlights that complemented her distinctive Asian features. With the exception of her bright red lips, her makeup was subtle, impeccably applied.

Phaedra took notice of her just as the woman took notice of Mason. There was no missing the woman's excitement that shimmered out of her eyes. The man who'd stepped in behind her noticed it as well, quietly admonishing her to calm down. Phaedra pressed a napkin to her mouth as the woman rushed toward their table, her companion following closely on her heels.

"Mason Boudreaux," the older man said, calling for Mason's attention.

Mason looked up in surprise. "Daniel, hello," he said, rising from his seat to shake the man's hand. "What a wonderful surprise."

"We did not know you were back in Thailand," the man said.

"You should have called, Mason," his female companion said, moving to wrap Mason in a deep hug. She kept her arms wrapped around his waist as if she were afraid to let go.

Mason smiled politely. "It's good to see you, Mali," he said.

Extricating himself from the woman's grasp, he moved to Phaedra's side, taking her hand in his. "Allow me to introduce you to my dear friend. Phaedra, this is Daniel Kasam and his daughter, Mali Kasam. Daniel is one of the most respected politicians here in Thailand. Daniel, Mali, this is my friend, and my traveling companion, Phaedra Parrish."

The man named Daniel gave Phaedra a wide smile. "It's a pleasure to meet you, Miss Parrish. Mason and I have been good friends for many, many years."

"Please, call me Phaedra. It's nice to meet you both, as well," Phaedra responded as Daniel took her hand and pressed a kiss to the back of her fingers.

His daughter eyed her from head to toe, her expression blank. When Mason dropped his hand to Phaedra's shoulder, gently caressing her warm flesh, the woman's face twisted in a harsh snarl. Mali glared and Phaedra held the harsh stare, hardly intimidated.

"How long will you be in town?" Daniel asked, appearing to not see his daughter's behavior.

"Just a few more days," Mason answered. "Phaedra has business back in the United States, so we'll be heading back home by the end of the week."

"Well, we must have dinner together before you leave. Are you two free tomorrow night?" the other man asked, looking from Mason to Phaedra and back.

Phaedra glanced up to see Mason eyeing Mali with reservation. He sensed her staring at him and tossed her a quick look. Taking a deep breath, he smiled sweetly, giving her a quick wink.

"We'd love to," he said as he gently squeezed Phaedra's shoulder.

"Wonderful!" Daniel said. "Then we'll catch up with each other tomorrow."

"We both look forward to it," Mason concluded, moving to shake the man's hand one last time.

As her father turned away, Mali moved herself against Mason, clutching the front of his suit jacket as she pressed her body to his. She leaned to kiss his closed mouth, moving her lips earnestly over his. "I've missed you, Mason," she whispered seductively. Before Mason could answer, Daniel called his daughter's name, admonishing the woman in their native Siamese language.

Mali huffed in annoyance as she stepped away. "Tomorrow," she said, tossing the man one last wink and as she turned to follow her father, she gave Phaedra one last glare.

When both were out of earshot, Phaedra shook her head. "Well, well, well," she said, bemusement shimmering across her face. "You didn't tell me about your ex," she said.

"Mali is not my ex," he said with a deep chuckle. "There has never been anything between me and her."

Phaedra tossed Mali one last look as the woman and her father joined a group gathered in the private dining room. "Well," she said, lifting her gaze back to his, "someone clearly forgot to tell her that!"

Phaedra hadn't missed Mali's blatant interest in the handsome bachelor. What she didn't know was that Mali had been vying for Mason's attention for as long as he could remember, but her brash behavior and brazen antics had been a complete turnoff for him. Despite the woman's obvious overtures, Mason only had eyes for Phaedra, clearly intoxicated with her, and he told her so. Phaedra was the sweetest addiction that had ever consumed him, and his only interest was the magnetic attraction between them. Shaking his head, Mason changed the subject.

The rest of their meal was uneventful. After a main course of rosemary lamb chops sitting on a mint salsa verde and lemon yogurt with herbed couscous, they finished their dinner with a decadent tiramisu. Sated beyond reason, Phaedra couldn't imagine them having a better time.

"Have I thanked you yet? Our time here in Thailand has been absolutely amazing," she said as she reached for his hand, drawing her fingers against his open palm.

"Many times, but you don't have to keep thanking me, Phaedra. I really haven't done anything."

Phaedra shook her head. "But you have and I think that couples sometimes forget to acknowledge each other and show their appreciation for what each does. I don't want that to happen with us."

Mason smiled. "And are we a couple?"

Phaedra was suddenly overwhelmed by the look he was giving her. His stare was eager and searching. She felt as if she were falling headfirst into his gaze, able to lose herself completely if she were willing to let go. She was grateful for the distraction when the waiter appeared at the table with the dinner bill.

On the ride back to the island, Mason took off his suit jacket, wrapping it around her shoulders to shield her from the cool night air. Phaedra rested her head against his shoulder, reveling in the soft light of a full moon and the dark sky littered with bright stars.

"This has been wonderful," Phaedra said, her voice floating through the darkness. She spun around, wrapping her arms around his waist as she rested her cheek against his broad chest.

As Mason leaned to kiss her forehead, there was nothing else he needed to say, everything about the moment agreeing with her.

Chapter 11

Mason had kissed her one last time before wishing her a good night. Phaedra had stood in the doorway of her bungalow, watching as he made his exit, returning to his own room. For a split second she'd thought about calling him back to her and then she didn't.

She couldn't help questioning where the two of them might be going with their relationship, a discussion they had yet to have. She knew he was ready for marriage and children and family, anxious for that next phase in his life. Yet, he knew that she'd never given those thoughts much consideration, her career taking precedence over all else. They had talked in generalizations, but now the discussion of how that affected the two of them together needed to be shared. Because Phaedra did feel like the other half of a couple, but when he'd asked, she hadn't been ready to say yes.

If they were moving too fast, she didn't want to be

the one initiating the race. Mason seemed content to let her set the pace, and Phaedra didn't want to rush if it were at all possible for the two of them to be thinking about forever with each other. Because Phaedra found herself thinking about forever with Mason Boudreaux.

Phaedra stepped out of her clothes, tossing her dress over a chair and kicking her shoes into a corner. She dropped down against the feathered mattress, her hands resting against her upper thighs. Music played softly from speakers in the wall, a slow, erotic tune with a deep, sultry base. The song seemed to have a certain power over her, the seductive lyrics and entrancing beat making her want to dance and make love all at the same time. Her body tingled, heat beginning to creep from her southern quadrant as she swayed from side to side.

Outside, a loud splash of water drew her attention. Phaedra moved to the open window to peer outside. Beneath the glow of moonlight she couldn't miss Mason, the man having dropped down into the lagoon for a late night swim. The water around him glistened, shimmering from the reflection of the light above as his muscular body floated atop the watery bed. Intoxicated by the music and wanting more from the man who had her full attention, Phaedra stepped out of her panties, took a deep breath, then headed out the door.

Mason was taken by surprise when Phaedra stepped out onto the edge of the dock. She was as naked as the day she'd been born. He'd been swimming laps between their two bungalows and when he saw her he stopped midstroke and began to tread water, taking a moment to appreciate the gorgeous sight as she posed seductively in front of him.

Phaedra loved the cool sensation of fresh air on her

exposed breasts, the dark chocolate areolas surrounding candy-hard nipples. A breeze blew like a fine mist between her legs, moisture beginning to pool between her creases. But the intense sensations were nothing compared to what she felt when she saw the look on Mason's face, the man looking as if he were experiencing the single greatest moment of his life.

Neither spoke, but there was no denying the rise of wanting that was spiraling between them. Even beneath the blanket of cool water, Mason's muscles tightened, blood surging with a vengeance below his waist. His erection stretched full and hard, feeling as if it might explode if he even thought about the woman. He bit down against his bottom lip, wanting to still the rise of nature between his muscular legs.

Holding on to the wooden ladder that dropped into the natural pool, Phaedra slowly eased her body into the water to join him. The chill of the moisture did nothing to ease the heat that was consuming her. Phaedra wanted him. She wanted him more than she had ever wanted any man in her life, and if that made her fast, she thought, then she was past ready to set a new record.

Mason swam toward her as she moved into his arms. He wrapped one arm around her waist as he maneuvered her against the dock where he could grab on to the structure with his other hand. The light floral scent of her perfume surrounded him, blending with the sweet ocean air. He seized her mouth hungrily, barely daring to believe that this moment had finally arrived. His mouth clung to hers, and he felt her tongue meet his own, the two dancing deep in her mouth. Tasting the sweet fullness of her lips, Mason couldn't help biting down on her bottom lip, then nibbling on her top lip. Their kiss was heated and intense, just a semblance of the hunger they had for each other.

Yearning for more, Mason braced himself against the wooden steps as Phaedra wrapped her legs around his waist. She pressed her pelvis against the length of his manhood and it took everything he had not to explode from the connection. His mouth did a nosedive and landed smack on her nipple, greedily sucking and tugging and pulling at her with his teeth and lips. Phaedra let out a loud gasp, the sound resonating between a moan and a scream. It was almost too much for her to bear as his hands followed his mouth, kneading and pulling at the fleshy tissue.

The duo dropped beneath the water. They both held their breaths, lost in the sensations of his touch and hers as they clung to each other. It was eerily quiet, their beating hearts all either of them could hear above the swell of the ocean. When they resurfaced, the sounds of their desire rose to a crescendo that echoed through the night air.

"We need protection," Mason whispered, thinking of a prophylactic before the moment consumed them and he wouldn't be able to think of anything except the pleasure the two were intent on giving each other.

Phaedra nodded as he lifted her from the water, setting her easily atop the wooden platform. He lifted his body from the water, reached for her hand and led her back inside his bungalow. Inside, he snatched the bed's coverings and tossed them to the floor. Lifting her into his arms, Mason kissed her again as he laid her gently down against the mattress. His swimming trunks tented eagerly between them.

"Do you really want me, Phaedra?" he questioned, stopping to stare down at her.

Phaedra responded by pulling him back to her, her mouth dancing like silk against his. Inhaling her scent, Mason ran the tip of his nose up and down the side of Phaedra's neck, then did the same with his lips and then his fingers. Goose bumps rose against Phaedra's damp skin as he teased her feminine spirit. His kisses became more and more intense until he was gently sucking on her neck, his teeth lightly biting her soft, pliant throat until tiny little marks began to rise against her flesh. Beyond any doubt he knew that she was his, and he couldn't help wanting to mark her and stake his territory.

Beneath him Phaedra was slowly grinding her pelvis against the rigid hardness between his legs. She reached her hands around his torso and raked her nails down the length of his back. It was the sweetest pleasure and most delightful pain. Snaking her way down into his wet swim trunks, she pushed the garment off the firm globes of his behind, squeezing and kneading the taut flesh.

Her touch was too much for him to handle. Every muscle ached with wanting for her. Mason lifted his body from hers and moved to the dresser and the leather toiletry bag that rested atop the marble surface. Pulling a condom from the side pocket of the leather case, Mason tore the cellophane pack open with his teeth, then rolled the rubber over his protruding member. Dropping his body back down against hers, Mason drew a slow path against her skin as he kissed her stomach, sinking his tongue into her belly button.

Phaedra pulled her fingers across his cropped hair, the silky curls tickling her skin.

She was grinding unabashedly as he kissed his way back to her breasts, suckling one and then the other, then biting the skin beneath her chin, until he reached her mouth and kissed her, his tongue darting back and forth with hers.

Mason grabbed one of her hands and then the other, pulling her arms high above her head. Phaedra gasped as he eased himself between her thighs, using his knees and body to pry her legs open. He held her captive with his gaze as he lifted himself ever so slightly to stare down at her. She called his name, the echo of it caressing his spirit.

"Mason!"

Nodding, Mason pressed his mouth back to hers and whispered against her lips, "I love you, Phaedra."

Tears glistened in Phaedra's eyes. The words were there, caught deep in the wealth of emotion that filled her spirit. She loved him, too. More than she'd ever imagined possible. She choked back sobs that obstructed her words. She loved him and every fiber of her being wanted to tell him so. Instead she responded with her tongue, voicing it in her kiss and touch and the easy caress of her body against his. Mason slowly eased the length of himself into her. As he pushed himself forward, moisture dripped past his thick lashes, mingling with the tears that rained down Phaedra's cheeks. The moment was surreal, the magnitude of the experience sweeping sensations through them both as neither had ever experienced before. It was more than Phaedra could ever have imagined, and with her arms still captured above her head, Mason's mouth locked with hers, his breath kissing her breath, Phaedra lifted her hips and welcomed him home.

Mason couldn't remember when they'd fallen asleep. They'd made love over and over again, their desire for each other almost insatiable. There'd been no place in the room that he hadn't taken her, their sexual aerobics moving from the bed to the floor, against each of the four walls and back to the bed again. He wouldn't have thought it at all possible, but he was still hard, desire still lengthening his manhood in anticipation. He shivered, his muscles quivering with want.

Phaedra slumbered comfortably beside him, her back curled against his body. Heat wafted off her skin, igniting a flame deep in his core. He pressed himself against her, savoring the sensation of her buttocks cradled against his crotch. He hardened even more, his male member twitching as he drew a light hand down the length of her arm, his palm coming to rest against her hip. He was in awe of just how beautiful she was, as exquisite inside as she was on the outside. As if she could read his thoughts, Phaedra snuggled closer to him, wiggling her body from the waist as she pressed her bottom closer against him.

Reaching across her body, Mason cupped her breasts in the palm of hand. They were absolutely divine, he thought as he gently kneaded one and then the other between his fingers. Phaedra stirred again, her body squirming against his. She turned in his arms, rolling onto her back, and he lowered his lips to her nipple, his tongue slathering one and then the other. He savored the sensation of them hardening in his mouth.

Phaedra moaned softly, leaving sleep behind as she

woke to the moment. She could get used to wakening to such delicious sensations sweeping through her body, she thought, and Mason was becoming an expert at eliciting the most enchanting vibrations from her. She clasped her thighs tightly together with desire from his ministrations.

Mason chuckled softly as he whispered good morning, and all she could do was moan in response. He slid a large hand between her legs, gently inserting his middle finger into her wet folds. Phaedra shuddered with ecstasy, his touch causing her to swoon. She wrapped her arms around him, a smile pulling at her lips as she embraced him tightly.

Moving up her body, Mason nuzzled and kissed her throat as she threw her head back against the pillow, sighing and moaning with delight. His continued strumming the spot between her legs, expertly playing her like a bass player with his instrument. He played notes on her labia, his fingertips dancing against her sweet spot until she was senseless with ecstasy. Sensing that her climax was imminent, Mason drove his fingers deep inside her while still stroking her with his thumb. He grinned, relishing the expression on her face as Phaedra exploded into a screaming orgasm that left her breathless and squirming.

There was vulnerability in her eyes when she opened them to meet his gaze, her breathing still coming in short gasps. Mason smiled as he shifted his body atop hers, his nakedness kissing her nakedness. He brushed his lips against her lips, kissing her softly, leading a damp trail of gentle kisses all along her cheeks, at the tip of her nose and across her eyes.

Their gazes locked, and both felt something stir

deep within them. Mason sought her mouth a second time, his hands moving furiously over the length of her body. His breathing became labored as his excitement increased, his erection so hard that he felt as if he were about to explode without being touched. But the moment wasn't about him, he thought, his desire to bring her pleasure outweighing the need for his own release.

He kissed a trail down the length of her body, back to her neck, across her stomach and downward as he sought out the rich scent of her femaleness. He then pushed her legs up and out, exposing her most private place. Phaedra's eyes were widened in anticipation. She inhaled swiftly as he gently slid his tongue into that soft, sweet wetness and then she moaned loudly with pure, unadulterated lust. She clamped her hands down against the back of Mason's head, willing him to never stop the heavenly sensations he was creating.

Mason was nearly on the edge himself, knowing how much pleasure he was bringing the stunning woman. He slid his fingers inside her and she moaned his name, a soft mantra chanted over and over again. He fingered her slowly, matching each thrust with the flick of his tongue across her swollen love button. Phaedra's hips bucked against his mouth and hand as he increased the firmness of his touch. He stroked her, feeling her open up more and more with each pass of his fingers. Phaedra's moans were reaching a frenzy as she clutched her breasts. In that moment, nothing existed but the two of them together and as Phaedra exploded in orgasm Mason's own release surged between his legs.

They lay together panting, both stunned by the intensity of what was happening between them. Mason lay with his head cradled against her abdomen, Phaedra gently caressing the side of his face.

"You're incredible," Phaedra whispered, leaning up on one elbow to look into his eyes. "I didn't think it could get any more amazing with us."

Mason pressed a kiss against her belly button. "Baby, we're just getting started. We haven't even tapped into amazing yet!"

Chapter 12

Phaedra had no idea of the time. The sun had risen, the day had passed and she'd been oblivious, focused only on Mason and what they were sharing between them. For most of the afternoon all they'd done was make love, talk, talk and make love. She couldn't remember being so happy and only briefly did she think that such might never have been possible if her mother had not been taken from her life when she had.

Phaedra would have loved to still be in bed with Mason, the two focused solely on each other and nothing else. Instead they were headed to Cape Yamu in Phuket to have an early dinner with the Kasam family. She stole a glance toward Mason, who was lost in his own thoughts as the driver of the private car they were in maneuvered his way through the streets of Phuket.

The man was absolutely stunning, she thought, a smile rising to her face. His attire was dress casual, black slacks, black blazer and a white dress shirt opened at the collar. He was impressive, the silk suit fitting him to perfection. Phaedra had chosen a halter jumpsuit from the collection of clothing Mason had made available to her, the red linen complementing the warm brown tones of her complexion. Side by side they made a beautiful couple. As if he were reading her mind and thinking the same thing, Mason squeezed her thigh, smiling sweetly at her.

"Are you sure you don't mind doing this?" Mason asked once again.

Phaedra gave him a smile back. "Of course not. Why would I?"

"Mali," he said, his eyebrows arched knowingly.

Phaedra laughed. "Are you sure there's never been anything between you and that woman?" she asked teasingly. "Because Mali Kasam seems to be of more concern to you than she is to me. Mali does not bother me!"

Mason laughed with her. "I just want to make sure," he said, kissing her lips. "Mali can be quite a handful."

"If I need to, I have no problems putting Miss Mali in her place."

Mason nodded, grinning broadly. "Claim your man, baby!"

She leaned to kiss his mouth as the driver pulled into the home's driveway. "I've done that already and I will make sure she understands that."

He winked at her, still chuckling softly as the driver pulled the door open for them to get out.

Overlooking Phuket's dramatic east coast and the natural beauty of famous Phang Nga Bay, the Kasam family villa overlooked a stunning vista of beautiful limestone islands, tiny beaches and secret coves. The location was secluded yet conveniently close to town. In one direction Phaedra noted the premier Mission Hills Golf Course and two marinas. The home was a melding of contemporary architecture with key elements of traditional Thai designs. The multimillion-dollar property was stunning.

Daniel Kasam greeted them at the door. "Mason! Phaedra! Welcome," the man said as he welcomed them into his home.

Mason shook the man's hand. "Thank you for having us, Daniel!"

"It's good to see you again, Mr. Kasam," Phaedra said politely as he kissed the back of her hand. He wrapped an arm around Phaedra's waist, guiding her to the center of the open space.

As they settled themselves down in his living room, a server came with a tray of cocktails, extending them in Phaedra's direction first, and then Mason's.

"Please have a drink," Daniel said, offering them two glasses of rice wine. "We must toast!"

Mason nodded as he clinked his glass with Phaedra's.

"So, are you enjoying Thailand, Phaedra?" Daniel asked.

"I am, very much so," Phaedra answered. "Mason has been showing me a wonderful time."

"My friend is very good at that." He turned his attention back to Mason. "So, did you return for business, as well, my friend, or has this just been a pleasure trip?" The man winked an eye at Phaedra.

"Strictly pleasure," Mason said, his comment eliciting a giggle from Phaedra, who sat beside him.

Daniel nodded. "Finally! You are good for him, then, Phaedra. Mason has not had much success letting go of the business and just enjoying the pleasure."

Mason laughed. "Well, I'll be getting a lot of opportunity to practice. I sold my company recently."

"Well, well," Daniel replied, a look of surprise crossing his expression. "That is definitely something. This will be a significant change for you."

"I'm really hoping so, Daniel. You know that I've been ready for a change for some time, but enough about me. What is this I hear about you seeking the prime minister's seat?"

Daniel smiled, his head nodding. "You've heard right. It is definitely under consideration. With the political unrest becoming more problematic, especially with our young people, I have to consider all options which will be of benefit to my country."

For the next half hour Mason and Daniel chatted easily about their mutual business interests and thoughts on Daniel's political run and regaled Phaedra with stories about their many antics together. It was only as Daniel's personal chef called them for dinner that Mali arrived, sweeping into the room like a monsoon that would not be tamed. Rushing through the home's front door, she moved directly to Mason's side, throwing her arms around his neck to hug him tightly. Her father shook his head in annoyance.

"Mali!" he chastised, voicing his displeasure with his daughter's behavior.

The young woman rolled her eyes. Mason reached

for her arms, disentangling himself from her grasp. He gave her a light kiss against the back of her hand, then spun her toward the other side of the room. Mali huffed as she threw herself down against a cushioned chair, her arms crossed in defiance over her chest.

"You don't love me anymore, Mason!" she cried, pouting.

Mason shook his head. "I have much love for you, Mali."

"We all do, Mali. But you are quite the nuisance, daughter," Daniel added. "And you need to politely say hello to our guests."

"Yeah, hey," she said as she cut an eye in Phaedra's direction, crudely chewing on a piece of gum in her mouth. She refocused her attention back on Mason.

"It's a pleasure to see you again, Mali," Phaedra said as she casually dropped her hand against Mason's knee.

The gesture did not go unnoticed as Mali glared, rolled her eyes and then stormed off in the direction of the dining room. Daniel shook his head as he admonished the girl a second time, tossing his hands up in frustration.

Mason looked at Phaedra, who was smiling slyly, clearly amused. He shook his head. The two men locked eyes.

"Women!" Mason said to his friend, chuckling softly.

Daniel nodded in agreement. "I apologize for that one. It is my fault that she is as spoiled as she is. Her mother died when she was just a baby and I have always given her everything she has wanted." He gestured for them to follow him into the dining room, promising a sumptuous meal the likes of which guaranteed to exceed every one of their expectations.

As Phaedra followed, Mason on her heels, she couldn't help thinking that Mali's daddy clearly hadn't been able to get the girl everything because Mason Boudreaux was high on the woman's want list and unable to be had.

Aloud, she spoke to Mali, who'd already taken a seat at the table. "Mali, I hear you're a fashion student in London. That's every exciting," she said as she took the seat beside the other woman, the seat that Mali had been holding for Mason.

Mali eyed her with disdain, not at all pleased as Mason sat down in the seat across from the two women. Daniel made himself comfortable at the head of the table.

"I don't do that anymore," Mali said, turning her attention back to Phaedra. "It bored me."

"Oh, well, I'm sorry to hear that."

"Mali drops out of school every other week," her father interjected.

"I'm coming to the States for school," Mali said. "Phoenix, maybe." She tossed Mason a look and a smile.

Mason shook his head.

"Phoenix is beautiful," Phaedra said. "What do you think you'd like to study?"

Mali shrugged. "What do you do?" she asked, responding with a question of her own.

"I'm a photojournalist. Professional photography is my passion."

"So you take pictures," Mali said unenthusiastically.

"Award-winning pictures," Mason interjected. "Phaedra is considered one of the best in the world," he said proudly.

"Hmmph!" Mali grunted.

Phaedra laughed. "You're still young, Mali. One day you'll figure out what you want to do and I'm sure you'll be the best at it that you can be."

Not bothering to respond, Mali pulled a forkful of rice into her mouth, her attention dropping to the food on her plate. The rest of the evening was uneventful and before they were served dessert, Mali politely excused herself from the table.

"Where are you going?" Daniel asked. He swiped a cloth napkin across his mouth, then dropped it back into his lap.

His daughter strolled to the other side of the table and leaned to kiss Mason on his closed mouth. As she pulled back, she lifted her eyes to meet Phaedra's and Phaedra smiled in response, not even bothering to blink an eyelash.

Mali sighed. "I have some things to take care of," she said. "I'll see you again soon, Mason?"

Mason cleared his throat, then shook his head no. "Tomorrow is our last day here. Phaedra and I have to be back in Texas by the end of the week."

Mali tossed Phaedra another look as she made her way out the door. "Well, until I see you again, then," she said.

"It was nice meeting you, Mali," Phaedra called behind her.

As Daniel excused himself to follow behind his daughter, Phaedra pointed her index finger in Mason's direction. She leaned across the table as she whispered teasingly just loud enough for him to hear, "We'll need to disinfect your lips the minute we get home."

His eyes widening, Mason swiped the back of his fingers across his mouth, and both burst out laughing as the home's front door slammed harshly in the distance.

Chapter 13

The sun was setting in the distance as Mason and Phaedra sat on the beach, where the clear blue water kissed the white sand. Phaedra was nestled between Mason's legs, her back resting against his chest. A warm breeze wafted through the air as the sky above their heads shimmered in shades of red, orange and yellow. Neither could remember the last time they'd been so at ease, completely relaxed and content in the moment.

Phaedra blew a soft sigh as Mason drew his hands over her shoulders and down the lengths of her arms, his caress a slow and easy touch that teased each of her nerve endings.

"This is nice," she said softly, her voice a low whisper.

He pressed a gentle kiss against the back of her neck, allowing his lips to linger against the soft flesh.

His eyes were closed as he fell into the simplicity of the moment. It was nice. Nice in a way that couldn't be sufficiently explained. So nice that there was no one, and nothing, on either of their minds but each other. Mason blew a soft sigh against her skin, kissing her once again.

Nestling closer to him, Phaedra couldn't help wishing that life could always be this pleasant. She'd been wishing for moments like this since she was a little girl believing in fairy tales and the possibility of happily ever after. Her mother had always assured her that her crown prince would come when she least expected him, riding in like a knight in shining armor to save her from herself. Phaedra couldn't help thinking he'd finally found his way to her, his arms holding her tight to him, the wealth of the emotion he had for her undeniable. She had hardly been looking, and just like that, with the snap of her camera capturing his magnetic smile, Mason had steeled his way into her heart.

Mason gave her a hug, rolling her down against the blanket beneath them. He pressed his body over hers as he met her lips in a deep kiss. When he drew back, joy was shining in his eyes and in hers. He had no desire to move, wanting only to hover above her and admire the beauty before him.

As if she'd read his thoughts, her rich, full lips stretched into the happiest smile he had ever seen, highlighted by a light sheen of lip gloss that accentuated her warm, creamy complexion. Her nose wrinkled slightly as she smiled and her eyes gleamed with lust that was waiting to be coaxed out. Her body was silhouetted against the plush blanket beneath them, the curve of her hips and shapely legs and the natural form of her breasts stirring something animalistic within him. He could feel himself lengthening in his swim trunks, his body craving every last ounce of her sweetness.

Phaedra pulled a hand through her tousled hair, yet every hair seemed in place, framing her face nicely. Mason suddenly had visions of their future together, them sharing a rich and full life, traveling the world, making love in unimaginable places. He suddenly had an endless list of places where he wanted to have her, against a volcanic waterfall, in the midst of a garden of wildflowers in a mountain meadow, in the backseat of his Maybach parked on the French Riviera. As he pondered the possibilities he remained motionless, his breathing shallow, as if him breathing heavily might interrupt the beauty of the moment.

Heat spiraled between them, so abundant that Mason felt as if he could cut it with a knife. Phaedra felt it, too, and she began to pant softly, her lips parting as she passed the tip of her tongue between them. She purred softly, a low hum seeping past her open mouth. She lifted herself up just enough to pull his mouth back to hers, kissing him deeply a second time. When she pulled away, Mason was rock hard, the length of steel between his legs flexing for attention.

"What are you thinking?" Phaedra whispered as she nuzzled her face against his neck, wrapping her arms around his torso.

"I was just thinking that you are so beautiful and that sky is so spectacular that I should be making love to you."

Phaedra giggled. "I kind of like how you think!" she said as Mason nibbled the spot beneath her chin, teasing up to plant another kiss on her lips. He grabbed both her wrists as he lowered his weight against her, his body kissing her body. Phaedra opened her legs as he dropped himself between them, her torso captured beneath his. She began to slowly grind her pelvis against his, his erection straining hard against her.

As Mason stared down into her eyes, he could feel his control starting to slip away, so enamored with her he felt completely lost in her intense stare. He drew the fingers of his right hand down the length of her arm and Phaedra shivered, a flash of heat burning deep between her legs.

Mason slid his left arm beneath her body, pulling her tight against him as Phaedra snuggled her face into Mason's neck. She inhaled the sweetness of his warm brown skin, almost tasting the scent of his smooth chocolate body. Unable to resist, she planted a trail of gentle kisses against his neck and Mason groaned at the electric shivers that coursed through his body.

"Stop teasing me," Phaedra whispered, eager to experience the moment.

Mason softly stroked her hair, her dark tresses cascading against her shoulders. "I'm not teasing," he answered, a wry smile pulling at his mouth.

Mason took a finger and traced soft circles down the side of Phaedra's face. He twinked her nose and Phaedra giggled softly. When he reached her full lips, Phaedra grinned as he gently tapped the moist flesh. She opened her mouth and captured his firm digit between her lips. She sucked softly on the sweet flesh, using her cheek muscles to draw him in and out. When she sucked harder on his thick finger, Mason moaned, warm waves of excitement passing through him.

"Now *you're* teasing!" he said with a low chuckle.

Phaedra slipped his finger out of her mouth, kissed his warm palm, then rubbed her cheek against his hand. Mason leaned in and pressed his mouth to hers. He moaned and panted as Phaedra's tongue entered the heat of his mouth, their kiss deepening as she gripped the back of his head and locked her fingers against his tight curls. The kiss was passionate and promising, nourishing each other's intense desire. Their deep hunger for affection consumed them, causing them both to moan in ecstasy.

It seemed like an eternity before Mason broke the connection, both of them gasping excitedly for air. He pulled at the ribbon that held up her bathing suit top, then snatched the garment from around her body. He began kissing down her body, running his hands down the length of her torso as he nuzzled his nose between her breasts. She had beautiful breasts, Mason thought, like fresh-picked vine-ripened peaches. He ran his hands back up her sides and kissed the inner curve of her left peach.

He looked up at her. Phaedra had her eyes closed and was breathing harder than she was before. He took one of her nipples into his mouth and started sucking and swirling his tongue around the sweet delight while he gently caressed and kneaded the other breast. Phaedra groaned with pleasure beneath his ministrations, the heat from his fingertips lingering against her skin. When he switched sides and began suckling on her other breast, Phaedra was completely gone.

With mastered skill Mason continued to slide down the length of her body, his moist kisses stopping at her belly button as he dipped his tongue into the slight well. At the waistband of her bikini bottoms, he paused and

Phaedra groaned at the loss of contact. She opened her eyes to watch as he hooked his fingers into her bottoms and pulled them down, his fingers connecting with precision against her flesh. She lifted her hips as he pulled them off, throwing them somewhere into the sand.

He paused as he looked at her. "God, you are so beautiful!" he said, his tone intoxicating.

Before she could respond he began to minister to the bundle of swollen flesh that pulsed between her legs, his fingers tapping with magic. Phaedra fell into a trance of pleasure. "Oh, Mason…" She bit down against her bottom lip, knowing that she wouldn't last long if he continued to stroke her so unabashedly.

Phaedra inhaled swiftly, the magnitude of him and the moment suddenly consuming. Never before had anything felt more perfect to her. She sat up, reaching to pull him back to her. She tugged at his shorts, running her hands across his stomach as she pulled the string to loosen his swim trunks while he kissed her. Mason stopped kissing her long enough to stand up, slide his trunks down and step out of them. Pulling out a condom hidden in his pocket, he sheathed himself quickly.

Grabbing his hands Phaedra guided him back down to her. She closed her eyes and moaned at the skin to skin contact as he rolled against her. She started to grind her hips with his, the two moving in perfect sync. Phaedra kissed his neck as he ran his hands through her hair. With perfect precision he entered her easily, the two dancing together as if they were one body and not two. She pushed as he pushed, pulled as he pulled, meeting him stroke for stroke.

Mason panted, his excitement building as sheer decadence surged through every nerve and muscle in his body. Phaedra lost all coherent thought, her body convulsing with waves of pure, unadulterated pleasure. She arched her back against him, calling his name into the night air.

"Mason! Oh, Mason," she screamed, her body juddering around his as Mason spilled himself deep inside her.

As they climaxed simultaneously, Mason clung to her, feeling as if he'd never be able to get enough of the exquisite creature. When he collapsed on top of her, Phaedra clutched him tightly to her. Her chest moved up and down against his as they both fought to catch their breaths. With stars spiraling above her head, love spilled from Phaedra's eyes as she met his stare, unable to miss the longing that shimmered in the dark orbs. Above them, sitting high in the darkened sky, a full moon gave them its blessing.

Mason and Phaedra spent hours on the beach, the night air beginning to cool comfortably. With one last dip in the warm waters of the lagoon, they strolled hand in hand back to his bungalow. Phaedra lay on her stomach, sprawled across his king-size bed as Mason nuzzled his body against hers, both unable to sleep.

"This feels too good to be true," Phaedra whispered.

Mason nodded his understanding, his hand stroking her lower back and the curve of her buttocks. "But it's all very real," he whispered back.

Phaedra smiled sweetly, shifting so that she could kiss the curve of his shoulder. "But all good things must come to an end," she concluded, a deep sigh easing out of her mouth.

"It doesn't have to," Mason said. "This can last as long as you want it to."

"What if I want forever?"

Mason laughed, a low chuckle that warmed Phaedra's spirit. "Then you can have forever."

"You have such a way with words, Mr. Boudreaux." She smiled.

"I am quite the wordsmith, madame, and your wishes are my commands."

"You could spoil a girl like that."

"Have no doubts, I plan to spoil my girl like that."

Phaedra eased herself farther into his side, heat wafting from his skin to hers. "I like how that sounds. I like being your girl."

Mason leaned over to kiss her forehead, brushing his lips gently against her. "That makes me very happy," he whispered against her skin, the warmth of his breath causing her to shiver ever so slightly.

"I want to make you very happy," Phaedra said coyly. She stroked his chest, gently grazing the broad expanse of flesh with her fingernails. Mason inhaled sharply at the sensation, blood surging in a southern direction. "Don't move," she commanded when he tried to reach for her.

His body tensed with anticipation as she pushed him back against the mattress. She drew her hand down past his belly button, pausing at the cusp of his pubic hair. Her fingers teased the tight black curls and his erection twitched eagerly, the protrusion stretching obscenely.

When he couldn't wait any longer Mason took her hand and wrapped it around the length of his manhood. Her hand quivered as her fingers touched the long, thick, rock-hard length. Phaedra began to stroke him gently, feeling the long shaft as her palm glided up and down.

Mason shuddered as her fingers danced over his flesh and he sighed audibly. Phaedra was in awe as she stared at him, his beautiful, big organ seeming to grow beneath her nurturing. He was so hard and hot, silky to her touch, and as she moved her hand gently back and forth she could feel his heartbeat pulsing rhythmically in the palm of her hand. The tips of her fingers glided against his testicles and Mason jumped from the sensation. The feelings were exquisite and he could feel himself weakening beneath her touch.

As she continued to stroke him, her motions becoming more intense, he lifted his hips to grind against her palm. His hands clutched the sheet beneath him as he allowed his body to give in to the intensity. His breathing began to quicken and Mason knew that he couldn't hold on as Phaedra took him over the edge. He suddenly shuddered, his body shaking all over. His orgasm flooded over her hand and arm as the woman continued to milk him dry.

As the last remnants of his climax lulled him to a comfortable slumber, Phaedra nuzzled her mouth against his ear and whispered, "Sweet dreams."

Chapter 14

Phaedra woke well before Mason, the man snoring comfortably at her side. Rising from the bed, she tiptoed into the bathroom. Staring at her reflection in the mirror, she couldn't believe that she was as wide-awake as she was. It had only been a few short hours since she and Mason had fallen asleep together. Any other time or place and she'd be a walking zombie, desperate for one more hour of slumber.

After splashing cold water on her face and brushing her teeth to a pearl-white sheen, she tiptoed back into the bedroom. Her clothes were in the other bungalow so she borrowed one of Mason's T-shirts, slipping the oversize top around her naked body. Sliding into a pair of rubber flip-flops, she grabbed her camera from the dresser and eased her way outside, mindful not to disturb Mason's rest.

Outside, the sun was rising, the beginning rays of

light just starting to crease the dark sky. Phaedra was glad for the moment, wanting to capture the morning's sunrise. They were headed back to Bangkok today, then back to the United States tomorrow, and despite the many hours they'd spent alone on the island, there was much Phaedra had yet to experience of the private landscape.

As she walked the length of beach, photographing the early morning imagery, she was taken aback by the sheer beauty of the lush landscape. The tropical topography was like nothing Phaedra had ever experienced before and she knew Thailand would forever be one of her favorite places in the world. She adjusted the fifty-millimeter prime lens on her camera to accommodate the low light conditions and capture the more minute details of the flora.

Maneuvering her way past the length of beach, she eased her way into the natural forest, snapping shot after shot of the diverse plant life. Before long she'd gathered a nice visual collection of the bamboo, coconut palms and banana trees posed against the morning sky.

Not wanting Mason to worry if he woke and couldn't find her, she eased her way back to the beach, a fresh-picked bunch of bananas in her hand. As she strolled casually across the sandy stretch she thought back to the evening before when Mason had made love to her right where she now stood. A bright smile flooded her expression and a shiver of heat coursed in the pit of her stomach. The man gave her butterflies and just the sheer thought of him sent her into sensory overload.

She paused, inhaling the scent of the ocean, the warm morning air a soothing balm to her spirit. In the distance she could hear a boat approaching, the deep roar of the engine out of place in the midst of all the quiet. Mason must have heard it, as well, because just as she peered across the lagoon in the direction of the approaching vessel, he stepped outside.

She waved excitedly at the sight of him, but Mason was focused on the speedboat, not looking in her direction. After resting the bananas on the sand at her feet, she switched out the lens for the two-hundred-millimeter telephoto lens and lifted her camera to her eyes. After making the necessary adjustments, she zoomed in on his face. His expression was pensive, an air of uncertainty seeming to drop down against the man's broad shoulders. She snapped the shot, noting the concern in his dark eyes.

Phaedra lowered her camera briefly, still staring, something about his demeanor giving her pause, her heart beginning to race. Mason hadn't said anything about expecting visitors, she thought, wondering if the boat's occupants were an unexpected intrusion. She was almost certain that it wasn't the island's elderly caretakers, Bahn and his wife, Rutana. They came every day by canoe, their arrival almost covert as the narrow boat cut through the water with an easy, quiet precision.

As the speedboat came to a quick stop at the end of the dock, Mason strolled casually in its direction. Phaedra lifted her camera a second time as two men hopped out of the boat, appearing to greet him. She snapped one photo and then a second and she was poised to take a third when there was a sudden rush of loud chatter, the trio appearing to argue. Phaedra looked over the top of her camera, her anxiety rising tenfold. She peered back through the lens just as the taller of the two strangers struck Mason with something in his hand. Phaedra gasped loudly, her heart skipping a quick beat, then two. As Mason fell to his knees the other man threw a canvas sack over Mason's head and, like that, they tossed his body into the boat, jumped in behind him and gunned the boat's engine.

Still snapping shot after shot, Phaedra struggled to keep her camera focused on what was happening. Then without thinking she began to run, desperation taking hold as she screamed out his name. By the time she made it to the other side of the beach and the end of the dock, the speedboat had rounded the north corner of the island, Mason disappearing from her sight.

Phaedra was at wit's end. She'd been in the custody of the Thai Royal Police for over three hours trying to get someone to understand that Mason Boudreaux was in trouble. But nothing she said could convince them of the urgency. She pulled her hands frantically through her hair, pacing the small interrogation room she'd been left in. The officer who'd taken her statement had been exceptionally cooperative when she'd mentioned Mason's name, but even that hadn't been enough to motivate him to start searching.

Dropping down onto a metal chair, Phaedra closed her eyes and tears began to fall rapidly. For whatever reasons, after Mason had been taken, she hadn't been able to get any reception on her cell phone. Waiting for Bahn and Rutana to arrive had felt like forever. Bahn had saved the moment, though, ushering her to the mainland and the police department, promising that he and Rutana would pack her and Mason's belongings and get her to wherever she needed to go when she needed to move. Now she was anxious to go do anything that would help find Mason. She jumped to her feet, the chair crashing from beneath her, the sound ringing like thunder against the concrete floor. Shaking, Phaedra clenched her fists at her sides, fighting not to scream out loud.

Just as she was about to throw a major tantrum, the door swung open, Officer Don Niran eyeing her curiously. "Is everything okay, miss?" he asked politely.

"No!" Phaedra screamed, desperately trying to contain her emotions. "Nothing is okay. Mason Boudreaux is missing and no one is doing anything to help me find him."

The officer nodded, his expression blank. "I assure you, miss, we are doing everything we can to corroborate your story. However, it is more plausible that Mr. Boudreaux simply left without telling you where he was going. As you said, you've just recently become acquainted with him. Perhaps you didn't know the man as well as you thought?"

Phaedra bristled, her eyes narrowing sharply. She took a deep breath. "Well," she said, "I can appreciate your opinion, Officer Niran, but I assure you, I know him very well and I know what I saw."

"That being so, miss, these things take time. So, if there is nothing else that you can tell us, I must get back to my duties."

It was on the tip of Phaedra's tongue to argue, but knowing that such would probably not be in her best interest she simply nodded. Clearly, she needed help, and help wasn't going to be found here.

The officer turned to the door, moving as if to make an exit, before Phaedra called after him.

"Yes, miss?"

"Please, is it possible for me to use a telephone to place an international telephone call? I need to call my family to let them know what has happened and to make arrangements to get back home," she said, meeting his gaze evenly.

Officer Niran paused briefly before nodding. "Certainly, miss," he responded after a quick second. "Whatever I can do to be of assistance to you."

Chapter 15

John's cell phone ringing pulled him out of a deep sleep. For a brief moment he thought he might be dreaming, but the ring tone persisted, disturbing the quiet in his bedroom. Beside him, Marah muttered incoherently, rolling onto her side as she wrapped herself around a pillow and pulled the sheet above her head.

Leaning toward the nightstand, John grabbed his phone, squinting to see the caller ID. The display read UNKNOWN. For a brief second he thought about ignoring it, but something in the pit of his stomach wouldn't let him. Flipping the device open, he pulled it awkwardly to his ear.

"Hello?" he said, the lazy drone of sleep punctuating his tone.

On the other end Phaedra's voice pierced the airwaves. She sounded as if she was on the verge of hysteria. "John, I'm sorry to wake you but something has happened to Mason and I can't get anyone to help me find him and I don't know what to do. I'm scared and please, I need someone to help me and I didn't know who else to call," she said, barely pausing to take a breath as the words rushed out of her mouth.

"Calm down," John said as he sat up in the bed. Tossing a quick glance toward Marah's sleeping form, he whispered into the receiver, "Tell me what's happened."

Phaedra nodded as if he could see her. Taking a deep breath, she told him what had happened from the moment Mason had stepped out onto the dock to when the Thai police had allowed her to use their office telephone to make a call. She repeated verbatim every conversation she'd had since waking, and with every other sentence she kept reiterating how scared she was. By the end of telling her story she fought back tears thinking of the worst possible outcome.

Wide-awake, John tried to be as consoling as the distance between them would allow. "Phaedra, I need you to relax, okay? I'm on my way and if Mason hasn't shown up by the time I get there, I promise I will do whatever it takes to find him."

Phaedra's head bobbed up and down against her thin neck. "Thank you," she whispered, the words catching in her throat. "Thank you so much!"

"How are you traveling?" John asked. "Do you have transportation?"

"Yes. Mason's housekeeper is being really helpful."

"Good. I want you to go to the Boudreaux Residence Resort and ask for the general manager. His name is Sean Martine. As soon as I hang up with you I'm going to call him. He'll take care of you until I can get there."

"Sean Martine," she repeated. "Okay."

"And, Phaedra, I do not want you running around Phuket trying to find Mason by yourself. I don't want anything to happen to you. Do you understand me?"

Another tear rolled over her cheek. "Yes," she finally answered, swiping at her eyes with the back of her hand. "John? He's going to be okay, isn't he?"

John took a deep breath as he swung his legs off the side of the bed. "Don't you worry. Everything is going to be fine," he said. "I'll see you soon."

As he disconnected the call, John released a deep sigh. He'd promised Phaedra that things were going to be okay, but truth be told he wasn't so sure. If Mason was in trouble, their being out of the country was going to make finding him difficult at best. As he shook Marah awake, he pressed the speed-dial button on his cell phone. He needed to round up the troops. He wasn't sure himself where to begin, but he imagined this was a mission that was going to take more than himself to accomplish successfully.

Three hours later the Stallion jet was fueled and ready on the tarmac, the pilot waiting for John to order their takeoff. Both John and Matthew were on their cell phones, still issuing commands and asking questions. Half a day would pass before they reached Thailand, and knowing how things could change in that amount of time, no one wanted to take any unnecessary chances.

Once John was assured that Phaedra was safely secreted away in the owner's suite of the hotel, he was better able to fathom what had actually happened and how they might discover Mason's whereabouts.

Matthew put one call on hold to answer another. John smiled ever so slightly as he heard his brother trying to calm his wife's nerves. "Katrina, you need to stop worrying, baby….I'll do my best….I promise, honey….Katrina, you just need to concentrate on taking care of yourself and our baby….I will…I will…I will make sure your brother is okay….Yes, dear! Yes… I'll call you as soon as we get there and find out what's going on," he finally concluded before disconnecting the call.

The two brothers locked gazes. Matthew shook his head. "This isn't good, is it?"

John took a deep breath. "I've spoken to the Thai police, who are less than helpful, to Mason's housekeeper, who knows nothing, and the hotel staff, who were close to him, and no one has any idea what's going on," he said firmly.

"When you speak with Marah, please make her promise to stay by my wife's side. I don't need her going into labor before I can get back here."

John nodded. "I've already handled it for you, brother. Marah will make sure Katrina takes care of herself."

"So will Mitch," Mark said as he stepped onto the plane, entering the conversation.

"Hey," John said, rising. He and Mark bumped shoulders in greeting. Matthew tipped his head, the two men slapping palms.

"What do we know so far?" Mark questioned as he took a seat in one of the leather chairs.

John gestured toward the pilot, nodding his consent. "Let's get in the air first and I'll fill you in," he said.

An hour or so later the three brothers had settled

down for the long flight, dozing comfortably in their seats. With the thirteen-hour time difference it would be late when they arrived in Thailand, and what they might be able to accomplish at that hour of the night would be slim. But each of them knew they needed to be as rested as possible if the next few days proved to be the challenge they predicted they would be.

Phaedra was stir-crazy as she stood at the front desk of the luxury hotel waiting for the general manager. Since her arrival the staff had been exceptionally gracious, extending her every courtesy. But she couldn't sit in the luxury suite one minute longer and not do something. She strummed her fingernails against the marble counter as she waited, her patience having worn thin.

Sean Martine greeted her warmly, the tall blond man with the strong Nordic features moving to her side. "Miss Parrish, I apologize for keeping you waiting. I hope everything has met with your satisfaction."

Phaedra nodded. "Yes, definitely. I have no complaints and I can't tell you how much I appreciate everything you and your staff have done for me."

Mr. Martine smiled. "So, what else might I be able to do for you?"

"I was hoping that I could get access to a computer and a printer. Preferably a color printer?"

Mr. Martine paused in a moment of quick reflection. "I think that's possible. We have a color printer in the marketing department and plenty of computers. Why don't you follow me?" he said as he gestured toward the office doors.

Behind the scenes of the hotel, the back office was

a bustling whirlwind of employees ensuring that the mechanics of the Boudreaux Residence Resort worked smoothly, no guests having a clue that their perfect vacations might have come with some major bumps along the way.

In the marketing area Phaedra was directed to a small cubicle and given access to a computer and printer. Mr. Martine smiled and nodded politely as he instructed the employees to give her any assistance she might need. After expressing her sincerest appreciation and watching until he was out of the room and no one was looking over her shoulder, Phaedra finally relaxed the hold she'd had on her camera case, the instrument secured over her shoulder and beneath her arm.

She took a deep breath as she pulled the sixteen-gigabyte SanDisk CF memory card out of the camera, inserted it in the computer's SD slot and accessed the digital images she'd taken earlier that day. She had briefly thought of telling Officer Niran about the photographs, but something about his attitude and demeanor had stopped her. Instinctively, Phaedra had been certain that if she'd told and he'd confiscated her camera and pictures, they would never again have seen the light of day.

One by one Phaedra printed each image that she'd taken, enlarging them as much as the system would allow. An hour later she had a stack of sixty-plus photos and duplicate copies that had captured Mason's kidnapping. Sixty-plus images that put faces on the two men who'd taken him and the boat the three had ridden away in. After emailing the files to herself and stuffing the images into a manila folder, Phaedra headed back to her room to lay her head on a pillow and cry.

* * *

Mason woke to the stench of dead fish and a raging headache that made him feel as if his head were about to combust from the pressure. He took a deep breath, wincing from the pain and the sour smell that filled the air. The room was small, sparsely decorated, a concrete shelter with a single door and one window. He lay on the only piece of furniture in the room, a wire-framed bed with a paper-thin mattress that had seen better days. There was also a small plastic bucket in the corner and a week-old newspaper on the floor.

Struggling to his feet, Mason braced his hand against the stone wall to hold himself upright. The floor was cold and damp beneath his bare feet, grime and sludge the floor covering of choice. He was still wearing the sweatpants he'd slipped into when he'd heard the speedboat earlier. He was bare-chested and grateful for it since the temperature in the room was sweltering. A glass of ice water and a cold shower would have been a welcome comfort if he had a choice. He felt as if he'd been run over by a Mack truck, the throbbing across his temples making him nauseated. He gently pressed his fingers along his forehead, his hand coming away with streaks of drying blood. He tried to take another deep breath, wishing for just one breeze of fresh air.

As he expected, the door was locked and there was no doorknob on his side. Moving slowly to the window, he stepped up on his tiptoes to peer outside. He was somewhere on the eastern seaboard, the sun setting in the distance behind the building. Wherever he was, he was right on the coastline of one of the fishing villages, the salt air spraying the scent of the day's catch.

He didn't bother to call out, knowing that if there was anyone outside, they were not there to do him any good.

Moving back to the bed, Mason eased his body down. He couldn't begin to fathom why he was there or who was responsible. The two men from earlier had spoken to him in Siamese, the gun that was pointed at him announcing their intent. And then he'd been slapped with the butt of the weapon, the strike rendering him helpless. In that moment there had been only one thing on Mason's mind and it was still haunting him. Where was Phaedra and was she safe?

Chapter 16

Phaedra was pacing the room when the Stallion brothers finally arrived, knocking at the entrance for her attention. Pulling the door open, she could only have been happier if it had been Mason himself.

"Thank you!" Phaedra cried, throwing her arms around John's neck first and then Mark's. "Thank you so much," she said as she hugged Matthew in greeting.

"Have you heard anything at all from Mason?" John questioned, moving into the suite as he looked around.

"Nothing. I called the police station a few hours ago and they weren't able to tell me anything more than it was still being looked into."

"I don't think they're going to be of any use to us," Matthew said.

"And you can't tell us anything else?" Mark asked, his eyes meeting Phaedra's.

"I can do better than that," she said, reaching for

the manila folder on the glass coffee table. "I can show you." She passed the folder to Mark, cutting her eyes from him to John and Matthew, then back. "I was on the far end of the beach when the boat pulled up to the dock. I was taking pictures of the landscape. I kept taking pictures."

Mark was flipping through the images, his brothers peering over his shoulder. "These are good," he said, turning to look at Phaedra. "Really good. They should help."

Before Phaedra could respond the telephone rang, startling them all. She moved to the other side of the room to the oak desk to answer it.

"Hello?"

"Yes, miss. This is Lina at the front desk. I'm trying to reach Mr. John Stallion, please," a woman with a soft voice said on the other end.

"One moment," Phaedra answered, gesturing toward John. "It's for you, John," she said, eyeing him curiously.

John moved to her side and took the receiver from her hand. "This is John Stallion," he said as the others stood waiting.

Phaedra chewed nervously on her bottom lip, her heart beginning to race. Sensing her rising stress, Matthew moved beside her, wrapping a warm arm around her shoulders. The gesture caught Phaedra off guard, but she was grateful for the compassion. She blew a soft sigh.

"Send them up," John said just before he set the receiver back onto the hook. "We have company," he said, looking from one curious face to the other. "The cavalry has arrived."

Matthew nodded, a wide smile pulling at his lips. "Just in time," he said softly as he gently hugged Phaedra to him.

Almost as quickly as Matthew had spoken, there was a knock on the door, a heavy *rap, rap, rap* looking for attention. He moved to the door and opened it, greeting their visitors warmly. "Please, come in," John said. "It's good to see you again. I just wish it was under different circumstances."

Three men and a woman stepped through the door and for a brief second Phaedra was certain that Mason Boudreaux had been cloned at least once if not four times over.

John made the introductions. "Phaedra, allow me to introduce you to Mason's sister Kamaya and his brothers, Donovan, Guy and Kamaya's twin, Kendrick."

The woman smiled warmly. "Hi, it's nice to meet you. We've heard a lot about you," she said, reaching to give Phaedra a warm hug.

"It's nice to meet you, too," Phaedra responded.

The brothers all echoed their sister's sentiments as they moved around the room shaking hands and reacquainting themselves with the family they'd first met at their sister Katrina's wedding to Matthew.

Guy Boudreaux was most anxious to get down to business. "So, where are we?" he said as they all settled down in the living room space. "What's the game plan?"

Mark pulled one of the images from the folder. "We need to track down these two," he said, passing the photo to Guy, who passed it on to his siblings. "And that means we need to hit the streets."

"Do we even know why someone would do this?"

Phaedra ventured to question, feeling as if she was missing something.

Donovan Boudreaux leaned forward in his seat. Of the brothers he looked most like Mason, the resemblance almost eerie. "Phaedra, Mason has a lot of history here in Thailand. Building this hotel required him to deal with a lot of people, some who might have been a little unsavory. And as I'm sure you already know, the political climate has some challenges. Although he made some great friends, there were just as many who didn't want him or the hotel here and who haven't been overly accommodating."

Guy nodded. "He owes a lot of his success here to Daniel Kasam. Daniel helped him navigate the political waters. The man pulled some strings that many thought were impossible."

"I met Daniel. And his daughter. We all had dinner the other night," Phaedra noted.

"He's a great guy but he's rumored to have some ties with the Bangkok crime syndicate," Guy said, adding the disclaimer, "not that we're sure that's true. He might not be a Mafia lord."

He continued. "I do know, though, that there were some who were not happy about the connection between them or that Mason was able to do what he did because of Daniel's help."

Phaedra stood up in frustration. "This is crazy. A crime syndicate? A Mafia lord? Really?"

Both Donovan and Guy shrugged.

"It is crazy," Kendrick interjected, "but they do things differently here. Traditionally, high officials were given gifts for rendering their services. In addition, they benefited from getting a percentage of their expenditures even if they didn't do anything. Obviously, the bigger the gifts they received, the bigger the payoff for the giver. The practice bred corruption. Unfortunately, Thailand has had a long history of dishonesty, from extortion and bribery to the use of insider information to even buy land. For many reasons, although it's not talked about, those practices are still deeply embedded in Thai society."

"So, do we need to speak with Daniel?" Phaedra asked. "To see what he might know?"

"Our first stop in the morning," John said. "Phaedra, you, Kamaya and I will pay Daniel a visit right after breakfast tomorrow. I've already called to schedule an appointment with him."

"Tonight, though," Mark interjected, "we need to hit the streets." He gestured with the picture in his hand. "Unsavory characters tend to keep their heads down during the day."

Kendrick stood up, reaching for the briefcase he'd arrived with. When he popped the lid, Phaedra was stunned by the amount of cash inside.

"We knew we were going to have to grease some palms to get some answers," he said, answering the question Phaedra was thinking but didn't want to ask. "We were able to exchange it for Thai baht at the airport."

Kendrick tossed two wrapped stacks of currency toward Mark and two toward his brother Guy, the men depositing the money in the breast pockets of their suit jackets. "Are you coming with us?" Kendrick asked, looking toward Donovan.

The man shook his head. "No. I need to follow up on some leads here in the hotel."

"I'll give you a hand with that," Matthew said.

"I'd appreciate that, brother-in-law," Donovan said as Kendrick closed the case and handed it to John.

John crossed over to the other side of the room. Sliding back a painting on the wall, he revealed a large wall safe. He pushed a series of codes on the digital panel, then depressed his thumb against the security guard. When the door swung open he deposited the case inside, closed the door, secured it and slid the painting back in place. "Everybody good?" he asked, turning to the other men in the room.

They all nodded.

"We ready to bounce?" Mark asked as he moved toward the door.

Kendrick and Guy were close on his heels.

"Stay safe," John admonished, pointing his index finger in their direction.

Kamaya then repeated John's wishes but with a hint of worry in her voice.

Guy leaned to kiss his sister's cheek. "We got this."

Donovan gestured for Matthew to follow him. "We need to move, as well," he said, winking at Phaedra.

Matthew and John slapped palms as the two men exited the room. When the door was closed behind them, John blew a deep sigh, tossing his head back against his shoulders. It had been an exceptionally long day and it was about to get even longer.

Phaedra was still wide-eyed awake, believing that she would never be able to sleep until they found Mason alive and well. On the other side of the king-size bed, his sister Kamaya was snoozing easily, seemingly without a care in the world. But Phaedra knew she was worried, too. They were all worried.

Much like with the Stallion family, there was no escaping the Boudreaux lineage. Their distinctive features hinted of an African-Asian ancestry, with their slight angular eyes, thin noses, high cheek lines and full, pouty lips. Donovan could easily have passed for Mason's twin, the low lines of their closely cropped haircuts complementing their facial features. Kendrick had the same facial features but had a full afro, boasting a retro, bad-boy facade. Guy was more bohemian in his look, rocking dreads that hung well past his broad shoulders. He had an artistic aura about him and even if she hadn't already known that he was in the entertainment industry, Phaedra would have easily taken him for a musician or an artist.

Like her sister Katrina's, Kamaya's features were soft, more delicate than their brothers'. But where Katrina's demeanor was exceptionally conservative, Kamaya was hard-core and edgy. And unlike the Stallion men who all boasted the same rich, dark, coffee-with-no-cream complexion, the Boudreauxes were a kaleidoscope of colorations that ranged from burned umber to milk chocolate.

Although she would have preferred to meet Mason's family under very different circumstances, it was what it was. Kamaya had emphasized that they'd heard a lot about her, and Phaedra couldn't help wondering what and from whom. Had Mason been there she knew it would have been a delightful laugh between them. She then curled her body into the fetal position as she clung to her side of the bed.

In the other room John was sleeping comfortably

on the couch, snoring easily. Phaedra was grateful for him, and for Mark and Matthew, the trio coming when she called without blinking an eye. Mark was still cautious, dealing with her at arm's length, but there was nothing hostile in his demeanor like before. She hadn't asked about the test results and no one had volunteered the conclusions. The question of her paternity and the familial connection between them still lingered in the back of her mind, but in that moment Phaedra wasn't interested in hearing the answers until Mason were there with her as he had been since she first came to Texas.

Chapter 17

Daniel Kasam rushed to greet them, almost pulling John and the two women through the front door of his home. Concern painted his expression, the man seemingly distressed to learn Mason was missing.

"This is very serious!" Daniel bellowed as he gestured for them to take a seat. "Very serious!"

"Obviously, you understand our concerns," John said.

"More than you know," Daniel said. He reached for an envelope resting on the table and passed it to John. "This was delivered to my office right after I spoke with you yesterday."

Taking the mailer from the man, John lifted a typed letter from inside and read its contents. He looked up to meet Daniel's gaze, then dropped his eyes back to the letter to read one more time. He took a deep breath as he passed the document to Phaedra and Kamaya to read.

"A million dollars!" Phaedra yelled. "They want a million dollars in ransom?"

"I'm afraid so, Phaedra. Unscrupulous, it is," the man said as he rose to his feet and paced the floor.

"Why did they send it to you?" Phaedra queried. "Does this have anything to do with Mason's business dealings?"

Daniel shook his head. "There are some people Mason had to do business with who were not good people. I'm sure with him selling his business one of them thought this would be a good opportunity to take advantage. However, I assure you it has nothing to do with any transactions Mason and I had between us."

John cut his eye at Phaedra, his stare moving her to reflect on the other man's tone. Daniel seemed insulted by her suggestion and Phaedra was cautious not to offend him further.

"Well, we should take this to the police," she said.

Daniel nodded. "I have already given a copy to Officer Niran. I was made to understand that he is handling this case? Is that correct?"

John nodded. "That's correct. I'll touch base with him as soon as we leave."

"You should do that," Daniel said. "The sooner you pay the ransom, I'm sure the sooner they will let Mason go."

Phaedra took a deep breath. "Do you think Mali might be able to give us any information about Mason's acquaintances? Is she here by chance?"

Daniel turned his back to the conversation, reaching to pass each of them a glass of fresh-squeezed mango-and-papaya juice. "I'm sure Mali knows nothing. And unfortunately, she has already left Thailand.

She's gone back to school," he said as he gave Phaedra a slight smile.

Phaedra's face skewed with confusion. She opened her mouth to speak, then closed it, shooting John a quick glance as she bit back her words.

John smiled politely. "Well, we certainly appreciate your time, Mr. Kasam. You've been a big help to us."

"Of course," Daniel said. "If I can do anything else to assist you, please just ask. Everything I have is at your disposal."

"We greatly appreciate that," Kamaya added.

"Where did you say Mali was going to school?" Phaedra asked as Daniel clasped her hand beneath his.

"Design school in London," he answered matter-of-factly. He kissed the backs of Phaedra's fingers. "I'm sure Mason will show up before you know it," he said, adding, "As soon as you pay their demands. I'll call you as soon as they contact me with the details of the exchange."

Phaedra lifted her mouth in a slight smile, her expression not as certain. "Thank you," she said, biting back what she wanted to say. "You've been a good friend," she added for conversation's sake, not believing one word.

Daniel waved his goodbyes as their driver pulled the car out of his driveway. As they headed in the direction of the hotel, Phaedra met John's curious stare.

"What is it, Phaedra?" he asked.

She shook her head. "What are we going to do? They want one million dollars!"

John nodded. His tone was consoling. "The money isn't the problem," he said. "We have the money. What we need to figure out is if we should pay it. The fact remains that we might pay and they might not let Mason go. We need to keep trying to figure out who did this and where they might be holding him."

She blew a deep breath, trusting that John knew best. She thought about their meeting with Daniel, everything about their conversation bothering her, and she said so. "Daniel never said why he thought they sent the ransom note directly to him. And he also lied. Daniel lied to us."

"What do you mean?" Kamaya asked, leaning forward in her seat.

"Mali didn't go back to school. At dinner the other night Mali told us she quit school. She had no plans to go back."

"Interesting," John pondered. "And something else. I spoke with Niran this morning. He didn't say anything about the ransom note or that he'd spoken with Daniel."

"I don't like that man," Phaedra said, "and there's nothing about him or Daniel that I trust."

"But why do you think Daniel would lie about his daughter?" John questioned.

Kamaya answered before Phaedra had a chance to. "Mali Kasam is obsessed with Mason. That girl has been like fungus since the first day Mason stepped foot in Thailand, and her father indulges her every whim."

Phaedra nodded. "What Mali wants…" she said, not bothering to finish the statement as she turned to stare out the window.

Mason had fallen asleep, the pain in his skull still throbbing with a vengeance. It was dark when he woke and he had no sense of the time. He could have been sleeping for hours, or days; he just wasn't sure.

He sat up slowly, his equilibrium clearly off-kilter. While he slept someone had paid him a visit. A cardboard box had been dropped in the center of the floor. A tray of food—two sandwiches wrapped in waxed paper, three pieces of fruit, a bag of Thai cookies and a gallon jug of water left for him to consume.

An old oil lantern was burning on low, emitting just enough light for him to see how to maneuver his way around. Mason sighed. He was still in the dark about what his kidnappers wanted. But clearly they didn't want him dead. Not yet. He thought about the people he knew and he drew a blank as he reasoned who might want to do this to him.

He'd always been as aboveboard in his business dealings as was possible in Thailand, determined to maintain his integrity. And even in those situations where he might have consorted with individuals whose tactics were questionable, he had kept those dealings on the up-and-up. So he was drawing a blank, and the pain in his head wasn't helping him.

He took a deep breath and then a second. The temperature had started to cool, a breeze of fresh air billowing through the concrete opening. It was quiet outside, the hiss of ocean water the only sound. Mason's frustration was rapidly rising. If nothing else he needed to know that Phaedra was safe from harm. It had been clear in the moments before everything went completely blank that the two intruders were only interested in him.

But where had she disappeared to? Waking to an empty bed shouldn't have been different, but without Phaedra by his side, his whole world felt as if it had changed. It had taken no time at all for him to find comfort in her presence, thankful to have her next to him when he fell asleep, grateful to wake up by her side. But Phaedra hadn't been in his bed that morning. Phaedra had been gone and Mason had missed her desperately. Wanting to find Phaedra had been the last thing on his mind before their peace and quiet had been stormed.

Mason closed his eyes as he lay back down. He need to rest, to soothe the hurt that beat like thunder behind his eyes. He anticipated needing his strength to free himself from captivity, and if any harm had come to Phaedra, he would need every ounce of his might to cause a world of hurt to whoever was responsible.

After John had called the rest of the family to share news of the ransom note, they all converged back at the hotel suite. When they arrived Mark's excitement was hard for him to contain.

"I think we found them," Mark said, tossing a Polaroid onto the table. "They were at Club Pattaya until four o'clock this morning."

"Where did they go from there?" John asked.

Guy answered. "An apartment in downtown Phuket. Above the fruit market."

"We need to go back. We need to talk to them," Phaedra said as she took the photo from John's hand. "We need to find out what they know."

Her eyes suddenly widened as she studied the picture Mark had taken, playing as if he were just a tourist enjoying the Thai nightlife. She tapped a manicured finger against the image, her own excitement suddenly infectious. "This woman here in the background, was she with them?" Phaedra asked, looking from Mark to Guy and then Donovan.

Mark shrugged as he leaned to stare where Phaedra was pointing. "They spoke like they knew each other, but she spent most of the night with someone else. Why?"

Looking over Mark's shoulder, Kendrick nodded. "They left together. Or rather, she left and they followed behind her."

"Who is she?" John asked.

Phaedra cut an eye toward Kamaya. "It's Mali Kasam. It's Daniel Kasam's daughter."

"Is she important?" Donovan asked.

"Something's up with that girl, and her father," Kamaya said. "We just don't know what that is."

"So, now that we know Mali is still here and that her father is hiding something, what's the game plan?" Phaedra asked, looking toward John.

The man hesitated for a brief moment. "I hope you girls brought your dancing shoes because I'm thinking that we're all going clubbing tonight."

Kamaya grinned. "Sleazy nightclubs! You gotta love 'em!"

Kendrick leaned to whisper in Guy's ear. His brother nodded his agreement.

"Under the circumstances I'm thinking that we shouldn't go back unarmed," Kendrick said out loud, looking around the room.

Phaedra raised an eyebrow. She wanted to ask about the legality of having a weapon in Thailand, but she didn't. She looked at John, who gave her a slight wink.

"We'll head to Mason's and get what we need. I have a key to the gun case," Guy said.

Phaedra's mouth fell open. "Mason has a gun case? With guns?" she asked.

Kamaya laughed. "Our brother is quite the marksman," she said. "Besides, tourist Thailand is quite different from underground Thailand. There are places here that can be quite dangerous if you're not careful. We learned that when Mason began building this property."

"Only because you didn't know how to stay put when we told you to," Kendrick said.

Kamaya shrugged. "Sometimes a girl has to do what a girl has to do. Isn't that right, Phaedra?"

Without giving it a second thought, Phaedra nodded with conviction. "Yeah, so you boys better get a good nap because tonight we're going to get some answers. I don't care what it takes, but we're going to find Mason and bring him home."

As Phaedra and Kamaya exited the room, strategizing in hushed whispers, John, Matthew and Mark all shook their heads, the other men chuckling softly.

Phaedra had retreated to the lobby of the hotel to regroup. She wasn't accustomed to the madness of so many family members in one place at the same time. Despite the severity of the situation and the resulting stress, they still found things to laugh about, humor easing their tension. It was too much and she found herself needing a moment of quiet to reflect.

When she'd been gone for a good length of time, each of the brothers sought her out, varying degrees of concern coming in a revolving door of Stallion men. John came first, his eyes skating around the space until he saw her sitting alone in the corner.

Taking the seat beside her, he took a deep breath, saying nothing as the two of them sat side by side watching the cast of characters that paraded in and out of the hotel.

"Are you going to be okay?" John finally asked, still staring out into space.

Phaedra shrugged. "I will be once we get Mason back."

"You two have become close since you've been here."

She tossed him a quick glance. "I care about him. He's a good man. I haven't known a lot of good men."

John paused, reflecting on her comment. "I hope we can change that," he said softly.

Phaedra turned to look at John, who was looking back at her. She took a deep breath. "Your father was a good man, too, wasn't he?"

John smiled. "One of the best. You would have liked him. And I know he would have liked you, too."

Phaedra swiped at a tear that managed to escape past her thick lashes. She swallowed hard, taking a deep breath.

John reached a hand out and patted her on the back. "When we get back to Dallas I look forward to telling you more about him," he said.

She smiled. "I'd like that."

Within minutes of John's departure, Mark lumbered across the lobby, pausing when he saw her sitting alone. He moved to her side and dropped down onto an upholstered seat across from where she was sitting. He leaned forward, meeting her curious gaze.

"What's up?" Mark questioned.

Phaedra shrugged. "I'm good."

He nodded. "You need anything?"

She shook her head. "No, I'm fine. But thanks for asking."

"Okay, then, but you know that if you need anything you just have to ask, right?"

Phaedra smiled. "I appreciate that."

Mark smiled back. "But ask John. He's better at things like that."

Phaedra chuckled softly as Mark trudged back across the lobby floor, heading out the doors to the outside.

Just as Phaedra was thinking about returning to the family's suite, Matthew waved at her from the other side of the room. Rising from her seat, she headed in his direction, waiting as he and the hotel's concierge had a brief conversation.

"Are you doing okay?" Matthew asked, turning his attention back to her.

"Yes, thank you," she said.

"We're all worried about you."

"Mason's the one we need to worry about," she responded.

Matthew nodded. "My brother-in-law's tough. I'm sure he'll be fine. And I know he wouldn't want you to worry."

Phaedra shrugged. "I can't help myself."

"I just spoke to Katrina and she asked about you."

"Your wife is very sweet. You're a lucky man."

Matthew grinned. "Yeah, I am. And so is Mason," he said, giving her a quick wink.

Phaedra nodded. "I guess I need to head back up," she said.

Matthew nodded as he studied her expression. He

reached to give her a hug, wrapping his arms tightly around her. "Family can be a good thing, Phaedra," he said. "Even one you didn't expect to have. Lean on us and Mason's family, too. I promise, we won't fail you or him."

Chapter 18

Daniel was furious, rage gleaming from his eyes as if he'd gone stark, raving mad. His shouts vacillated between English and Siamese, as if his screaming in two languages would better get his message across.

But Mali was apathetic, her expression blank as she focused on a spot on the wall behind her father's head. As she chomped on her signature piece of chewing gum, her father's tirade went in one ear and out the other, the young woman clearly not concerned with his unhappiness.

"I told you to go to London. Why are you here?" Daniel screamed for the second time. "Why can you not do what I tell you to do, Mali?"

Mali sighed, her mouth pushed out in a childish pout. "I wanted to be close to Mason. He might have needed me. Those goons of yours, they hurt him," she said, snarling at the duo who stood in the doorway, waiting for their employer's next order. "They should not have hit him like they did!" she said emphatically.

Her father shook his head. "They will do what is necessary and right now they are spending far too much time babysitting you."

Daniel paused as he crossed over to the bar and poured himself a jigger of bourbon. After tossing back the first shot and pouring another, he turned his attention back to his daughter. "Now, Mason's family has come and they are asking questions. They cannot find you here, Mali. I want you out of Thailand tonight."

His daughter rolled her eyes. She rose from her seat and moved to the man's side, wrapping her arms around his waist as she pressed her head against her father's chest. "Don't be angry with me, Papa! I hate when you yell!"

"You make me yell. You know how important this is. I need this money!"

Mali shrugged. "And you will get your money. And when I rescue Mason it will all be perfect. That's why I have to be here, Papa, so that I can rescue him and he will know how important he is to me."

Daniel stared at his daughter intently. Mali was spoiled beyond reason and he had no one to blame except himself. Mali's mother had died in childbirth and his precious baby girl had been all he'd had left. Giving her everything she wanted had made her unreasonable and selfish and had finally taxed him into financial ruin. Hoping to scam money for holding Mason hostage was his last hope to turn his and Mali's lives around.

There had been a time when he had hoped Mason would have loved Mali as much as he did, the two partnering as in-laws. But Mali's disregard for other

people and her constant tantrums had done nothing to
inspire the man to want a relationship with her. Mali's
shameless pursuit had turned Mason off, and as much
as Daniel loved his only child he hadn't been able to
blame the man for his disinterest. Even at her very best
Mali could frustrate a person senseless.

He shook his head, his tone hardening. "There is
much more at stake here, Mali. Without that money
we will lose everything. When we have that money,
then I will decide what we do with Mason Boudreaux.
Now, do what I ask, please."

Mali bristled in defiance as her father stormed out of
the room, his two flunkies following on his heels. She
stole a quick glance at the watch on her wrist. Grabbing her purse, she headed in the direction of the front
door. Her father knew her better than anyone, and he
knew that Mali did what Mali wanted. No more and
no less. And in that moment, all Mali wanted was to
ensure that no one and nothing came between her and
her want of Mason Boudreaux.

Timing was going to be the key to their success,
Phaedra thought, sipping on a glass of cola. Donovan was sitting beside her, his eyes skating around the
room. They had all been in the club for over an hour,
hoping against all odds that the two men who'd taken
Mason, or Mali Kasam herself, would show.

The Stallion brothers were seated at a table in the
back of the club, three Thai dancers vying for their attention. Guy and Kendrick were both at the bar with
Kamaya, everyone pretending to be interested in nothing but a good time. The music was loud, the *thump,
thump, thump* of a 1970s playlist vibrating around the

room. Any other time or place Phaedra would have been enjoying herself, but in that moment she was nervous, believing that they were running out of time to get Mason back safe and sound.

As if reading her mind, Donovan said, "He's going to be fine." He met Phaedra's anxious stare.

Phaedra nodded. "I just hate that we can't get any help. The police have been useless. We're just running on instinct and what if we're wrong about the Kasams? What if we're looking in the wrong direction and something happens to Mason? I'll never be able to forgive myself."

"Let me tell you a story about my brother," Donovan started, his voice a loud whisper. "Him being the oldest of nine kids, with a father in the military and on deployment as often as he was home, put a lot of responsibility on Mason. I was only six or seven when I realized just how much pressure being the oldest had on him. He was trying to help our mother and be a surrogate father, big brother and best friend rolled up into one. And one day I asked him why he did so much. What made him want to work so hard?

"Mason said that our father told him to follow his gut instincts and always do what felt right for him to do. It's a philosophy that Mason continues to live by. He was barely out of college when he decided that he wanted to go into the hotel business and build an empire. And he sold that empire because he said the timing just felt right. He knew that there was something else in this world that he was supposed to be doing. Mason has always stepped out on faith, trusted in God and succeeded."

Donovan paused as he took a quick sip of his own

drink. "Did he tell you that he called me the night he met you?" the man asked.

Phaedra shook her head. "No, he didn't."

"Well, he did and I haven't heard him that excited in a long time and all because this beautiful woman took his picture and made him smile. And something about you and that moment felt right. His instincts told him that you were special, and Mason always trusts that gut feeling. And I tell you all this to say, trust those instincts. Mason trusted his when he followed you here. Trust yours and help us get him back. If you don't feel right about the Kasams, then there's a reason."

"Thank you," Phaedra said, pausing to reflect on his words.

With a wink, Donovan resumed his watch, his gaze skating back around the room. Phaedra saw them first, Mali entering the room behind the two thugs. The men headed to a table on the other side of the large room as their companion headed straight to the dance floor. Turning an about-face, Phaedra leaned to whisper into Donovan's ear, "As soon as I start talking with her you need to get up and leave. Don't let her catch up to you. She needs to think that you are Mason."

Donovan nodded. "No problem. I'll be in the alley with the car. As soon as she bolts we'll be right behind her."

Phaedra smiled. "Dear God, please let this work," she whispered as she gestured for Kamaya's attention. Kamaya, who'd been eyeing them intently, nodded as Phaedra gave her a thumbs-up.

Rising from her barstool, Kamaya made her way to where the two kidnappers sat, both men having distanced themselves from Mali. She sauntered easily in a seductive red dress, her hips swaying in invitation as she took a seat beside them, gesturing for a waiter to bring them each a round of drinks. It took no time at all before they were both completely entranced by the beautiful woman before them. With her coquettish laughter and overt seduction, Kamaya was like a black widow spider luring her prey.

Mark had made his way to the dance floor, his large palms resting easily against the line of Mali's narrow hips. She was dancing seductively, her head tossed back against her thin neck as she laughed, clearly amused by the attention the handsome man was showing her. Mali thrived on attention and Phaedra and Kamaya both had banked on her wanting to be the object of some man's desire before her night was done. Mark was the perfect man for the job.

When Kamaya gestured for a second round of drinks, Phaedra watched as the bartender slid two of the glasses toward Guy, the brother dropping two small white pills into the amber-colored liquor. If anyone had been paying attention, they would have noticed Kendrick slipping money into the bartender's palm and then the waitress's just before she delivered the drug-laced drinks to their intended targets.

Phaedra closed her eyes and took a deep breath. Opening them again, she watched as Frick and Frack both gulped their spirits, the duo spurred on by Kamaya's encouragement. Kendrick had assured her the drug's effects would be minimal, the two not remembering anything once they recovered. With no color, smell or taste, neither man would even be able to tell that anything at all had happened to him. They would both soon become weak and confused, or even pass out so they wouldn't be a threat to the next phase of the family's plan to rescue Mason. In the morning they'd have one hell of a headache for their indiscretions.

John crossed the room, headed in the direction of the door. As he passed Kamaya's table, he purposely bumped into the shorter of the companions. As he apologized profusely, offering to buy them all another round of drinks, there was no way not to notice the man's clear lack of focus, his head rolling awkwardly. Evenutally he laid his head on the table, appearing to fall off to sleep. Kamaya turned to Phaedra and winked, her head bobbing against her shoulders.

"Wish me luck," Phaedra said as Donovan gave her hand a quick squeeze before purposely pushing his full glass of drink into her lap. Phaedra jumped to her feet, squealing loudly enough to draw everyone's attention. She brushed at the offending moisture, her head shaking as Donovan pretended to assist her. Spinning away from the table, Phaedra crossed the room still muttering profusely as she headed past the dance floor toward the restrooms.

Mark was laughing as he pointed in her direction. Mali turned to stare where he stared, her eyes widening as she noticed the man who was following Phaedra with his eyes. Her gyrations came to a fast halt, her heart suddenly beating with a vengeance. How was such a thing possible? she thought, her mind suddenly spinning with questions, unable to fathom how Mason had managed to free himself. Unable to fathom how she was going to explain that to her father.

"Mali!" Phaedra cried as she suddenly blocked the woman's view. "What a surprise!" Phaedra leaned to give the girl a hug, then extended her hand in Mark's direction. "Hi, Phaedra Parrish. I'm a friend of Mali's."

Mark nodded politely. "Looks like you had a little accident," he said as he pointed to the spill down the front of her dress.

Phaedra shrugged. "My boyfriend, Mason, was a little clumsy," she said as she turned to point in Donovan's direction.

"Mason is here?" Mali questioned, unable to hide the look of surprise across her face.

"Yes," Phaedra said, a brilliant smile painting her expression. She shifted her body to block Mali's view a second time. "I know you heard about him disappearing, but he was able to get away and we're celebrating. We're leaving tomorrow, though, so we can put all of this bad business behind us."

Mali shook her head as she made a motion to move. Mark caught her about the waist. "Don't you want to keep dancing, pretty lady?" he said sweetly.

Mali brushed him off. "I need to say hello to my friend," she said as she moved to step past Phaedra.

Mark grabbed her by the arm and swung her back against him. "But we're having such a good time!" he said excitedly.

As Mali pushed him from her, snatching her arm from his grip, she didn't notice that Donovan had risen from his seat and was exiting the club, the man stealing out of the spotlight he'd been placed in. Kamaya, Kendrick and Guy followed closely behind him.

As the door closed on their departure, Phaedra cut a quick eye in Mark's direction. "Well, it was good to see you, Mali," she said, still swiping at the wet spot that had darkened the silk print she wore. "Please give your father my regards."

Before Phaedra's last words were out, Mali was searching the room, frantic to spy the man who looked like Mason Boudreaux. As she rushed in the direction of the club's entrance, she shouted in Siamese to the two men who'd arrived with her, both sitting alone, heads bowed as they slumbered comfortably at their table. Not bothering to wait for them, Mali rushed outside.

John stood at the door's entrance, blocking her quick exit. "Excuse me," he said as he stepped left when she stepped right, and right as she went left, the two looking as if they might be dancing.

"Get out of my way!" Mali shouted, clearly perturbed.

"I really am sorry," John said, feigning an apology. He stepped out of her way to allow her to pass.

Rushing past him, Mali looked left and then right, and the only thing in her view was the empty street.

Chapter 19

"Don't lose her," Kamaya said as Donovan maneuvered the car through the dark Thai streets.

"I'm not going to lose her," he responded, annoyance on the tip of his tongue. "You need to relax."

From the backseat, Guy and Kendrick admonished them both. "Stay focused," Guy said, Kendrick echoing his sentiments.

Ahead of them Mali was racing her car as if she were late for an important meeting. Just as Phaedra and Kamaya had both predicted, the combination of alcohol and dim light had successfully deceived her. Seeing Mason's brother had thrown her for a loop; the woman had lost control. After exiting the nightclub she'd headed straight for her vehicle, not bothering to wait for her two bodyguards. Anticipating that they were following close behind her, Mali didn't give the car in her rearview mirror a second thought. And both families were banking on her negligence, hopeful that she would lead them directly to where Mason was being held. The one unknown in their plan was whether or not they'd be able to rescue him without incident. And everyone was hoping that wherever Mason was, the area would be secluded, with little interference to get in their way.

In the vehicle behind them, John navigated at a safe distance, not wanting to draw any attention to the fact that there were actually two cars in hot pursuit of the young woman. Mark rode shotgun, one hand gripping the dashboard. Phaedra and Matthew held court in the backseat.

"I don't have a plan from here," Phaedra said, her eyes skipping from the back of John's head to Mark's.

"The plan is that you are going to sit in the car and stay out of the way," Mark said. He looked to the backseat.

"You are not the boss of me," Phaedra shouted, bristling with indignation.

"I didn't say I was the boss of you, but you need to listen. Why are you being difficult?"

"I'm not being difficult," Phaedra countered. "Why are you?"

John cast a quick glance in the rearview mirror, meeting Matthew's amused stare. The two brothers chuckled softly to themselves.

"I'm the boss of everybody," John said, "and you two need to play nice."

Annoyed, both Mark and Phaedra fell into the silence, sulking in their seats. Matthew laughed out loud, and Phaedra, who was totally perturbed, punched him in the arm.

"Ouch! What did you do that for?" Matthew cried out as he rubbed the rising bruise.

Phaedra rolled her eyes. "It's his fault," she said, pointing at Mark.

"Apologize, Phaedra," John said. "I don't care whose fault it is."

Phaedra bit her bottom lip, crossing her arms over her chest.

"Now," John admonished. "Say you're sorry."

She took a deep breath. "Sorry, Matthew."

For a brief moment a blanket of silence dropped down over them and then all four burst out laughing, the moment alleviating the stress that was fighting to consume them.

Mali fumbled with the key to the master lock that secured the door to the storage shed. Frustration was clouding her view, her anxiety obscuring every ounce of rational thought. There was no way Mason had gotten out, she thought, but how else would that explain how the man had found his way to Club Pattaya to spill a drink on Phaedra's dress?

Pushing open the door, she flicked on the oversize flashlight, shining it inside. Mason lay on the bed, his back to the door, exactly where he'd been the last time she looked in on him. Nothing had changed; even the food her father had left for him was undisturbed. She rubbed her hand across her eyes, swiping at the perspiration that had risen over her brow. Taking a deep breath, she held it as she eased her way inside the small enclosure, the heels of her Chanel pumps clicking loudly against the cement floor.

Shining the light on Mason, she leaned over his

body, her heart beating rapidly as she waited to see him breathe, relief coming when he took a breath, his body shifting with the exhalation. She reached a tentative hand out, brushing the backs of her fingers along the side of his face. He was running a fever, his body temperature spiked high. Knowing that there was no way Mason could have been in that nightclub, realization set in that she had been played.

A wave of anger suddenly flooded Mali's spirit. Phaedra had played her, stringing her along like a guitar player. Mali didn't take kindly to anyone besting her, and she was suddenly outraged, determined to get revenge. Spinning about on her high heels, she turned just as Mason rolled onto his back, lifting his head to stare at her. He brought his hand up to shield his eyes from the light, squinting to focus.

His voice was low and craggy, the fever evident in his tone, delirium blanketing his perception. "Phaedra? Is that you, baby? Phaedra, are you okay?" he asked as he tried to sit up.

Turning to stare at him, Mali grimaced, unable to hide her dismay. He was calling Phaedra's name, and not hers, and that made her even angrier. It was on the tip of her tongue to cuss him, but she didn't. Instead, she switched off the light as she eased her way backward to the door. And as she turned to make her exit, Mali slammed harshly into Donovan and Guy Boudreaux, who were standing like stone in the entrance.

As she lifted her arm to swing the flashlight at his head, Donovan grabbed the woman's wrist and pushed her back against the wall. "I wouldn't do that if I were you," he said as he turned the flashlight back on and waved the light around the space, resting it on Mason's reclined frame.

Guy moved past him, rushing to his brother's side. Kamaya and Kendrick followed on his heels. Noticing the lantern, Kamaya dropped to the floor, fiddling with the wick and a pack of matches that rested beside it. In seconds, a stream of light flooded the room. "Is he okay?" she questioned, concern spilling past her lips.

"We need to get him to a doctor," Guy said. "He's burning up and it looks like he might have lost a good amount of blood." He pointed to the stained mattress beneath his brother's head.

Kendrick called his name. "Mason…can you hear me?"

Mason struggled to focus. "Who…I…" he sputtered softly, his eyes closing as he fell back into a stupor.

"I found him," Mali said loudly. "I was trying to save him. I was just going to call for help. I wouldn't let anything happen to Mason!"

"We need to move," Donovan said, ignoring her. "Get him to the car."

With Kendrick bracing his brother's weight on one side and Guy on the other, the two lifted Mason to his feet.

"Everything is going to be fine now, Mason," Kamaya said, bringing up the rear. "We've got you, big brother."

They heard him just seconds before they saw him enter the room. He spoke in Siamese, his words meant only for his daughter's ears. As Daniel Kasam stepped into the room, he fired into the midnight air, the gunshot ringing loudly. They all came to a standstill in anticipation of a second shot, panic blowing through the space as the man pointed a large gun squarely at Mason's heart.

The silence was thundering. Donovan released his hold on Mali, the woman pushing him harshly in the chest as she moved to stand beside her father. Daniel was not amused by the smirk on her face, his daughter sneering as if everything was going to be okay.

"I am very sorry for this," he said, looking from one Boudreaux to the other. "This was not how things were supposed to go. You were supposed to pay the money and we would have let him go."

"So, what now?" Donovan questioned, easing himself slowly in front of Kamaya. "Do you plan to shoot us all, Daniel?"

The man swiped the back of his hand across his brow. He shook his head. "I just needed the money," he said. "You don't understand."

"But we do," Guy said. "And that's not going to happen now. So the only choice you have is to kill us all or let us go."

"Don't listen to them, Papa," Mali demanded. "We can fix this. We can make them get us the money. We can—"

"Shut up, Mali!" Daniel shouted. "I have to think. If you had just done what I told you to do, we would not be in this position."

"You need to decide now," Kendrick said. "Because Mason needs a doctor and the only way we're not leaving here is if you shoot us."

"You leave when I say so," Daniel shouted back, turning the gun to point at Kendrick's head.

"Not this time," John said as he and Mark moved in behind the father and his daughter, surprising them both.

Deborah Fletcher Mello 179

Mark pointed his own pistol to the back of Daniel's head. "You might want to put that down, friend," he said softly. "We don't want any blood to be spilled tonight."

It was a standoff and that brief moment felt like a lifetime. The silence was consuming, so harsh that every heartbeat resounded like thunder. Taking a deep breath Daniel finally acknowledged defeat as he lifted his hands, opening his palms in submission. John reached for the gun Daniel was holding, pulling the firearm from the man's hand. "In the corner," he said, gesturing for Daniel and his daughter to move.

Daniel moved to the other side of the room as he and Mali both turned to stare, watching as the brothers carried Mason out the door.

Phaedra met them in the entrance, wrapping her arms around the man's waist. "Mason!"

Opening his eyes, Mason met her eyes and held the gaze for a brief moment. A slight smile pulled at his lips as he whispered her name. "Phaedra?"

Phaedra nodded. "I love you, Mason," she said as she kissed his lips, pressing her cheek to his. "I love you," she whispered before stepping out of the way so that they could get him to the car.

"We'll meet you at the hospital," Kamaya said, dropping a warm hand against Phaedra's arm. "Good job," she finished, giving Phaedra a quick wink.

Inside, Mali persisted. "What are you going to do with us?" she questioned, her eyes widening.

Phaedra pushed past the brothers, coming to a stop in front of the woman.

"I thought we told you to stay in the car," Mark admonished.

"I have some unfinished business," Phaedra said, looking at him. "And I told you, you are not the boss of me!"

"Let's go, Phaedra," John commanded. "We need to check on Mason."

"What about us?" Mali asked again, leveling her gaze on Phaedra.

Phaedra looked from her to Daniel, who'd sunk to the floor, visibly sobbing. Mali's father was broken. There was no denying the wealth of hurt that consumed him, everything he had ever valued gone with a series of bad decisions. Phaedra shook her head. "Your father needs you, Mali," she said. "You are all he has."

Mali sneered, twisting her mouth to sound off. A torrent of expletives flew past her lips, but before she could get the second wave out, Phaedra balled up a tight fist and busted the girl in the mouth. Mali fell back in surprise, landing flat on her behind on the floor beneath her. "And if you come anywhere near me or my man ever again, I will hurt you," Phaedra said, her index finger waving erratically.

"Damn!" Mark shouted as he pulled his own fist to his mouth. "Nice right cross!"

John shook his head. "Phaedra, move it. Now!"

Mason was diagnosed with a concussion, heatstroke and severe dehydration. After a day of intravenous fluids and some serious bed rest, the doctors at the Phuket International Hospital released him. Back at the hotel, both Kamaya and Phaedra were smothering him with attention.

"Girls, I'm not handicapped," Mason said, admonishing them both to give him a break.

"You better enjoy this," Kamaya said. "It won't last much longer 'cause we're leaving this afternoon."

"Uh, pay your sister no mind," Phaedra said, smiling. "I'm not going anywhere."

"Don't be bringing him into any bad habits," Kamaya teased. "You'll regret it once he gets better."

The men in the room all laughed. "I could use a cool drink of something," Mark quipped, "in case one of you would like to wait on me hand and foot."

Phaedra rolled her eyes. "Uh, you've got two good hands." She looked at Mark as he eyed her back.

Matthew laughed. "Y'all two are funny."

Mason chuckled softly. He turned his attention to John. "So, what's happening with Daniel?"

John shrugged. "Officer Niran took him and Mali both into custody, but it seems that they have a long history between them. I don't anticipate that much will come of it. He's actually charged the two men who took Mason with assault to cause bodily harm and detaining by force. They'll see more time than Daniel will."

"Daniel called me," Mason said, the pronouncement surprising them all. "He called to apologize."

"He's got some nerve," Kamaya said. "He kidnaps you, demands one million dollars in ransom and he thinks all he has to do is apologize?"

Mason shrugged. "Desperate times will make people do desperate things, Kamaya. I can't discount that without Daniel's help I would not have been able to accomplish half of what I accomplished here in Thailand. Daniel is not a bad man. He just made a very bad decision. In his eyes one million dollars wouldn't make a dent in my bank account, so it wasn't going to be missed."

"That she-devil he calls a daughter isn't much help to him, either," Phaedra muttered under her breath.

Mason smiled, pulling the woman's hand to his lips as he kissed her palm. "Mali has some issues, there's no denying that."

"Some issues?" she repeated, pulling her hand to her hip as she stared down at him.

Mason lifted his hands as if in surrender, laughing warmly. "Sorry, sensitive subject."

"Watch her right cross," Mark teased. "Mali found out the hard way that Phaedra packs a mean punch."

Phaedra flipped her hand at Mark, moving to take the seat at Mason's side.

"So, you're not going to do anything about him?" Kamaya persisted.

Mason sighed. "If he accepts it, I'm going to extend a helping hand both emotionally and financially to help him get back on his feet."

"You're crazy!" his sister yelled, throwing her hands up in frustration.

"Maybe, but sometimes we have to remember that our good fortune isn't everyone else's good fortune. As a family we have each other to lean on for support. We have an excess of financial security. Our blessings have been plentiful. Sometimes we have to look past people's mistakes and focus on their needs."

Kamaya rolled her eyes. "Yeah, yeah, yeah," she said, tears misting her eyes.

Phaedra nodded her understanding as she met John's gaze.

John came to his feet. "Mason, we're going to give you and your family some time together. If you don't mind, my brothers and I would like to steal Phaedra away from you for a minute or two."

He locked eyes with Phaedra and smiled warmly. A twinge of anxiety wafted through her stomach. She took a deep breath as Mason squeezed her hand.

"She'll be in good hands," Matthew interjected.

Mason nodded. "Be easy with my girl," he said softly. He leaned to kiss her cheek.

Meeting Mason's gaze one last time, Phaedra followed the Stallion men out of the hotel suite and down the hall. Matthew used a security pass to open the door to the second suite that the two families had been sharing. John led the way to the outside patio, taking a seat in one of the cushioned chairs. He gestured for Phaedra to follow, four chairs pulled up into a tight circle.

As Matthew sat down he pulled a sealed envelope from out of his breast pocket, passing the mailer to his older brother. Leaning forward in his seat, John rested his elbows against his thighs, flipping the envelope over in his hands. Phaedra took a deep breath. She twisted her hands nervously in her lap, suddenly wishing that she was still sitting by Mason's side, leaning on the man for support.

John started the conversation. "We've all been anxious to get the paternity results, and they came shortly after we left Texas. I asked the office to express them here to us and with everything that's been going on we really haven't had any time to review them."

"What about Luke?" Phaedra asked, her voice a hushed whisper.

"We'll share the news with him when he gets back from his honeymoon, but it's not fair to you to wait any longer."

John looked from Matthew to Mark as he passed the envelope in his hand to Phaedra. She took it tentatively, her hand visibly shaking. Tears misted behind her eyelids. Just as she slid her thumb beneath the sealed edge, Mark stopped her, dropping his own hand over hers. He shook his head. Phaedra eyed him curiously as he pulled the envelope from her grasp.

Meeting John's stare, Mark tore the envelope and its contents in half. Moving back inside the lavish hotel room, he returned with an empty trash can. Pulling a lighter from his pocket, he ignited the corner of the paper and once it was lit dropped the two halves of the flaming paper into the canister. The family sat in silence as they watched the document burn until nothing but gray ash remained.

Phaedra turned to stare at Mark. "Why—" she started, the words catching deep in her heart.

"Because I don't need that piece of paper to tell me who my family is," Mark said, casually shrugging.

John and Matthew both smiled widely. John nodded. He stood up, extending an outstretched hand. Matthew stood with him, dropping his hand atop John's. Mark added his to the mix, the three brothers turning to stare at Phaedra.

"What are you waiting for, little sis?" Mark asked.

Phaedra looked from one to the other, her tears beginning to seep past her lashes.

"She's crying," Mark said, his eyes spinning skyward. "And she's doing that ugly cry that Luke used to do."

"Sisters cry, little brother," John replied with a slight chuckle. He nodded his head at Phaedra. "So, what are you waiting for?" he asked a second time.

Coming to her feet, Phaedra dropped her hand on top of the pile. John placed his other hand on top of hers, squeezing it warmly. The others followed until they were all hands in.

"Welcome to the family," Mark said softly, tossing her a wink.

"Once a Stallion," Matthew chimed in.

"Forever a Stallion," John and Mark echoed.

"Once a Stallion," Matthew repeated, his gaze meeting Phaedra's, his eyebrows raised.

The three brothers all grinned at Phaedra.

"Forever a Stallion," she answered, knowing that from that moment forward, those words would always be true.

Chapter 20

"So, you two are headed where?" Mark questioned, his eyes narrowing suspiciously.

Mason laughed. "I'm thinking that we might fly to Greece before we head back to the States."

"And how long do you plan to be in Greece?"

"One, maybe two days."

Mark nodded, his expression moving Phaedra to laugh.

"Why are you giving Mason the third degree?" she asked.

Mark looked at her. "It's what big brothers do," he answered.

Matthew and John both laughed heartily. The two leaned to kiss Phaedra's cheek.

"You're coming back to Dallas after Greece, right, Phaedra?" John asked.

Phaedra nodded. "I need to stop in N'Orleans first, but yes, I'm coming back to Dallas."

"We'll talk more then," he said as he gestured for his brothers to get on the Stallion jet. "Let's move it," he said, heading in the direction of the private plane.

Mark moved to Phaedra's side, wrapping her in a deep hug. He met Mason's amused gaze over the woman's shoulder. "Take care of my little sister," he said sternly. "I think we're going to keep her."

Mason laughed, giving the man a quick salute. "Yes, sir."

Mark laughed with him as the duo slapped palms.

Phaedra stepped into Mason's arms as they watched the siblings board their plane for home.

"Greece?" Phaedra said as Mason led her by the hand to his own private aircraft.

"Would you prefer Italy? We can go wherever you want to go."

"You're killing me," she said, giggling softly.

"With love, baby. Just with love!"

Phaedra reached to kiss Mason's lips. "In all honesty, what I would like to do is just go to N'Orleans. After everything that's happened I need something familiar. I really just want to go home."

Mason nodded his understanding. "Then we're going home," he said.

An hour later the pilot confirmed the change in their travel itinerary and the duo was on their way back to the United States. As the Gulfstream G450 ascended into the midday sky, Phaedra blew a sigh of relief, grateful that she was still standing because for the past month all she had wanted to do was lie down and pull the covers over her head.

Since her mother's death, every aspect of her life had felt like something out of a novel, feeling unbelievable. She'd gone from having no family to having four brothers, and a man who loved her and talked about spending the rest of his life with her. The week before she'd been pointing a camera at pretty things taking pictures, and just days earlier she'd witnessed guns being pointed at people she loved, threatening to take their lives. She'd traveled from New Orleans to Dallas in economy class to Thailand on a private jet, and with Mason the next stop would be wherever her heart desired, by whatever mode of travel she wanted.

She'd had to make life-changing decisions on the fly, and just days after her mother's passing a grief counselor had warned her not to make any major resolutions for at least six months. She'd been blessed beyond measure, but she couldn't stop thinking that all of it was just a phenomenal dream and she would soon wake up from it.

"A penny for your thoughts," Mason said, his fingers gliding down the length of her arm.

Phaedra shook her head. "You really don't want to know what I was thinking."

"Yes, I do. I don't want you to think that you ever have to keep anything from me. And right now you look like your world has just fallen apart. I don't like that look and if I can do something to take that kind of worry from your heart I want to do it," Mason said.

"I guess I was just worried that my world might want to fall apart," Phaedra answered. "A lot has happened and I keep waiting for the other shoe to drop."

Mason nodded, his expression reflective. "Do you believe that good things come to good people, Phaedra?"

"Sometimes."

"Maybe this is your sometime. Maybe your blessings are coming because you are deserving of them."

Phaedra shook her head. "How are you such an optimist?"

"How are you not?"

Mason leaned to kiss her, his hand cupped gently against the side of her face. His lips were soft and teasing, stirring a rumbling of heat in the center of her core. The last time they'd made love had been the morning Mason had been taken, and Phaedra admitted to having been scared that he would never make love to her again.

Mason broke the connection, staring into her eyes as he pulled himself away. He took a deep breath, a wry smile pulling at his mouth.

"What?" Phaedra asked, smiling with him.

He leaned to whisper in her ear, stealing a glance toward the galley to ensure that they didn't have an audience. "I'm hard," he said, brushing his face gently against hers. "Every time I think about you I get an erection and we haven't had a moment alone," he whispered.

Phaedra laughed. "That sounds like a deeply personal problem, Mr. Boudreaux."

Mason nodded. "It will be if I have to spend the next sixteen hours in this airplane, excited, without getting any relief."

Still giggling, Phaedra pointed to the plane's restroom. "You might want to go take care of that problem," she said.

Mason grinned. "I didn't think you'd ever ask," he said, rising from his seat. He grabbed Phaedra's hand and pulled her along behind him.

Her eyes widened in surprise. "What...I..." she sputtered as he pulled her into the bathroom and locked the door. "Mason!" Phaedra cried out. "We can't—"

Before she could complete the thought, Mason pulled her into his arms and kissed her hungrily, his mouth consuming hers. When he licked the fullness of her lips, moving her to open her mouth to him, his tongue danced past the line of her teeth, swirling in sync with hers. He pressed his body against her, Phaedra's softness cushioning every one of his hardened muscles.

"Well, maybe this one time," Phaedra purred as Mason nuzzled his face into her neck, planting a line of kisses from one ear to the other. She shivered in ecstasy as Mason painted circles with his tongue across the soft, supple skin of her neck. Phaedra closed her eyes and lost herself in the delicious feelings swirling through her. Heat rose with a vengeance in the small enclosure, perspiration rising fiercely in every crack and crevice of both their bodies.

Mason teased her for what seemed like an eternity. Phaedra moaned as Mason's lips and tongue danced sensually against her blazing skin. She felt as if she could collapse from the intense pleasure.

"Take this off," Mason ordered as he tugged at the bottom of Phaedra's blouse. He twisted the buttons and she slipped off the silky material. As Mason hung it over the door handle, Phaedra unlatched her bra, releasing her breasts. Her firm chocolate nipples stood at attention.

"Mmm," Mason whispered as he captured one rock-hard candy in his mouth, his thumb and forefinger pulling at the other.

"Ohhh," Phaedra gasped, sucking in air at the intense sensation, shivering as Mason teased her sensitive flesh. Every ounce of sensibility was gone from her, the woman barely able to remember her own name as she focused on the sensations sweeping through her body. Mason's tongue flicked and teased her as he sucked hard on the sweet gem, sending sparks of heat deep into her feminine core. Phaedra sighed in ecstasy as her body began to shake and her moans intensified.

Wanting him to feel what she was feeling, Phaedra glided her palm down the front of his chest to his belt and unbuckled it. Before Mason realized it she had eased his zipper down and was sliding her palm over his crotch, the heat from her hands igniting a firestorm in his erection. He was brick-hard, the length of his manhood pulsing for release. Mason inhaled swiftly, humming as Phaedra began to stroke him earnestly. Suddenly Phaedra stopped cold and Mason shuddered, his body quivering for more. He looked at her, his desire washing over his expression.

"Drop your pants," she said.

Mason smiled as he let his pants and boxers slide down to the floor, releasing the protrusion of flesh that was desperate for her ministrations. She grasped him firmly in both hands, manipulating him with an intensity that had him fighting to stand, his knees threatening to buckle beneath him. Mason still had a firm grasp on her breasts, his mouth and tongue continuing to tease her.

"I need you," Mason whispered. "I need to be inside you," he gushed, his hips pumping in time with her strokes.

Phaedra kissed him again, the passion of it consuming them both. Mason suddenly spun her toward the sink and mirror, looping his arm around her waist. He pulled her to his chest, gently biting the back of her neck. Phaedra sank into him as he cradled his pelvis against the round of her bottom, grinding heavily against her. Pulling at her pants, Mason snatched them from her around her buttocks, his hands eagerly stroking the softness between her thighs. Stepping out of her G-string, Phaedra parted her legs, moving eagerly against his fingers.

As Mason bent her forward, Phaedra braced herself against the pedestal sink, holding tightly as Mason entered her from behind. His strokes were urgent and searching, driving her to a level of ecstasy that she had not known was possible. She bit down against her bottom lip to keep from crying out loudly, the sweet sensations drawing every ounce of breath from her.

Mason hugged her to him, his arms tight around her torso, one hand still stroking each nipple as Phaedra drew the fingers of his other hand into her mouth and sucked the appendages with vigor. His pelvis pushed and pulled against her, her bottom colliding into him with each stroke, and then with an intensity that rocked every nerve ending the two of them exploded together, their orgasms erupting in one tumultuous wave after another.

Collapsing against her back, Mason was panting, fighting to catch his breath. Phaedra was breathing heavily as well, her body still twitching with pleasure. Minutes later, their clothes adjusted back onto their bodies, the two of them eased their way out of the restroom. Returning to their seats, they strapped themselves back in, holding tight to each other's hand.

Outside, the plane seemed to be floating on a snow-white cushion of thick clouds. Peering out the window, Phaedra leaned her head against Mason's chest as he wrapped his arms tightly around her. Every ounce of doubt that had flooded her spirit earlier had dissipated into thin air. With it feeling like home in Mason's arms, the moment was heaven and Phaedra was grateful for it.

With Phaedra feeling as though all was well in the world, their landing at the Louis Armstrong New Orleans International Airport was simply the sweetest cherry on top of the best confection. Stepping out of the plane, she took a deep breath, inhaling the familiar scent of home. A limousine sat in wait at the end of the tarmac.

Phaedra shook her head. "Mason, we could have taken a taxi," she said, amazed at how he always seemed to have a pulse on what they needed before the thought even crossed her mind. "When did you arrange for a car?"

Mason shrugged. "I have a very adept staff of employees," he said as the driver opened the car door to let them inside.

"I need to meet this staff," Phaedra said.

The man smiled. "You will, and very soon, I'm sure."

Traveling through the streets, the duo compared notes, both having stories about growing up in New Orleans. Phaedra's excitement incited his, Mason seeing his hometown in a different light. The last time he'd been in the city for any length of time had been shortly after the hurricane when the shine had been considerably dimmed. The stopovers since had been quick and sweet, lasting just long enough to check on the renovations of his family's home.

When the car stopped at the quaint house on S. Claiborne Avenue, Phaedra's excitement was palpable, the woman bursting with glee as she rushed to open the front door. And Mason was excited for her, her joy like a sweet balm to his spirit. After he and the driver had gotten their luggage to the front porch, Phaedra called for him to come inside. As he entered the comfortable space, her smile was a wide explosion across her face.

"Welcome to my home," she said, her arms thrown out to her sides.

Mason laughed. "Very nice," he said, his eyes darting around the room. "This looks like you."

"It looks like my mother," she said, pointing to a photo of a woman that sat on the mahogany end table.

Mason eased his way to stand in front of the fireplace, examining the collection of family photos that decorated the mantel. Photos of Phaedra as a baby. Her high school graduation picture. Formal portraits of mother and daughter together.

Her mother had been a beautiful woman, and he told her so. "I see where you got your good looks from."

"Thank you. She would have adored you," Phaedra responded, laughter shining in her eyes.

"I'm sure she and I would have been great friends," Mason said.

Phaedra grabbed his hand. "Let me show you around," she said, guiding him through the dining area and kitchen, then to the bedrooms on the second floor.

"We'll sleep here," she said, leading him into her bedroom.

Mason smiled, his eyebrows raised mischievously. "I imagine we might not be getting much sleep," he said teasingly as he wrapped his arms around her torso and hugged her to him.

Phaedra giggled as Mason blew warm breath against the side of her neck, following the warmth with his tongue. "Are you trying to get something started, Mr. Boudreaux?" she quipped.

"Yes, ma'am. I am definitely trying to get something started. Are you going to let me?"

Phaedra giggled again. "I've never had a man in my room before. My mother would be having a fit if she knew."

"I assure you that your mother would have loved me so much that my being in your room wouldn't have been an issue."

"Mmm," Phaedra purred as Mason assaulted her mouth, kissing her voraciously, their tongues twisting wildly together.

Without a moment's hesitation Phaedra wriggled out of her slacks and top and stood in front of Mason with nothing on but her tiny black thong. Mason grabbed her by her thin waist and lifted her up onto the wooden dresser. Phaedra gasped, her arms wrapped around his neck. Her thin brown legs instinctively spread open, wrapping around his waist, and Mason licked his lips in anticipation. Guiding her movements, Mason pushed her legs up until her feet were resting on the dresser top. Spread open in all her glory, she was absolutely delicious, a sweet expectation at the ready.

"Do you have any idea what I'm going to do to you?" Mason asked.

"What?" Phaedra whispered.

The man smiled, not answering out loud as he took his index finger and teased the mound that pressed against the black triangle of fabric. He was staring in her eyes when he ripped the garment with his hands, tossing the remnants to the floor. Still staring into her eyes, Mason drew his fingers in bold strokes through the folds of her femininity, blatantly teasing her.

Phaedra inhaled swiftly, lust sweeping in bold waves through her. Every time Mason touched her she was in awe of the sensation. Every muscle in her body quivered for more.

Taking a quick glance around the room, Mason reached for a desk chair and pulled it to where she sat on the dresser. As he rested his knee against the cushioned seat, settling himself comfortably in front of her, he inhaled the sweet fragrance of her intimate scent. Phaedra's eyes widening in anticipation, he licked his index finger, sucking on it slowly. Phaedra took a deep breath and held it, her body beginning to convulse with wanting. She watched in wonder as Mason slowly slid his moist finger across her swollen nub with wanting.

Phaedra gasped. "Mason! Oh, baby."

Phaedra was on fire and when Mason placed a damp kiss against her inner thigh she thought she might combust. He started slowly, allowing her temperature to rise to an unreasonable level. As he dipped his tongue into the sweetness of her inner folds, he began to lap at her more furiously. Phaedra ran her hands over his head as her body shook with pleasure. She screamed his name, her body twisting and turning as every inch of her flesh tingled.

Savoring the intimate delicacy, Mason pushed his tongue deeper into Phaedra's private garden to savor the sweetness of her nectar. As Phaedra rode the tumultuous waves, speeding closer and closer to her orgasm, Mason pulled her to him, clamping his arms around her thighs to hold her steady. She arched her back and cried out with joy.

"Ohhh!" she screamed, locking her hands behind his head. "Don't stop! Please don't stop! Ohhh, baby!"

Mason doubled, then tripled his efforts, desperate to bring Phaedra to the explosion of a lifetime. He quickly licked his finger and slid it deep inside her. She was hot and tight and as he pushed a second and then a third finger in, Phaedra bucked hard, loving the sweet intrusion into her secret box.

She moaned, calling his name over and over again. Mason held her tight as he maintained his oral assault, lavishing long, wet strokes against her swollen button.

Phaedra screamed, her senses on overload. She raced higher and higher toward ecstasy, giving in to the wanton abandon. Suddenly Mason stroked her deeper and deeper, hitting her sweet spot until her passion crested. Phaedra bucked, her back arching as her legs locked behind his head, holding him hostage between her legs. She sobbed as he buried himself into her wetness.

"Ahhhh!" Phaedra shuddered as Mason lapped every drop of her sweet liquid. As her passion ebbed and flowed he gently stroked her damp thighs, continuing to kiss the soft, damp skin. He smiled as he felt her continue to shiver in ecstasy. Rising to his feet, he lifted her into his arms and carried her to the bed, laying her gently against the handmade quilt that decorated the bed. Lying down beside her, he curled into her warmth, the lovers drifting off into a sound sleep.

Chapter 21

Mason woke to the aroma of fresh-roasted coffee and thick bacon sizzling in a cast-iron frying pan. The smells wafting through the small bedroom were transforming, shifting him from a state of total unconsciousness to bright-eyed cognizance. Taking a deep breath, he rolled over onto his back, taking in the sight of Phaedra's childhood bedroom. The decor was an amalgamation of black-and-white photographs, remnants of college paraphernalia, trinkets from her travels and rich, lush fabrics in bright, vibrant colors. The space was warm and inviting, invoking the spirit that Mason had come to love about the beautiful woman.

Making his way into the bathroom, he tossed off the clothes he'd slept in and stepped into the shower stall, turning the water to superhot. Moisture rained down over his head and shoulders, the invigorating stream pulsing over his muscles. As he soaped his body, rinsing the suds down the drain, he was excited to start his day with Phaedra, anxious to see where they would be headed together.

As he stepped out of the shower, Phaedra knocked on the bathroom door, calling his name. "Hey there, do you want some breakfast?" she asked, peeking inside.

"Good morning," Mason said, grinning brightly.

"Good morning. I thought you might be hungry," she said as she stepped into the room and passed him a plush white towel.

"I could eat," he said as he swiped the towel across his body. "How long have you been up?"

"Not long. You were sleeping soundly, so I figured I'd let you rest."

He smiled as she reached to help him dry his back, her fingers lingering longer than necessary as she swiped her hands across his skin. She stepped in and planted a moist kiss against his back and shoulders. Turning an about-face, he wrapped his arms around her and kissed her gently, relishing the comfort of the embrace. He kissed her cheek before releasing the hold. "So, what would you like to do today?" he asked, wrapping the towel around his waist.

"Actually I really don't want to do much of anything. I have a stack of mail I need to go through, the paperwork to settle my mother's estate that needs to be completed and I need to figure out where my next photo assignment is going to be. I figured we'd just hang out for a while and then maybe head downtown later?"

Mason nodded. "Sounds like a plan. I actually have a few things I need to do, as well."

"Well, you get dressed and I'll go pour your coffee." Phaedra smiled. As she turned to walk out of the room, Mason gave her a swift pat against her backside.

Down in the kitchen the two enjoyed a breakfast of bacon, eggs, toast and coffee. Their conversation was easy and relaxed, the two enjoying each other's company. Mason asked questions about her mother and their history, enjoying the slide show of photo albums that documented them together. He sensed that Phaedra was missing her mother, and talking about the joyful times they'd shared clearly lifted her spirits.

After breakfast Phaedra retreated to her office and Mason to the screened porch that bordered the backyard. Neighbors had kept the grass cut, flowers blooming in no particular order around the perimeter of the fenced area. With his laptop resting against his knees, he accessed the home's Wi-Fi to retrieve his emails, responding to a lengthy list of messages. Turning his cell phone on for the first time since leaving for Thailand, he returned some necessary telephone calls. At some point he dozed off, a cool breeze wafting comfortably through the space. When he woke Phaedra was curled up at the opposite end of the sofa, her electronic reader resting in her hand.

He stretched his body upward and yawned. "How long have I been asleep?" he asked.

Phaedra shrugged as she answered, "Most of the afternoon. I think the time difference and jet lag finally caught up with you. Plus, you're still recovering from your trauma."

She rested her e-reader against the floor and shifted her body easily over his. Mason wrapped his arms around her as she leaned to kiss his mouth. "Ready to get out into the sunshine?"

Mason smiled as he glided his hands over her buttocks, sliding them beneath the T-shirt she wore. "I can think of something else I'd rather be doing," he said as he kissed her again.

She grinned, moving her pelvis to meet his. "Are you trying to get some again, sir?"

He lifted his eyebrows, his fingers still teasing her flesh. "Yes, ma'am."

She giggled softly as she lifted herself from the sofa, stretching out her hand to take his. Following her lead, Mason trailed after her as she led him back into the house and up the stairs, both leaving a trail of clothing behind them.

Phaedra couldn't have imagined a more romantic evening as they strolled through Woldenberg Park, enjoying the evening sunset. The sun danced across the mighty Mississippi as they strolled along the river. A procession of ships floated by on the river, and interesting sculptures dotted the landscape near the docks. As they sat on one of the many benches, a violinist stopped to serenade them, the enchanting strings setting a starry mood.

As the sun disappeared in the distance, the sky gleaming in vibrant shades of red, orange and purple, Mason led the way to the Napoleon House. Cocktails at the dimly lit, rustic bar were a quiet preamble to dinner at the restaurant Lola's, where they enjoyed a tantalizing meal of Spanish food, Mason insisting that the paella was the best he'd had since visiting Spain. The restaurant was charming and quaint with only a few tables and a strict no-reservations policy. As they'd waited for a table, Mason had held her close, his arms wrapped warmly around her.

After dinner they swung by Jackson Square and grabbed a late-night ride around the French Quarter in the back of a horse-drawn carriage. The picturesque views reminded them both of what they loved most about the exotic city, and by the time they'd found their way back to Phaedra's home, the mood was set for a night of making sweet, sweet love.

Hours later Phaedra slumbered comfortably against him, her naked body curled around his. Every so often she'd draw her fingers along the curve of his buttocks, the gentle sensation against his skin soothing. She snored ever so slightly, and listening to her breathe made him smile.

In that concrete room, delirium clouding his thoughts, he'd been afraid that he'd lost her, and the thought of her being gone from him when she had just moved into his life and heart had left him broken.

Phaedra had been fearful of them moving too fast, their relationship coming on the heels of too many obstacles. He'd been more confident about the two of them, believing that God had heard and answered his persistent prayer, blessing him with a partner who would fill the emptiness that had been his life. And the more time they spent together, the more they discovered about each other, the more convinced he was that he was right.

Phaedra shifted her body closer against his, seeking out his body heat. Her breathing shifted as she tossed one leg over his. Mason smiled into the darkness.

"Are you asleep?" she whispered, wrapping an arm around his waist.

Mason shook his head against his pillow. "No, I'm wide-awake."

"Is everything okay?"

"Perfect. I was just thinking about you. About us."

"I like us," she responded, caressing his side and abdomen. "I like us a lot."

Mason rolled onto his back. Phaedra cradled her body over his, resting her head against his chest. "Me, too," Mason said, tracing his hand along her profile.

Phaedra closed her eyes and relished the sensation of his touch. She took a deep breath, then lifted her body above his, straddling him comfortably. "So, what's next with us, Mr. Boudreaux?" she asked as she palmed his chest.

"I know what I want, Phaedra. I guess the question is, what do you want?"

Phaedra paused. She took a deep breath, blowing it slowly past her lips. "There's so much for us to consider," she said, reflecting on their two situations. "Where is business going to put you?"

"What I need to do for your brothers is going to keep me traveling for a while. I don't see myself settling down in any one place for at least the next year. Maybe two. And I'm sure you will want to spend time in Dallas getting to know your family. Have you given any consideration to moving there? Because I'm sure John is going to bring the idea up to you. I know I would."

"I've thought about commuting between here and there, but no, I hadn't thought about moving."

"It's something that you might want to consider," Mason said matter-of-factly.

Phaedra nodded. "So, where would that leave us? Will this be a long-distance relationship?"

"It doesn't have to be. Depending on our schedules, you can travel with me wherever I go or I can travel with you. Money isn't an issue for us, so you'll be afforded the opportunity to take pictures all around the world if that's what you want to do."

"Money isn't an issue for *you,* Mason. I make a comfortable living, but that's all it is, comfortable."

"No, it's not an issue for us because whatever I have, you have. Most especially after we're married."

Phaedra laughed. "And you're planning to marry me?"

"Was there any doubt?"

She paused, taking a quick moment before she responded, "In all honesty, Mason, I hadn't thought about marriage. I've just gotten used to the idea of us being a couple."

"Well, I have thought about it and I can't imagine us being together and you not being my wife. And I'm not saying we have to be married tomorrow or next week, but when it feels right and you're ready, I want to marry you. I want you to know that I am committed to our being together forever. I love you, Phaedra."

Phaedra leaned to kiss him, her lips gliding like silk against his. "I love you, too, Mason," she said as he wrapped his arms around her.

His wiggled his pelvis beneath her. "So, just how much do you love me?" he said, his voice dropping to a seductive whisper.

Phaedra squirmed against him, feeling the rise of nature that surged anxiously for her attention. She grinned widely as she stroked him with her body, his erection hardening like a rod of steel between her legs. "Let me show you," she said as she reached a hand be-

tween them, her fingers wrapping around the length
of him.

Mason reached toward the nightstand and the box
of condoms that rested behind the lamp. He pulled a
prophylactic from the container and passed it to her.
Tearing the wrapper from the rubber, she shifted her
body to give herself enough room to sheathe the length
of him. Mason's smile pulled ear to ear in anticipation.

Dropping her mouth down to his, she kissed him
sweetly. She teased him, taunting him with anticipation as her body glided firmly against his. As Mason
began to thrust himself upward, grinding his body
against hers, Phaedra lifted her hips and plunged her
body down against him. Mason gasped at the sensation, pleasure surging through him like a wildfire that
refused to be contained.

As Mason grabbed her by her hips, guiding her motion, Phaedra rode him in earnest, propelling herself
up and down against him. With the length of himself
nestled nicely between her legs, Mason savored the
sweet sensations, Phaedra hot and delicious around
him. The feelings through his body were out of this
world. Mason knew that he wouldn't last long. He could
feel his orgasm slowly building as Phaedra sped up her
strokes. At the point of no return, Mason pushed himself into her, hard, causing her to cry out, and a second
later he felt her contracting around him as she had her
own climax. Collapsing against him, Phaedra nestled
into his embrace, reveling in the love that spiraled in
deep swirls around them both.

Mason kissed her ardently. It was like kissing an
angel, he thought, nothing else nearly as perfect. Phaedra was beautiful and delicate, graceful and lithe. As he

explored her body with his hands, he was drunk with
lust after what they had done and what else he planned
to do before the night was over.

Chapter 22

The ringing cell phone startled them both from a sound sleep. Mason jumped and Phaedra jumped with him, her body sprawled over his. She laughed huskily. "I think that's for you," she said as she rolled to the other side of the bed, pulling a pillow over her head.

Reaching for the device that rested on the night-stand, Mason pulled it to his ear. "Hello?"

The familiar voice on the other end moved him to sit upright in the bed listening intently. Phaedra peeked up at him, curiosity pulling her awake.

"Yes, sir…yes…I…but…" Mason heaved a deep sigh. "Yes, sir, I will," he repeated as he disconnected the call. The man shook his head, a smile pulling at his mouth.

"Is everything okay?" Phaedra asked, concern rising in her tone.

"We have been summoned," Mason said with a deep sigh.

Phaedra sat up in confusion. "Summoned?"

He nodded as he threw his legs off the bed. "Don't worry, it's not as bad as it sounds. Let's get dressed," he said as he tapped her gently against her backside. "We've been invited to brunch."

An hour later, Mason was maneuvering Phaedra's Toyota Camry uptown into the 14th Ward. With her efforts to pull any information from him fruitless, she was still in the dark about who had called for them or where they were going. When he pulled past the wrought-iron gates of the Broadway Street home, she looked at him, a wave of anxiety filling the pit of her stomach. Her eyes widened.

"Is this your family's home?" she questioned, eyeing him with reservation.

Mason nodded. "Yes, it is. And my parents are here. It seems that one of my siblings couldn't keep their mouth shut and they now know about the incident in Phuket."

Phaedra laughed. "And Mom and Dad are pissed, aren't they?"

"Very!" Mason said with a deep laugh. He leaned to kiss her lips. "But meeting you is going to make them forget all about it."

She shook her head. "I wouldn't place any bets on that if I were you," she said as they stepped out of the car.

Mason's mother met them at the door, pulling the entrance open before they stepped onto the porch. Katherine Boudreaux threw her arms around Mason's body, hugging him tightly. Tears misted the older woman's eyes.

"How dare you frighten me like that, Mason?" his mother said.

Mason hugged her tightly, shaking his head in earnest. "Mom, I am fine. There was nothing for you to be frightened about."

"That's not what we heard," Mason's father said, stepping out to greet them. "To hear your brothers tell it, things were pretty sketchy 'cross dem waters. Nearly got yourself killed."

"It was not that serious," Mason said, trying to alleviate the concern. He kissed his mother's cheek before extending his hand toward his father.

Mason Boudreaux Jr. shook his son's hand and then pulled him into a hearty embrace. "It's good to see you, son."

"It's good to see you, Senior."

Mason's father tossed a look past his son's shoulder, spying Phaedra, who was standing nervously on the top step.

"Good morning, pretty lady!" Mason Senior chimed, extending his hand. "Mason Boudreaux Jr., but everyone calls me Senior," he said as he pumped Phaedra's arm up and down.

Mason looped his arm around Phaedra's waist, pulling her to him. "Mom, Senior, this is Phaedra. Phaedra, this is my mother, Katherine, and my father."

Katherine wrapped Phaedra in a warm hug. "I am thrilled to meet you," the woman said excitedly. "We've heard such nice things about you, dear!"

"Thank you," Phaedra said, a smile brightening her face. "And it's so nice to meet you both."

Still holding on to Phaedra, Katherine gestured for the two of them to follow her into the house. "That was some nasty business in Thailand. I am so glad that you both are back here safe and sound."

Phaedra smiled as Mason tried to transition the topic. "The house looks great, Mom," he said, glancing around the large living room. "Are you happy with everything?"

Katherine shrugged. "I'm not unhappy, but with you kids all over the place it still doesn't feel homey yet."

"Well, I'm sure once you two settle in, it won't take long for everyone to find their way back home," Mason said.

He and Phaedra both sat down against the upholstered settee.

His mother rested on the arm of the chair his father sat down in, wrapping her arms around the man's shoulders. "Well, Senior wants to go back to Arizona for a few months since all you kids are on that side of the country. And of course once Katrina has that baby, we'll be in Dallas for a while to help her out."

"I have to keep that grandson of mine in check. You know how teens can get," he said, referring to his daughter Katrina's oldest son. "Have you met Collin yet, Phaedra?" he asked.

She nodded. "Yes, sir. He's a wonderful young man."

The proud grandfather nodded. "That's my boy!"

Katherine slid her hands across the tops of her thighs as she stood up. "I need to go get the food ready. I hope you two are hungry," she said, looking from one to the other.

Mason nodded. "Starving," he said.

"Mrs. Boudreaux, can I give you a hand?" Phaedra asked, rising to her feet.

Katherine nodded, reaching for Phaedra's hand. "I'd love some help," she said as she pulled Phaedra in the direction of the kitchen. "It will give us some time to get to know each other while my boys catch up."

Intrigued, Phaedra tossed a glance over her shoulder. Mason winked at her as she followed behind the matriarch. His smile was canyon wide. When the two women were out of earshot, his father chastised him.

"I didn't like hearing from other folks about you getting into trouble, son. Why didn't you call me?"

Mason apologized. "I didn't want to worry you and Mom. It really wasn't that serious."

Senior raised his eyebrows, his expression voicing his disbelief. Mason smiled, his head nodding ever so slightly.

"I promise, Senior, I won't let it happen again," he said.

Satisfied, Senior leaned forward in his seat, his hands clasped together in front of him. "So, tell me about your new friend," he said, gesturing with his head toward the kitchen.

"She's incredible," Mason said, grinning broadly as he gave his father an edited version of his time with Phaedra since the two had met at the Stallion wedding. "She's the most amazing woman I have ever met," he concluded.

His father nodded. "She sounds very special. And she's been through a lot. I know your sisters haven't stopped talking about her. Kamaya and Katrina have been giving your mother an earful."

Mason shook his head, only imagining how the

women in his family had been gossiping. The two men sat in conversation for some time, catching up with each other, while in the kitchen, Phaedra was becoming acquainted with his mother. The young woman stood at the kitchen counter breaking eggs into a bowl.

"Mason's been wonderful to me," Phaedra was saying, sharing the story of how he'd been so supportive since the two had come together.

"My son is a good man," Katherine said proudly, pulling a pan of biscuits from the oven.

Phaedra smiled, nodding her agreement. By the time she helped carry the meal to the kitchen table, Katherine calling her husband and son to come eat, the two women had become fast friends. Katherine reminded her of her own mother, and Phaedra was grateful for the time with the woman, noting how much she had missed the maternal companionship.

The rest of the morning flew by, laughter ringing soundly through the home as the family enjoyed the midmorning meal. Mason's parents regaled her with stories of Mason's childhood, his many antics moving her to shake her head.

"Stop, stop!" Mason cried, holding a hand up. "Don't tell that story," he said to his father, shaking his head. "Phaedra may not like me anymore if you keep telling her these stories," he teased.

Phaedra leaned to kiss his lips. "I'm enjoying this," she said. "Definitely don't stop!"

He shook his head, everyone trying to catch their breaths from laughing so hard. Hours later, Phaedra excused herself to go to the restroom.

Katherine crossed over to her son's side and hugged him warmly.

"She's perfect for you," she intoned. "She is absolutely delightful."

Mason nodded. "I love her, Mom," he said softly. "I didn't know it was possible to love any woman the way I love Phaedra." He met his father's stare, the man smiling contently.

Katherine hugged him a second time as she whispered into his ear, "She loves you, too, but just take it slow and enjoy your time together. She's still fragile and you don't want to scare her."

Nodding his understanding, Mason grinned, joy shimmering out of his eyes over his parents' approval of his and Phaedra's relationship. Moments later Phaedra stood in the doorway, staring at the bond between the parents and their son as they sat laughing easily together. Delighting in the moment, she lifted her requisite camera to her eyes and snapped a photo, capturing the moment for her and Mason's family album.

Chapter 23

John Stallion had dispatched the limousine that picked the family up at the airport. Phaedra was feeding off their excitement, Mason and his parents bursting with elation as they headed in the direction of Dallas's new Parkland Hospital.

Matthew had called hours earlier to say that Katrina was on her way to have the baby, and with a private plane at their disposal it had taken them less than two hours to get from New Orleans to Dallas, their arrival beating the new baby's.

Mason laughed warmly. "Your brother is so excited. He sounds like he's about to bust," he said as he disconnected his cell phone. "She's still in labor. No baby yet!"

Katherine laughed. "I told Katrina that baby was going to take his dear sweet time coming here. Collin was a slow baby, remember? Katrina was in labor almost eighteen hours with him."

Mason shook his head. "If I knew it was going to take that long, we could have taken our time getting here," he said.

His father nodded in agreement.

Phaedra chuckled. "Do you think it's a boy, Mrs. Boudreaux?"

"I'm sure it's a boy. Katrina was carrying this baby low, just like Collin."

Her husband shook his head. "What you gon' do if that baby is a girl?" he asked teasingly.

Katherine tossed him a look that spoke volumes, and both the Boudreaux men burst out laughing.

At the hospital, the families were gathered in the waiting room outside the maternity ward. Their laughter could be heard down the long length of corridor. It was a Stallion-Boudreaux reunion, the likes of which Phaedra had never seen before. She smiled brightly as they rushed into the room to join in the wait.

Her brothers each greeted her warmly, hugging and kissing her easily as they exchanged dap with Mason. The Stallion women were just as welcoming, pulling her into their conversations with ease.

"Where we at?" Senior asked, his arm draped over young Collin's shoulder.

"It's close," John said as Marah stepped into his arms, hugging him around the waist.

"This is so exciting!" Kamaya said as she pulled Phaedra into the empty seat beside her and her sister Tarah, introducing them to each other and Phaedra to the other members of the Boudreaux family.

The noise was abundant and every so often, Katherine and Juanita would shush them to a low murmur. At every opportunity Phaedra snapped pictures with her camera, wanting to capture as many of the memories as she could. Time passed swiftly and before the sun began to set outside, Matthew entered the room, still dressed in the required scrubs expectant fathers donned in the delivery room. Tears misted his dark eyes, his hands wringing excitedly.

"It's a boy," he shouted. "Nine pounds two ounces!"

"It's a big boy!" Katherine said with excitement as she and Juanita both rushed to give him a hug.

"How's Katrina?" Katherine asked, her husband moving to wrap his arms around her waist.

"She's doing great. Tired but she's just fine."

"So, do we get to see it?" Collin asked anxiously.

Matthew laughed. "Your little brother is not an it. And yes, you can see him." He smiled, gesturing with his hand for them to follow him to the maternity ward's viewing window. When the family was assembled in front of the glass enclosure, he gestured at the pediatric nurse, who smiled warmly. The woman pushed a white baby basket to the front and center of the nursery. She mouthed congratulations at the family as they all pushed forward to get a glimpse of the new baby.

"We've named him Matthew Jacoby Stallion Jr.," the new father said proudly. "We're going to call him Jack."

John reached his arms out to hug his brother. "Nice job," he whispered into the man's ear. "Nice job!"

As the family stood admiring the new bundle of joy, the beautiful baby resting with a thumb pulled into his mouth, his eyes squinted as he struggled to focus, Phaedra tugged on Mason's arm, gesturing for him to follow her into the hallway.

As the two stepped outside, she tossed a quick glance back over her shoulder, smiling brightly at the love and joy that blessed the space.

"What's wrong?" Mason asked, concern falling over his expression.

She shook her head. "Nothing," she said as she reached to wrap her arms around him. "Everything's perfect."

She kissed him keenly, her mouth skating with pleasure over his. "I just wanted to tell you something," she said, the excitement ringing in her tone.

Mason eyed her curiously. "What, baby?"

"I want that," she said, gesturing back to where the family was gathered.

Mason smiled, joy shimmering in his stare as she continued.

"I want family, and you. I want us to have babies together. Lots of babies. I want this life with sisters and brothers and us being a family. I want us to be like your mom and dad, and my brothers and their wives.

"I love you, Mason, and I want to be your wife more than anything else!" she said as she kissed him again.

Holding Phaedra tightly, Mason closed his eyes, pressing a damp kiss against her forehead. He held her as they reveled in the beauty of their love for each other and the love their families had for them both.

Across the room John stood watching them, sensing his sister's happiness, a bright smile blessing his face. Mark met his gaze and nodded his approval as Matthew gave them two thumbs-up. As Phaedra's brothers turned their attention back to the family's celebration, they knew that they would be Stallions forever, forever a family bonded by much more than blood.

* * * * *

LET'S TALK
Romance

For exclusive extracts, competitions
and special offers, find us online:

 facebook.com/millsandboon

🐦 @MillsandBoon

📷 @MillsandBoonUK

Get in touch on 01413 063232

For all the latest titles coming soon, visit
millsandboon.co.uk/nextmonth

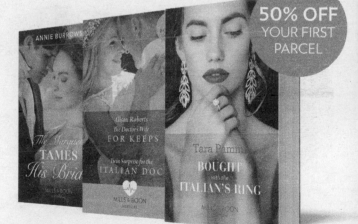

MILLS & BOON
True Love
Romance from the Heart

Celebrate true love with tender stories of
heartfelt romance, from the rush of falling in
love to the joy a new baby can bring, and a
focus on the emotional heart of a relationship.

MILLS & BOON
MEDICAL
Pulse-Racing Passion

Set your pulse racing with dedicated,
delectable doctors in the high-pressure
world of medicine, where emotions run
high and passion, comfort and love are the
best medicine.

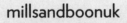